The Casinghead Company

Volume II of The Golden Lane Trilogy

The Casinghead Company

▼

Linton Morrell

Authors Choice Press
San Jose New York Lincoln Shanghai

The Casinghead Company

All Rights Reserved © 2001 by Linton Morrell

No part of this book may be reproduced or transmitted in any form or by any means, graphic, electronic, or mechanical, including photocopying, recording, taping, or by any information storage or retrieval system, without the permission in writing from the publisher.

Authors Choice Press
an imprint of iUniverse.com, Inc.

For information address:
iUniverse.com, Inc.
5220 S 16th, Ste. 200
Lincoln, NE 68512
www.iuniverse.com

This is a work of historical fiction. Some characters in this story are real. Some events are real. The plot is fictional. Resemblance to actual circumstances is coincidental. Language reflects popular usage in these times.

ISBN: 0-595-17784-0

Printed in the United States of America

Nicholas Gray

Contents

Prologue ix
Acknowledgements xi
Chapter I. The Merger 1
Chapter II. Amanda Macabre 26
Chapter III. The Casinghead Company 64
Chapter IV. Rojo Olimpio Torres 86
Chapter V. Vaduz And Ventimiglia 103
Chapter VI. The Copper Bar 122
Chapter VII. Drilling 159
Chapter VIII. A Call for Dynamite 179
Chapter IX. Dereliction of Duty 201
Chapter X. Work Print 223
Chapter XI. Orchid Island 233
Chapter XII. St. Theodore 248
Chapter XIII. Secret Policeman 263
Chapter XIV. Gaceta Ofical 282
Chapter XV. Tyler, Texas 302
Chapter XVI. 1957 322
Chapter XVII. Abduction 346
Chapter XVIII. High Noon at the Hotel Negresco 361
Chapter XIX. Melee at the Miramar 376
Chapter XX. Oil in The Tanks 391
Chapter XXI. The Casinghead Tower 421
Epilogue 439
About the Author 445
Glossary 447

Prologue

From: *The Yellow Peril*
By Wanda Wannamaker
June 30, 1957

Los Ladrones de Piedras Negras had its premiere yesterday afternoon at Grauman's Chinese Theater. Some show! They say that if you have seen one oater, you have seen them all. Well if you see this one, you'll see four others, or at least parts of them. The chase was extracted from *Thunder at Thorny Bluff*. The barroom bust-up came out of *Sin Beneath the Sage*. The shoot-out at the corral first saw light of day in *Massacre at Fort McMack*. The bell tower blast-out was originally filmed in Monument Valley for *Pecos Pete Peters*.

Still, if you like westerns, and many do, this one had nearly sixty minutes of thrills. It also had some oddities. Big Alphonse Malbecco, who co-starred in the role of a Mexican villain, has to be a cowpoke curiosity. How could a man of such bulk ever find a horse he could sit? Let alone, ride. We didn't spot him in the chase, by the way.

Sixto Cigone, the hero's sidekick speaks no lines. Strong silent type. But Oh Boy! If you have what he has and you display it in Toreador pants one size too small, you don't have to say a word. The girls will see for themselves what they don't have to be missing.

A treat for starlets of all ages is Flint Westwater, a new find, sort of. He is a neat broncobuster in spiffy cream-colored chaps and a really white hat. He looks just groovy when he has that six-shooter in hand and a hard stare in his eyes. Watch out you bad guys in black hats! Flint has a fine future in flicks of this genre. We can't wait to see his next effort.

Of course, seeing that remarkable Helen O'Reith is worth the price of the ticket. Not a famous role but she played it with her usual aplomb and distinction. Perhaps a bit long of tooth for a heroine, as she would no doubt, be the first to admit, but as a character actress, take care all you wranglers. While you're stealing cattle, Señora Elena is stealing scenes. As a co-director, along with the Neapolitan mystery man, Frederico Bolletti, la O'Reith cannot be faulted. This movie moves, especially along the canyon rim.

An inside source reveals that the real heroine of the production is our own hotshot astrological wizardess, Alice Ridley. Welcome home, Alice! We await your next daily horoscope in the pages of this newspaper.

Dust clouds surround this film outside the cinema as well as inside. There is talk that a scene was to be shot in the Miramar Hotel in Biarritz. That never happened. But *something* happened. When we know what it was, you'll read it right here. What we do know is that some of the personalities in *Los Ladrones de Piedras Negras* are making themselves mighty scarce, podner. This kind of skull-duggery fits right in with the kind of life that Helen O'Reith's globe-trotting husband leads. General Clive Colin O'Reith seems to have vanished. He usually attends his wife coming out flicks but not this one. Maybe he's drilling a well in the jungle somewhere. Nor have we seen anything of Frederico Bolletti or Sixto Cigone since the movie was put in distribution. We hear Big Alphonse Malbecco is not doing well at all in a clinic in, of all places, Ventimiglia, Italy. So the movie may be made but not all of the story has been told.

Okay kids. Curtain time. Hurry along. Get a large coke and a super sack of salted popcorn. Slip in your ear plugs and sit back for…

Acknowledgements

Maria C. Lynch prepared the manuscript for publication.

Chapter I

▼

The Merger

It was an immense office by any standard, the size of two tennis courts on the 39th floor of the Calitroleum Tower on Sepulveda Boulevard, a penthouse. He could, if he liked, look west and see Catalina Island, look south and see downtown Los Angeles or he could look east and see Hollywood and Beverly Hills, including his mansion in Holmby Hills and his bungalow on Summit drive, a gift from his mother the late Rae Regan, famous actress of the Silver Screen.

General Clive Colin O'Reith, President of the Calitroleum Oil Corporation preferred the western view, the ocean, the yachts, the sailboats, the water-skiers, fun-seekers, much like himself although his preferred game was golf. He often stood at one of the clerestory windows and pondered his good fortune, that being family and friends. Helen, Maxine, Little Clive Colin his son just out of the army, Rae Regan his daughter, married to a rising young Douglas Aircraft Company executive by the name of Clifford Thorneberry, Helen Simpson, his seven year old second daughter and Monique in Paris, Helen Simpson's half-sister, technically his third daughter but they were born about the same time. Such was his family.

As far his friends, General Hardy Harold Tarbutton was one of them. Tarbutton, a battle-tested comrade in arms, was his personal aide and the man who knew all there was to know, legally and financially about him. Colonel Hunter Hawke Holland, his executive vice president for production was also battle-tested, by the same enemy. Down in Maracaibo, he considered Amanda Macabra Schaeffer to be a good friend too, although a rather dangerous one. She was like the black widow spider that lived in a web in the corner of his garage, one that had been there a long time and that he had grown accustomed to. They respected one another. But his best friend and of longest duration was right down the hall. Vincent Barkett Blake was Chairman of the Board of the company.

O'Reith had been president for four years now, since the management was reorganized following the death of the founder, Harvey Holmes Halliday in the spring of 1951. Most of the time, Blake stayed out of his way, let him run with the ball wherever that led. After all, the two had been drinking companions for many years. If Blake needed to know something, he was confident that O'Reith would tell him. And in fact, O'Reith was to the point of having to tell him something. Now, in the late autumn of 1955 he was, in his own words, in the soup. The first three years of his presidency had gone all right. But the hand he was holding right now was mostly deuces and treys. Blake would have to know this soon, but not just yet. He had until the end of the month to present the budget for the coming year. He rose from his vast paperless desk and rubbing his chin, walked across to an eastern window, looking for the roof of the Holmby Hills mansion. There Helen his wife, if she were not sleeping, would have her nose in a shooting script.

Clive Colin O'Reith was six feet tall, slender, and resembled Adolphe Menjou, a matinee idol of years past. O'Reith had on a midnight-blue tuxedo with a white silk shirt and a carelessly tied black silk bow tie. On his left wrist was a Rolex GMT Master. Beyond that, a golden wedding band and a square-cut emerald decorated his hand. He paid a thousand dollars in Bogota for the stone. His hair was jet black, dyed, as was his pencil mustache. He was 48 years old and his eyes were crystal blue although not as blue as they once had been. A distinguished face, atop a lean, athletic body that had a military bearing. Once, in a moment of pique, Helen had suggested his icy countenance could be rendered even more frigid by a monocle. He gave her a sharp look when she said this, but he remembered her words. O'Reith was January's child, a Capricorn in good standing. A tenor, he speaks with a musical, rhythmic, calibrated flow of words, precise and rapidly enunciated; calculated such that one must listen closely to connect word with thought. He can speak in another voice when the occasion requires it, a voice an octave lower, with no music, just cold authority. His son, little Clive Colin, calls this, *'the Voice'*. It is often accompanied by *the Stare*.

His disasters, his disappointments, some of them heart-wrenching were behind him, right behind him in fact when he was sitting at his desk. Hanging between the clerestory windows on the south was a grainy black and white enlargement of the *Holly No.1*, snapped by a Halliburton cementer with a Brownie camera at the exact moment that the derrick collapsed. Then there was an elevation view of the B-17 *Okie from Fenoki* cruising along in level flight with all four engines running normally, everything just fine except that the "*from Fenoki*" was sheared off along with the rest of the cabin. An FW-190 with a dead pilot at the stick had slashed through the formation while they coming off the target at Big-B. The cabin crew, two pilots, the navigator and the bombardier were incinerated in the collision. Six parachutes appeared before the decapitated bomber fell off into a shallow spin, like a sailed hat. The photograph was a *still* from a roll of 30-mm film shot by the crew chief of *Dangerous Delilah*, the bomber from which he had commanded the Air Division that day. Completing the melancholy triptych was a Technicolor picture of the *Lago Poniente No.1*. Yellow and orange flames shooting skyward, black smoke billowing up and drifting toward Lagunillas. The ruin of the rig draped *Daliesque* over the concrete platform, crown block dipping now in, now out of the green water of Lake

Maracaibo. Holland had taken that one with a Leica camera from the deck of a Loffland Brothers work barge.

His triumphs, his most pleasurable moments hung on the west wall where he could see them easily without getting up. A 1930 wedding photo with Helen in her white gown and dotted lace veil smiling in apparent ecstasy, as brides usually do and he standing straight-faced beside her in the dress uniform of a brand new first lieutenant. There was a poster of Helen as *Pecos Lil*, a comedy in more ways than one. Another poster of her as she appeared in *Women at War*. In that one, she had on a skimpy, non-regulation Airwac uniform and more bust than she really had was *bustin' out all over* as the song went. She was in spike heels *'truckin' on down the avenue'*. Finally, the one that always made him feel proud. Helen, in a long black gown wearing silken gloves, with her Oscar in her arms, tears filling her lovely hazel eyes, beaming at an applauding crowd of her associates. That for her role as *Estelle* in *Neon Lights*.

Today his most pressing concern was the Tidikelt Field in Algeria. On production since May of 1951, it was a depletion drive reservoir with a high gas-oil ratio. Originally capable of producing 500,000 bopd, now it was down to 400,000 and declining all the time. The problem was that they had to flare the gas associated with the oil. Compression and reinjection costs were prohibitively high at such a remote location. A complicating factors with regard to this field was that Paris Petroleum Company owned a 25% interest. Paris Petroleum, an agency of the French Government, was under the sway of Charles de Gaulle.

If Tidikelt had been in the San Joaquin Valley, West Texas or Oklahoma, O'Reith would not have thought twice. He would have presented the Crude Oil Committee a proposal for pressure maintenance and gas conservation. They would have rubber stamped it without comment.

But for over a year now, an organization which called itself *Front de Liberation Nationale*, headed by one Belkacem Krim, was in armed revolt against the French Government. Rioting and civil unrest, of course, was hardly new in that part of the world. Such incidents went all the way back to the *Setif Massacre* of 1945. French military strength was paramount. The oil field as well as the pipeline to Oran was guarded like family jewels. But the original spontaneous revolt was spreading, becoming more organized, occurring all across the country. The troops, stretched thin, were coping with it but at some point, things could come unglued. So any proposal for Tidikelt that required capital expenditure would have to be qualified by an opinion of the political risk involved, a red flag to the committee.

His great strength was his care in putting forth controversial projects of high financial risk. Sometimes it was necessary to do this but he always thought long and hard before he did it. He did not enjoy seeing the directors squirm in their seats. *Le Grand Charles*, as deGaulle was often called wanted to arrest the pressure decline in Tidikelt and increase oil production at the same time. In that respect, O'Reith thought, he was like an American politician.

If that were not enough, *Ain Mutra*, their first big foreign oil field, was now making water not only in the edge wells but also, here and there, in the very heart of the field. An extension to *Ain Mutra*, which they had thought at one time to be even larger, had turned out to be a disappointment. With less than half the structure drilled up, they had stepped out across an undetected fault and found the pay wet. So he had to recommend funds for water shut-off in 1956 or risk premature abandonment of the field. *Ain Mutra*, in the Neutral Zone, was directly affected by events in Persia, just a stone throw across the desert. The new Consortium in Persia, which included all of the international giants, had gone on the line in the autumn of 1954 with big oil. They had already knocked five cents a barrel off the price of Middle Eastern avails.

Finally, prorationing in Texas, Oklahoma and Louisiana was cutting into domestic profits. A complex bureaucratic system represented by the Texas Railroad Commission, The Oklahoma Corporation Commission and The Louisiana Department of Conservation, employing so-called "discovery allowables" and "non-producing" days, had effectively cut offtake by about 30%. All this to protect the small "mom and pop" oil producers around the country.

But Sumatra was doing okay. Venezuela too. In fact Lago Poniente Field in Lake Maracaibo was doing better than it should be considering how long it had been on production. It just kept on flowing oil without any decline at all. Sumatra and Venezuela. Two bright spots on the map.

So here he was, looking out the window, mulling the Capital and Exploratory Budget for 1956, wondering how Blake would react when he saw it. The draft version would shortly be atop his desk. The Widow Halliday was typing it. Presently she would bring it in. The budget reflected the thinking of engineers, geologists, refiners and marketers from Calitroleum operations around the world. Each department had reported their needs with an estimate of funds required to fulfill them. Each technical option to maximize income had been considered in minute detail. All O'Reith had to do was initial it and send it down the hall to Blake. This he was reluctant to do. It didn't have to be on Blake's desk until 1 December so he had ten days to ponder it.

It was at this moment that Susie Halliday entered his office. Susan Simms Halliday, nee Briscoe, was thirty-five, hazel-eyed, svelte and stylish. She had been a platinum blonde for as long as O'Reith could remember which was 1939 when she had been the Drilling Department secretary down on the 10th floor. Some weeks before the war started, she caught the eye of Harvey Halliday, at that time a widower of long duration. She moved up to the 39th floor, to become his private secretary. They married after the war and their son was now seven. Whatever money could buy, she could buy it. She was in white. Silken business suit. Velvet pumps. Pearls in her ears. She resembled Jo Stafford and had a smooth, torchsong voice to match the looks.

O'Reith thought she was bringing the budget but she was bringing the Daily Drilling Report, just up from the 10th floor. A one page affair when O'Reith used to take it with a telephone, a yellow pencil and a legal pad, now it was five pages of typescript taken by four drilling superintendents and as many clerks. Although he had long ago ceded responsibility for all drilling operations to Holland, he still read the Daily Drilling Report as if it were holy scripture. He quickly scanned the pages looking for big trouble, found none. Then he read it more carefully, foreign first and then domestic. He started at news that they had just spudded the John McLarssen Estate No. 1 in the Beaver Lodge Field of North Dakota. "Christ!" he muttered. That name brought a bitter memory. Drilling a well up there this time of year would be pure agony for the roughhands. He remembered Block 37 in Ector County, Texas long years ago when he was pushing tools. An Ellenburger test in December of 1935. A howling blue norther whipped across the the *Llano Estacado* from the west, wet and freezing. Overnight the derrick was encrusted with rime and icicles two feet long hanging from the girts. The sand line had a two inch thick cylinder of ice around it that went all the way up to the monkey board where the derrickman worked. A fifty mile an hour wind whistled through the derrick like a banshee singing a siren song. How those men managed to handle pipe in all that misery was a miracle. But work they did. They didn't shut down for a minute and when it was time to pull the pipe out of the hole for a new bit , when the driller broke the kelly off, put it in the rat hole, latched on to the top joint of drill pipe and pulled, the derrick groaned and squatted and hundreds of shards of ice fell to the floor, like crystalline shrapnel as it hit the derrick floor. But then it was all right again. Rid of its icy burden, the derrick became quiet. The trip out of the hole was routine.

If it was like that in West Texas, how must it be in North Dakota? It was the significance of the name that upset him. John McLarssen was the U.S. Congressman on the House Un-American Activities Committee that had given Helen hell about being subversive; who had brought about the suicide of Fritz Harrington, a director of many of the movies that Helen had made in that era and who in the end, involved O'Reith in an affair with tragic consequences. He said, "Susie, call down to the Land and Legal Department and ask them for the file on the McLarssen Estate lease. Find out who signed on behalf of the estate and let me know." Rubbing his chin, he watched her depart.

Just then, his office door swung wide open and Vincent Blake strode rapidly across the thick gray carpet and dropped like a rock into an easy chair in front of O'Reith's desk. Blake, a heavy-set, bull-necked man with a florid face that resembled that of Broderick Crawford, had on a navy blue serge suit, white cotton shirt, stiffly starched. He wore a blue and white striped tie clipped to his shirt front with a diamond stickpin. The tie was pulled into a tight knot. O'Reith would have liked to go over and loosen it for him, maybe even unbutton his collar which seemed to be choking him. But he resisted that urge. Instead he smiled and waited.

Blake was fifty-three. His salt and pepper hair was thinning rapidly and he combed it with a left-hand part that accentuated his approaching baldness. O'Reith kept a combination barber, manicurist and makeup artist in one of his side offices. He had often offered her services to Blake, suggesting that a nice toupee might make all the difference in the world. But Blake just glared at him. He was a growling baritone, brisk, crisp, a voice that crackled with authority, like a burst of static from a short wave radio on a stormy summer day. He always came quickly to the point and was a desk-pounder *extraordinaire* with zero tolerance for dissimulation or procrastination, a right-now guy. O'Reith knew him like the back of his hand and had already assessed his mood before the door swung shut.

"Clive, Harry Collier just called. Invited me to have a drink with him and R.G. Follis at The Top of The Mark. I stalled. Told him I had to review my calendar with you. What do you think?"

"That's a pretty strong signal," O'Reith answered. "Sounds like they want to get right down to it."

"Yeah, that's what I thought too," Blake said, frowning slightly. "If it was a lunch invitation, they'd have to wait for dessert to spring it."

"Vince I've been sitting on the budget until I could think it through more carefully. Too much gas in Algeria and too much water in the Middle East. Take some heavy sugar to fix things up. The committee may choke on it. Those Standard Oil hands know what we're up against. We're wounded and they smell blood." He pushed the switch on his interoffice phone and in his musical tenor said, "Susie, call Brent Lankford over at Merrill Lynch and get us the opening quotes on SD and COC. When you get 'em, bring 'em in." Then he did some quick arithmetic on his legal pad. He said, "Vince, you and I and the Widow Halliday have controlling interest. What do you say we put it to Susie when she comes in with those quotes."

"Let's you and I kick it around first," Blake suggested with authority.

The Widow Halliday came through the door and handed O'Reith a buck slip, departed quickly, wordlessly.

O'Reith studied the back of the buck slip, said, "Standard Oil is trading at 75 1/8. We're up fifty cents at 215 1/2. Vince I've noticed our stock has been trading up for about a month. Suppose they're nibbling?"

"Could be but why the hell would they want to buy us when oil markets all over the world are coming under pressure? Standard has crude oil coming out of the gazoo. Now that they are in that Consortium in Persia, they'll have even more. Where are they going to sell it? I don't get it at all."

"Vince, Tidikelt is the finest gasoline grade crude oil in the world. It'll be the first to snap back out of this little slump we're in. Another thing. Standard Oil is in much better political shape to deal with Charles deGaulle than we are. They know how to pinch his balls when he acts up. And at *Ain Mutra*, we're looking at eight cents/bbl to mount a sustained water shut-off campaign. For them, *Ain Mutra* is a hop, skip and a jump away. They can move six workover rigs in from Saudi Arabia and shut that water off for three cents/bbl. Considering that we've got some of the best long-term crude oil contracts in the country, we're a bargain at $400/share."

"That's what you think?"

"Until they turn over their hole card."

"Something else there you think they know that we don't?"

"We offset them in Venezuela. They know Venezuela like you and I know Ted Schaeffer. Unfortunately Carolyn is out of the country. If she were here, we could get a quick reading on any possible interest they might have in those concessions."

Blake fell silent, sat looking across the desk at O'Reith. His frown slowly turned to a half-smile. He mused out loud, "Little Ted. What do you suppose that rascal is doing?" He didn't wait for O'Reith to answer. Instead he rose and walked over to the same window where O'Reith had stood earlier. Instinctively O'Reith joined him. Together they looked out at the roofs of Holmby Hills, where they both lived.

Blake said, "Clive, I'm ready to throw in my hand. I never have been comfortable in this job. I wouldn't be here if Harvey hadn't jacked me up into it, with you pushing from behind, I might add. That brush with the Justice Department in 1952 when Harry Truman got after us with a criminal antitrust suit. All of us. Jersey. The Texas Company. Gulf. Standard Oil... Well, you remember... One night I picked up an copy of *The Yellow Peril* and there was my name in the headline. '*Calitroleum's Vince Blake to go to Jail*'. Jesus Christ Clive! Virginia was hysterical."

O'Reith laughed, said, "Vince that's the only time I've seen you rattle ice cubes so hard you sloshed the gin out onto the table. Boy were you ever torqued up!"

"Well it wasn't very goddamned funny. We're lucky that little Kansas City slicker didn't run for another term. That civil suit, that restraint of trade suit that Ike's guys filed was bad enough. And that's not over yet. Where the hell is that going to end?"

"Not in jail."

"Clive it has been one thing after another since I became the Chief Executive Officer. I know that you've carried the ball. Kept me out of trouble. Seems like we always come out smelling like a rose... But Clive, it's my tail that's on the line. You can never relieve me of that burden. So we've got a chance to sell the company and I want to do it."

"Fair enough, Vince. I don't object. Shall we summon the widow?"

"Under the terms of the trust that Harvey established for her and little Briscoe, we don't have to ask her. I can vote her shares."

"And if she didn't like it, she'd challenge it in court. Good chance she'd win. Then where would we be?"

Blake's eyes were glazed over. He was far away. Uncharacteristic behavior, O'Reith thought, wondering what was on his mind. Then he asked, "Clive, do you remember Mimi Martell? She sang at Harvey's wake. A pretty little twist."

"I remember her."

"I dated her a few times," Blake continued, reddening slightly. "First time it was half business. Wanted to thank her for singing at the wake. We went to the Union Club. Had a few drinks. Found out we had things in common. I got to like her. How old do you suppose she is? Thirty-five?"

"How about 44."

Blake changed his stance, looked directly at O'Reith. "You sure? She looks younger."

"She's the same age as Helen."

Blake recognized authority speaking. He continued, "She carries her age elegantly. Clive, I came away from that lunch feeling twenty years younger." He sighed. "Well, to my supreme surprize, a day or so later, I got a card from her. I was up in the air, Clive. Before I knew what I was doing I had the phone in my hand. I had her on the line. We had another date set up. I took her to the Forty-Niner Club. Harvey got me in there a couple of years before he died. I didn't tell Virginia about it. Don't know why exactly. I guess subconsciously I was already thinking about straying off the reservation. Or maybe I just wanted a place to hide out. So we drank champagne, danced and put on the Ritz."

"You get some of it?"

Blake looked at the floor. He was reddening again and when he looked up at O'Reith, he seemed bashful, even a bit dejected. "I guess I could have but I just took her home in the limousine and we necked. Kid stuff. I spent the night at the Ambassador and sent my clothes out to a dry cleaner. Sure as hell didn't want Virginia smelling strange perfume."

"She was wearing Tabu the night of the wake," O'Reith mused. Then he added, "Vince, she likes rich, powerful men."

"Yeah, I know. I remember a scandal with that big band leader. Another with that Crocker Bank guy."

O'Reith snorted. "That one was more than mere scandal, buddy. His wife plugged him six times with a Police Positive 38 Long. They say it's the only murder case in Los Angeles County where a woman fired a pistol so fast she corkscrewed the barrel."

Blake shuddered. "Clive I just can't imagine what would happen if Virginia came after me with a pistol. She's never shot one. Bullets would fly everywhere."

"She might use a sawed-off. Doesn't make a hell of a lot of difference as long as you get close. And even if she missed, you'd be deaf for a week."

"Christ, Clive, don't even talk like that. My skin crawls. Anyhow, I broke off with Mimi. Haven't seen her for quite some while."

"Good for you babe," O'Reith said. "But before you start fooling around again, you better let Sharon fit you out with a toupee."

Blake glared at him. But then his expression softened. "Clive, you know that you're the only one I can talk to like this."

"Vince, I'm flattered. What do you say we whistle up the Widow Halliday ?"

Blake nodded. "You do the talking. She's your secretary."

O'Reith rang for her and when she came in, he motioned her into a chair next to Blake. "Susie, you remember the night of the wake? You and I were dancing to the *Wang Wang* Blues. You hit me up for a job. Vince and I were kind of cross-threaded at the time. I thought that I would be out on my tail the next day. I hired you conditionally."

She laughed. "Yes sir. I remember but I knew better. I knew they had to have some guys who knew how to run the company. Calitroleum Oil Corporation was not about to let you go."

"It's looks like I may be going now."

"General O'Reith! Clive, I...!

"Susie, Vince got a call from Harry Collier this morning. Remember him?"

"Chairman of Standard Oil? Nice guy. I danced with him at Harvey's wake."

"He's retired now. He has the reputation of a tyrant but then so did Mr. Halliday," O'Reith continued. "Collier wants Vince to fly up to San Francisco and have a drink with him at The Top of the Mark. R.G. Follis, Gwyn Follis, will be there too. He took over as CEO from Collier. The only possible reason for the invitation would be an offer to buy the company. Vince wants to sell. The three of us have controlling interest. What do you say?"

Her mouth fell open. She stammered for a moment. Then she said, "General O'Reith, I'm floored! I don't know what to say. What are you going to do? And Mr. Blake...?"

"Susie, I'm going to retire," Blake replied somberly. "You remember those headlines of a while back. I've had enough of this pressure cooker."

She turned to look at O'Reith and waited expectantly. After several silent moments, O'Reith volunteered, "Susie, I'm not going to retire. Helen doesn't know about this turn of events. I'm going to call her in a minute. Tonight we'll discuss it. But Calitroleum Oil Corporation will soon be history. We can't win a fight with Standard Oil."

"If Mr. Blake retires and you took his place and we still control over half the stock, we could win."

"Susie," Blake said in a tone of voice that could not be misunderstood, "I want to own Standard Oil stock. And if you're thinking about little Briscoe, as you should be, you want Standard Oil stock too. Calitroleum is in the second tier of oil companies. Standard Oil is a blue chip. It's a big company in the big league. It will pay a steady dividend far into the future."

The widow put her hands together. She trembled slightly, first looked down at the floor and then looked up at O'Reith. She said, I'll agree to sell the company. But if you keep on working, General, I want to keep on working too, for you."

"Susie, I'm flattered," O'Reith said. "The job could be in Paris or more likely, in Caracas."

She smiled and laughed. "I can pack in a couple of hours."

O'Reith winked at her. He said, "Then it's settled. Vince will vote your shares. We'll get the best deal we can. After I talk to Helen and the smoke has cleared, I'll tell you where we're going and what we're going to do. In the meanwhile, take some Spanish lessons."

She rose from her seat, smoothed her dress and offered a hand to Blake. She said, "You two are right guys." As she was leaving Blake said, "Susie how about getting Harry Collier on the line for me. He's in the office at 225 Bush Street with Follis. They're waiting for a call. I think the number is SUTTER-3000 but you better check it."

When they were connected, Blake said, "Harry, I'm with Clive in his office and we're pretty open. When would you guys like to get together? Tomorrow. Sure. We'll fly up. Meet you around eleven o'clock. That okay?" He nodded to O'Reith that they were on and hung up.

O'Reith called Helen. Although drowsy from lack of sleep when he left her, she had her nose in a script. He was pretty sure she was still into it. He said, "Baby, you okay for cocktails on the terrace at six?"

"Sure. Something up?" The music in his fine tenor voice told that an important change was in the works.

"Yeah but it's tight. I may be out on the street in a couple of weeks. As George P. McDonough would say, it is a bit of a flutter." Helen was fond of the portly Englishman, a director of Calitroleum who always spoke in fluid, dramatic tones. "We're back rolling the dice," O'Reith added.

Helen laughed. "When were we not, Ace? I'll be glad to see you. I want your opinion on this script. I'll try out a few lines on you."

O'Reith chuckled. "See you at six, baby."

As he hung up, Blake looked at his watch and asked, "Invite Larry for lunch?"

"Have to," O'Reith answered.

"What do you think he'll say?"

"He'll want to stay with Standard Oil. He thinks they hung the moon. He's a little guy that wants to be a big wheel in a big oil company, bigger than Calitroleum."

"That suits me fine," Blake said with emphasis. "I don't trust that half-pint and he doesn't trust me. I've spent most of my adult life keeping him a couple of steps behind me. I often feared Harvey was going to make him the Chief Operating Officer. When Harvey finally agreed to make you the executive vice-president, I let out a long Hip Hip Hooray."

"I owe you for that, babe."

"Holland?"

"He's home. Resting up. Indisposed."

"Got the flu?"

"He's got a hole right below his rib cage where Ines pinked him with that frogsticker she wears in her garter-belt. And the son of a bitch is lucky to still have his testicles. She was swinging for 'em. She was going to give him the wound of wounds. But she missed."

"Jesus H. Christ! What the hell happened?"

O'Reith's eyes lit up. "My guess is he got caught. Happened last night. I was coming in to tell you later, after I got through with the budget.

Helen and I were in bed. After midnight. We'd been fooling around and I had just rolled off to the side and gone to sleep. Phone rang. Helen answered. Ines. Hysterical. Said she'd killed Holland. Sounded suicidal. Helen told her to get herself together that we were coming right over. I phoned Max. Woke him up. Told him to put some sedatives in his bag. He said he'd hotfoot it over there. So we got there and the door was off the latch. The Mexican maid was crying and wringing her hands. But I give her credit for keeping the kids out of the bedroom. In the bedroom there were a couple of empties on the floor. Haig Pinch. Ice bucket turned over on the carpet. Ice cubes everywhere. Some half melted. Holland not in good shape, dazed, pressing a towel against the cut, stanching the flow. Blood on the carpet and on one side of the bed. Ines had on a fresh nightgown, pink. Other one, light blue, on the floor in the blood. She was kneeling on a pillow in front of her vanity. Little black candles burning, one on each side of the mirror. Crucifix hanging down. Little doll on one side of the vanity. Holland in uniform. Pin sticking in his heart right below his *Croix de Guerre*. She was sobbing and wailing "*mi amor, mi amor, mi amor, pobrecito, mi amor. Matica de Café.*" Then she went into a babble. Her hands clasped tight. Her head down. Praying as fast as she could rattle the words out. Helen attended her. I sat Holland down on the bed, on her side where there wasn't any blood. Holland said she'd lunged at his balls but he sidestepped her. It didn't look to me like she had cut anything vital. I asked him if he had spit up any blood. He said no and that he was all right. Just shaken. About that time, Max shows up. Gives him a local. Swabs the wound and sews him up. Then he sedated Ines and called a company nurse out to spend the night. Helen gets the maid going and between them, they clean the place up. All the bloody clothing and bed sheets went into the washer. They have one of those fancy vacuum cleaners that squirts water into the pile of the carpet and then picks it up again. Helen cleaned the carpet. Nurse shows. Helen piled the kids into the limousine. We go home and back to bed. That's four o'clock in the morning."

"Jesus! What a night!"

"Life in the oilfields of California," O'Reith shrugged.

"Have you talked to him this morning? He still shook up?"

"Hung over," O'Reith said. "Holland's been fucked around the horn more than once. That starlet bit a hole in the head of his dick the day the Japs bombed Pearl Harbor. A Zero pilot nearly took him out over New Guinea and he shot himself down in the ETO. He's a tough cookie. He'll be all right. He just underestimated that little Colombiana."

"How in the hell did he shoot himself down? I never heard of anything like that."

"Got in a Lufberry with a FW-190 around Hanover. Tailgated him at the turn and powdered the piss out of him. Point blank range. As he flew through the debris, junk hit the fan. Bent the shaft. Started running rough. Engine seized. Prop sheered off. He was lucky. Those English girls did a good job packing his parachute. But he'll sure as hell think twice before he cheats on Ines again."

"So just the three of us for lunch."

"Yeah."

They ate in the Calitroleum Executive Dining Room on the 38th floor. Larry Teague, who was affectionately known as 'Pup Joint' because he was only five feet and three inches tall, was the highly educated son of *Gasoline* Teague, a crony of the founder of Calitroleum. In fact, Calitroleum Tanker Corporation had named a vessel after him. The elder Teague had owned a tea kettle refinery in the 1920s and merged it into Calitroleum. A shrewd operator, it was common knowledge that he got his start stealing casinghead gasoline from Standard Oil traps in the Midway-Sunset Field. When he died of stomach cancer, it was said that it was a result of his siphoning gasoline out of automobiles when he was a kid to get his carrying-around money. The son, 'Pup Joint', was a graduate chemical engineer from The Case Institute of Technology. He had an advanced degree in accounting from Yale. He was slender, had square shoulders, emphasized by pads in his coats. He was nearly always smiling, even when he was angry. His face was boxy, with dark brown hair that he combed with a part, intense brown eyes that could be intimidating if you happened to be one of his subordinates. He often stretched as if that would make him taller. O'Reith, thought he looked like Jerome Cowan, the motion picture character actor and sometime leading man in B movies. Teague and Holland were both executive vice presidents, reporting to O'Reith. Holland was in charge of Exploration and Production; Teague, Refining and Marketing. They despised each other.

Over coffee, after O'Reith had explained the situation, Teague confirmed that he would like to become an executive in the Standard Oil Refining Department. He did his best to get himself invited to the meeting in San Francisco so he could make his own pitch. Blake put him down gently. Told him there would be two Standard Oilers and two COC men. Teague asked O'Reith why he wanted to leave.

O'Reith laughed. "Larry, how long would a guy like me last at 225 Bush Street? They'd put me in a broom closet on the fifth floor and forget about me."

Blake grinned. He was feeling expansive after a snifter of Hennessy cognac. He said, Clive, you could be wrong. Gwyn Follis probably can recognize talent just like Harvey."

O'Reith shrugged. His mind was far away. In Venezuela in fact.

"Clive, we haven't talked about Carolyn," Blake said. "Think we can protect her job?"

"I'm sure we can," O'Reith rejoined, his focus returning to the business at hand. "She knows Collier from the wake. That's a plus."

"Magaly was there with her," Blake added. "That's a minus."

Teague said, "Magaly. Odd name. I remember her. I wondered who the hell she was. She was the dame from Caracas togged out in a black bullfighter suit. Wearing a black sombrero with tassels hanging from the brim. When I first saw her I thought it was Leo Carillo just off the set of a mule-blaster."

"She's Carolyn's *friend*." O'Reith said.

"She was smoking a cheroot," Blake added.

"And Harvey was turning in his coffin," Teague speculated.

"He knew about her, Larry," O'Reith said. "And I'm sure that by now, Harry Collier has figured out who she is. That means that Carolyn may have a job but she's sure as hell not going to run the Standard Oil Company Exploration Department. At least not as long as Ken Crandall is around. They'll put her out in the provinces somewhere. Louisiana. West Texas. Some place like that. I doubt if she will wish to stay on after the merger."

"Are you going to stay, Vince?" Teague asked.

"Maybe long enough to see that it all gets pasted together. Depends on how things turn out tomorrow. I can't refuse if they want me in an advisory capacity for some extended period."

The waiter cleared their table, asked if they wanted more coffee or brandy. Blake nodded not and they all got up. On the elevator going up to the 39th floor, Blake asked, "You fellows be able to put a valuation on the assets this afternoon?"

"Book value of refineries, terminals, cat-crackers and tankers is just a couple of phone calls." Teague said.

"I'll scratch out a reserve estimate, count the wells, pipelines and production equipment," O'Reith added. "Larry give me what you've got by four o'clock. Susie can put it together for us. Vince can look at it on the plane in the morning."

Back at his desk he found the McLarssen Estate file on his desk. Susie had noted that the lease had been signed by one Donald McLarssen and one Eileen McLarssen, brother and sister of the deceased congressman from North Dakota.

The lease covered several hundred acres, enough for a dozen or so wells. The location map showed that they were on the south end of the Beaver Lodge Field and the geologist's appraisal was good. When drilled up, they could be running three or four thousand bopd. Donald and

Eileen McLarssen would have some good money coming to them. Enough to give him a hard time if that was on their mind. Well, he'd get into that with Tarbutton. Not much else to do right now. He put the file on the edge of his desk, asked Susie to return it to Land and Legal.

Right after the war, Clive and Helen O'Reith bought their mansion in Holmby Hills. Fixed up, with a new coat of paint, they had a million dollars in it. Their little bungalow on Summit Drive was now occupied by their older daughter Rae Regan, and her husband. Little Clive Colin, a year younger than Rae Regan had some time back, fallen in love with Blake's youngest daughter, Marilyn. They promptly shacked up in Santa Monica when he got out of the army. They surfed by day and hung out at a beer joint by night. Virginia Blake was not amused.

When O'Reith got out of the back seat of his Cadillac limousine that night just before six, he was greeted at the door by his second daughter, Helen Simpson, who had been born in 1948 while Helen was in deep trouble with the House Un-American Activities Committee. In spite of that, little Helen Simpson was a happy, cheerful child and brought great warmth to her father. He swept her into his arms, turned her over his shoulder and carried her inside as she giggled and tittered. After the customary kisses and affections, he returned her to the governess and climbed the stairs to the suite where he and Helen spent most of their time together. She was on their private terrace overlooking the swimming pool, standing at the rail, in a black silk pantsuit trimmed with rhinestones with dime-sized silver discs in her ears. Her ash blonde hair was cut in a pageboy. At forty-four, with three children, she still retained her elegant appearance. She exercised every day, played golf on weekends and rode horseback on Saturday afternoon. With the help of her cosmetician of twelve years dedication, she looked as good now as she had years ago when she stood-in for Joan Bennett for whom she came close to being a dead ringer. Helen Huntington Simpson had been a Wampas Baby of 1928 and Helen Huntington O'Reith was an Oscar winner of 1948. She was a Pisces, a democrat, a martinet as far as her children were concerned, and a clotheshorse. She stood in awe of her husband, considered him to be a nonpareil stud of Grecian dimension. She had frequent sexual fantasies of him when he was away. She knew he was vain, complicated, and that he carefully hid from her whatever feet of clay he might have. She was now and always had been jealous of him and took offense even when other women admired him at a distance; became furious when one of them brazenly appraised him at a cocktail party. Other than that, she was a normal American woman.

O'Reith kissed her, fondled her bottom and led her to the terrace table upon which was a pitcher of martinis, cocktail glasses and an ice bucket. As she poured his drink she said, "Well Ace, they're lovey-dovey again so I sent the kids home. Ines just called. Said thanks. She sounded repentant. Ace, you remember during the war I offered to finance a *Rio Limon* test for you from my first real movie money?" Her voice was husky, modulated, a vivid voice that suggested sensuality. O'Reith likened it to that of Chris Connor, the canary, now famous for her cool rendition of Cole Porter's ballad, *Get Out of Town*.

He replied," *Women at War* . Yeah I remember. You offered me a hundred grand. About enough to set surface pipe. I appreciated the offer even if I was in no position to take you up on it."

"If I want you to finance a venture of mine, would you?" She sounded a bit uncertain.

"It's all community property baby. "You can write a check as easily as I."

"Big bucks, Ace."

"Like how big?"

"Five million."

He shrugged, said, "chickenfeed."

"I'll need your emotional and intellectual support too. I want to start making movies. Oaters in Italy."

O'Reith sipped his martini. "What kind of gin are we drinking tonight, baby?"

"Booth's High and Dry."

"Good name for a western. High and Dry. Hero standing on a tall rock with his six shooter in his hand looking down on the bad guy down in the gulch with water up to his knees."

"Funny. Ace, I met this guy, his name is Frederico Bolletti. He makes Italian movies. Has his studio in a town called Ventimiglia. Know where that is?"

"Not too far from Monte Carlo."

"Ever heard of Alberto Garcia de los Ladrones?"

"Mexican writer. The Zane Grey of the Border. If it were me, I'd shorten the name. That the guy?"

"That's him but he's not down on the Mormons like Grey was. He's down on gringos mostly. He writes about all the misery that the white men give the Mexican peasants in towns like Matamoros, Nuevo Laredo and Piedras Negras. Characters are derelicts. Drunks. Whores. Pimps. Quacks. Failed priests. Rumdum gunfighters. People like that, on the edge of nowhere."

"I haven't read any of his books," O'Reith said. "I'm more of a Raymond Chandler man."

"You remember John Howard Lawson?"

"The Hollywood Ten guy. He was in the sneezer a while back. Blacklisted. Not too bad of a scriptwriter as I recall. What's he doing now?"

"He can't find work. Wants to throw in with us. Frederico has bought rights to a couple of Garcia novels. Lawson has already converted the first one into a shooting script. I've got it here. Been into it. Ace, Frederico says that my old movies, oaters especially, are all the rage in Europe. Spain. Italy. Greece. Even in France although that's hard to believe. I get furious when I think about it. I don't get a cent of royalty. I want you to set me up in a penthouse in Monte Carlo, one with a view of the sea. I want to be part of a new production company with these guys. I'm bored with Los Angeles. I'm bored with the kids and I'm bored with Virginia wanting me to do something about little Clive Colin. And I'm totally; I mean 100% bored with the Internal Revenue Service. In the motion picture company, I'll be part owner. I'll be a director. And I get to play those parts that suit my age and personality."

O'Reith smiled. "In those kind of movies the women must be ... Well, you know."

"I won an academy award for that kind of role. Remember Estelle. As a lady, she was pretty marginal."

They laughed together.

"So in these movies, I'd have roles like that. Saloonkeeper. Bordello operator. A woman married to a wife-beater."

"Kind of a limited range, baby. Miss Helen."

Helen smiled at him, refilled the glasses. "How about Señora Elena?" Helen continued, joking. "This is Piedras Negras, remember."

"Sound's neat."

"See that script on the floor. I'm a nurse working for this quack doctor out of Omaha, Nebraska. They've run him out of town for some reason or other. Mopery on the prairie, maybe. You know what that is, Ace?"

"Yeah. Staring at a women on the high plains by the light of the moon in the nude with a coyote howling on the horizon."

"This quack is a half-assed abortionist by night, usually with a snootful of Tequila. Daylights he's an undertaker. He also digs slugs out of the hero's bottom."

"What kind of hero gets plugged in the tail?"

"Mexico, Ace."

"Helen that reminds me of something. I'm having trouble with my leg again. I called Max this morning. He's going to look at it just as soon as Vince and I get back from San Francisco."

"You're going to San Francisco. When?"

"Tomorrow. That's why I called. But go ahead with what's going on in Piedras Negras. I'll fill you in after that."

"Clive Colin, if you had gone to the flight surgeon after you creamed out that bomber, that *Flat Foot Floogie*, you wouldn't have all that goddamned leg trouble. But you were so hot for that little Limey guttersnipe… You just couldn't wait to go down in the smoke to roll around with her. Oh! That slutty little twist! Every time I think about her I become unglued. And she was just a child!. A mere child!"

"Baby, what do you say we hotfoot it back to Piedras Negras?"

"Well you know how I feel!"

"1943 baby. All that was a long time ago. It was a public affair, a Guy Fawkes soiree at the Gloucester. Lots of big brass. My brother. Ismay. Arnold. Ike. Clark Gable. Jimmy Stewart. David Niven. The little guttersnipe married a Signals officer of the Army of the United States and they live happily in Richmond, Virginia. Furthermore, she's a dame. Heroine of the British Empire. Finally, all you have are suspicions. No facts. None."

"She's a husband stealer just like Mimi…"

"Helen. Do we continue the discussion or not?"

"You're right Ace, why should I lower myself?"

"Another drink?"

"No. I've had enough. Why are you and Vince going to San Francisco?"

"Standard Oil wants to buy the company."

"I don't believe it!"

"Susie didn't either. But it's true. Vince says he's had it. Says he wants out. I don't blame him. He took some heavy flak over that antitrust suit."

"And you?"

"We wouldn't fit in at SOCAL with our notorious past. I want to do something else anyhow. When the merger closes, we'll find you a place in Monte Carlo. Then I'm going to Caracas. Go into the oil business. *Production*. None of the rest of it, the things that drive Vince nuts." He looked at his watch. It was after seven. He said, "How about dinner at the club?"

"Let's go."

The Limejuicers Club in its heyday, was the most exclusive watering spot in Hollywood. Most of the members were in the motion picture industry, a disproportionately large number of them from Great Britain, thus the name. O'Reith inherited his membership from his mother. Now there were fewer Englishmen. The polo grounds had been sold off. Half of the vast orange orchard that surrounded it was under development. The club was no longer so exclusive and the clubhouse had lost most of its art deco charm in a remodeling. Still, no newspapermen were allowed on the premises so it was a haven for those seeking privacy. Clive and Helen O'Reith definitely fell into that category. While Helen bathed, O'Reith changed into a fresh tuxedo, put on dancing shoes and slipped a 9mm *society* Luger into his shoulder holster. Helen joined him. Soon they were in the tonneau of his limousine, laughing and telling jokes.

Chapter II
▼
Amanda Macabre

O'Reith was flying the converted C-47 to Oakland. Of a dozen war surplus aircraft that Calitroleum had bought from the U.S. Government in 1946, ten were C-47s and two were B-17Gs with gun-turrets removed. All were brand, spanking new, unpainted except for the serial numbers on the tails. O'Reith personally picked out each airplane. When the auction closed, he had bought them for something less than the value of the high-octane gasoline in their tanks.

Blake was his 'co-pilot', sitting in the right-hand seat, smoking a Pall Mall and studying the corporate balance sheets that Susie had given them that morning before they left the office. The regular pilots were in the executive passenger cabin drinking coffee and playing gin rummy. Blake asked, "Clive, how are we going to cue this up?"

"I'd say that after we get past the formalities, once we're down to it, we tell them that we want their best offer. No haggling. No dickering. No horse trading. It's yes or no. As far as I'm concerned, any offer over $400/share is a winner."

"Job protection?"

"Yes," O'Reith agreed. "Get into that right away. Make it a condition of the sale. If they are not prepared to do that, then no dice."

"You want to do that part?"

"OK."

"What will it be? Cash? Common stock? Some of each?"

"That's a tough one, Vince. For me, SOCAL common is fine. I think it will go up forever. For Susie, maybe some preferred and some common. She told me this morning she had plenty of cash. Doesn't want any more."

"I want some cash," Blake said with emphasis. Will you help me find a place to put it, somewhere I can use it when I want it and nobody will ask me any questions about it? I mean N-O-B-O-D-Y!"

"Yeah, I'll help you set up a bank account in Zurich and show you how to tap it."

"Can we structure this to leave the tax man out of it?" Blake asked, his voice indicating that he was nervous."

"We should be able to do that OK, Vince. We get back to the office, we'll huddle with the tax accountants. The corporation is a holding company. Its single largest asset is *Compagnie du Petrole Saharien S.A.* Registered in Liechtenstein. We can arrange to sell that directly to *California Arabian Standard Oil S.A.* We'll have to check the registration but I think it is in Switzerland. You and I and Susie can get ours out of that transaction. We'll close in Vaduz or Zurich. The rest of it can be done however the merger experts want to do it."

"That's legal?" Blake asked.

"Happens every day, my friend," O'Reith assured him.

"I'm ready to get it over with," Blake muttered. "I didn't sleep a goddamned wink last night?"

"Virginia after you?"

"She's pissed off about the change of life. Hot flashes. Irritability. She's after Marilyn to marry your boy. Some days it's hell on wheels." Blake stopped abruptly. O'Reith sensed he was in thought. Some moments later, Blake resumed, "Clive, I'm still thinking about this. I'm not ready to do anything yet. You know how I am… But if I wanted to find someone, well you know… Not like Mimi … She's dangerous.

Would you help me? You know about these things. I'm a babe in the woods. I don't want to make a fool out of myself. I don't want to embarrass Virginia or the girls."

"O'Reith's voice dropped an octave. He began to speak slowly. He said, "Vince, when the merger is made, Helen and I go to France. She wants a change of pace. I called LeBel yesterday. Felt like I had to let him know something was in the works. He said he wanted to throw in with me. Said he could get some backing from Charles de Gaulle if I wanted to take a flyer in Venezuela. That's exactly what I plan to do. Anyhow we'll have to explain all the merger details to him. *Le Grand Charles* will be his usual *Cross of Lorraine* to bear when he hears he's got to deal with SOCAL. So you and Virginia can come along. At some stage of the trip, you and I can slip away for a look at the Eiffel Tower. Find a place for a quiet drink and… What say, babe?"

Blake looked at him, almost with tears in his eyes. His mood began to change. A grin crossed his rugged features. He asked, "The offer of help with a toupee still good?"

O'Reith winked at him, rang for the regular pilots. They were getting into the Oakland traffic pattern and his leg had gone to sleep.

Harry Collier and Gwyn Follis were sitting at a corner table in the cocktail lounge at The Top of the Mark. A few couples were downing Bloody Marys. At eleven o'clock only a couple of dedicated topers were at the bar. The lounge was bright and glittery in the morning sun. As O'Reith and Blake entered, Collier and then Follis rose and came forward to greet them. Collier said, "Vince! Clive! When was the last time? When we laid Harvey to rest? Yes indeed! That's when it was!" His voice was a cadenced, rolling, and almost a heroic baritone. Collier continued, "Fellows like for you to meet Gwyn Follis. He took over from me some time back. I'm here unofficially. But I do own a few shares of SOCAL stock so I guess it's all right." Everyone laughed heartily.

As the four of them, walked to the table, Collier continued, "Clive, how's Helen? I so remember dancing with her at the wake. Dream about doing it again some time."

"She's fine Harry. Got her nose in a script. She's a nurse working for a jake leg quack in Piedras Negras digging slugs out of no-good Mexican cowpokes."

More hilarious laughter as the waiter approached. "Vince, name your poison," Collier boomed out heartily. He was in fine fettle.

"Dry martini on the rocks with a twist," Blake said. "Make it with Booth's and Nouilly Prat."

"Clive?"

"The same."

Follis said, "That's a Standard Oil drink." He dismissed the waiter. "You fellows fly up?"

"Clive flew," Blake said. "I was the co-pilot, looking out the window. Regular pilots got in some gin rummy time. Nice flight. Head wind about half way up. Clive had to goose it. We left LA at eight o'clock, came up over the Santa Ynes and right up the valley till we hit the Oakland Traffic Lane. Clive let the regulars land it."

When they were rattling the ice cubes in their martinis in a preliminary way, Collier, eyes atwinkle said, "Let's drink to that exquisite creature that Clive sleeps with and to Virginia, that elegant hostess of rare charm."

Blake and O'Reith raised their glasses. Blake said, "Harry, you're a flattering son of a bitch. But thanks anyway."

Collier tasted his drink, said, "I got that off of Harvey, God bless his soul. You know I ran into him one morning in the barbershop at the St. Francis. I asked him when he was going to come up and see us. He said he was free right then so I took him up to the top of 225 Bush Street and introduced him around. He could hardly keep his eyes off our little Negro boys in livery padding around on crepe-soled shoes delivering memos on silver salvers. Harvey said, 'By God, Harry, when I get back to the Tower, I'm going to start doing that.' And damned if he didn't."

Another roar of laughter rose from the table. Collier signalled the waiter for refills. Blake said, "You fellows know that Clive run all those little jigs off when we set him up as executive vice president. He announced that the bellhop era at Calitroleum Corporation was over."

"Vince, I didn't run 'em off. Some of 'em went to pulling slips in the San Joaquin. The rest went to work in the Bakersfield Pipe Yard."

Collier continued, "Did you fellows know that we tried to get Harvey to throw in with us back in 1937? We wanted his Venezuelan concessions. Harvey laughed. Said he didn't know what they were worth and he never sold anything if he didn't know what it was worth. Pretty sage old boy."

Follis took over, said, "So here we are damn near twenty years later and ready to ask the same question. Big surprise to you fellows, no doubt."

They laughed again, but not so loudly this time. The conversation was getting serious, voices steadier and softer. The topers at the bar could no longer follow the conversation.

O'Reith said, "Gwyn, if we were to get together, we'd have to have job protection for all that want it. We feel pretty responsible about that. Harvey would turn in his grave if he thought all those loyal men and women who made the company what it is had to go out on the street."

Collier turned and said to Follis, "Gwyn, these fellows run a real skinny company. Not like us. Calitroleum doesn't have an old soldiers home." To Blake and O'Reith, he continued, "Fellows, COC doesn't have a monopoly on forward thinking. SOCAL is doing that too. We've got a job for every swinging dick that wants to come along." Then he looked directly at O'Reith, added, "Even those that haven't got one."

O'Reith ignored the implication and said, "The most important one is Larry Teague. He wants a slot in the Refining Department."

Collier looked at Follis, said with a smile, "Gwyn, Larry is the son of old *Gasoline* Teague. He used to rob our drips down in Midway Sunset. He'd lace that natural gasoline with iodine crystals and sell it as Ethyl. He was a wild, wild guy."

"Larry's smoother, O'Reith continued. "He's a chemical engineer from Case Institute with a master's degree in Finance from Yale. Sharp. Charming. He negotiated the merger with Far Eastern Petroleum. He handled those Limeys just right."

"Well, we can sure as hell use him!" Follis said with enthusiasm. "You can tell him he'll have all the horsepower he needs to trim off the fat loitering out in the provinces. California is a big place. Easy to hide."

"Larry won't trim, Gwyn. He'll axe," Blake said.

They chuckled. "That's OK too," Follis agreed. "He can go down to Taft and chop some of those loungers off the main line. We're so big here in the west that we've got hands stumbling over one another. But in Texas and Louisiana, we're clean. In fact, Clive, we're keeping open the presidency of The California Company for you. Live in New Orleans. Be a corporate vice president. Couple of years from now, when the smoke has cleared, we'd put you on the board. Ten years from now you could even be running the company."

"Gwyn, I'm flattered," O'Reith answered, smiling. "But I'm going to say '*Adios Muchachos*.' I have the greatest respect for the Standard Oil Company. Sadly, I'm a maverick. I wouldn't fit in."

Follis went on, "Vince we have to keep you on board for a year or so. Could be longer."

Blake said, "I'll stay until we get it sewn together. After that…"

Follis said, "You fellows got any idea of what you need to make the deal work?"

Blake said, "Clive made a back-of-the-envelope estimate of what we've got. Book value downstream and reserve estimates upstream. It's here and I'm going to hand it to you in a minute. Clive and I are going to sit at that empty table that looks out on Alcatraz Island. We'll check up, see if any of the prisoners are escaping. You fellows look the numbers over and when you're ready, make us an offer. We'll tell you yes or no. Cold Turkey. No bargaining." Blake handed Follis the balance sheets. He started to rise.

"Sit down, Vince," Collier said, "Those yard birds aren't going anywhere. We don't need to look at those numbers." He nodded to Follis.

"Five hundred dollars a share and we'll pick up any debt on the books," Follis said in a machine gun burst of words.

Blake looked at O'Reith. Follis looked at Blake. Collier rattled the ice cubes in his empty glass until the waiter got his signal. Finally after some long, delicate moments, Blake said, "Fellows, you just bought the Calitroleum Oil Corporation."

Hoisting his new drink, Collier proposed another toast. "Gentlemen, when the final roll of honor is put up on that great cloudy bulletin board in the sky, the Standard Oil Company of California and the Calitroleum Oil Corporation will be there. Strong hands on the master valve. We're going to put some crude oil in the tanks!"

The oil men lunched in the SOCAL Executive Dining Room at 225 Bush Street. King crab cocktails with mayonnaise, filets of sole in lemon butter, baby lima beans and Caspian Sea long-grained rice, steamed with fresh dill and sliced red peppers. Flan with crème caramel sauce washed down with Colombian coffee and Remy Martin Cinq Etoile. Since it was a celebratory occasion, Pomery Greno Brut was substituted for the usual California zinfandel.

Thus at the end of the day, after three martinis, three flutes of champagne and a snifter of cognac, the terms of the merger were lettered out neatly in engineer's script on the back of the balance sheets that Blake had presented and were pushed back at him unread.

For the most part, it would be a stock swap. Basis of calculation would be the $500/share for each share of Calitroleum stock. After that, the computation would, become arcane beyond description to satisfy the requirements of Blake and the Widow Halliday.

Follis insisted that O'Reith agree to become a consultant to SOCAL for six months following the close of the deal, saying "Clive, you're the only person who knows where all the bodies are buried. We want you to help us settle existing lawsuits against the company and other matters where your detailed knowledge of a situation can keep us out of trouble."

O'Reith said," Gwyn I don't object to that but I plan to become an independent oil producer. We don't want to find ourselves in conflict of interest."

"We'll put some language in the consulting agreement to hold you harmless on that point. Hell, we encourage you. Get big! We'll buy you out too! Now, what do you need in the way of remuneration?"

"How about $10 million as an exit fee, the 1951 Cadillac limousine that I use now and four airplanes out of the Calitroleum fleet. I'd like to have two B-17s and two C-47s."

"Why don't you take the entire fleet?" Follis suggested. "We sure as hell don't need them."

"Neither do I," O'Reith said.

Larry Teague would become a SOCAL vice president in the Refining Department with a contract for five years and an option for five more. Blake would become Vice Chairman of the Board, reporting to Follis. His duties were unspecified. As for the other members of the Crude Oil Committee, O'Reith would sound them out and report to Follis those who wished to remain with SOCAL.

So it was settled. The regular pilots flew Blake and O'Reith back to Los Angeles, both men napping from the effects of food and booze. That night a groggy O'Reith, his leg giving him hell, told Helen the barest of bones about the agreement. She understood. He went to bed without dinner, got up at six the next morning and left her asleep. To his surprise, Blake was already in the office. Seeing the light on, O'Reith went in. He sat yawning, asked, "Sleep okay last night, Vince?"

"The sleep of the damned. Virginia met me at the door and wanted a complete rundown. We didn't get to bed until after midnight. I went out like a light. I just got here. I'm making a list of everything I've got to do. It staggers me."

"You'll walk through it. I have to get cracking too on that consulting agreement. That has to be right. Max is going to look at my leg at ten. If he's going to cut on me, I may just go home. I didn't get into it with Helen last night. Too much booze. So I have to tell her the details. You going to put out an announcement?"

"High noon. Same time that SOCAL releases it in San Francisco and New York."

"What about our people here in the tower? Will you give them the word?"

"I guess I better," Blake said. "I'll circulate a memo. Set up a question and answer session for tomorrow."

O'Reith went to his office. Susie had not yet arrived. It was five o'clock in the afternoon in Paris. He hadn't spoken with Maxine in several days, ached to hear her voice. Ached to have her in his arms too. But that would have to wait. He'd give the world to hoist little Monique over his shoulder, pat her little bottom and listen to her soft babble in French. He had planned to go back to Paris over the weekend but the business with SOCAL had interrupted that scenario. Not the first time his schedule had been thrown out of kilter, so Maxine would understand. He was not quite ready to tell her that COC was finished; that it would soon be time for another venture. Because he didn't know, at this stage, what it would be, she would in all likelihood, rebel at the idea of leaving Paris. In the end, he called, said he was delayed, possibly needed minor leg surgery and would call again when he had more information. He expected to spend Christmas with her; suggested they attend midnight mass at the Madeleine."

Then he called General Hardy Harold Tarbutton USAAF (Ret.) whose office was just down the street in the Fullerton Building. "Hardy, I've got an appointment with Max Parkinson at ten for X-rays but I should be finished by ten thirty. How's your day shaping up? Can you come around eleven?"

"Sure, Clive. What's the doc going to do? Look for more shell fragments?"

"Well, it's in that same place, top of my calf right under the knee. I'll let you know more later. See you."

"Something not right," Parkinson said, gently feeling of the muscles in the upper calf of O'Reith's right leg. "Could be a hematoma in there. Signs of subcutaneous bleeding. Remember anything about the original wound?"

"Only what the flight surgeon told me. He said it was a shell fragment that hit the bone below my knee and caromed downward. He removed an inch long steel splinter. The wound healed quickly but it was sore a long time. That's the same leg where I pulled a muscle jumping off the derrick floor of the *Holly No.1*, back in 1935. Maybe the problem is related to that."

"Well, we'll X-ray the entire leg, tibia to fibula. That should tell the story."

After he was finished, Parkinson advised O'Reith that he would give him a report that afternoon. O'Reith set up a lunch with Blake, then took the elevator up to the 39th floor to await Tarbutton. He called Holland at home. "Hunter, how's a-boy?"

"A lot better, sir. Appreciate what you and Helen did."

"Forget it. Hurt when you stir?"

"Some. But I can come in. You need me?"

"How about two o'clock. If I'm not here, I'll be in the infirmary with Max looking at X-rays."

"Yes sir, see you then."

Susie announced Tarbutton, led him in. Fifty-seven years old, an ace, he had first flown with the *Lafayette Escadrille* in 1917 and was decorated with the *Croix de Guerre*, among other medals, the former being a distinction he shared with his one-time subordinate, O'Reith. After

World War I, Tarbutton became a pilot with American Airlines. On the day the Japanese bombed Pearl Harbor, he was flying the Las Vegas to Los Angeles run. Recalled to active duty as Commander of the 97th Heavy Bomb Group, he first met O'Reith when the flight surgeon of that group invited several called-up reserve officers to a cocktail party. As the air war in the ETO turned deadly, O'Reith became his favorite and he pushed him ahead as circumstances and a steadily lengthening casualty list permitted. When the war ended, Tarbutton commanded the Combat Executive Officer Pool at Widewing. He had stayed in the army for a year or so, stationed at Eglin Field, Florida, attached to the Adjutant General's Department where he successfully prevented the courts martial of a dozen officers who refused to fly after the disaster called *Second Schweinfurt*. Now he was O'Reith's personal aide. A Leo, ramrod straight, stocky, six feet tall with steely, piercing eyes, crew-cut gray hair to match and a granite plug of a face. But for the gray, he could have passed for Frank Lovejoy, the movie star. At cocktail parties, unless toned down by his wife, Marjorie, his stentorian voice overrode all other voices as it reverberated around the room. Although he and Marjorie had been married 30 years, they had no children.

Tarbutton handled all of O'Reith's financial and legal affairs, was the executor of his last will and testament and took care of miscellaneous chores that had to be done correctly and confidentially. He knew more about O'Reith than Helen did.

When Tarbutton was comfortably seated, O'Reith handed him a slender leather-bound volume with gold lettering, titled *Witchcraft in Eastern Venezuela: A Survey of Practices from Antiquity to the Twentieth Century* by Megaera Melpomeme Micawber. O'Reith said, Hardy what do you know about the Wupperman family?"

"Never heard of them?"

"Ever hear of Frank Morgan?"

"The Wizard of Oz?"

"That's him. He's a Wupperman. Has a brother, Ralph. Not as well known but a pretty fair actor. Frank is expecting a call from you. He'll give you the name of their company lawyer in Ciudad Bolivar."

"What's the connection?"

"Angostura Bitters. Like in pink gin. What we used to drink in London at the *Club of XX*. The Wuppermans own a spread on the Orinoco, an Angostura plantation. Citrus trees with an aromatic bark that turns purple when soaked in alcohol. Back in the 19th century the town was called Angostura. Now it is Ciudad Bolivar, famous for, among other things, the training and education of high-class witches. The sharpest in South America. You hire one of those harpies, you pay an arm and a leg but you get what you came for. Or so they say. But that's a side deal. The guy Morgan will line you up to see is a buddy of Colonel Marcos Peres Jimenez, the dictator. When you get in to see him, tell him you represent a new American oil company that wants an oil concession on Lake Maracaibo."

"When do I leave?"

"Next week. Susie will help you get a visa. Take a company plane. Travel with Holland and Carolyn Cook. Oh yes. As of today, you're on the payroll of Calitroleum Oil Corporation as a consultant. You just became a merger expert with regard to the pending deal with the Standard Oil Company of California, Inc. Ten thousand a month plus expenses until the deal closes. When that happens, you'll join The Casinghead Company, which does not yet exist but it will by then. When you're finished in Ciudad Bolivar, go to Caracas to see the *colonel* and when you're done with him, find me a nice, penthouse flat in the Las Mercedes district, within walking distance of the Hotel Tamanaco."

"Clive, you're carrying me along a bit too fast, "Tarbutton objected. "What's with this merger?"

O'Reith beamed brightly, showing Tarbutton his pearly white teeth. He said in his musical voice, "Vince and I had a drink yesterday in San Francisco with the SOCAL brass. We sold 'em the company. So I'm thinking about my future. I'm confident that Holland and Carolyn will throw in with us and we need them. I talked to LeBel the other night and he's with us too. I have not talked to McDonough but this is his kind of play. So that's our team. Carolyn is on her way back from Sumatra. She knows Lake Maracaibo like you and I know London. There's a sea change in petroleum policy down there. They're putting out new concessions. First such in years. We have money. We have a team. We still have to get the concessions. That's for you and Carolyn. Calitropical has a lawyer in Maracaibo named Emilio Garcia. Knows his way around the Ministry of Mines and Hydrocarbons. He and Carolyn have worked together for several years. They click okay. I want you to recruit Emilio for our side. Also, visit Alan Prescott and his wife, Sally. I'll give you a letter to him. And I'll need a place to stay too. Find me a flat on Milagro Avenue not too far from the Hotel Del Lago. While you're at it, rent an office in the new wing of the hotel. Then, when all that is done, Holland will take you to see a woman named Amanda Macabra Schaeffer."

"Schaeffer? That rings a bell."

"Ted Schaeffer, Theodore. Was on the Crude Oil Committee. Involved in the automobile accident that killed Harvey's boy. Harvey blamed Ted. Wanted him exiled. I put him out on the lake pushing tools. Ted met Mandy on his days off and one thing led to another. They got married in Carmel some years back. He retired from the company. They live on a *finca* that used to be out on the edge of town. Maracaibo has grown a lot. Now they're in the suburbs. Pretty good-sized spread. Four or five acres. They built an inn next to Mandy's house. Trying to pump up some tourist activity. I don't know how it's doing. Not a hell of a lot of sightseers in that town."

Tarbutton ran his finger over the gold letters of the book O'Reith had given him. He thought aloud, "Micawber? Macabre? Any connection?"

O'Reith's face became arch, his voice musical, "Yeah, sort of. Mandy comes from Ciudad Bolivar. I met her right after the war, when we had that fire on the lake. She was a high-octane witch then. She'd give a guy a jolt of optical energy that would turn his limp dick into a casehardened bull plug. A fellow had to be careful around her, not look her directly in the eye. Then she took up with Ted. He's a half-assed Catholic and I guess she was too, once. He conned her into getting exorcised. Ted had this buddy, a monsignor up at Carmel who did the trick. Drove out the evil spirits in the morning. Had a good, long, liquid lunch with them. Married them that afternoon. They went back to Maracaibo and that's where they are now. In her salad days, as she tells it, she was a promising young sorceress. But a missionary priest got a grip on her. He tried to drive the devil out but it didn't take. She kept on with her magic spells and incantations. Got so bad the Bishop of Caracas kicked her out of the church. She went to Paris and studied medicine and psychiatry at the Sorbonne. *Diplome Superiore,* or some such. She returned to Venezuela, moved lock stock and barrel to Maracaibo and went into high gear. She and Maxine and Ines are bosom buddies. She fixed both of 'em up with passports when they needed to get out of the country. To be the chief bagman in Maracaibo for the Casinghead Company, a fellow needs to be on good terms with a broad like la Macabra."

"And whom might that distinguished gentleman, that bagman, be?"

"Hardy H. Tarbutton, retired four-star General of the Army of the United States." O'Reith laughed and laughed until his eyes were full of tears.

"Clive you got me mixed up with some other guy. For sure."

"Hardy, you've been running in idle for too long. As Holland would say, it's time you got a little hair in your teeth. Remember Stanley Ethering, our guy in Washington, our Booze and Pussy coordinator? He worked his way through St. Mary's Law School in San Antonio dealing stud poker for Red Barry in a joint behind the tobacco stand in the Gunter Hotel lobby. Stan knows a winning hand when he sees one and he's met a few four-flushers in his time."

"I thought he was a lobbyist?"

O'Reith smiled again. "That's him. Nice guy. Knows some good jokes. He and I were together on an API committee. Vince hired him off of Pure Oil Company during the war. He'd been with them since 1929, title attorney for the Van Field south of Dallas. In the mid-30s, Pure sent him to Washington in connection with the Connally 'hot oil' Act. From there he began a lobbying career. He's at ease with politicians. Keep's 'em jollied-up. Recognizes the powerful ones. Ignores the castrati. From Palacios, Texas. Speaks good Spanish. SOCAL needs him like they need a dry hole in the Golden Lane. Give him a ring. Hire him. Line him up to go to Caracas. In Venezuela, black magic goes right along with booze and pussy, they call it *poontang* down there, by the way. You better take Marjorie with you. You get tangled up with some strange stuff and you'll be *hors de combat tout de suite*, before you even get started."

"Marjorie will like that. And I'll be glad to have her company. This Macabra woman sounds pretty dangerous?"

"She is if you ruffle her feathers. Treat her gently. Alan and Sally think the world of her. She and Ted look after their kids when they're up here."

"Sally know about her background?"

"I'm sure not."

"Clive, let me repeat. I'm too old…"

O'Reith cut him off. "Hardy, it's a chance for you get a Mustard Cluster on your *Croix de Guerre*. You might as well settle back and enjoy this. It isn't every day that a fellow gets a chance to wrap himself in clover. Time'll come when you and Marjorie both will appreciate a little nest egg. Pensions are okay but they tend to get thin over the years. Besides my affairs are too complicated. There it is."

"Okay." Tarbutton growled. "I hope you know how to make all this come true."

O'Reith nodded authoritatively, continued, "On the way back, stop in Mexico City. Call on a guy named Juan Pablo Alfonso. I'll telephone him you're coming. He was Minister of Hacienda in the old government, before the colonel took over. He formulated oil policy. Alfonso is a flag-waver. Thinks the gringos have fucked Venezuela around for years. Cheated the people blind. False-bottom tankers. Short measurements. Usual rhetoric. He's probably half-right. But he and I are friends. We'll pitch it to him we're going to run a clean company with no fol-de-rol. One, in time, he could come to like. All we want is that they adhere to the contract. No seizures of assets. No force majeure. No number fudging. Beyond that, we'll play ball. Hire lots of locals. Give out scholarships. Training programs. Jobs for those that complete the scholarships. Engineers. Geologists. Geophysicists. Sound him out. See if he wants a consulting contract. You'll have to be careful. He could be suspicious. But if he rises to the bait, sign him up. Even if he refuses, which I expect he will do, even if he keeps his distance, make it a point to keep calling on him – with some regularity. Keep him in the picture as much as you can without revealing any secrets."

"Clive, I'm having trouble getting all this in focus. Are we starting an oil company or making a movie?"

O'Reith laughed. "Hardy, don't think too much about it. By the time you get back, it will begin to make sense. But I'll give you a little background. You can take some notes if you like." O'Reith waited for Tarbutton to get paper and pencil ready. He continued, "Hardy, when I first went down there, it was late 1936 and there was a hell of a labor strike going on in the oil fields. Lasted well into January of 1937. There had been some changes in the legislation regulating oil production. That may have been what precipitated the strike. Anyhow, because of the changes, Halliday decided the time had come to start drilling up some of those old Calitropical leases. About a year before I went down there, the guy who had been running the country for decades died. His name was Gomez. He was a strongman, a dictator. When he died, riots broke out all over the country. The worst of them were in Maracaibo. Mobs sacked the stores, strung up anybody that was connected to the Gomez Government and generally raised hell. Went on for days. They burned the Foreign Club where the Limeys and the Gringos hung out. Oil company families were evacuated. It was a bad scene. But the army held together, a guy by the name of Lopez Contreras took over. By the time I arrived, things had settled down. But there was still plenty of criticism of the big oil companies. Shell and Mene Grande and Jersey especially. Calitropical Oil Company was a detail of the game. We were not producers. Weren't even drilling. Nobody paid much attention to us. I was by myself for several months. We were building a camp but it wasn't ready so Helen stayed here. It was about that time that the Venezuelan Congress, which had been no more than a rubber stamp under Gomez, decided to completely overhaul the oil statutes. They established a *Direccion de Hidrocarburos* to look over the shoulders of the oil companies, forcing them to measure oil volumes properly, clean up oil spills and utilize the natural gas that was being flared off. All that made Harvey Halliday sit up and take notice. That's why I was down there. Provisions in the new laws allowed them to revoke idle concessions. All of the Calitropical concessions were. I was the tool pusher and the drilling engineer and the geologist all rolled up into one. We built the camp fifty miles south of Maracaibo on the road to Machiques, not a famous place. We drilled our own water well, set up a light plant. Noisy as hell. Had to boil the drinking water. Helen came down. We were running two steam rigs up in the jungle country bordering the Perija Mountains. Rough duty. Every month or so I'd get a few days off. Helen and I would drive into town for a nice dinner at the Hotel Granada, see a Mexican movie and go shopping. Summer of 1937, Helen went to San Francisco to stay with her parents. That fall she put the kids in boarding school. I was in the jungle most of the time but once in a while I'd get into town. There was a ballet school in Maracaibo. Pretty neat stuff, some of it. I fooled around with one or two of 'em. Nothing serious. Helen returned in late September of 1937 but her heart wasn't in it. She was unhappy. I was in my element. She tried to make the best of it but in the summer of '38, she went home for good.

I stayed with her for a couple of weeks but I had to go back to work. We found oil. Those wells would flow over a thousand barrels a day. Big time. In the summer of 1939, war broke out. The U.S. was awash in crude oil. The British declared a blockade on Germany. The German submarines attacked British tankers. Halliday got cold feet and shut everything down. The oil business in Venezuela cooled off. I returned to Los Angeles and began working for Vince. All the time I was down there, I was vaguely aware that the new government was unstable. A guy named Medina took over in 1941, another military man. He tried to sell crude oil in the U.S. but didn't get anywhere. Things hit rock bottom in Maracaibo. But by 1945, things were picking up. Halliday was ready to have another go at it. Medina got kicked out. A so-called *Revolutionary Junta* took over. I was back in the picture. Suddenly the tax laws were important. Read the file on it. You'll have to understand the law governing concessions before we negotiate a contract. To finish the story, the *Military Junta* collapsed and the present guy came to power in 1952. He's tougher than an army mule. Been in there for three years now. There are signs of further unrest. So we have to be careful. Still it is a great opportunity. I want to grasp it. Susie will help you plan the trip. Stay at the Tamanaco in Caracas and the Del Lago in Maracaibo. I don't know Ciudad Bolivar but Morgan can help you there. One thing to remember all the time. Never forget this. *Seguridad Nacional.* They weren't too bad in the old days but under Colonel Marcos Perez Jimenez, they've become a terror. A Gestapo with a Latin flavor. Tough cookies. They hang around the popular bars and hotel lobbies. When you've got business to discuss, Holland will take you to a quiet place. Peters Hotel. Stalingrad Bar. Couple other places. Better carry a gun. Still got your .45?"

"Yeah but I haven't fired a shot in twenty years."

"Clean it up. Buy new ammunition. Get new distance glasses. Ear plugs. Go out to the thousand inch range at the club and make sure you can bull's-eye the target. The day you leave, have Max tape it between your shoulder blades. He'll give you a letter in Spanish saying you've had a growth removed. When you go through Customs and Immigration, there'll be a *Seguridad Nacional* man there to pat you down. They are pretty casual when it comes to Gringos. If they look at your back, show 'em the letter. Holland will be at your side so not to worry.

"What else?"

"I want you to hire some bodyguards. I need round the clock surveillance on Holmby Hills, Summit Drive and that place in Santa Monica where little Clive Colin lives with Blake's youngest. Hardy I want guys with front-line experience. See if you can find some former MPs. Guys out of the 82nd or 101st Airborne. I want 'em armed. You'll have to run them by the Los Angeles Police Department. Tell 'em they're movie star guards. Work it through an attorney or maybe a private eye. Don't let this leak out."

"Clive, can I get off somewhere by myself and pull all this together? I'll come back later today and review it with you? Go over everything. Make sure I've got it all."

"Holland is coming in at two. Can you be ready then?"

"Sure."

"If I'm not here, look for me in the infirmary."

"See you then."

*   *   *

As they were sipping their first martini at the California Club, Blake asked, "Can we close by December 31?"

"Yes," O'Reith answered. "Lawyers and accountants are all lined up. Follis called. He's sending his guys down to see everything fits. We'll have some weekend work but we'll make it."

"I need to do anything?"

"Take some singing lessons," O'Reith suggested with a chuckle.

"What for?"

"We get this all wrapped up, you can start singing in the choir at the Methodist Church on Sunday."

"Virginia would smell a rat."

Both men laughed and O'Reith signaled for menus. "Clive, I don't know when I've been so excited," Blake said, rattling ice cubes. "I really look forward to this. Big load gone. How about you?"

"Max made some pictures of my leg. He'll give me the word this afternoon. Meanwhile I'm gazing into my crystal ball."

"See anything interesting?"

"I see an oil company operating out of Maracaibo with nothing but crude oil running to steel storage at Punto Fijo. No refineries. No gasoline stations. No tankers. No criminal antitrust suits. No restraint of trade filings. No Texas Railroad Commission and…"

"No booze and pussy," Blake interjected.

O'Reith grinned. "Well, Vince some things never change. We have to be realistic about the fundamentals. But down there they call it Pampero Rum, Poontang and Black Magic."

"Ted's wife on the payroll?"

"Yeah."

"Clive, how much you going to sink into it?"

"Don't know for sure. Maybe a hundred million clams. Depends on the cost of the concession. Tarbutton goes down next week to scout things out. Could be more. Maybe $200 million."

"All that out of your own pocket?"

"LeBel wants in. Maybe McDonough."

"What about me?"

"That's fine. But it's conflict of interest with SOCAL."

"My worry. It gets to be a conflict only if I tell 'em."

"You're in. Five percent?"

"Maybe more. When you know what it looks like, we'll settle it. Larry has some loose change too."

"I think not. And I really don't want to risk any of the Widow Halliday's money. But she hit me up. She's going to be my private secretary so I can't shut her out."

*   *   *

After lunch, he was back in the infirmary. Parkinson showed O'Reith the X-rays, said, "See that blank in the film up under your knee? Looks like a nail without a head. That's it. Look closely at the bones. See that calcium build-up? That shell fragment has migrated over the years, worked itself up into the joint. When you walk it irritates the bones and the calcium accumulates."

"Why does my leg go to sleep?"

"Pinched nerve or a collapsed blood vessel." Parkinson turned off the light behind the film. "Clive, I'm not set up for it here. I booked you into Hollywood West. Be there at eight in the morning. We'll be finished by noon. General anesthetic."

"You the surgeon?"

Parkinson nodded. The nurse entered, told O'Reith that both Holland and Tarbutton were in the waiting room. Parkinson said, "See you in the morning, Clive."

Hunter Hawke Holland was a graduate of The University of Texas, a petroleum engineer. His home was in Gladewater, which he visited only when his parents pressured him. After ROTC at San Antonio, Texas, he became a second lieutenant in the Air Corps and joined Calitroleum in 1939 when he was released from active duty. Like O'Reith, he was called up right after Pearl Harbor. As a fellow aviator, he caught O'Reith's eye. After the war, O'Reith pushed him ahead as fast as he could. Now, Holland was a member of the Crude Oil Committee in charge of Exploration and Production. His blond hair had faded from youthful gold to mature ash. But his eyebrows, long, flattened vees were still bright and luminous. By contrast they gave his bullet-like gray eyes a coldness that made him seem more distant than he was. A long, jagged scar ran from his right temple to his jaw. For several years it was flaming red but now most of that color was gone. He had been gashed by a shard of aluminum railing when the bullet-riddled open canopy of his P-40 slammed forward during a crash landing at Darwin, Australia. His face was still hatchet-thin but growing wider. His voice was above a bass, but not much and it lacked texture. He was handsome in a rugged way, like John Wayne. He was an Aries, thin as a rifle barrel, wild as natural gasoline. His wife Ines was murderously jealous and with considerable reason. Holland had a roving eye, to put it in its best light. He recognized no higher authority in the universe than General Clive Colin O'Reith. Indeed, he had idolized him since he was a mere captain. In matters of ethics, morals, politics, intellect and fine art, Holland considered O'Reith to be the supreme authority. Only in courage and the ability to assess feminine beauty did Holland consider himself on a par with his master. Holland, not a philosopher, recognized that going with O'Reith would get him where he wanted to go.

He knew everything there was to know about drilling oil and gas wells, no matter how deep, how hot, or how high the pressure at the bottom of the hole. From the San Joaquin to the Sahara, from the jungles of Sumatra to the shallow waters of Lake Maracaibo, he could drill them faster, cheaper and safer than most of his contemporaries. His name was a legend in oil fields around the world. Even Gwyn Follis had heard of him. After the ruckus with Ines two nights earlier, Holland was concerned that O'Reith might order him to 'keep his peter in his pants,' which, of course, he would surely do if it were so mandated. He was relieved when O'Reith, as usual, got right down to business.

In the elevator on the way up to the 39th floor, O'Reith briefed him on the merger, asked him where he stood and accepted his decision to throw in with The Casinghead Company. When the three of them were seated in O'Reith's office, he told them of the morrow's surgery and that he expected Carolyn Cook back over the weekend. On Monday he wanted to lay out the general strategy with them all. He was sure Carolyn would join them. On that basis, he wanted her to select the concession that they would seek. This was no time for dry holes. Looking Holland in the eye, he asked, "You and Ines okay? Will she let you go to Maracaibo by yourself?"

"I better not ask. I'll suggest she pack her bags. She'll stick to me like glue for quite some long while. Until…"

"O'Reith looked at Tarbutton, said, "You could the take a B-17. It has Tokyo tanks. Get you to Mexico City in one pass. Check Holland out as co-pilot. Pretty comfortable airplane. Pisser installed in the tail and another one in the galley where the radio room used to be. Couple of half beds back in the fuselage. What do you say?"

"Suits me," Tarbutton responded. Holland nodded.

O'Reith dismissed Holland; asked Tarbutton to stay. He began, "Hardy, the surveillance we talked about has to be discreet. I don't want the family to know. They'd worry. And the emphasis is on their safety. The boys you hire will need good judgement. They see something that's not right, they must act on their own initiative. We can't give them much guidance."

"Let me work it down to a short list. Then we can interview them. That way, we'll have lads we trust."

"Good idea. Hardy, the other night Helen hit me up for a move to Monte Carlo. Still under discussion. I have to get into it again with her. In the meanwhile, I want you to check out a guy named Frederico Bolletti, an Italian movie maker with a studio in Ventimiglia. I want to know if he's on the level. Helen would like to set up a production company with him and a couple of other guys, neither one of 'em first class citizens. It's okay with me but if he's not a right guy, maybe I can head her off at the pass. Bill Wyler can help. He'll know all of those guys who are worth knowing."

"I'll get on it this afternoon," Tarbutton replied. "I've got myself a plate full."

That night on the terrace after he had briefed Helen on the merger and his session with Doctor Parkinson, he said, "Baby let's take another trip down Piedras Negras way. Have you and Bolletti and the others worked out a program? You're putting up $5 million. What is Bolletti putting up?"

"He's putting up 5 million Lira. And, of course, the studio."

"Lawson?"

"Stone broke. Lawyers cleaned him out. He agreed to work for room and board until the first flick is in the can. After that…"

"How did you get acquainted with Signor Bolletti?"

"Ace, is this the beginning of the third degree or something?" Helen asked, irritation rising in her voice.

"I don't want you to make a mistake. I don't want to get into the soup again. We don't need another scandal. Helen, I'm a political animal only in a subjective way. That business with the Committee for Un-American Activities unsettled me greatly. I want those pols to do what I tell them to do, what I pay for. I don't like it when they act up. As an observation, and I don't want you to read anything into it, I wonder why these people, the Hollywood Ten and all those they ratted on, why would communists seek out the best paying jobs in the richest country in the world? Do they send all that money back to Moscow? So, has this guy Bolletti got anything to hide? Another thing, while we're on the subject of mistakes, I got quite a start the other day when I learned that we were drilling the John McLarssen Estate No. 1 in Beaver Lodge Field, North Dakota. What do you think of that?"

He could see the blood draining out of her face. She took in a sharp breath. He detected a tremble in her hands. She said nothing, just looked at him intently. He continued, "I asked Susie to get me some details. Donald and Eileen McLarssen, brother and sister signed the lease, which covers several hundred acres. She runs a ranch. Brother is a lawyer and a lay preacher."

"What do you think?"

"I don't know what to think," O'Reith replied. "After the indictment against me failed, I got a threatening letter from Eileen. She was fourteen then so I ignored it. I didn't tell you because I didn't want you to worry."

"Now she's eighteen," Helen said. "Some good money coming in from the wells on their property. Why would Calitroleum lease their land in the first place?"

"Routinely, I'm sure," O'Reith answered. "Those Land and Legal lawyers wouldn't have made the association with us. In 1948 there was no oil in North Dakota. Now there is a boom. It's just a crazy coincidence. I hope that they get their money and leave us alone. I'm somewhat concerned because I had to agree to a six month consulting contract with SOCAL. If something went wrong up there, a blowout or a fire, a lawsuit might result. I'd have to appear in court. If that happened, it might bring out the worst in them. Many people in that part of the country are convinced that I shot Congressman John McLarssen."

She refilled his empty glass, trying to regain her composure. Color began returning to her face. She said "Ace, I'm not in great shape today. Still thinking about the way Ines sliced up Hunter. Virginia called again this afternoon. Worried that little Clive Colin is going to knock her daughter up. Wanted to know if I had talked to him."

"What did you tell her?"

"I told her I hadn't and that I wasn't going to. She gave me the usual. A half hour of it."

"Well, leave that to me. Soon as Max has me fixed up I'll speak to our son. If you're determined to go to Monte Carlo we'll have to straighten him out. Now back to Bolletti. What kind of a guy is he? How tall..."

Helen cut him off. "Goddammit, Ace I really resent it when you refer to my business associates as runts. Really! Ace, I look to you for emotional support."

"We still drinking High and Dry, baby?"

She drained the pitcher of martinis. Looked at him sullenly.

"Helen, the movie industry in Italy is well-developed. Why don't you ask Jack about him? Ask him what he thinks about the whole affair. He made you what you are today and you're not under contract to him. He can tell right away if you're going in the right direction. He'll know what kind of a guy Bolletti is."

"Why are you always so maddeningly right?" She asked between clenched teeth.

He smiled and said, "Let's dine in tonight. My poor leg is throbbing like a broken heart."

"What are you going to say to little Clive Colin?"

"I'm going to put the squeeze on him."

"About Marilyn?"

"That too."

"His wayward life getting on your nerves?"

"No. He's only been out of the army a few months. He didn't have an easy time of it over there. Front line signals officers in the dead of winter earn their pay. I'm glad he got back in one piece; that he's not in a Chink clink. But the clock is running out. If Rae Regan moves in here, I want him and Marilyn to be in Summit Drive. If he loves Marilyn and I can't imagine that he doesn't, hell they've been fooling around now for years, they need to get married. My intention is to get him off high center. Maybe even offer him a job."

"Really? Doing what?" Helen was, for once, interested in her son's future.

"Well, my dear, if you're in Monte Carlo and I'm in Caracas, we'll need some means of communication. A phone call would take a week given the chaotic condition of telephone lines in Venezuela. It takes two days to call Los Angeles. Clive Colin knows short wave radios. He can start there. Plenty for him to do."

"If he marries Marilyn, we'll have to throw a blast. Can you cope with that?"

"I can after Max is done. Before I forget, be sure and put Harry Collier on the guest list. He sent you his regards when we were in San Francisco. Hinted he'd like another dance with you."

"Well he'll certainly get his chance. How about Follis?"

"Yeah, him too."

"The sooner you talk to little Clive Colin, the better. I'd like to be straight with Virginia again."

"I'll call him in the morning after I get up. Ask him to come in on Monday. I'll keep you posted."

* * *

It was Monday morning and O'Reith was in a wheelchair behind the vast expanse of his mahogany desk. Susie had already placed his schedule before him and served coffee. His chauffeur sat in a side office reading the sports pages from the *Los Angeles Times*. His son was due momentarily. Halfway through the cup of coffee, Susie ushered him in. He was wearing rumpled fatigues, a faded green fatigue hat and army low cuts, scruffy and mildewed with salt encrustation around the heels. His black hair was grown out far beyond what army regulations would allow and he had a scraggly black beard. The skin of his face was weather-beaten and peeling. Above his lips was a black, ratty mustache. But his brilliant blue eyes, like his father's once were shined luminously and beneath the facial clutter, he was still handsome. Cleaned up and properly attired he could attract a higher class of women, his father concluded. O'Reith ignored his appearance, greeted him warmly, extended a hand and beamed broadly as the boy came around behind the huge desk. "How have you been keeping, son?" he asked in his musical tenor.

"Okay Dad," little Clive Colin replied, studying his father's face for clues as to his destiny. "And yourself?"

"Well as you can see, I'm not 100% up to par but I expect to be shortly. Marilyn?"

"She's okay." He twitched a bit, began to see what was looming.

"How long have you been out of the army now, my boy?" O'Reith asked. He was quite friendly as if he really wanted to know.

"Since June. Seems longer."

"Given any thought to stopping doing what you're doing and doing something else?"

"Not really. Surfin' and singin'. Anything wrong with that? I'm free, white and twenty-one."

"Twenty-four." His father corrected him. "Where do you do the singing?" O'Reith asked. He knew where he did the surfing.

"Beachcomber Club in Santa Monica. The Surfer Quintet. Bongo. Trumpet. Clarinet. Saxophone and piano. I play the sax sometimes when we're short."

"Thought about your future with Marilyn?"

"Some."

O'Reith was silent, looked at him fixedly, pursed his lips to let him know he expected a more extended answer. A steely gaze slowly replaced the fatherhood countenance. It was a glassy-eyed stare that had once wilted many a group officer. His son felt the tension building. He knew a better answer was expected of him. Finally he continued, "Well, the subject comes up from time to time."

"She that way?"

"I don't think so but it could happen. We get into the booze bag pretty often. Careless."

"You love her?" O'Reith's features softened somewhat.

"I love her. I just don't want to be pushed. You know Dad it isn't easy to just come out and pop the question. We're getting along just fine..."

"You were. You're not anymore. Things are changing. You should marry her. Shack-ups have a way of coming apart. In our society, the time comes when a man, especially an army officer, has to face responsibility."

"I resigned my commission. Anyway, what's the big rush?

O'Reith ignored the insolence. He remembered that day after Victory over Japan when Holland was in his office to get his old job back. He recalled that you could take the boy out of the army but you could never take the army out of the boy. He knew that this was as true of his son as it was of Holland. He continued, "You know son, that SOCAL is buying Calitroleum. Deal to close by the end of the year."

"Yes. I know. It's in the papers. Marilyn heard it from her mother. I heard it from my mother." His tone of voice bordered on exasperation. "So what?"

"Son, your mother wants to make a change. She…"

"Wants a divorce." His son interrupted.

"No, goddamn it. Son, don't cut your father off like that." His face became hard again. "She wants to start making movies in Italy. Rae Regan will move into Holmby Hills. I'm going into the oil business in Venezuela. You're caught up in circumstances beyond your control. So I want to know if you plan to marry Marilyn. If so, you can move into Summit Drive."

"Dad, are you trying to organize a shotgun wedding?"

The cold piercing gaze returned. The two men glared sullenly at one another. At last O'Reith said, "You could call it that."

His son was silent for a few moments, shuffled his scruffy shoes in the pile of the gray carpet. Then his face became friendlier. He said, "All right Dad. We'll get married. Are we finished? Can I call Marilyn and tell her to get ready for the beach?"

"You can call her and ask her to marry you. Then we'll get on with our affairs. No beach today, my boy."

His son reached for the telephone and soon Marilyn was on the line. O'Reith listened, pleased, to the conversation. As they spoke, O'Reith asked Susie to send in Sharon Mills, his cosmetician.

Mills was a tiny, mouse-like woman, forty or so, with a Mediterranean complexion and large eyes below plucked eyebrows and a cloud of lustrous brown hair. Attractive but far from beautiful, she had been involved in several minor biological scandals with B-movie leading men. Now that was behind her. She was exquisitely presentable in a black, satin business suit and high heels with a white apron. She had her makeup kit in her hand. O'Reith had recruited her from 20th Century Fox when he became president of Calitroleum. Now her small salon adjoined Susie's office. Before important meetings she "tuned him up," as he put it. She looked at his son and said affably, "Hello, Clive sweety-face. Long time, no see. How are you doing?"

Little Clive Colin returned the greeting, smiled tentatively.

O'Reith rubbed his hands together vigorously and with a twinkle in his eye said, "Sharon, Clive Colin here has plans to call on Mr. Blake later this morning. He needs a total make over. Three-piece suit with a silk shirt. Ivory cuff links. Dark blue bow tie to match the suit. New shoes shined up spiffy. Military haircut. Shave. Manicure. Facial. The works. He's going to ask Mr. Blake for the hand of his daughter in holy matrimony and he does not want to get turned down."

"Yes sir!" Sharon said gleefully, rubbing her hands together in anticipation of a job that she knew exactly how to do.

"Dad, why do I have to ask Vince for Marilyn's hand for Christ' sake. He knows…."

"My son, you are beyond the pale. You must follow orders."

"Jesus H. Christ, Dad. Nobody does that anymore!"

O'Reith gazed at him until he began to wilt. Little Clive Colin turned to Mills, said sheepishly, "Sharon, I guess we better get started."

As they were leaving together, O'Reith said, "Son after you've spoken with Vince, you and I are having lunch downstairs. I need a signals man and you're a leading candidate for the job."

Even as the two of them left, the telephone was ringing. It was Helen to tell him that Marilyn had called and with her mother Virginia, was on her way to Holmby Hills to begin planning. O'Reith said he was glad to get the news. Then Susie announced Miss Carolyn Cook.

"How were things in Sumatra?" he asked as Susie showed her in.

"Ticking like a clock, General O'Reith. I'm shaken by the merger news, I must say. What's to become of me?"

In 1943 with a dire shortage of geologists, Blake had hired Cook. In 1945, the regular geologists began returning from service. To conceal her from Halliday, Blake asked O'Reith to use her in Venezuela. Blake worried that Halliday would blow a gasket over his hiring a woman. She turned out to be gifted. O'Reith pushed her to the top of Exploration as he had pushed Holland to the top of Production. She was thirty-three, slender, modestly endowed with auburn hair, green eyes, a pointed nose in a triangular, pixie-like face. She vaguely resembled Veda Ann Borg. Her voice was soft and flat and lacked resonance. One had to listen carefully to catch everything she said.

"Carolyn, in the deal with SOCAL," O'Reith began, "we got job guarantees for those that want them. So if you want to keep on with them, you're OK. Of course Ken Crandall runs their Exploration Department. So you'll have to settle for a lesser appointment. But the pay will be the same. That's not too bad."

"Will I still be working for you?"

"No. Carolyn, I'm going to strike out on my own, open a Laundromat down the street in the Fullerton Building."

"What?" she said, jolted. She clenched her small fists until her knuckles turned white. She trembled ever so slightly. Then seeing the grin on his face widen, she relaxed, smiled and said, "you're putting me on."

O'Reith continued, "I plan to organize The Casinghead Company. Tarbutton, Holland and LeBel are in. You're invited to join. The aim of the company will be to get a good, solid concession in the lake. It is a gamble, of course. You'd be much safer with SOCAL, but I'd dearly enjoy having you."

"Count me in," she said quickly, as if he might change his mind.

He had watched her carefully as she regained her poise. He could see that she was relieved. Her future was once again secure. He asked, "Carolyn, have you an idea about which concession we should seek?"

"Yes, of course," she answered. She suddenly put her hand to her mouth. "Sir, have you reviewed the E&P budget for 1956. I reported $50 million to acquire Blocks 9 and 16. West of the zero line running due south from the La Cañada Cross. Both blocks offset *Lago Poniente*. They've got to be good."

"Carolyn, the production report shows a zero decline rate for *Lago Poniente*. I was going to ask you about that."

"Well that's why. Oil migration from those undrilled blocks. The water table hasn't moved an inch since we began running oil. The formations slope upward to the west. There's a crest out there somewhere…"

"And a secondary gas cap no doubt," O'Reith speculated.

"Yes. Holland and I discussed that. He ran a material balance. Concluded a high probability of a gas cap under Blocks 2 and 3. Those blocks are included in the call for tenders."

"That's a checkerboard area. SOCAL has a small part of *Lago Poniente*. They will know about that play."

He smiled broadly at the young geologist, added, "Carolyn, Gwyn Follis'll spit a snake if we snatch those two blocks out from under them."

"With the merger, will they see our 1956 E&P budget," she asked.

"If Follis asks for it, I'm sure Vince will show it to him."

"Can you recover it? So we can doctor it up."

"He doesn't have it yet."

They grinned together like possums in a persimmon tree heavy with ripe fruit. He rang for Susie, said, "Susie, give Carolyn back the portion of the budget for Venezuela. She wants to recheck some figures before we send it to Mr. Blake." Then he addressed Cook again. "Carolyn, Holland is home resting. Had a dust-up with Ines but everything is jake-a-loo now. Line up a meeting for this afternoon, the three of us plus Tarbutton. Work up a budget on the assumption we will win Blocks 9 and 16. Get the maps out. What say four o'clock in your office?"

"I'll confirm it as soon as I've talked to them."

As she departed, the telephone rang and it was Blake. "Clive! Virginia just called. Happy as a ruby-throated hummingbird in the morning glory patch. Little Clive Colin just popped the question to Marilyn! Best news since Harry Collier called. How are you doing?"

"Got the wheelchair blues. Max took a couple of splinters out. Said I shouldn't have any further problems. I'll be on crutches by the end of the week. He says I'll be ready to run the marathon by Christmas. I should have bet him some money on that. My son is coming in to see you in a bit. He wants to ask your per…"

"I'll give it! Ho Ho Ho!" Blake interrupted joyfully.

O'Reith laughed. "You ought to give him a hard time for dalliance."

"I'll give him the *Calitroleum Cross* with the *Crown Block* cluster. You free for lunch?"

"I'm dining downstairs with my boy but you may join us. I plan to hire him as my communications man. He was in the Signal Corps. Went to Army Radio and Telephone School at Fort Gordon, Georgia. With Helen in France and me in Venezuela, I'll need him. Come listen to my pitch."

"I better pass," Blake said chuckling. "Could be conflict of interest. By the way, when will you charter the new company?"

"January, after we close the deal with Standard Oil. That reminds me I've got to get some language in that consulting agreement to hold me harmless."

"Clive, Follis called this morning. Asked for a copy of our 1956 C&E budget. Are you sitting on it?"

"I have been. Tidikelt was on my mind. But we'll let them worry about that. It will be on your desk after lunch."

During lunch, O'Reith briefed his son on The Casinghead Company, hired him; told him to clean up his Army .45, begin regular practice at the club and to wear it at all times. He explained that Tarbutton would provide him with a license. His tailor would make him a chamois-skin stomach holster. At two o'clock, he called Helen about the guest lists for the wedding parties. They agreed to review them over cocktails that night. Then he called Maxine in Paris. It was late evening there. She would be preparing for bed. When she answered, he asked, "Sweetface is Monique still up?"

"No. Shall I wake her?"

"I just wanted to hear her little voice but it can wait. Sweets, I'm in a wheelchair. The company doctor cut a couple of war souvenirs out of my leg. So I won't see you until after the first of the year. You okay?"

"Lonesome. Maurice and Gabrielle had us for dinner the other night. He said he'd been talking to you."

"Yeah, Standard Oil Company is buying Calitroleum. I had to let him know. Deal set to close on New Year's Eve. Big changes. What would you say to a move to Caracas?"

Sure, that's fine with me. What's the reason?"

"I'm going into the oil business. Try to get a couple offshore blocks in the lake."

"Why not move to Maracaibo then? I'd prefer that. I could see Mandy from time to time. After all, that was my town for quite some while."

"Maracaibo it is then. Sweets, I'll be in your arms no later than the middle of January. Until then, watch the watch. Next time I'll call earlier so I can say hello to Monique."

He looked at his watch. Called for his chauffeur to roll him to Cook's office.

After an hour of map reading, cost estimation and general discussion, the four of them came up with a budget for 1956 of $100 million dollars; $40 million for Capital and Exploratory expenditure; $40 million to acquire the Blocks 9 and 16 and another $20 million for operating expense. They planned to drill a dozen oil wells, lay a pipeline to Punto Fijo and build a terminal with a storage capacity of 600,000 barrels. Their business concluded, O'Reith asked Tarbutton to roll him back to his office. In the elevator he asked, "Hardy, when can we talk to those bodyguards?"

"In the morning, Clive. I've got a dozen of the toughest birds that ever snubbed down the barrel of a Thompson sub-machine gun."

"We'll do that at your place, say ten o'clock?" Tarbutton nodded agreement. He rose to depart. O'Reith buzzed Susie to bring his Tuesday schedule. When she came with it, he asked for his chauffeur.

Helen waited on the terrace in a midnight blue dress that fell well below her knees. It had long sleeves and lace trimming at the bust. Pearl earrings with Chanel No.5 behind her earlobes. If his leg were not taped up, he thought, he would have skipped drinks and whisked her into the bedroom. The telephone conversation with Maxine had made him horny as hell. But he and Helen had much to discuss. Knocking off an early piece would render them both *hors de combat*. So instead he kissed her, fondled her, and rolled his wheelchair up to the round table. She poured his martini with care, gently lowered an oversized ice cube into it with the tongs, taking care not to splash the gin.

He said, "Helen, in a month I'll be out of my office. I'm going to take the conference room at the Fullerton Building. There is space for Susie but not Sharon. What do you say we set her shop up in guest quarters here? She can come to the office if I need her. I won't require much from a makeup artist, at least not for awhile."

"I was going to hit you up for her. My girl is under contract to the studio. Let me take Sharon to Monte Carlo. Are you going to keep your office in Paris?"

"Yeah. LeBel is retiring from Paris Petroleum. He'll move into it. We'll charter the company in Europe and keep the books there. Money too. If I need Sharon to fix my face for a meeting, she can catch a plane in Nice. Fly back the same day. What is our December schedule?"

"Wedding the Saturday before Christmas, the 24th, at St. John's Episcopal. The bride's father entertains on Saturday, the 10th, two weeks before the wedding. The groom's father will entertain on Saturday the 17th, one week before the wedding. Guest lists the same for both. Both Collier and Follis are on the list. So are the Prescotts. Can you bring them up?"

"Sure."

"Marilyn and little Clive Colin want us to hire The Kingston Trio. They sing at a joint in San Francisco called *the hungry i*."

"Fairy hangout."

"You sure?"

"Pretty sure. But they're popular as hell. Attract big crowds. The Kingston Trio is OK by me. For intermissions I'd like to hire a group I heard in Buenos Aires last year. They call themselves *Los Cinco Latinos*. Four hombres and a chica. Pretty smooth quintet. Suit you?"

"Why not? To finish out, my regular Christmas party is on Friday night. You get to meet Bolletti et al. Stan Kenton and June Christie for music."

"Then the Calitroleum Christmas party," O'Reith said. "Vince can squeeze it in somewhere. What about Christmas day? Usual open house for family and friends?"

"OK."

"Merger closes at eleven o'clock on the 31st at 225 Bush Street, a Saturday. Champagne lunch to follow. You're invited. We can fly up the night before. St. Francis or Mark Hopkins?"

"St. Francis," Helen answered quickly. After that, what? How long will it take you to get the ball rolling in Venezuela?"

"Tarbutton, Holland and Cook leave for Caracas day after tomorrow. They'll be down there three weeks. Back in time for the festivities. I'll know then. Government opens the tenders on March 31, 1956. If we get what we want, we'll be drilling in June. Say a year to lay the pipeline and build the terminal. Run oil 2nd quarter of 1957. That's assuming everything goes smoothly."

They dined at home on steak and potatoes with a red Pinot Noir. His leg was throbbing. He had an extra snifter of Martell cognac, which he knew he would regret. They slept in a king-sized bed. He lay on his back with Helen close beside him. Then she moved away, curled up and fell asleep. He woke after midnight wishing he'd skipped the cognac altogether. He'd had a bad dream. Going to Berlin on three engines with a faceless copilot. In his dreams comrades whose faces he could not see were dead men. This disturbed him. He awoke in a melancholy mood, remembered Maxine. He couldn't understand why this longing to see her again was so intense. They were often apart for longer periods than this. He was not hard up. Helen was at hand and even with a game leg, he knew they could make it if they wanted to. He reached over, touched her, and moved closer so he could smell her scent. He loved her, loved to be with her, to talk to her, even when she was difficult, to listen to her adventurous plans and to be beside her in the night. He would never tire of her. But Helen and Maxine were not alike. Helen was always on the go, always with a new scheme, a grand design with new friends, usually one of which he disapproved… Maxine was nothing like that. She was a good mother and a splendid cook. She lived for him and Monique. She patiently awaited him, tended the garden and watered her plants. Little Monique, he thought. How he would like to toss her over his shoulder as he listened to that soft French patois that so captivated him. In the final analysis, Maxine and Helen were more alike than they were different. Maxine was younger by seven years. But they were the same size, dressed similarly and in his eyes, both were exquisitely beautiful. On nights like this when he'd wakened from a nightmare, in that time of reorientation, that period when he was not sure where he was, he could never be quite sure which one of them slept beside him. Time back when Helen wore Chanel No.5 and Maxine wore Parure, it was easy. But now they both wore Chanel. Maxine had a mole on her left thigh. That was really the only way he could tell when it was dark, like now. It seemed to him that Maxine slept easier than Helen, that she was not so restless did. Helen had spells of tossing and turning. Maxine never did that, lay supine all the night, hardly moving at all once asleep.

He wondered if he should begin wearing a monocle. They went over big in Europe. Helen liked the idea. But Maxine would giggle. He became drowsy and as he fell asleep he could hear in the back of his mind Dinah Washington singing, "Roll me Daddy, Roll me over slow…"

Chapter III

The Casinghead Company

O'Reith was taking one last fond look at Los Angeles and the Pacific Ocean from his tall office windows. It was the middle of the morning of December 30, 1955. Thanks to the exercise regime set by Dr. Parkinson plus the herbal medicine and hot sea water baths, he was getting around nicely, with only a slight limp. No crutches. No cane. The wheelchair was gone. After the night he drank too much brandy, he had sharply cut back on liquor. Now it was just one double martini with Helen in the evening and a glass of wine with dinner. Helen had followed his lead. Gone was the martini pitcher from the lawn table. Brandy snifters gathered dust in the liquor cabinet. Their conversations were somewhat more rational too. Both of them realized a turning point had arrived. She needed her wits about her, as did he. The office was stripped. Early that morning Susie had seen to the removal of all his personal effects to the conference room in the Fullerton Building, that same room where just days ago, they had hired the bodyguards. The penthouse was not the same without the pictures. He missed them although he knew they would quickly reappear on the walls of his new office.

So it was goodbye to what represented the pinnacle of success. He sighed, took one last look out of each window, tossed his office keys on the desk and walked out to the elevator landing. Blake had not come in that day. They would meet later, with Helen and Virginia, for the flight to San Francisco. That night, the four of them would dine in the *Crystal Room* of the old Palace Hotel, the last meal he would ever put on a Calitroleum expense report. Tomorrow, at eleven, in the Executive Conference Room at the top of 225 Bush Street, San Francisco 20, California, he and Blake would sign the merger agreement. Calitroleum Oil Corporation would cease to exist. A busy month draws to a close. Four big parties, a wedding and a reception. The first party had been a drag. In a wheelchair, he could only watch the swirling couples. He liked to dance so this was a deprivation. But he watched the young people doing the *twist* and perhaps it was just as well that he was chair bound. The following fete was better. Up and around with the aid of a cane, he could circulate and shake hands. He was on the wagon. With the wedding looming, he'd have to be nimble and alert. The wedding went smoothly. He overheard Virginia complaining to Helen that the youngsters today 'had no shame'. Helen had replied, 'in five minutes dear it won't matter'.

Helen's blast for her motion picture associates was more interesting. When he saw her bringing a rather short man over, he whipped out his brand new monocle and deftly inserted it, mere moments before they came face to face. Helen for an instant, was at a complete loss, but she recovered nicely and made the presentation gracefully.

Francisco Bolletti was nothing like the picture O'Reith had of him in his mind. He was graying, handsome with a face similar to that of Tyrone Power. His hair had been professionally done. His eyes were brown, his complexion Mediterranean. His long nose made him look prying. His ears were perfectly centered in his squarish head. He spoke English with some hesitancy but quickly took control of the conversation, telling of his grand plans for the new motion picture company. O'Reith's impression was somewhat more favorable that he thought it would be. He sipped a flute of Mumm's Cordon Rouge with Signor

Bolletti before Helen led him away to meet other guests. Just then Tarbutton approached. "That the guy you wanted me to check out?"

"Himself. Let's stretch our legs," O'Reith said, his voice muted. A colonnaded cloister ran alongside the ballroom on the swimming-pool side, right below the terrace where he and Helen held their tête-à-têtes. Tarbutton followed O'Reith through one of the French doors that lined that side of the ballroom. They walked along the cloister to a pool side exit. They stopped at the rim of the pool by the diving board. Wavelets from a breeze blowing in from the Pacific danced on the surface of the water. O'Reith continued, "Hardy, some years back, Helen worked for a director named Fritz Harrington. Sharp guy. Jack Ford thought a lot of him. Fritz committed suicide in the back seat of his Rolls Royce. The House Un-American Activities Committee got after him. You remember… Some months later the FBI tried to hang that McLarssen murder on me. Well, you were in the court when the indictment failed. You know… But I never gave you the background on it. I guess it's natural that I compare Signor Bolletti with Fritz. Fritz was a little guy. Like Larry. Like Ted Schaeffer. Fritz was gracious, nimble, charming. A natty dresser with tiny feet, he could dance like Arthur Murray. I can always remember his shoes. Polished to a mirror finish. At heart he was a propagandist. Possibly that's why he was so successful. Those were the times. He reminded me of Joseph Goebbels. The way he held his shoulders. He was vain. Those little guys often are. Look at Napoleon. I have difficulty understanding why Helen turns that type of guy up with such regularity, as if she'd dug him up out of the garden. Well, I don't know why I should be down on a guy because he's not a six-footer. But Fritz got Helen into a fix. And I worry Bolletti will do the same. So what have you got on him?"

"Seems to be a typical Italian post war-movie maker," Tarbutton commenced. "Comes from the back streets of Naples. Somehow got a connection with the Mussolini Government. That goes back to the '30s. Made flag-wavers during the war depicting the British and the

Americans as dogs. Story ends around D-Day. Rome fell. Mussolini dead, hanging upside down. Bolletti goes back to Naples. Drops out. Story starts again in 1948. Some evidence he had a tie to the Camorra. They may have financed him. After the AMG was gone, he began making black market movies. Obviously he couldn't have done that with Uncle Sam and John Bull breathing down his neck. At least he couldn't have shown them. Made six of 'em altogether. Same story every time. High ranking U.S. Army officers selling commissary supplies to the *Paisanos*. Americans are all big, fat, swaggering guys wearing loose-fitting, muckledy-dun uniforms with huge stars on their epaulets and oversized caps with lots of scrambled eggs. All of 'em four star generals except the company clerk and he's a colonel. Pretty girls but they ignore the generals and go for the good-looking undercover cop trying to break the racket. Generals snarl at each other. In the end they all go to the sneezer. There's always an abduction scene. One of the pretty girls snatched because she rats on one of the generals. Cop saves her at the eleventh hour and they clinch. Ditto *ad nauseum*. Bolletti is married. Three kids. No scandals, at least none since the end of the war. In debt all the time. Borrows from Peter to pay Paul. He's probably not anti-American. He was just making the kind of movies he knew how to make. As wartime conditions retreated into the background, his films made less and less money. So now he's trying to rustle some up so he can get going again."

"What kind of a spread does he have in Ventimiglia?"

"Maybe four acres. All of it would fit behind Andy Hardy's house on the MGM back lot. It's a co-op studio. Several producers own it together. That's the story, Clive."

O'Reith nodded, went on, "There are some other things in connection with that problem we had with the committee. I'll fill you in later. When Helen gets set up in Monte Carlo, I want her under surveillance. Just like here. Maurice LeBel in Paris will be a shareholder in the new company. He has connections in the Foreign Legion. When you come over, bring those guys that have been watching out for little Clive Colin and Marilyn. They're surplus now with the newlyweds living at Summit Drive. They can look after Helen until LeBel recruits a couple of Legionnaires. When we're finished, you and I and Maxine and Monique will fly to Maiquetia in a converted B-17. It's hangared at LeBourget. Has Tokyo tanks. I get it as part of the termination settlement. It once had a target camera over the bomb racks. When we rebuilt it, we put the camera in the ball turret hole and used it to map a right-of-way for the pipeline to Tidikelt Field. We'll use it similarly in Venezuela. We'll take the old Southern Ferry Route out of Le Bourget as far as Dakar. From there we'll have to work out a flight plan to Maiquetia. Bring Marjorie if you like. There's plenty of space. Galley in the radio room. Two army beds in the waist. A pisser in the tail turret. Another where the bomb racks used to be.

"Marjorie will enjoy that. She's never made that kind of a trip. When do we go?"

"Pretty quick. I want you down there right away. In Paris next week, we'll charter the company, arrange the finances. We' plan to bid $18 million for each of those two blocks Carolyn is so proud of. Four million reserved for *lobbying* if that's the word for it. That money probably will support a side-letter agreement that guarantees the official contract.

Line Ethering up to go to Caracas. His wife's name is Merle. Good bridge player. If you and Marjorie play with them, make it the girls against the boys. When they're playing together, you can't win."

"Clive, in Ciudad Bolivar, the *Angostura* lawyer gave me the name of the guy who would help us. Rojo Olimpio Torres, an inside man to the *colonel*. He assured me that we could have those two blocks but we didn't get into any details. I have to see him again. I rented two flats in Caracas, in *Las Mercedes*, like you wanted. I'll let Ethering take one of them."

"You take the other, Hardy," O'Reith said. "When I talked to Maxine the other day, we decided to live in Maracaibo. She wants to be close to Mandy."

"I was going to bring that up, Clive. Mandy didn't strike me as anything out of the ordinary. Regular hausfrau. Seems devoted to Schaeffer. He seemed tame too. Not at all what I expected."

"Ted still wearing a toupee?"

"Not while I was there. He's bald as a billiard ball, except for a gray fringe. Hard for me to imagine an avuncular looking guy like that could get into the kind of trouble you've described."

O'Reith laughed in the darkness and it reverberated back from the walls of the cloister. "Well, appearances can deceive. That fellow can get into some funny fixes. Mandy show you around?"

"Grand tour of the inn. Upstairs and downstairs. Quiet dining room. Interesting pictures on the walls. Scenes from the Andes. Natives spearing fish in the mountain streams. That kind of stuff. Big black buck named Cansor mixed drinks for us in the bar. Had a good dinner. Shrimp Creole and rice. Chinese cook. He'd come out and hang around as we began each course. Wanted to make sure it was okay. Smiling son-of-a-bitch. We had brandy in the bar upstairs. Coy little nook with a window that looks out on the garden in back. Gas lamps lit the place up. Couple of bubbling fountains. Banana and mango trees. I could see the ripe fruit shimmering in the light from the lamps. I wanted to go out there but Mandy said it was snake-infested. Said after she got it exterminated, maybe next trip…"

O'Reith had been listening quietly, intently. When Tarbutton stopped talking, both men stood silently. The breeze had a chill to it. Stars twinkled above. The music and din of the party drifted out to them. Finally O'Reith asked, "You read that little book?"

"I did. Fascinating. Hard to believe optical energy with an electric component that a witch, even one as deft as Mandy seems to be, can jolt a guy down to the size of a beer bottle. Miniaturization as a consequence of sexual transmogrification. I have to laugh."

"That's the title of one of the chapters," O'Reith said.

"Ridiculous," Tarbutton scoffed. "Like an H.H. Munro tale."

"Like *Foo Fighters* too," O'Reith commented, almost idly.

Tarbutton started, regained his composure. "But we found out what they were. Jets. Me-262s. Rocket planes. *Komets*."

"Not all of 'em, Hardy. When you went to see Mandy, who was with you?"

"Marjorie. Ines. Holland. Carolyn and her friend. Magaly, isn't that her name?"

"Yeah. What did Marjorie think about Mandy?"

"Deceptive. Perceptive. A woman with something to hide."

"Close assessment," O'Reith agreed. "Hardy, when we get down there together, I'll give you a tour of that garden. Mandy always talks of getting rid of the snakes but she never does. By the way, they call them *Guayacons* in the lingo. They're *fer-de-lances*. Venom breaks down the lining of your veins. You bleed to death through the pores of your skin. They rarely strike above the ankles. We'll wear combat boots."

"Clive, Mandy Macabra and Megaera Melpomeme Micawber. One and the same?"

"Yeah", O'Reith said with a laugh. You spot any parrots in the garden?"

"Couple. Pretty raucous. I could hear 'em in the bar and they must have been fifty feet away with a closed window in between. They were swinging around in the mango tree."

"The male is named *Obregon*, like the one-armed Mexican general of the 1920s. Fifinela is the female. The mango tree. That's where they go to do it." O'Reith looked at his watch. It was long after midnight. The music had stopped. Intermission. Tarbutton yawned.

He said, "Clive, I'm going to find Marjorie and say goodnight."

"As they walked together back to the ballroom O'Reith asked, "Did you get us lined up with an office in the Hotel Del Lago?"

"I did. Also rented a villa for you near the Hospital Coromoto."

O'Reith and Helen flew to Paris on a Pan-Am Stratocruiser in the bridal suite. Before dinner in the bar, which had been the navigator's place when the airliner was a B-29, O'Reith asked, "Helen we never did finish our discussion of Signor Bolletti. Jack give you a glowing report on him?"

Helen was quiet, gathering her thoughts. She looked at her husband, eyes flashing, annoyed; she knew that he was relentless when it came to hard facts, getting answers to difficult questions. "Jack says he's no Pandro Berman. But he had a promising start as a young man. He was a member of *L'Unione Cinematografica Educativa,* kind of like the Ministry of Propaganda. He's a distant relative of Clara Petacci, the woman who was Mussolini's sweetie. She got him his first job, editing propaganda films for the government. He was a *caporal* in the *Camorra,* took orders from on high. Petty extortion. Blackmail. In fact he is said to have blackmailed his fellow fascists. Threatened to turn them over to AMG if they didn't come across. Used blood money to finance his 'bloaters', that's what Jack calls his black-market movies. Jack called him a son-of-a-bitch. Says he owes money. Left wing politics. He can only make one type of movie."

"Well there you have it. He offer any alternatives?"

"He asked me to come back to the studio. But I said no. He said it would take awhile to find the right guy. Italy, you know… I don't want to wait. I look at it like this. We're going to make westerns. Formula movies. Bolletti can work the formula. After all, he made six of 'em. Must have made some money. So it's a flyer. Far less expensive than yours. Besides, he and Jack are competitors. Ace, in spite of it all, Bolletti comes across as not too bad of a guy. Overlooking your bias about short men, consider the positives. He's an up and running producer. Stands on his own two feet, even if they are small, even if they're made of clay…"

"I'm not trying to discourage you. Watch your step, baby. You're drilling in dry hole country. Stay out of the soup. When do you start shooting?"

"Just as soon as I get settled and Helen Simpson is in school. I have a script in my bag, the one where I'm a nurse in Piedras Negras after a shoot-out at the *Cantina de los Tres Ladrones*. The hero plugs the bandito in the bottom. I'm digging slugs out before they haul him off to the sneezer."

"Some hero that plugs the bad guy in the tail."

"He was trying to get away."

"Ace, you know what would be really neat?"

"What?"

"If George McDonough would make a cameo appearance. He's so big and menacing. Absolutely drips evil. He could be Big Nick McNickle, a renegade Englishman that runs a string of joints on the river."

"Why don't you ask him?"

"Let's fly over to London before we go to Monte Carlo and I will."

"I need to think about that. We'll sleep on it".

"Helen, little Clive Colin will be in Monte Carlo to set up a long range single-sideband radio in your flat. He'll show you how to use it and hire an operator if you want one. With similar equipment in Caracas and Maracaibo, if you get in too deep and need help, you can whistle me up. I'll come quick. I'm sure you can cope. But the ball can take a funny hop… I can be there in less than twenty-four hours."

"What if I'm just hard up?"

He smiled. "Call me."

"I'm hard up right now, Ace. Let's grab a quickie in our compartment before dinner."

* * *

In Paris they were at the Ritz. While Helen and Virginia shopped, O'Reith and Blake went to see LeBel at Paris Petroleum Company in Malesherbes. The two oil men rode up in an ancient steam-driven elevator that jerked and hissed before coming to a rattling stop on the fourth floor.

LeBel, of average height, met them at the landing. He had an oblong face with sad, dark eyes and bushy gray eyebrows with a full head of silvery hair, not a toupee, and a waxed, silken mustache, carefully maintained in a thin rectangle of silver. When he smiled, he faintly resembled Charles Boyer. A reserved, distant French gentlemen with the walk of a soldier, his voice was soft and smooth, a tenor, like O'Reith. He had on a gray suit, a white cotton shirt with nacre cuff-links and a black tie to match. His shoes had heavy, thick soles. LeBel, veteran of General LeClerc's Army in North Africa, decorated at *Bir Hakeim*, became friendly with O'Reith in London during the days leading up to the invasion. After the war, he had helped O'Reith with the legalities of buying his place in the rue de Surene, where Maxine now lived. He had also helped him establish an alternate identity. O'Reith carried a French passport under the name of *de Troisetoiles*, an ex-legionnaire. LeBel's wife, Gabrielle a *pied noir* from Oran, was friendly with Maxine.

When they were seated with the inevitable small cups of black coffee and croissants before them, Blake explained how the merger with Standard Oil had come out of the blue with out any preliminaries, often the case in America. LeBel had a slate of questions, many of them originating with deGaulle. Blake told him that, as Vice Chairman of the Board of SOCAL, he would be the liaison with Paris Petroleum and would keep deGaulle fully informed of developments. LeBel expressed his desire to cooperate. Blake was aware of LeBel's involvement with O'Reith in The Casinghead Company but said nothing.

After lunch, O'Reith went to see Maxine. Little Monique met him in the foyer on the ground floor and he hoisted her up over shoulder. Together they rode up the electric elevator to the penthouse. She was giggling and calling out, *"Maman, Maman! Mon Pere! Mon Pere! Il est ici de nouveau!"* O'Reith frolicked with her until she was off to school. Then he and Maxine got right down to it. She liked to tease him, to play the siren, stripping slowly down to her panties and brassiere. Letting him strip off her hose. Kissing him and checking out what he had, clucking with satisfaction when it was suitably erect. Then when they were down, she would tell him if he were a good boy, she'd give him a taste. When he had fully penetrated her, she would say, "Sweetie, you have to take it out now. A taste is all you get." At that point, he really put it to her.

Afterwards, when they were up, showered and dressed, he explained that he had to go to Monte Carlo but that he would return shortly. She was to prepare for the flight to Venezuela. They would shutter the penthouse but keep the utilities paid up so they could move back in on short notice. The ground floor would become the offices of the new company.

Then a second meeting with LeBel. The Casinghead Company would be a *societe anonime* with accounts kept at the BIL in Liechtenstein. Paris Petroleum would put up $25 million. LeBel, $2 million. The Widow Halliday would put up $10 million and move to the Fullerton Building. Blake invested $10 million in the form of Swiss Franc bearer bonds, convertible into common stock after 5 years. Thus was his anonymity preserved. Holland and Cook participated to the same extent as LeBel. Tarbutton, not a rich man, had few savings, a small government pension and a somewhat larger American Airlines pension. Of course, O'Reith paid him well. A stock option was created for him. Over three years he would earn an interest equivalent to that of LeBel et al. A similar plan for fewer shares was established to cover Stanley Ethering and Alan Prescott. O'Reith put up $150 million, two-thirds of his fortune. Prescott was now the General Manager of Calitropical Oil in Maracaibo. On February 1, 1956, he would become the one and only drilling supervisor of The Casinghead Company. Prescott had married his childhood sweetheart, Sally Bierce, during the war while he was on leave in Los Angeles. At the time he was an artillery officer in Vth Army. The marriage had taken place at Summit Drive under Helen's careful attention. Sally had replaced Susan Briscoe as Drilling Department secretary in 1941. Now Alan and Sally had three children, one boy named after O'Reith another after Holland, and a girl was named for Helen. Prescott had a platinum plate in his skull, a gift from a German Army surgeon who removed a grenade fragment from his head in Hammelburg Prison in 1945.

Before the war, when Holland was a drilling foreman in the San Joaquin Valley, he had tried to put the make on Sally but she always refused him. Prescott and Holland were friends even then. Prescott knew Holland was predatory. Sally told him of Holland's passes at her. But during the war, Holland had helped him when he needed it badly. Prescott would never forget that. Neither would Sally. Anyhow, he and Sally trusted each other. Holland had Ines and that was that.

When he concluded his affairs with LeBel, O'Reith rejoined Blake in the lobby of the Ritz. Helen and Virginia were still shopping. O'Reith suggested to Blake that they visit the *Tour Eiffel* Looking out over the city towards the *Sacre Coeur* from the railing of the second stage, O'Reith said, "Vince in your capacity as an officer of SOCAL, come down to Maracaibo once in a while. You can visit Ted. Meet Mandy. See Alan and Sally again and…"

Blake interrupted, "I'd like to see that pert little twist again. She was the best help I ever had and she sure is easy on the eyes."

"Well there you are then," O'Reith rejoined, his voice musical and melodious. "I'm acquainted with the director of *Escuela de las Bellas Artes* in the Creole district of town. Not too far from where you'll be staying at the Del Lago. We used to give the hands Spanish lessons there. Down the hall from the classrooms is the ballet school. Girls from all over the country, indeed, girls from all over South America come to study. So when you visit me, I'll take you around and introduce you to the director. Many of those girls speak good English. You can take a look around. Then you'll be on your own. What say, babe?"

Blake nodded, blushed and smiled at his friend. O'Reith patted him on the back, said, "We better get back to the hotel. May have some steamed up ladies on our hands if we're late. Wives tend to suspect the worst in Paris."

That night, to Helen's delight, they were joined for dinner by George P. McDonough, a former director of Calitroleum, whom she considered to be one of the masterful actors of the 20th Century although he had never, to her knowledge, trod a single board. McDonough, tall and portly with a large, egg-shaped head and a mop of grayish-white hair that covered his dome like a thatched roof had sinister lemon-colored eyes. His eyebrows were fading arcs of ashen wisps. His cheeks were pink with rosy spots. His full lips were Epicurean. He swaggered across the room, projecting first one shoulder and then the other, his huge head smiling as it oscillated to and fro, like an electric fan. Helen was mesmerized by his somnolent, cavernous bass that produced an endless string of doomsday-like pronouncements. McDonough had been Sir John Masterman's lieutenant during the war. He was supremely confident of his ability to penetrate deception. He had dispatched countless German spies who failed to cooperate with him often summoning the firing squad officer with a snap of his enormous fingers to shoot the offender right there in his office. When he appeared, as if by magic, behind Helen's chair, sensing his presence she turned, looked up and saw his beaming face. She squealed, rose and threw herself into his voluminous arms. She said gaily, "Oh! You wonderful bag of a man! How glad I am to see you again!"

McDonough had on a white linen suit, heavy white oxford shoes with white socks. He wore an ivory tie with a gleaming pearl stickpin, his usual evening attire. In his hand was his floppy bleached-out Panama hat. He looked as if he had just stepped off the banana boat from Guayaquil. He also looked a lot like Sydney Greenstreet.

After the embrace, he held her at arm's length, gazed into her enraptured eyes and began, "Oh, thou beauteous fair maiden from across the endless, blue ocean…"

O'Reith, with mock impatience, cut him off with, "Actually, George, she's the girl from the other side of the mountain."

They were all laughing and rearranging the table for five. Helen asked, "Am I the only one who didn't know you were coming?"

"Vincent telephoned me," McDonough rumbled melodiously, rattling the glassware. "Of course I knew about the merger. I thought how grand it would be to see all of you again. And London is dreary now. I also had an ulterior motive. I wanted to petition Clive to let me subscribe to the capital of that unusual creation, The Casinghead Company. Clive, that's such a romantic name for an oil company. Does it have significance?"

"Only in the sense that nothing transpires after the crude leaves the casinghead. No refineries or gas stations. Just production to steel storage."

"Ah." McDonough droned on, voice rising and falling as he continued, "Wonderful notion. A great limitation of worry. No downstream and little or no government interference. How much will you put me down for, Clive? What an extraordinary, new tropical adventure. Directors meeting in Caracas. At the Tamanaco. Such cuisine. Superb in every way. And cocktails. That heady Pampero rum! Oh, if only it didn't go so directly to one's head. So how much, Clive?" McDonough produced an enormous Cuban Claro from inside his coat and let the waiter light it for him. As the fragrant smoke wafted across the room, O'Reith said, "George, we'll get into the finances after dessert."

"Ho Ho Ho," McDonough answered. He snapped his fingers for the waiter and they all ordered drinks.

Helen, entranced by the cadence of his voice and his remarkable stories of intrigue and espionage, hung upon his every word and encouraged him to continue when he seemed to slow down. He entertained them throughout the meal, the five of them listening and talking and laughing. Some smoking, some drinking and all enjoying each other's company and the splendor of *L'Espadon* restaurant in the Ritz. It was never better even in the *belle epoch*.

Next morning, the O'Reith's groggily took an Air Inter DC-4 to Nice. Tarbutton, little Clive Colin and Marilyn, with Sharon Mills in tow, met them at the airport and all of them rode together in a limousine to the Riviera Palace Hotel in Monte Carlo. Tarbutton had lined up a penthouse for Helen on the 10th floor of the Carleton towers on Blvd. Princesse Charlotte. Workmen were getting it ready, installing furniture and hooking up the utilities. She moved in three days later and when settled, called Frederico Bolletti in Ventimiglia to line up a tour of the studio. O'Reith went along, discreetly observing that Tarbutton's men were on the job. Bolletti showed them around. Somebody was directing a movie about life in the 17th Century. Lavishly costumed actors and actresses performed under the lights, sweating and hamming it up. After a long vinous lunch, they returned to Monte Carlo to find little Clive Colin installing the single side-band. O'Reith left Helen's affairs in the hands of Tarbutton and flew back to Paris.

Finally, he could get caught up with Maxine. O'Reith owned the entire building. The vacant ground floor would soon be occupied by the new company. The second story was storage. His office was on the third floor and connected to the penthouse flat where he lived with Maxine by a wrought iron spiral staircase. From that office, he had coordinated the development of the Tidikelt Oil Field. Shortly, little Clive Colin would retune this radio for trans-Atlantic reception with a separate crystal for communication with Monte Carlo.

From a distance, it would be difficult to distinguish Maxine from Helen. They were identical in size, had the same bust and hip measurements and the same hair color. Up close, they were not the same. Helen *was* Joan Bennett. Maxine, Mylene deMongeot. Maxine's voice was an octave higher than Helen's, a contralto, lyrical and melodic. She tinkled and chimed when she spoke. Maxine was rarely excited, refrained from earthy comment which was common coin to Helen. She drank, but not much and like Helen, had never smoked. Born in Paris, her father, a failed priest, took her to Buenos Aires when she was an infant. Her neurotic mother, committed suicide by jumping from a fifth floor window of the Plaza Hotel when Maxine was four. Packed off to a nunnery by her grandmother at puberty, she remained penned up until, at sixteen, she ran away, eventually falling under the sway of Mandy Macabra in Ciudad Bolivar. Holland introduced her to O'Reith in late 1945 after the extinction of the flaming *Lago Poniente No.1*, at a party to celebrate the event. Then, under Mandy's guidance, Maxine ran a house of assignation called *El Techo Rojo*, located at the corner of Calle 70 and Avenida 11 in Maracaibo. Oil field patrons of the house referred to her as *Miss Maxine*. Employees of Calitropical Oil Company, after she became O'Reith's lover, called her *Max the Mouse*, the moniker being related to the fact that her family name was deMoustier.

Formalities and legalities complete, with McDonough's draft for £7.5 million safely in the *Banque des Allemands* in Zurich, documents with the French government duly filed, O'Reith, Maxine, Maurice LeBel and Gabrielle, took train to Vaduz, checked in to the Park Sonnenhof in Maree Strasse and enjoyed the delights of that remarkable establishment while they attended the required formalities of the Liechtenstein Government. *Casinghead Anstalt*, a subsidiary was set up and a second bank account was opened. Operating expenses would be charged to the account at *Banque des Allemands*. Matters related to the acquisition of the concession, including side-letter agreements would be handled through *Banque en Liechtenstein*. Then it was back to Paris where the recently retired LeBel took up his new offices in rue de Surene, not far from the Madeleine, where Capitaine Gerard Chameleon de Troisetoiles had married Señorita Georgina Marie de Cahors d'Ampere of Caracas.

Now, in late January, it was time to go to Venezuela. He called Helen, advised her that all formalities were complete, learned that she had hired Alice Ridley, most recently astrologer for *The Yellow Peril* and that she too, was now installed in Monte Carlo. O'Reith had followed her column with some regularity, noticing that her prognostications for Blake were usually closer to the mark than those for himself. Helen was fond of Alice. O'Reith was pleased that they could enjoy each other's company. Tongue in cheek, O'Reith asked Helen if Alice could squeeze in for him, a day-to-day astrological prognosis for 1956. The Casinghead Company was a big project. Why not get a starcast, a divine guideline? He didn't have to pay any attention to it and Ridley was a gifted writer. Helen agreed on condition she could edit out any part that forecast possible love affairs. O'Reith told her, "Helen, ask Alice to leave out all that business about the phases of the moon and the conjunctions of Mars and Jupiter. I only want the facts."

"Ace, in astrology, there are no facts," Helen said acidly.

That matter was settled. Then he spoke to Tarbutton, arranged for him to come to Paris and then his son, to retune the Paris radios.

Little Clive Colin had just finished retuning the radio in the office, unaware that his father lived in a flat three stories above. O'Reith, beside him and said, "Son, now you've finished up here, you and Marilyn can return to Los Angeles, see how your sister is getting along in that big house. If everything is jake-a-loo with her, meet me in Maracaibo, say February the first. Bring Marilyn. Let us know so we can book a hotel room for you."

"Jesus H. Christ, Dad. What's the big rush? Marilyn and I want to roll in the surf for a few days. Maybe a couple of weeks."

"Make it a couple of days. I'll need your help getting set up. Lots going on and anyway, I plan to expand your job description."

"Yes sir, Dad sir! General sir. General O'Reith, sir!"

"That's your name too. And don't be snappy with me." It was *the Voice*.

When his son had departed, O'Reith's oculist fitted him with steel-rimmed reading glasses, a similar pair for driving and flying, and sun-shades for tropical service. He had been having trouble with fine print for a couple of years and here lately he was also experiencing a problem with street signs. The monocle didn't help much in these matters. He thought the heavy rims made him look like a banker. Next time he was in Monte Carlo, he'd consult Sharon. She would know what to do."

*   *   *

It was cold and windy, a steady rain blowing across the runway at LeBourget. Tarbutton, in the left seat was setting up for an instrument take-off. O'Reith, in the right seat, was running through the pre-flight check list. Maxine, Monique and Marjorie Tarbutton were strapped into the cushions of the seats aft of the radio compartment that was now the galley. The waist gun ports were covered by double-ply Plexiglas with aluminum bar reinforcement. They took-off at eight o'clock. Prognosis was low cloud, rain and scud all the way up to nine angels. Scattered cloud and clearing after that. And so it turned out to be. Rough and bumpy for the first few minutes, when they were leveled out at an even ten thousand feet, the plane settled down. Smooth flying. The B-17, that Gabrielle LeBel had named *L'ame de France*, like all B-17s, was not pressurized. O'Reith had considered it at the time of the purchase but it would have been expensive. There were structural problems as well. So if they had to go much above ten angels to get over the weather, they'd have to take oxygen from rubber tubes. He hoped to spare Monique that experience. This was her first flight and once they were cruising, Maxine strapped her into one of the bucket-seats facing the left waist window. The tot kept her eyes on the murky skies below, uncertainty in her young face but when they broke into bright sunlight, she smiled and laughed, clapped her hands and called for her mother to come and see.

All four engines were purring along. No red lights on the panel. Instruments normal. Tarbutton had set the throttles for 2,300 rpm and hooked up the AFCE. Monique, bored with the monotony of the clouds below, came forward to sit in her father's lap. Thrilled when they crossed the snowy Pyrenees, she thought she could just step right out of the plane and be atop one of them. Clearing the mountains into Spain, the undercast disappeared. The countryside was green. Soon Tarbutton was throttling back for the descent into Lisbon. On final approach, O'Reith lowered the gear, returned Monique to her mother and got ready to land. As soon as the B-17 rolled to a stop on the parking stand, O'Reith chopped the throttles, pulled off the rpms and shut down the engines. They lunched while the plane was refueled and then flew to Rabat and from Rabat to Dakar. Here they would deviate from the old Southern Ferry Route. From Dakar they flew to Cayenne in French Guyana, arriving late, staying the night in the Grande Hotel Atlantique. They were in the air again at daylight.

Maxine was introduced to Marjorie as a friend of Mandy Macabra. Marjorie could not understand French, could not follow the conversation between father and daughter. But Monique had his bright blue eyes and black hair. In any event, the nature of the relationship must have been clear to any woman of perception and Marjorie was sharp as a tack. Besides, it was unrealistic to think Tarbutton would have kept such an interesting bit of *on dit* from his wife. Officially, Maxine was what she was represented to be. Nobody would ask any questions.

The weather was perfect from Cayenne, high pressure with a few fluffy cumulus clouds here and there, several low squalls of limited extent which they easily overflew. The engines were still purring softly, as they were designed to do. The superchargers idled. No red lights on the panel. A thoroughly enjoyable flight across the South American littoral to Maiquetia. They spent the night at the Hotel Tamanaco.

During this last leg of the flight, Tarbutton filled O'Reith in on his visit to Ciudad Bolivar. "Clive, the guy I met, the wizard's lawyer, was a shrunken old geezer, still sharp but not active. His place is right on the river. From his front porch we watched the boats hauling iron ore. Odor of boiling sugar everywhere. Sweet. Heady. Like a poison you know is deadly but cannot resist. The workers were squeezing cane and boiling it down just a few steps away. We had a rum and bitters over ice. The maid brought a tray of brown sugar blocks about the size of a deck of bikes. Soft and wet, dripping caramel. That rum must have been fifty years old. The old guy is named Esteven Armas. He told me the history of eastern Venezuela. Emphasis on the evolution of government. How things worked today. He said that in Venezuela, loyalty to the flag, to the government, was a concept beyond the grasp of the average citizen. Down there, in that country, you can only be loyal to a man. Loyalty to a political concept like democracy is, well, when you bring it up, all you get is a shrug. After we covered the waterfront on that subject, and it began to sink into my slow brain, we had a long lunch with lots of mangos and papayas and platanos and lamb in a hot, peppery sauce, all that washed down with beer brought in from Caracas, *Cerveza Cristal*, they call it. Smooth as Pabst Blue Ribbon. Then more rum. Coffee so thick and strong that my hair stood straight up. He gave me the name of the guy to see in Caracas, one Rojo Olimpio Torres. Said he would send him a message of my impending visit. At that point in the conversation, he reached over and tapped my knee and he said, 'I remind you sir that all alliances are temporary. All friendships are tenuous. Remember that the Military Junta could not function. Jimenez squelched it. A dangerous man. There are external pressures on him. Alcabalas all over the country restrict movement of the people. The police are universally resented. Rojo Olimpio Torres works in the Ministry of Mines and Hydrocarbons. He has close ties to Colonel Jimenez. But be prudent. Don't trust him too far. Test the relationship. Do your best to form other relationships. When you have negotiated your concession contract, it is essential that it be published in the *Gaceta Oficial*.' Those were his parting words. So I went to see Torres. Modest office. Shares a secretary with another guy in the same room. Telephone hangs on the wall outside in the hall. People wandering in and out, shuffling papers. Not doing a goddamned thing. Just yawning and scratching their buttocks. I had to wait out in the hall for half an hour just to see him for maybe three minutes. He read the letter from Armas. Each time I tried to state my business he held up his hand. Stopped me. He put the letter down and wrote an address on a piece of note paper. Folded it, handed it to me, got up and showed me out, smiling and saying how pleased he was that I came. Out in the street I read the note. It was a street address. Below it, he had written 'midnight' and circled it for emphasis. So I went back to the hotel, remembered what you told me about the *Seguridad Nacional.* I hadn't a clue of where that address was. I sure as hell was not going to ask the hall porter. So I checked out my .45, made sure it was loaded and that none of the cartridges had corroded in the humidity of the Orinoco delta. It had a smooth action. I had confidence in it. It was around noon. I changed into my suit pants with the sewn in chamois-skin holster. Fitted the pistol into the holster. Stood in front of the mirror. I looked okay. Put my coat and hat on, went downstairs, through the lobby out to the street, just walking around looking for street signs. A Shell gasoline station caught my eye. On a hunch I asked the attendant if he had a city map. Sure enough he did. Back in the room, I located the address that Torres had given me. About ten blocks from the hotel. After lunch I checked it out. Just a number on a door in a five story building with a bell button and a light fixture over the button. I figured they would turn it on at night. So I was set."

"Place turned out to be a joint?" O'Reith asked.

"Yeah. Pretty gaudy one at that. I was there *en punto,* as they say. Punched the bell, door opened. Young guy in a tuxedo. Maybe twenty. He looked me over good. If he spotted the cannon, he didn't say anything. I told him that I had an appointment with Señor Torres. He nodded, let me come in, closed the door behind us. Place full of men and women, all ages. Drinking. Dancing. Smoking. Laughing. Big dance floor. Kids really shaking a leg. We skirted the dancers, got through the crowd. I spot Torres sitting in a booth, door open, with a girl, a looker. When I arrive, she scoots. Waiter brings a glass full of ice, pours me a jolt of Johnny Walker Black whether I want it or not. I wanted it. We close the door. Torres and I click glasses, pull hard on the scotch and get right down to it. I told him what we wanted. He drew a little map of the lake on a napkin, sketched in Blocks 9 and 16, asked if that was it. I nodded. So he asked how much we were prepared to pay."

"What did you say?"

"I told him we'd be competitive. Depended on the deal. He nodded. Said he'd have to confer with the *colonel*, he called him *El Caudillo*. He suggested we meet again the next night at the same hour. I nodded, got up to leave. His girl came back. So at the following session, we settled the price and drafted the side-letter agreement. It is as we planned at this stage of the game. We agreed to meet again with you in Maracaibo to remove any remaining uncertainty and ink it. You'll get to size him up for yourself."

Chapter IV
▼
Rojo Olimpio Torres

They checked out of the Hotel Tamanaco early the next morning and taxied to Maiquetia. This time O'Reith was the pilot, Tarbutton in the right seat. They flew along the littoral and two hours later, when O'Reith glimpsed the lake, he called the tower at *Grano de Oro* to request landing instructions. Holland met them with a ground crew to attend the B-17 and hangar it next to its sister, the *La Cañada Cruz*. Holland came in Mandy's limousine with Cansor, the seven foot black Trinidadian behind the wheel. A two-hundred pounder, he was silent and stolid. O'Reith suspected he was a eunuch. Cansor, devoted to Mandy, never spoke a word, responded to nods and gestures, was chauffeur, bar-tender, major domo and her bodyguard. Cansor hired a taxi for their bags. When all was arranged, the five travelers in the tonneau and Holland in the Chevrolet taxi behind, departed the airport and pulled out into *Cinco de Julio* for the drive to Mandy's *finca*. It was a broad avenue lined with Bougainvillea trees. Passing *El Redondo Cemeterio*; they turned south on *Bella Vista*, through the port area, near the ferry landing; turned west on *Libertador*, crossed a dry creek over the *Punto de Espana* bridge and motored south on *Los Haticos* until they reached *Calle 100*. Then Cansor turned up a hill with the V-12 motor scarcely laboring. The pavement ran out and became a red clay road, dusty and dry. Now in an old section of town called *Santo Domingo,* the road was curving and becoming steeper. Cansor pushed the accelerator. Even with more gas, the big engine began to ping and lug down. The trailing taxi was obscured by the dust. They were no longer climbing. The motor was purring again and they were in a green countryside. Occasional small villas, yellow with blue trim, like Zulia beer signs appeared on both sides of the road. Now they were among trees and shrubs, rolling along the high bluff overlooking the lake, higher even than the gray turrets of the Hotel Granada, visible far in the distance. Down below, a Jersey lake tanker, low in the water, plowed slowly up the narrows with a cargo of *Tia Juana Light* on the way to the North Terminal.

Presently Cansor parked the Cadillac on a graveled driveway beside an 18th Century Moorish mansion. Green vines curled through the grilled ironwork covering the windows. Cansor pushed a button near the lock of the moss-covered door. It creaked open. They were looking into a garden. Before them, a flagstone path overgrown with fine grass, like a putting surface on a golf course, opened out. It ran down the center of the garden. Some distance ahead, they saw a bubbling dragonhead fountain. Cansor directed them to the right along a branch path of recently poured concrete that led to the side entrance of the inn. Mandy Macabra Schaeffer and her husband, Theodore, greeted them. Maxine embraced Mandy, giggling and laughing and presented a baffled Monique to her. O'Reith shook hands with Schaeffer and introduced him to the Tarbuttons. Cansor and the taxi driver brought in their bags. When they were settled, little Monique coping with her greatly changed environment, Mandy led them into the dining room where the Chinese cook was smiling and bowing, beckoning them to their places. Holland said goodbye and took the taxi back to the company offices in the Hotel Del Lago.

Mandy, who resembled Gale Sondergaard, had inky black hair streaked with gray piled in a bun atop her head. Her black, penetrating eyes seemed sinister and speculative, like the spider checking out a newly arrived fly. Her sensuous mouth was lip-sticked dark red to match her crimson shift. Her voice was sonorous, seductive. The texture of her skin was fine and her complexion olive. A little fellow like Schaeffer would get lost in her svelte figure and probably enjoy it. She asked if they would like a drink before lunch, knowing what to serve to everyone except the Tarbuttons.

From his musette bag, O'Reith extracted two cartons of Chesterfield cigarettes that he had bought in Los Angeles. In Maracaibo, American smokes were often dried out from long storage in hot warehouses. He was sure that Schaeffer would enjoy fresh ones. As he handed them to his old foe, he said, "Ted don't chain smoke these up all at one time."

After lunch, while the ladies were visiting, Mandy said, "Theodore dear, show General O'Reith the improvements we've made to the garden. Don't forget to don your high-top shoes."

Schaeffer put on cowboy boots. O'Reith was still in flight boots. In any event he was not worried about snakes at this hour. They were most dangerous after the sun had thoroughly heated the stones in the garden. As they entered the garden, Schaeffer's wizened face lit up, his eyes became lively. Schaeffer without his toupee, covered his bald dome with a blue and yellow baseball cap with a *Cerveza Zulia* emblem on the crown. His ferret-like face with a small mouth, small teeth and a narrow, tapered chin topped off his five foot, six inch frame. He said, "Clive you're in for a surprize. They were at the front entrance of the inn. Schaeffer looked up and pointed up to a sign that said '*El Escondite*'. "What do you think of *that*, Clive? Cost ten thousand bolos. When we turn that baby on at night, you can see it from the middle of the lake."

O'Reith took in the splendors of the huge neon sign. "Fabulous, Ted. Does it attract any guests?"

Schaeffer cackled, "Not a swinging dick. Nobody! Who in the hell would come to a place like this in a country like this?"

"Somebody who wanted a quiet place for a drink and a chat," O'Reith answered. He had already fathomed Mandy's motives.

Schaeffer led him around to the gate they had entered earlier and into the garden that he knew so well, indeed, long before Ted Schaeffer had ever set foot into it. Schaeffer opened the mossy gate with a long iron key. As they walked the flagstone path, toward the fountain, O'Reith saw right away that it was a different garden from the one he remembered. It was tidy for one thing. Not so many tufts of grass growing around the flower trays. The weeds were gone. The hedges that created the mazes were trimmed. Around the dragon-head fountain were more flowers, fewer vines. A Japanese silk screen, red, green and gold, depicting water falling into a rock basin concealed the colony where once dwelt the miniatures and presumably, still did. The large gilded bird cage was gone. Obregon now a trusted member of the family, lived at liberty in the trees.

Schaeffer saw O'Reith studying the screen. He said, "Clive, you can't look behind there. That's a taboo. Mandy's orders. Whatever is back there is not for us to see."

O'Reith nodded, continued his survey. The gas light over the fountain was the same, perhaps a little more verdigris on the bronze casting. The banana tree was the same, but with a thicker stalk, heavy with fruit now and the long, oscillating, obscene red tassel that so excited the fruit bats. Around the stone table where he once contracted malaria and suffered from it in a London hotel room, he saw four electroliers, ten feet tall with curving tops. From them hung open boxes, each with a fine grid inside and a four-bladed fan.

Schaeffer said cheerily, "Bug burners, Clive." He flipped a switch under the table. The fan blades began to turn, slowly and silently. "The draft pulls 'em right through the grid. Juice in the wires. Bug hits and *psst!* Nothing left but a wisp of smoke. Four more of 'em down at the other fountain and a couple of dozen spotted around the garden walls.

All them babies running at one time, it's like the Fourth of July. Knocks those mosquitoes down pdq."

"Mandy's idea?"

"Mine. We had bug-blowers when we were drilling down in the Macao swamps. Plenty of bugs down there where the *Rio Limon* dumps into the lake. Not just mosquitoes. I've seen flies as big as sparrows. Big bug go through one of them high-powered blowers and it's mush. Bug shredders. Hell of a mess at night when the lights were on. We had a driller down there who had worked for Gulf Oil on a power rig in Mozambique green jungle. He came down with some African disease. When he was back on his feet he figured to change his luck on the lake. He told me about these burners. They're made in Germany. Tuffy Marks at Loffland Brothers got the poop on 'em for me. Mandy thought it was a great idea. She's hot for new stuff."

O'Reith nodded with approval. "Incineration instead of pulverization," he mused. "Ted, how is Tuffy doing? His legs holding up? And Lila?" He sat in a canvas-backed chair at the stone table. Schaeffer hoisted himself up, perched on the stone, looking down upon O'Reith.

"They're OK. Legs doing fine. Lila keeping him good company. Like Mandy does me."

O'Reith noticed that the paths through the garden had new curbs with a green strip on the top. "Ted, what the hell is that?" he asked.

"That green goo is snake-bane. Fer-de-lance will think twice before he slithers through it," Schaeffer advised. "Got arsenic in it."

O'Reith nodded his approval. Snakes were a principal worry in the old days. Of course Cansor was always standing by with a machete sharp as a razor. O'Reith had seen him flick many a snake head into the garden underbrush. But the *Guayacon* was as fast as lightning. One had to take care. He said to Schaeffer, "A fellow doesn't have to keep his feet up any more."

"The frogs jump right over that stuff," Schaeffer added. "Doesn't bother 'em one bit."

"Well I'm glad of that," O'Reith said. The garden at night was luminous with tracings of frog eyes arcing across the path, hopping into the catch basin at the foot of the fountain. They were of all sizes; big frogs, green with yellow undersides; gray frogs, smaller with yellow eyes and purple palps and tiny red and blue frogs that spun like a top when they hopped, their gleaming eyes pinpoints of spiral light.

O'Reith and Schaeffer reminisced about the old days in the California oil fields. Even though O'Reith had heard most of the stories, they still sounded good. The afternoon passed. The light was fading fast as it always did in the tropics at twilight. Schaeffer rose, signaled for Cansor to start the gas lights that gave the garden its eerie appeal. O'Reith followed behind him along the path to the side entrance to the inn. He said, "Ted boy, you're in the lush green. That's for sure."

The wrinkled little man smiled over his shoulder, speared a new Chesterfield out of a fresh pack in his shirt, thanked O'Reith again for bringing them. Cansor lit it with the electric glowbar. Schaeffer blew a long plume of turbulent smoke across the hedge. He said, "I can't complain, Clive. She treats me good. Sleeps nice and warm. Sometimes late at night she has some girls in and I go to bed. She doesn't like for me to look at 'em. She said she'd zip me through one of those burners if I so much as smiled at one of 'em."

O'Reith tensed. Did Schaeffer know something about his old friend Molloy, long ago lost in this very same garden? Then he relaxed as Schaeffer went on. "Clive, Mandy believes in reincarnation."

"Over half the population of the world does, Ted," O'Reith replied. "If you throw in those who believe in salvation of one sort or another, nearly everybody does."

"Mandy believes you come back in the same way as you go out," Schaeffer continued. "She thinks she can change me into a bug. Said if I fooled around with one of those *poulets*, she'd change me into a glow worm. Like the song. *Glow Little Glow Worm.* You think she could do that?" Schaeffer had stopped and turned around to face O'Reith on the path right in front of the door to the inn. The smoke of his cigarette spiraled up from his right hand, which trembled slightly. There was a bug-burner over the door that caught the column of smoke and dissipated it into a cloud over their heads. "She's a funny lady, Clive. I mean *extra* funny. People think I'm a dumb little fucker. And I'm not overly smart. Christ, I could never understand how those whipstock guys with their azimuths and departures deflect a directional well. And I don't understand Mandy when she says she'll shrink me down if I don't do right. I'm afraid of her…" His voice lost its tone, trailed off.

"Your imagination is working overtime, Ted," O'Reith admonished.

Schaeffer tried to grin in the purple garden light but it was a grimace of desperation. "Clive, I've always considered myself to be a pretty fair country-boy Catholic. I've been through most of the rites and sacraments. Circumcised okay. No burrs or ragged edges. Baptized okay.

Sprinkled down, as they say. First Holy Communion. Wearing a white suit and a tie. Ate the little white wafer. Not much to it. I didn't really have any sense of communion with God. But I didn't make an issue of it. Just went on about my business. Confirmation. I sweated that one. I'd heard that the bishop slapped your cheek and I hoped it would just be a tap. And it was. He was a big bruiser of a guy in his finery with a staff made out of heavy hickory; he could of knocked me to my knees if anything went wrong. But nothing did. Just smoke and incense. So there I was then with four of 'em under my belt. Then I married Mandy. Made five. Clive, Harvey had me drilling morning tour on a steam rig in the winter of 1935 down in the Louisiana swamps. I got friendly with this *cajun* boiler man. Around four o'clock in the morning, when it was nippy, the derrickman ran the rig. I'd slip off behind the boilers for a jolt of the local firewater that *cajun* carried in his overalls. He was a strong Catholic. Had a string of kids. He told me, he said 'Ted, if you want to go to heaven, just work your way through that list of sacraments, you'll make it okay. You get out near the end and you get *extreme unction* under your belt and well, buddy, you're on your way.'

I've thought about that over the years, Clive, for a long time I thought that *cajun* was on to something. Harvey was a religious guy. He was big enough to forgive and forget a lot of things. Especially my screw-ups, well, except maybe that last one. And the Almighty is a much bigger guy than Harvey. Clive I'm getting on down the trail. Damn near bald. Can't see a thing without my glasses. Wear a hearing aid sometimes. Some nights I can hear the church bells ringing, the flutter of angel wings. I've studied the Ten Commandments. They're not too tough, at least as written. It's the interpretation those bishops tie onto 'em. The way they've got 'em pumped up, they include everything, just about, including mopery on the high seas. The path to heaven is booby-trapped to where the average guy can't make it. Doesn't have a Chinaman's chance. Clive you have to be damn near perfect or you're a fucked duck. Only a saint can get in. Can you see Theodore Schaeffer committing a miracle? She said she'd make a glow worm out of me and put me through head first. Big glow then no glow. Smoke. Ashes. Finito for Mrs. Schaeffer's only son, Ted." He was trembling. Far to the south, now that it was dark, the *Catatumbo lights* were flashing.

O'Reith said, "Ted let's go inside. Cansor'll mix us a drink. Some Ron Pampero on the rocks. What say?" As they opened the door to the inn, far away in the distance, the lights of Maracaibo lit up the sky."

After dinner, Maxine, Monique and Marjorie Tarbutton retired. It had been a long day for them. Schaeffer, on signal from Mandy did likewise. The Chinese cook and his helper cleared the dessert dishes. Mandy rose, nodded to Cansor to prepare the cognac and beckoned to O'Reith. "The bar or the garden?" she asked.

O'Reith got up, stretched, said, "The bar. I've seen enough of the garden today." He followed Mandy upstairs, Tarbutton in tow. When they were seated, O'Reith motioned to Tarbutton, "Hardy, tell Mandy where we stand."

Tarbutton began with his meeting in Ciudad Bolivar and when he got to the one in Caracas with Torres, Mandy interrupted him. She said,

"His first name is Rodrigo. When he was young he had red hair. That's why he's called *Rojo*. I know him socially, well, sort of socially. There is an American expression for people like him. Is it wishy-washy? He comes here occasionally when he's in Maracaibo. He's never been in the garden. But he's seen it from the window."

Tarbutton completed his account. O'Reith said, "Mandy, tomorrow Maxine and I move into our villa in the *Distrito Creole* near the Coromoto Hospital. Hardy and Marjorie go to Caracas to take up residence in a flat in *Las Mercedes*, near the Hotel Tamanaco. We have two flats. A fellow named Stanley Ethering will be in the other. He was a Calitroleum lobbyist in Washington. No stranger to trouble, he was in the Texas National Guard during the riots in the East Texas oil field in 1932. Some drunken roughneck broke his back. He knows how to keep the wheels greased but you can give him insight into Venezuelan politics. Here we are in February. Clock running fast. It'll be the end of March *toute de suite*. That's when the government opens the tender offer. Next week, Hardy will fly back here with Torres. Could Cansor meet us? We'll conduct our business in the garden and go back to town. If we're lucky, we'll sign the agreements then. We'll be on our way. What do you say?"

"My dear General O'Reith. As always, I am at your beck and call."

"Mandy, the company has set aside a block of common stock in your name. You earn it the day we begin running crude oil. The dividends will keep you off the street when you're too old to do what you're doing now."

"More than I deserve," she said modestly.

O'Reith smiled. From the same musette bag that had produced the Chesterfield cigarettes, he removed a short barreled 7.65mm Mauser. Mandy I have the deepest respect for your remarkable powers but the occasion could arise when they would be inadequate. If you should ever need this, you will need it desperately. It's loaded. And here's a box of cartridges. Try it out on the garden snakes some afternoon. Make no mistake, we play a dangerous game."

"I know that. Should I need the little pistol, you may be sure that I will use it properly."

O'Reith finished his cognac, rose. He said, "Mandy, can Cansor take Hardy and I to town? We need to bring Holland into the picture."

"But of course." She snapped her fingers. Cansor appeared. She motioned to the Cadillac. With her flashlight in hand, she walked ahead, scanning the grass for snakes. Cansor opened the door to the tonneau. Tarbutton got inside. O'Reith stood beside Mandy. She said, "You had a nice visit with Theodore? He showed you the improvements?"

"Yeah he showed me that silk screen too." It was the *Voice*.

"Oh! Not much has changed there, my dear general. Not to worry. All's well." Her voice was agile, glib, nonchalant.

"Ted know what's behind that screen?"

"Silly question. Of course not. He has definite instructions not to look."

"Mandy, Ted can be a naughty boy."

"La La La, my dear general. I wouldn't harm a hair on that dear boy's head."

"He has no hair on his head. You tell him you were going to change him into a glow worm and zip him through the bug-burner?"

"Figuratively, perhaps. Or is it allegorically? I have such difficulty with those English words of obscure meaning. You may rest content sir."

"Mandy, we have never spoken of this but all of Ted's disasters involved young girls…"

"*Poulets?*"

"Yeah."

"Well you needn't have a care, sir. Theodore and I have a transparent marriage. We see through these things. Of course he knows that I have hegemony —- or is it autarchy? I'm not getting the words out right tonight."

"Let's not quibble, Mandy. Ted is pushing sixty. He may have learned a few things. Certainly his glands are less active, i.e., unless you've tampered with them."

"Sir, you'll have me blushing."

"Mandy, as I told you before, Schaeffer is no great friend of mine. He was a thorn in my side for many a day. But I brought him down here. Even if it was exile. I knew you were interested in him from what Molloy told you about him. Molloy, well, that's history. But I feel responsible for Ted. If I thought for one minute that you would actually change him into a glow…"

She cut him off. "He will be all right. General O'Reith, in this imperfect world, some must lead, must dominate, must rule, well, like the *Raj*. You know about the *Raj*?"

"Yes. My older brother served the *Raj* for a lifetime, with distinction, I might add."

"Well, there you are. Theodore, although I love him a great deal, is one of God's *little people*. He must be supervised and protected. Cherished, of course but…"

O'Reith entered the tonneau and sat beside Tarbutton. Cansor closed the door. O'Reith said simply, "Goodnight Mandy." As the Cadillac drove along the high bluff, the lights of the lake winking in the distance, he muttered to himself, "Well, I have more important things to think about than that little bastard."

"What's that Clive?" Tarbutton asked.

"Nothing Hardy, just the echo of a bad dream."

*   *   *

It was the last week of February. Little Clive Colin had come and gone. Radios installed and working. Communication with Helen was difficult. Static and interference most of the time. But late at night, some nights, he could raise her. So far all was well. They were shooting the Piedras Negras movie. McDonough had gracefully turned down the cameo role but said he would be sure to see the picture when it premiered in Rome.

O'Reith, eyeing his wrist watch, and drumming nervously on the arm rest of the easy chair, sat beside Holland in the lobby of the Hotel Del Lago. It was after six in the evening and they were monitoring the revolving door under the marquee. Holland was smoking a Lucky Strike, flicking the ashes on the floor, annoying the bell captain. Across the room in an easy chair sat a large man with a bulbous, purple nose in a humpty-dumpty like head. His eyes were closed. His head was back against the cushions. His mouth was partly open. A gold front tooth reflected light from the chandelier hanging above the reception desk. He reminded O'Reith of Thomas Gomez, the B-movie heavy.

In a whisper, O'Reith asked, "Holland, who's the fat guy in the white *liqui-liqui* with the floppy Panama in his lap? I've seen him before."

"That's Riva Marcelo Cordero. *Seguridad Nacional* brass hat. Hangs out here all the time. That hat covers the rod in his belt. Little .32 Beretta. You probably remember him from *El Techo Rojo*. He's put on some weight since then. Mandy threw him out so often, he quit coming. She must have had a strong stroke to do that. He's as dangerous as a scorpion. Why are you meeting Torres right here under his nose?"

"What he wanted. Original plan was to meet at *Grano de Oro* and go straight to the garden. Torres changed it. He wanted it like this. Part of the drill maybe. Cordero will report back that he met his party as planned. Torres is running late. Supposed to have been here at six. Could be bad weather out of Maiquetia. When Tarbutton comes through that door, you can take off. But get a good look at Torres. You may have to deal with him one of these days."

Holland nodded, put his cigarette out in the ash stand beside his chair. The bell captain approved. Holland said, "He'll show okay. A half hour down here is nothing."

At that moment the revolving door began to turn and Tarbutton strode through. Holland departed. O'Reith rose to meet the newcomers. Tarbutton said, "Clive, like you to meet Señor Torres. *Rojo* Torres. O'Reith shook his hand. Tarbutton said, "We're running late. Shall we be on our way?" He guided them through the revolving door and into the tonneau of the Cadillac. Cansor closed them in and pulled out into *Milagro Avenue* .

"Where are we going?" Torres asked.

"To a garden that adjoins the inn known as *El Escondite*." O'Reith answered. "We can talk there in comfort and privacy."

Torres smiled. "I know that inn. A good choice."

When the Cadillac pulled up to the wooden gate, Cansor alit, helped them out, closed the car door and unlocked the gate. The beam of his flashlight played on the path as he led them to the stone table near the dragon-head fountain. He lit the gas lamps and turned on the bug burners. As the three men sat, he went for drinks. Shortly he returned with a tray bearing bottles of Pampero rum, Gordon's gin and Johnny Walker Black Label with an ice bucket and glasses, soda and Coca Cola. Under his arm was a bottle of dry Vermouth. Torres touched the Johnny Walker. Cansor made martinis for O'Reith and Tarbutton, poured a jolt of Johnny Walker into a glass for Torres and opened the bottle of Coca Cola. Torres added a finger or two of it to the scotch. When the three men had their drinks ready, Torres lifted his glass and said, "*Caballeros. Exito!*" They clinked glasses and drank, the two gringos echoing the toast. The sounds attracted the attention of Obregon and his mate in the mango tree. The two birds pushed their heads through the leaves. Obregon a big parrot, was in the lingo, a *Huacamayo*. From the shoulders up, he was crimson except for a yellowish oval flecked with red spots around his black, bead-like eyes. His manila-colored beak was hooked. His expression was a glassy glare. His wings, red and green, had blue tips. His tail feathers, hidden in the leaves, were red and yellow with a blue clutch of feathers underneath.

His talons were pointed, flexible and businesslike. They curved around a tree limb like a Stilson wrench. Obregon now, lived with Fifinela, his girl friend. Maxine had named her the night she and O'Reith were kissing and smooching in the garden so long ago. It was clearly an enduring relationship as evidenced by the presence of many more, younger, less arrogant, parrots who dwelt, here and there, in the several trees, shrubs and bushes enclosed by the high stone wall with shards of broken glass embedded along its wide top. Obregon had been a bachelor the night O'Reith saw him for the first time, over a decade ago. Then he lived in the gilded cage where he usually perched on a broomstick that ran from end to end. In that era he was a guard and jailer. The night O'Reith first saw him, Obregon was in charge of two naked, miniaturized black men on the floor of the cage who quaked under his steely gaze. Holland, more frivolous then than now, facetiously called the prisoners, *minijigs.* All that had happened long ago when they were much younger and the trauma of war was still heavy upon them. Today, Obregon was a free parrot, had the run of the garden, a good companion whose eggs he fertilized with regularity, many offspring all of which, if they were males, looked exactly like him and he had no specific duties or responsibilities. His notorious reputation was history. No one would have thought that he ever could have been cruel. Obregon was wary when Mandy was in the garden; kept still and silent, huddled beside Fifinela in the luxuriant green foliage and let the clock run until Mandy was gone again.

"And so," said Torres in the gloom. "How do we proceed?"

"Nine and sixteen," O'Reith said. "Are we agreed on that?"

"Yes. Exactly," Torres said.

"We'll pay the first installment when the when we sign the contract. We'll pay again when we get permission to begin work. A third time when the contract appears in the *Gaceta Oficial* and a final payment when oil runs into steel storage at *Punto Fijo* "

"Do you agree to the model contract?" Torres asked. "Fifty-fifty split?"

"Of course, after we recover the investment. Standard royalty up to that point." O'Reith said. "And other specific obligations set forth in the model."

"So quickly we get down to the testicles of the deal," Torres observed. "What, sir, are the numbers?"

"Ten million U.S. dollars as a signature bonus, five for each block. Another ten when we get the *permisso de trabajar*. Another ten when the gazette appears. Final ten when we run oil."

"Forty million all told," Torres said, adding the numbers as O'Reith spoke them.

"Just so."

"My dear gentlemen. I have in my briefcase several documents, all in triplicate. They are complete except for the numbers. We can write them in with India ink. Customary in this country. The official documents bear a government seal and are dated 31 March 1956. The other documents, side-letter agreements, as you call them are written to be parallel to the official documents. There are two side-letters. I think you were only expecting one. Can you up the amount to $44 million?"

O'Reith sipped his martini. Rubbed his chin. *Como no, mi amigo*."

Torres produced the documents. O'Reith read the official award. Then he read the production contract. Tarbutton read the side-letters. Torres produced a fountain pen with a broad point and filled in the numbers. $36 million to the official contract, to the Government of Venezuela. $4 million to a second party and $4 million to a third party. O'Reith quickly signed. Tarbutton signed as a witness.

Torres said, "Please ask your banker to stamp the extra copies of the side letters. Then return them to me."

O'Reith nodded. When briefcases had been snapped shut, they signaled for Cansor to refill their glasses. They drank another toast. Torres continued, "You read the language of the side-letters carefully, General Tarbutton?"

Tarbutton nodded. "You're referring to the payments for ten years once production has reached one hundred thousand bopd?"

"Yes."

"In the event of a *Golpe de Estado*, should we lose rights to our concession, then payments will stop," O'Reith said. "We don't need any language in the agreements to protect us. The possibility of a lawsuit is remote indeed."

"You noted the bank account numbers and the name of the banks." Torres continued.

"That too," Tarbutton said.

"O'Reith said, "I'll wire Paris tomorrow. The first payments will be made immediately." Final dregs of diluted drinks were quaffed back. Many an insect had been converted into vapor as they conducted their affairs. Many a frog had jumped the poison–topped curbs. The *fer-de-lances* were sleeping on the ground beneath the labyrinths. Obregon and his mate had long ago lost interest in the proceedings and had returned to their amatory activity. A good night's work had been done, all around. On the morrow, money would change hands. O'Reith continued, "Rojo, Hardy and I, now that we've done our work, are going to dally for a bit in *El Escondite*. Will you join us?"

Torres rose, smiled briefly then allowed the heaviness of duty to cloud his features. "Nothing would please me more, "he replied. "But the *colonel* expects me at a good hour tomorrow. I must catch the early LAV Viscount to Maiquetia. Would your chauffeur be so kind as to take me to my hotel?"

Cansor turned off the gas lights and the bug burners. The three negotiators followed him out of the garden, stood by as he locked the gate. He closed Torres into the tonneau of the Cadillac. The tail lights of the car diminished as it rolled along the bluff. When the car vanished around a bend, the two friends walked beneath the garish, flashing sign that read *El Escondite*. Inside, in the darkened hall, they climbed the stairs to the second floor. It was long after midnight. In the dining room, the dinner tables had been replaced with cocktail tables. Each had a black candle in the center, in an amber glass chimney. The overhead lights were off. On a small bandstand, a Cuban trio was playing a beguine. Piano. Saxophone. Clarinet. A pretty girl with smoky skin and an orchid in her hair was waiting her signal to sing. From nowhere, from behind them, Mandy appeared. "All is well?" she asked.

"Yeah, O'Reith said. "Jake-a-loo."

"A drink?"

"Cognac."

They followed her to her office behind the bar. O'Reith let her read the documents that he had signed. She made a note of the bank numbers. He said, "That's it for now. In the morning Holland will begin to line up the platform rigs. I'll order pipe. I want that contract published in the gazette. Think you can help there?"

"Normally six months pass before a contract appears in the *Gaceta Oficial*. What's the urgency?"

O'Reith was tired. His lined face was sagging more than usual. He was feeling rumdum. He said, "I worry about a *golpe de estado*."

Mandy nodded. With the contract gazetted, a new government would honor it. Ungazetted, it was an orphan. "I see your point, sir. Well, of course, it is a question of a little money. Say ten thousand bolivares?"

"That's fine," O'Reith said. Cansor returned and took them to town. O'Reith slept in the cushions of the tonneau.

Chapter V
▼
Vaduz And Ventimiglia

In his dream, Maxine had decided to go away to live with her sister for awhile, had already done so in fact, and O'Reith was vainly trying to remember where he'd written down the telephone number in Caracas. He wanted to call her and plead with her to return home. He was hard up and needed some of what she had. He looked everywhere; in his diary, his billfold and on the pad at his desk in the office. He couldn't find the number anywhere. He was in a sweat, desperate, distressed. The rattle of rain against his window awakened him from the melancholy dream. A woman slept close beside him. As he stirred, confused, he didn't know if he were in Los Angeles with Helen or in Paris with Maxine. The scent was Chanel No.5, no help. Then he remembered that he was in Maracaibo. It was Maxine. Still apprehensive, he fondled her, found and caressed a mole on the inside of her thigh, confirming her identity. He was relieved. She was not in Caracas but at his side. He reflected that it was a silly dream. Maxine didn't have a sister. To call Caracas from Maracaibo was pretty close to impossible. Indeed, there were no lines running across the lake. Anyhow, why would she even think of going away? Then he began to remember the events of last night. Meeting Torres. Drinking toasts to success. Signing the documents. Going over things with Mandy. He knew then he had to get up and get going. It was almost eight o'clock, late in the afternoon in Paris where LeBel awaited news. He had a meeting with Holland at nine. He gave Maxine a parting caress, got up, took a quick leak, shaved in the shower, donned his bathrobe and slippers and went to the kitchen for orange juice, papayas, mangos and toast. Coffee could wait until he got to the office. He dressed in khakis and field boots, saw that it was still raining, borrowed one of Maxine's many umbrellas and started down the hill. The walk did him good and his leg didn't act up.

Holland served O'Reith coffee. A bellboy brought him two messages. The first one was from Blake.

FOR CLIVE COLIN O'REITH
THE CASINGHEAD COMPANY
HOTEL DEL LAGO
MARACAIBO, VENEZUELA
March 1, 1956
CLIVE, A BIT OF BAD LUCK. MCLARSSEN ESTATE NO. 1 IN BEAVER LODGE FIELD, NORTH DAKOTA CUT AN UNEXPECTED SHALLOW GAS SAND RIGHT OUT FROM UNDER SURFACE PIPE. WELL KICKED AND CAUGHT FIRE. DERRICK DOWN IN FIVE MINUTES. RED ADAIR PUT THE FIRE OUT AND SINCE CONTRACTOR WAS OPERATING ON THE FOOTAGE RATE, ALL EXPENSE IS FOR HIS ACCOUNT. HOWEVER MCLARSSEN ESTATE HAS FILED SUIT AGAINST STANDARD OIL CLAIMING PROPERTY DAMAGE AND LOSS OF LIVESTOCK (SIX COWS GRAZING BEHIND THE DERRICK SUB-STRUCTURE). WE OFFERED TO SETTLE CLAIMS BUT THEY INSIST ON GOING TO COURT. LOOKS LIKE YOU WILL HAVE TO APPEAR AS EXPERT WITNESS FOR THE COMPANY UNDER TERMS OF THE CONSULTING AGREEMENT. NOT MUCH GOING ON IN NORTH DAKOTA THIS TIME OF YEAR AND WE EXPECT CASE WILL BE ON THE DOCKET IN A COUPLE OF WEEKS. CAN YOU COME TO SAN FRANCISCO FOR DISCUSSIONS? NEXT SUBJECT. BARNEY

DONNEGAN IN TOWN LOOKING FOR A JOB. HAD THAT RED-BIRD FELLOW ALONG, THE ONE THEY CALL THE FEATHER-MERCHANT. YOU MAY REMEMBER DONNEGAN IS RELATED TO THE LATE JOHNNY KNOBLES WHO WAS HARVEY'S BAGMAN FOR MANY YEARS. WE CAN DISCUSS THIS WHILE YOU ARE HERE. COME SEE ME PAL. IT'S LONESOME NEAR THE TOP.
REGARDS
VINCENT B. BLAKE
VICE CHAIRMAN
STANDARD OIL COMPANY
SAN FRANCISCO

The next message, from Helen, said she'd tried to get him on the radio without luck, that all was going okay in Piedras Negras. She was standing short and could use some expert fooling around. He told Holland that he would be going to San Francisco and from there to Monte Carlo. Then he cabled LeBel to make payments according to a coded system they had worked out in Paris. He wired Tarbutton and Ethering to meet him tomorrow in the Tamanaco. He cabled Helen that as soon as he was free, he would come see her in Nice.

He wondered about the reference to Donnegan. Blake, aware of what happened in Maracaibo in late 1945, was warning him. Blake knew Donnegan was kin to the late, little lamented Knobles. So what was that all about? The fire in North Dakota was a nightmare come true. He'd have to face one or both of the McLarssens in the courtroom.

So he'd have to explain to Maxine about his need to travel. He decided to fly to Miami from Maiquetia. Then to Los Angeles. Visit the kids. Confer with Susie. Brief her on the case. She could organize the files he would take to the trial. Then to San Francisco to see Blake at 225 Bush Street. Find out when he was required in court. Get to the bottom of the Donnegan puzzle. Fly to New York and on to Paris. See LeBel and then proceed to Nice and Monte Carlo for some extended stud service.

At the travel desk in the hotel lobby, he asked the girl to make airline reservations and started out the revolving door. It was still drizzling. He went back to his office, got Maxine's umbrella, went out the side door and twenty minutes later he was home.

He killed time with Maxine until lunch, ate sparingly with nothing to drink and then they tumbled around in the hay for an hour. She walked with him back to the Del Lago as he had a late afternoon appointment with Holland. Maxine had her hair fixed while he attended business. Then they went by taxi to pick up Monique. Normally she came home on the school bus, but this was a special occasion since he was leaving the next morning. In Caracas he advised Tarbutton that he would have the 3rd copy of each side-letter bank stamped in Vaduz and back in Caracas before March 31. Then he was on his way to Miami and Los Angeles.

*   *   *

"Clive, I know that most of this is old hat but I'll repeat it for perspective," Blake said magisterially. "Congressman Johnny Knobles, from California, district of Los Angeles, unfrocked, became Calitroleum's bagman while you were pushing tools in Texas. He and Harvey were pals. Harvey supported him when he was a politician, overlooked his many peccadilloes, including the one with the high school girl, the one that lost him the election of 1932. Knobles, while a congressman, became friendly with Sam Rayburn, presently Speaker of the House. He seems to be a solid citizen. But he is linked to the McLarssen family, maybe by marriage, and the new, young Congressman John M. McLarssen fell under his aegis. As you, better than anyone know, Congressman McLarssen's bright, blossoming, political career was short, abruptly terminated by decapitation with a machete, or so it was alleged at the time, when they were trying to pin it on you. After all the hullabaloo, Rayburn denied that he was in any way related to

McLarssen, which for all I know, may be true. Carrying you along too fast, Clive?"

O'Reith chuckled. "Vince, I really didn't know where the hell Johnny Knobles came from. Most of the rest is still vivid in my memory. I assume this ties in to the lawsuit. Go on." O'Reith shifted in his chair, noticed his hands were moist, dried them on his handkerchief.

"Barney Donnegan is a cousin of Knobles. He took the money he extorted from us, that Macoa block..."

"I remember that all too well, Vince" O'Reith said rather sharply.

Blake continued, "He took the money and set himself up as an old time revivalist in Oklahoma City. Part of it he used to send his buddy, that *Redbird* guy, to school at The University of Oklahoma. He got a law degree. I naively thought that anyone with a record could not be certified as a practicing attorney in the United States. But apparently you can and he is. He was in prison on two occasions, fraud and embezzlement. And now we find him across the bar from us in McLarssen Estate Vs The Standard Oil Company. Tie that, pal!"

"What a comic opera," O'Reith said, grimly. "If it were not so close to home, I'd laugh. Vince, I have places to go and things to do. Minot, North Dakota is not one of the places and a lawsuit is not one of the things. But I'm on the hook. Where do we stand?"

Blake had a mixed expression on his face, part amusement, part concern. He continued, "Donnegan organized the *Triangular Church of the Holy Jesus.* Bought a 1,000 watt, near-bankrupt radio station in Oklahoma City and began banging the Bible on the air. Like some of those guys down in Mexico. You know how those guys are?"

"Like Harvey in his dotage."

"Yeah," Blake affirmed. "Well this guy Donald McLarssen, brother of the late lamented congressman, is of the same stripe, a preacher of some description. I guess he knew about Donnegan through the Knobles-Rayburn connection. So he set up a branch of the triangular church, but not in North Dakota. He couldn't make it work up there where they have all those Lutherans. He set it up in Omaha, Nebraska, complete with a hill-billy band and a radio station. The church is clicking along just fine. Now they want to organize number three. Where? Los Angeles. They see big money. Even now they're ventilating over the air from Oklahoma City and Omaha that the great fuzzy spider of the west, The Standard Oil Company is hammering a poor, humble man of the sod into the ground. Why do this? My guess is that they will settle. But not until we're in court with a jury seated, one that the *feathermerchant* helped select, and not until the eleventh hour when attorney for the plaintiff has made an impassioned cry for justice against the crude oil monster. Naturally the settlement will be greatly out of proportion to the damages cited in the complaint and ten to twenty times, maybe a hundred times, what we've offered. How do you like that?"

"Kind of like the way things were before we sold out to SOCAL," O'Reith answered. "Any idea when it will go to trial?"

"May the 10th. U.S. District court in Denver Colorado. Our legal team got a change in venue on account of all the unfavorable publicity."

"Well that's something," O'Reith said. He was marginally more cheerful. "Beats Minot. Timing not too bad. Gives me enough space to get my affairs arranged. There's a nice hotel in Denver too. Brown's. Good food. Nice big bar with a copper top."

Blake made a wide grin, showing his teeth. "Clive, all we need is for old *Triple A* Agnew to horn in on this and it would be just like old times. We'd have the same cast as for the *Macoa* drama."

"That wasn't too long of a ride and we came out of it pretty good. At least pretty cheap. *Triple A* isn't likely to make this party. He went down the tube in Maracaibo some years back."

"I didn't know that!" Blake exclaimed. "I thought he was back in jail. You think he's in the lake with a rock bit tied to his ankles?"

"If so, the little fishes long ago stripped his bones." O'Reith speculated, knowing exactly what had happened to him but not wanting to get into it.

Blake's eyebrows went up. "Are there fish out there? Venezuelan Government says we gringos have polluted it so bad there's no life left in it. There's a bunch of 'em in Washington right now trying to get Uncle Sam to finance a clean up. They say the Americans spilled the oil and the Americans should clean it up."

"Propaganda," O'Reith replied. "Lake's full of fish. Sting rays. Turtles. Even alligators in some of the backwaters. Every time we run a velocity survey, dead fish cover the surface."

"Government lets us shoot dynamite in the lake?"

"It's in the contract. They send a *Fiscale* out to observe. He lines up a boat for the fish. Fringe benefit." O'Reith yawned, said, "Back to McLarssen Estate Vs Standard Oil. I'll read the file while I'm here. Copy crucial documents and send Susie whatever she needs. I may take her along. Help out with files and cue me for testimony."

"Be careful with her. I've always thought she'd give you a little piece if you got close enough for her to grab you."

"I've had it on my mind for twenty years or so. But I better not. She's my secretary. Vince, it looks like an interesting case. Any other funny factors I need to know about?"

"Yeah, there is," Blake said slowly.

"Tell me, pal" O'Reith said, alarm in his voice.

Blake grinned. "Gimp. Gimp Flagherty. Remember him? He was pushing tools on a Boyd and Bowen power rig out of Bakersfield."

"I remember from the Drilling Report that it was a Boyd and Bowen rig," O'Reith said. And I remember when Gimp was a no-good driller in West Texas."

"Standard Oil lawyer took his deposition last week," Blake continued. "Said he was a guy with a face like bad news. He's reborn. Got religion. Wants to confess his sins in court. Recant. He'll be an expert witness for the plaintiff."

"Figures," O'Reith commented. "Donnegan's people'll tell him what to say."

"Standard Oil lawyer says he stammers pretty bad. Cries a lot. Wipes his eyes with a big, red bandanna and asks the Lord for mercy. Says he's got it down pat. Dresses in a black suit and gray shirt with a string tie. Both of his shoes special made. One of 'em with an extra high heel. Like a Kansas undertaker."

"You know why he stammers?" O'Reith asked.

"No. I don't know much about him. I never saw him. Just heard the hands talking about him. He had his right foot crushed in a casing swarm. Drilling for Gulf in the Goldsmith Field. I suppose that's why they call him 'Gimp'."

"He never worked for us," O'Reith explained. "He worked for George P. Livermore, out of Lubbock. After he got his foot crushed, he left the oil fields. Took to shooting pool. Hustling greenhorns in Odessa. He was *abbreviated* one night in *The Ace of Diamonds*, a beer joint. Like the *Barracuda Club* in Los Angeles but tougher, they say. I was never in it. Gimp's real name is Clyde O'Flagherty, but he dropped the 'O' after he got to stammering. He couldn't get it all out of his mouth in one breath. He was standing at the bar, with his foot on the rail, as they do out there. He got into a contretemps with a derrickman. Called him a stump-jumper or something insulting. Derrickman worked for Loffland Brothers on a big rig drilling for The Texas Company in Block 45. Gimp was wearing a Smith & Wesson .44 revolver in a belly-button holster, all six cylinders loaded and the hammer down on the cartridge looking into the barrel. Derrickhand took a swipe at him with an empty *Grand Prize* bottle, that's a popular beer in Texas, brewed down in Houston next door to Hughes Tool Company. Well, Gimp took a half step back and the beer bottle smashed on the hammer of his pistol. It went off. Shot the head off of his dick, punctured one testicle, severed his kneecap and the big toe on his left foot. Bullet hit the concrete floor, turned around, came back up through his left pants leg. He had on heavy duty, blue denims. Bullet cut a groove in the calf of his leg, furrowed the cheek of his ass, scraped his backside, went up through his arm pit, snapped his collar bone, shredded his ear and knocked his hat off. All that in about a second and a half. Derrickman was stunned. Didn't know what to think, said Gimp just stood there hammering on the bar with one hand and yelling 'OOOOOeeee! OOOOeeee!' Created a furor. So Gimp is crippled up. And I suppose it also affected him mentally. That's when he began to stammer. I hadn't heard about the weeping and moaning. He may have picked that up in church. Gimp has had quite a few things happen to him that any normal man would regret. He got caught in the draft during the war but he flunked the physical. I heard that he went back to working in the oil fields. Shortage of hands, I guess Boyd and Bowen thought they could make a pusher out of him. I don't know how he landed on a rig that was working for us. Hiring that rig would have been a 10th Floor decision. We've used their rigs before. Nobody in the executive suite would have had an inkling it was old Gimp pushing tools. Holland knows who he is. He would have had him run off immediately if he'd known."

"Well, you'll get to renew your acquaintance with him." Blake said. "How about lunch?"

Afterwards, Blake took O'Reith down to the Land & Legal Department and introduced him to the Standard Oil lawyer in charge of the case. He read the files and copied documents that afternoon. Late in the day, he caught a Western Pacific DC-6 to Los Angeles and took a taxi to Holmby Hills for an evening with Rae Regan and her family. Little Clive Colin, and Marilyn, the Widow Halliday and her son, Briscoe came for dinner. Later they played bridge while the children watched *Gun Smoke* on television. Seeing Miss Kitty on the screen, he wished he were in Helen's arms. Susie Halliday, indicated she wouldn't mind if O'Reith escorted her home, but he declined, pleading the lateness of the hour and travel-weariness. "See you in the morning at nine," he told her at the door.

Next morning he was blunt with her. He said, "Susie, I appreciated the invitation last night. I could have used what you've got. It's occurred to me more than once during the last twenty years. But you're my secretary and I'm not a mixed metaphor man. Won't work. Not only that, with Hardy in Caracas, you'll have to do a lot of his work. In his office, scotch-taped to the back of that fireproof filing cabinet, you'll find the combination. Files related to my private life. You can review them. Mail comes in here you don't understand, things from Europe. Bank statements. Security statements. Bills of one kind or another. Look in the files. You'll find the reference. If you can't find it, let me know. Shoot me a cable." He rubbed his hands together as if he were getting ready to pick up an axe handle. "Now, some years back, the McLarssen affair made the headlines in Washington. Also in *The Yellow Peril* out here on the coast. I got some hate mail. Most of it from North Dakota. Only letter I read was written by McLarssen's sister. She was just fourteen then. That's why I read it. In the bottom drawer of the cabinet you'll find that letter and all the others. I want you to read them all and make a list. Many will be anonymous. Doesn't matter. List 'em anyhow. Date. Postmark and content, especially if threatening. I'm flying to Europe in the morning and then to Caracas. Be back here a week before the trial in Denver. Study the case. Call the Standard Oil lawyer in San Francisco. Make sure we know exactly what I'm to do. You may have to go up there and review it with him."

"Yes sir."

He then briefed her about the meeting with Torres. He said, "Susie, in my briefcase are copies of the side-letters that run parallel to the model contract. Photocopy them for the file here and put 'em back in my briefcase. They have to be stamped by the *Banque en Liechtenstein.* That's the guarantee for Torres that everything is OK. When he has them in his hands, he'll give us a work permit and allow the contract to go for publication. So this is a matter of some urgency. The contract is in force as of 1 April even though not published. We'll begin operations. After that date, expect a steady flow of orders for tools, casing, well heads, separators, tubing and tanks. Everything. You'll need help. Call Vince in the morning. Ask him if some of those extra Standard Oil buyers can come to work for us. Move 'em down here and put 'em to work. You'll need extra office space. Call my son and tell him you want a teleprinter installed, another just like it in the Maracaibo office and a third in Tarbutton's flat in Caracas. Tell my son to get cracking on that. We need them working by 1 April."

She was scribbling furiously in her shorthand notebook. He waited for her to catch up. When she looked up at him, he said, "I want you to hire a private detective. Ask him to go to Oklahoma City and find out all there is worth knowing about Barney Donnegan. Explain that it is in connection with that lawsuit. That *Feathermerchant* guy too. I forget his name, Donny Bob something–or-other. When that's done, send him to North Dakota to check out the McLarssens."

She looked again at O'Reith, studied his face, now grim and unsmiling, flat-mouthed, lined. While still a remarkably handsome man, the years were catching up with him. The war. Two bad oil field fires. The indictment. Yes, lots of stress and strain eroding the beauty she saw in him. She said, "Clive, I know a private eye that Harvey used to check out Ted Schaeffer's private life. He's a sharp guy, doesn't talk except when he has to. He's your age, about. Worked in the oil fields when he was a kid. Name is Phillip Marlborough. Office just down the street."

"Hire him," O'Reith said. "Line him up for Spanish lessons. We get past that lawsuit I've got plenty of work for him in Venezuela."

So he was on his way again, like the wandering Jew. TWA Super-Constellation to Idlewild. Another one just like it to Orly. LeBel met him. Next day they took the train to Vaduz, had the side-letters stamped and photocopied. Then back to Paris. Cables to Tarbutton. Air Inter to Nice. Helen's limousine took him to Monte Carlo. That night they got down to it. After a four day weekend, he was totally pussy-whipped. Helen, for the moment, was satisfied. In between while resting up, he had enjoyed the tender delights of his daughter, Helen Simpson. When the essential copulative communication was temporarily suspended as a result of mutual exhaustion, over drinks on Helen's broad terrace, he asked, "Baby, how are things going down in Piedras Negras?" The sun was behind the mountains. It was twilight. The brighter stars were popping out in the purple sky over the calm Mediterranean.

"Disillusion setting in," she answered. "I'm coping with it."

"Bolletti not the right guy?"

"He's okay. But not exactly what I thought he would be. He's slow. Likes late starts in the morning. Long liquid, talkative lunches. Sort of boring to tell the truth. And then early quits.

The actors are all his pals. Guys he was using in the black market movies. The big fat guys. Older and heavier. Ace, this is supposed to be an English language movie. Those guys have accents that would drag down the *Andrea Doria*. Heavy. I guess it's okay to have one of those bloated guys in a movie. But the *Old West* was tough. The Mexican border even tougher. A square meal was hard to come by. Probably why they drank so much. Washing down that beef jerky. To have even a flavor of the times, the merest hint of realism, you've got to have some hard-eyed, rangy guys quick on their feet. Especially the hero. Hell Ace, the lead in Piedras Negras must weigh three hundred pounds. Not a spring chicken either. When he goes for his gun, he has to look for it, tucked away under all that avoirdupois. Slow. Ponderous. Ace, this flic has all the promise of a farce. All we need is Buster Keaton as the bad guy. We may never get it in the can."

"What does Alice prognosticate?"

"You know Alice. Rosy scenario. Everything OK but 'to the stars through difficulty'".

"Money holding up?"

"Not like it should. I don't know where it goes. Looks like this turkey will cost a million bucks. Hell, Jack would shoot it for two hundred grand." She sighed. "I suppose I'm easily discouraged but I can't see the end of the trail yet."

"Throw your hand in, Helen. Call it a bad job. Write off the investment and return to Los Angeles. Maybe Jack will put you under contract again. Wave at Bolletti and say *Ciao*."

"I'm not ready for that yet. Alice may be right. Maybe it *will* turn out OK. I want to see it through. How much longer can you stay?"

"Not long. I've got some papers in my briefcase that Señor Torres wants quickly, before March the 31st. His insurance policies. Today is March the 25th. In a week the contract becomes official. Got to get the iron lined up and moved out to the platforms. By the way, our son will be in Maracaibo when I get back. I'll give him your fondest regards."

"See that he shaves, too. He and Marilyn getting along OK?"

"As far as I know. Why?"

"I don't know. Mother's intuition. Something funny there."

*   *   *

Tarbutton met his flight at Maiquetia in a new Citroen limousine. O'Reith was in white, a tropical linen suit, silk shirt, bow tie, shoes and a Panama hat. He had his monocle in, carrying his briefcase in one hand and a small bag in the other. The chauffeur closed them into the deep soft cushions, imperial purple and satiny. "Hardy, you go to heaven, this must be how you get around. I'll ask LeBel to buy a couple of these babies when we get on the rich list. Boul Mich! Not going to bankrupt us is it?"

"No, but Torres may," Tarbutton said it like a joke but the tone of his voice suggested something more serious.

"Yeah, O'Reith responded, an edge in his voice. "What now?"

"He rang early this morning. Said it was imperative that we meet tonight. I told him you were arriving. He said, 'the three of us then'. He seemed pretty nervous."

"You tell him I was bringing the stamped copies of the side letters?"

"No. But he would have expected that. It's something else."

"The night of March 30th. That's not good," O'Reith sighed. "So where and when?"

"Same joint, same hour. We go armed?"

"For sure." O'Reith slumped in the soft cushions, polished his monocle with his handkerchief. He replaced it in his eye. They were entering the first of several snakelike curves on the highway from Maiquetia to Caracas. "You get me into the Tamanaco OK?"

"Yeah. A suite."

"Hardy, while I was in Los Angeles, I shifted some of what you've been doing over to Susie," O'Reith began pensively. "Thought it through. I've known her a long time. She used to work for Vince and me down on the 10th floor of the tower. I've always played it straight with her, stood up for her when she was getting into Halliday's nest. Most of the men in the executive suite thought she was an A-Number one gold digger and it showed. Harvey let her in on most of what he knew. She may already know about Maxine. If not, she soon will. I gave her the combination to the safe in your office. Sooner or later Helen will find out about Maxine too—and promptly blow a fuse. I'm not worried about that. After the inevitable fireworks and melodrama, nothing will happen. At her age, she knows only too keenly where her interests lay. I am worried about having to face those two McLarssens in a court of law. It's the unpredictability of it. Well, I asked Susie to open the safe. Read that old hate mail. Make a list of those with threats. Asked her to hire a private detective to check out the McLarssens. A couple of jokers that were tied in to the late Johnny Knobles have popped out of the woodwork. Knobles was Halliday's bagman. Not a great person to know. This case is shaping up as a nightmare. Trial set for 10 May in Denver. Whatever is bothering Torres, barring a total disaster, we can fix with more money. If not, he wouldn't have called you. I'm concerned but not alarmed. I am distressed that a long entanglement with revenge-seeking McLarssens may ensue. When all my attention should be focused on the affairs of the company. I tell you this because you are a seasoned, battle-tested executive who won't wilt when the cartridge cases begin chinking through the propeller blades. But you don't know anything about running an oil production company. We'll change that. We'll teach you the basics, the nuts and bolts. Hardy, have you ever stood on the derrick floor of a big platform rig cutting fast ditch?"

"No."

"Well, pretty soon you will be."

*   *   *

At ten minutes to midnight, the phone rang. It was Tarbutton. "In the lobby, Clive."

"I'm on my way, Hardy," O'Reith answered. He took a last look in the door mirror. He was in a midnight blue, tropical-weight tuxedo with a silk cummerbund and a 9mm Luger in a two-ply silken shoulder holster. He had a 7.65mm Steyr in a leg holster just in case. No monocle tonight. Distance glasses for the walk and reading glasses in his pocket in case there was anything to read, which he doubted.

Coming out of the elevator from his suite on the fifth floor, he spotted Tarbutton in pinstripes standing near the entrance to the lobby. His coat was buttoned. He looked OK, no bulge over his pistol. O'Reith quickly spun through the revolving door out to the street. Tarbutton fell in behind him, caught up with him. The two men walked to the rendezvous. At the address, Tarbutton pushed the button below the dim, red light. The door inched open. A young man in a white *liqui liqui* looked out at them, not the same one Tarbutton had encountered previously. "Señor Torres," Tarbutton said. They were carefully looked over, then waved inside. They followed the young man through the revelers to the familiar booth. He turned and said, "Señor Torres has not yet arrived. You may wait." He opened the door of the empty booth and waved them in. As he left, Tarbutton closed the door.

"Not good, Hardy," O'Reith exclaimed, voice flat and worried. He sat at the table, adjusted the hang of his piece so he could get to it in a hurry. "This a set-up?"

Tarbutton rapped on the door with his knuckles. "Take a .50 to shoot through this door. Let's give it a few minutes."

A waiter came to take their drink order. They sent him away. Two girls came around, were dismissed summarily. The joint was really beginning to jump now. Through the ventilator above the door came the sound of a bolero, laughing girls and the clink of glasses. Expensive-smelling cigar smoke drifted in under the door. The lamp on the wall in the paneled booth began to vibrate ever so slightly, moving with the music. The young man in the white *liqui liqui* returned and opened the door. A man entered. But it wasn't Torres. It was *Capitan* Riva Marcelo Cordero, the secret policeman. He closed the door, beamed at O'Reith and Tarbutton, showed them his gold tooth and sat across from them. He said, "*Caballeros, Buenas Noches.*" Cordero had on the same draping, gray, *liqui liqui* and floppy hat as when O'Reith spotted him in the lobby of the Del Lago. Up close, his sallow face was pock marked, with a scar running down his right cheek. His jowls sagged. Brown bulges hung over his eyes. He wheezed softly like a tire with a slow leak. With bushy gray eyebrows, he still looked like Thomas Gomez. O'Reith put him at fifty or so. "You were expecting Señor Torres. But as you see, I am not he. In fact Señor Torres has been detained. He may even be shot."

"We're disappointed to hear that," O'Reith said. "Torres seems to be a nice, decent fellow. Why would he be detained? Why would he be shot?"

"Nice indeed but greedy, " Cordero said. "If you don't know it, I am a policeman. I am in charge of the *Seguridad Nacional* in Maracaibo. I have seen you before, sir, more than once. You have a liaison with a woman whose pedigree is, shall we say, defective. Hardly my affair of course, but I notice things. The four million dollars that you plan to pay Señor Torres is *my* affair. He is a simple civil servant. He works for the government. At least he did until quite recently. Now he is in disgrace.

In irons. In prison. And soon…" Cordero held his right hand up and snapped his fingers for emphasis. "*Finito!*"

O'Reith was thinking in high gear. On their side, only Mandy could have betrayed Torres and he didn't think that had happened. He recalled the circumstances of the first meeting that Tarbutton had with him. Torres was obviously wary then. Any of those people wandering through the offices of the Ministry could have been agents of the secret police. He remembered too that Torres himself insisted on appearing at the Del Lago so Cordero would see them together. So what next? Finally he said, "*Capitan* Cordero, I am a man who believes that all business problems can be resolved by negotiation. Señor Torres has a wife, a family, is respected. I, for one, would like to see him released from detention, unmanacled and returned to this very table so that we could conclude our negotiation. What do you suggest that we do?"

Cordero said, "General O'Reith, I wish that I could find a way to help you. But the hour is late. The charges against Señor Torres are serious. *Lese Majeste*, well almost that. Tomorrow is March 31, the day the tenders will be opened. Perhaps if you would give to me that certain document, that stamped agreement, the so-called side-letter. Perhaps then we could see what, if anything could be done, so that your two precious blocks could be awarded."

Reflexively, automatically, before they could think, Tarbutton and O'Reith looked at one another, stifled their mutual desire to smile. Cordero was unaware that there were two side-letters. He did not have the complete details of their negotiation. He was unaware that the contract was already signed, sealed and delivered. So there was a bit of light, a glimmer of hope.

O'Reith, spoke slowly and deliberately, "*Capitan* Cordero, we have no intention of abandoning Señor Torres to the tender mercies of the *Seguridad Nacional*. Shooting him is unacceptable, as is his further detention. Let me give you something to think about. When we came to Venezuela to seek an oil concession we approached a distinguished, senior member of society whose political credentials were impeccable. More than that, he is a friend of the *colonel,* can see him without intermediaries. An American businessman with large interests here recommended him. This American has long experience in Venezuela. He walks the corridors of power. This gentleman, this friend of Colonel Marcos Perez Jimenez, directed us to Señor Torres. So I propose to you the following. Either we resolve whatever problem exists, or we adjourn permanently. General Tarbutton and I will then seek redress with the *colonel* through our intermediary."

Cordero was suddenly, cordial. He said unctuously, "Tomorrow night then at the same hour. The four of us."

O'Reith nodded, said, "I see a telephone jack there beneath the lamp. Let's request a telephone. You can release Señor Torres to go home, to spend the night with his family."

"Excellent idea," the policeman agreed.

The two oil men were walking back to the Tamanaco. In Caracas in early spring, at one o'clock in the morning, the air is pleasantly cool and soft to the skin. A faint odor of frangi-pangi and mimosa adds to the ambiance. The altitude of the city, combined with the time of the year makes for an exhilarating stroll. With no traffic to speak of, O'Reith felt comfortable in his tuxedo, even with the tug of the Luger beneath his armpit. He said, "Hardy, I've heard some old-timers say that around the turn of the century, in the higher elevations of the city there were early morning frosts in December and January. Can you imagine that?"

"With the weather like it is now, I can. Clive, where do you think we stand?"

O'Reith's voice turned musical, as it often did when he was elated. He said, "Hardy, I think we're o-o-o-k-a-a-y. We've smoked Cordero out. The question now is whom *else* have we smoked out. We may find that out pretty quick. We must penetrate this mystery. This is not the last time we'll fight for our rights. We absolutely have to know who our friends are. Short term, we're in the clear. Cordero would not have caved in if he'd been holding trumps. He was running a sandy, as the card players say. Longer term, we have to know how Torres stands with the *colonel*. Cordero doesn't know we have a signed contract. He thinks it's still to come, won't come if we don't cooperate. So far, Torres hasn't told him everything. That's hopeful. We'll have a better fix on it tomorrow night." They were at the marquee of the Tamanaco. O'Reith said goodnight, watched as Tarbutton headed home to his flat in *Las Mercedes* in a taxi.

O'Reith rode the elevator to the fifth floor. In his room, he undressed, showered and went to bed. Even though travel-weary and exhausted by the rigors of the evening, he couldn't sleep for a long time. He kept going over in his mind the pieces of the puzzle, seeking to see a coordinated whole. But it would not come to him.

Chapter VI

The Copper Bar

O'Reith slept late, rose, showered, dressed and breakfasted in his room on orange juice, papaya and lime with a pot of strong black coffee. He telephoned the *Ministerio de Minas y Hidrocarburos* and asked for Torres.

A girl said, "*momento*."

Minutes later a man's voice asked, "Whom do you wished to be connected with?"

O'Reith said, "*Señor Torres, por favor*".

The man said, "*momento*."

Then a woman came on the line and said in English, "Señor Torres does not speak on the telephone. I take him your message."

O'Reith said, "Would you kindly ask Señor Torres to prepare a letter addressed to The Casinghead Company authorizing the commencement of exploration and production activity on Blocks 9 & 16 in Lake Maracaibo with effect 1 April 1956? The letter should be to the attention of General Hardy H. Tarbutton."

The woman said, "Just one moment please."

O'Reith waited, from time to time looking at his wristwatch. The woman returned to the line, asked, "Is this General Tarbutton speaking?"

"It's Clive O'Reith," he answered civilly.

"Just one moment, Señor O'Reith." He waited. Presently she was on the line again. "Sir if you would like to call at the Ministry in one hour's time, your letter will be waiting for you."

"Thank you," O'Reith replied. "Would it be possible for me to see Señor Torres to express our appreciation for his co-operation?"

"Just one moment, sir," she said. He waited again. When she returned to the line, this time, her voice was more cordial, "Señor Torres will receive you sir."

O'Reith thanked her, broke the connection and dialed Tarbutton. "Hardy, it looks OK. Come over to the hotel." He drained the pot of coffee, swigged it down, put on his coat and hat and rode down to the lobby. While waiting, he scribbled out two notes for Torres. The first was to confirm tonight's meeting. The second note said: "4 April 1956 in the garden at ten p.m. OK?"

Tarbutton arrived. The two men taxied to the offices of the Ministry, a half-hour drive in morning traffic. In the cab, Tarbutton asked, "Clive, are we any closer to solving the mystery?"

"While I was waiting for you in the lobby, I took another look at those side-letters. You'll recall I was bit startled when Torres presented the second one. If he were acting in strict accord with his instructions, there would have only been one side-letter. We're paying into six accounts in the first letter. If sanctioned by the *colonel* to get paid, one of the six accounts would be his. In the second side-letter, we pay into two accounts. One of them is also in the first letter. Why would somebody get paid twice? I'll ask him to a private chat in Maracaibo in Mandy's garden. Try to find out what we're up against."

The letter was ready as promised, in duplicate. O'Reith kept the original, to take to Maracaibo, gave the duplicate to Tarbutton for his file. Torres received them. O'Reith looked him over carefully for signs of abuse. Found nothing to arouse his suspicions. Torres nodded positively when presented the first note. The second note he read, then consulted his desk diary, and again nodded positively. He circled the date and the hour, made a check mark beside the word 'garden' and handed it back to O'Reith. They bade him goodbye and took their leave. In the taxi on the way back to the hotel, O'Reith looked at Tarbutton, said, "So far so good."

Tarbutton nodded. He was reading the letter Torres had given them, slowly working his way through the Spanish. O'Reith helped him. He said, "Basically the *permiso de trabajar*, as the letter is called, tells any interested party that we are legitimately pursuing our business. Holland will post it in our office, on the rigs, work-boats, automobiles etc. Also each member of the staff should carry a copy, including yourself. It is useful when the cops stop you at the *Alcabalas*. In Venezuela in those days, many police checkpoints, existed. Manned by youthful, often intoxicated, military policeman, they were the bane of the gringo oil workers. The *Alcabalas* located where traffic was dense, often required a half-hour wait to be waved through.

Midnight approaching, the two Americans were walking to their rendezvous. The evening was cool, the night cloudy, mist in the air. "Clive, you think those two birds will show?"

"I think they will. For the short term, we've got our business under control. Longer... Well, let's say we have more diplomatic work ahead. Bring Stan into this tomorrow. Once I see Torres in Maracaibo, I'm off to Los Angeles again. I want you to go with me. Bring Marjorie along, if you like. No point her staying down here by herself. Hardy, for a few moments last night, while Cordero was ventilating, the thought occurred to me that it was all staged for our consumption. Now I have a different theory, but still a theory. Untested. We've seen that Torres, judging from his humble office, is far from the top of the power structure. And even if he were, Cordero would be reluctant to put the squeeze on him. We think that Torres is a spunky guy. If Cordero had him in detention, which, I don't doubt, then Torres would have been in a hell of a sweat. The *Seguridad Nacional* is bad, bad news. Their methods of torture are as sophisticated as any you'll find in the modern world. They've got a gadget they hook up to your peter and balls called the electric whore, *puta electrica*, in the lingo. They throw the switch on that baby and it's spillikins in spades. You'll tell everything you know. I've been told that Juan Peron perfected the device. Gave one to the *colonel* just to be neighborly. So Torres, sitting on a rusty army bed in the sneezer, knowing a great deal about Blocks 9 & 16, would have a lot he could tell. They'd hang a 200 watt light bulb six inches or so above his head. He'd fear the worst. Of course we really don't know what he told Cordero. But I think he kept his poise. Gave him enough to get by on. We may learn more tonight. The rest has to wait until I talk to Torres in the privacy of Mandy's garden, that event in itself being of a speculative nature."

At the appointed hour, Tarbutton pushed the bell button. O'Reith continued, "I looked this joint up in the phone book. The name of it is *La Casualidad*, means accident or hazard or chance. Good name for it, don't you think?"

Tarbutton nodded. The same young man as last night opened the door, waved them through. He said, "*Buenas Noches, Caballeros,*" They found their own way following the hall between the glittering bar and the dance floor, deftly avoiding the swirling skirts of the *señoritas of the night*. At the row of booths at the back, Tarbutton rapped on the heavy oaken door. Cordero admitted them, closed it again. Torres sat at the table between the two benches drinking Johnny Walker Black Label and Coca Cola. Besides the whisky bottle was an ice bucket. Several glasses and bottles of Coke and soda surrounded the bucket. The waiter came and was dismissed. So there they sat, O'Reith and Tarbutton on one side of the table, Cordero and Torres on the other. A driller, an aviator, a policeman and a bureaucrat. O'Reith checked out Cordero's pistol as he took his seat. He had the same Beretta .32 in a front-pocket holster with a snap-down leather strap across the butt. The hammer was down but it was a double action so it didn't really matter. O'Reith had released the safety of the Luger in the hotel. He figured he could outdraw Cordero if it came to that, hoped it wouldn't, made a mental note to tell Helen about this scenario, maybe something she could use in her movie.

Formalities concluded, he began, "Gentlemen, we are here tonight to resolve a problem that has arisen in connection with our pursuit of an oil concession. *Capitan* Cordero, how do you propose we begin?"

Cordero, offered them his nicest gold-toothed smile. It was a smile that bordered on the comic as most police smiles do. O'Reith had noticed that in the army, concluded that there must be a school somewhere that teaches policemen how to smile grotesquely.

Cordero said, "As I suggested last night, we could look at the stamped side-letter. Compare it with the unstamped one. See if they are in precise agreement, as they should be. So you may now, at this moment, pass it across the table."

O'Reith said, "I presume that one of you can produce the unsigned letter."

"I have it," Cordero said.

O'Reith asked, "Before we proceed Captain Cordero, have all charges against Señor Torres been dismissed? Is he now in good standing with rights as a citizen restored?"

"But of course, sir," Cordero said, suavely, sincerely. It was all a mistake. One of those, what do you Americans call it? A screw up? Things like that happen in police investigations especially when conducted by junior personnel. We rely on informers. They don't always check their information, as they should. As you see now, and as you saw earlier today, Señor Torres is in the pink and in complete possession of his liberty."

O'Reith gazed directly at Torres. He had already been appraising him as discreetly as he could, looking for signs of abuse, for the kind of wear and tear you get in a secret policeman's prison. Torres looked OK. O'Reith asked, "Rojo, how long were you in durance vile? How long locked up?"

"Just a matter of hours. I was released shortly after midnight."

"How'd they treat you?" He looked at Cordero, just to see if he was squirming.

"All right. Not like at the bar in the Tamanaco. But one can't expect that. I was not mistreated."

"You agree with Captain Cordero that it was a mistake?"

"Yes."

"O-o-o-k-a-a-y," O'Reith began musically, light-heartedly. He withdrew an unsealed hotel envelope from inside his tuxedo jacket and removed the stamped side-letter, smoothed out the creases and laid it out on the table so that both Cordero and Torres could read it. Just a single sheet, signed by himself, Torres and Tarbutton as witness. Now it bore the embossed seal of the *Banque en Liechtenstein.* "Gentlemen, you may compare this with the other one. In view of the controversy that arose last night, which we now appear to have laid to rest, I have decided that the best interests of all concerned will be preserved if we retain possession of this document. Please make your comparisons. Satisfy yourselves that it is proper and that it is unaltered. Not emended in any way. Annotated only by a bank official to show that payments have been made and that they are as specified. You both already know that this was done. You have the money, or somebody has the money. Now, so long as the scene continues to unfold in a regular way, all forthcoming payments will be made promptly. However, should there be any irregularity and, even more importantly, should the civil liberties of Señor Torres be impaired, then payment will be suspended until such irregularities are resolved."

Torres paid no attention to the examination. Cordero placed the two documents in apposition and read them together, line by line, with a show of suspicion, rolling his small bloodshot eyes at O'Reith from time to time in what he imagined to be a sinister way. When at last he was satisfied, he reluctantly shoved both documents back to O'Reith. With just a hint of sarcasm he said, "You may as well keep them both."

O'Reith folded the two papers and placed them in the hotel envelope and returned it to his inside pocket. He said, "Gentlemen, in accord with the contract, we will notify our bank that the work permit was issued. You can expect the second payment. We bid you a good night."

On the way back to the Tamanaco, O'Reith said, "Hardy, I'm going to Maracaibo in the morning on the Avensa early flight. Call Torres every day. Make sure he's OK. Take Stan along. He's an expert at deciphering legislative gibberish. When the time comes, he'll have to take a close look at the *Gaceta Oficial.* Meet me in Maracaibo on 5 April. I'll bring you current on my meeting with Torres. Next day, you and I will fly to Los Angeles. See how Susie's getting along. Then we'll call on Vince at 225 Bush Street. I'm going to ask him to give you some exposure to their Geological and Geophysical Section, a few days of looking at cross-sections and seismic surveys. You'll become acquainted with that part of the business. Then go down to Taft and ride around with a SOCAL production superintendent for a few days. Visit some wells, learn the lingo and see how the crude oil comes out of the ground and goes through the separator and into the tanks."

"Separator?"

"Yeah, when crude oil comes out of the ground, it has a lot of gas in it. Not a good idea to put that gas into a pipeline. Down there at Taft, most of what comes out is reinjected into the formation. Keeps the pressure up and makes the well flow longer. All you need is a rudimentary education. When you get back to Maracaibo, Holland will see that you get the full treatment. Before you realize it, you'll be *all knowed up* as the rough hands say." He laughed softly.

*   *   *

O'Reith was in Maracaibo. It was the evening of 3 April 1956. A cable from Helen with news about the movie, included an invitation to Grace Kelly's wedding. *Tuffy* Marks, Manager of Operations for Loffland

Brothers Drilling Company, was entertaining important executives of The Casinghead Company, his newest customer, at a garden party on the immense lawn of his hacienda in *Las Delicias,* one of the more fashionable addresses in the city. Maxine and Monique were there with O'Reith. Holland and Ines with their three children; Alan and Sally Prescott, also with three children; Carolyn Cook and her *friend* Magaly; Mandy and Ted Schaeffer were there. O'Reith, Schaeffer and Marks had all known each other since they worked on the Avenue in Ventura in the early 1930s. Holland and Prescott had known Marks since right after the war.

Thomas Jefferson Marks was a Veteran of Foreign Wars but had actually participated in only one battle and that for about twenty minutes. He had been shot through the legs by a Japanese machine-gunner while wading through the surf at Iwo Jima. His nickname, *Tuffy,* had nothing to do with his Marine Corps service. It derived from his occasional bellicosity in the face of dereliction of duty on or around a drilling rig. In the early decades of the 20th Century, the drilling business attracted many of the dregs of society, as it did only a few of the elite. The riffraff, men who liked the good money but didn't like the hard work required to get it, called for special attention in the interests of practical economics. Marks, short and stubby with a weatherworn, angular face, whose demeanor was that of a Bantam rooster, was famous for his ability to extract a sweaty, oily, hot and often dangerous day of work from the most scurrilous, dirty, low-down, no-good, back-sliding roughneck. A taciturn supervisor, a finger pointed up meant work in the derrick, down, work in the cellar. Whomever was the object of the pointing had better know exactly what to do when he got where he was pointed to, because Marks was not going to tell him. Marks had only a high school education but not a dozen men were in his class when it came to drilling. He had courted Carolyn Cook briefly and unsuccessfully in 1945. Some months after she had turned him down, he met and married a pretty American schoolteacher who taught the fourth grade in the foreign student section of the *Escuela Bella Vista*. Her name was Lila and they had two children, one eight and one six.

The party celebrated the signing of a two-rig contract. Holland had first mentioned it in December of 1955 when he was in the scouting expedition with Tarbutton and Cook. In February, he told Marks the deal was getting hot. After the meeting with Torres in Mandy's garden, he gave Marks a *letter of intent* which, in due course, resulted in the contract just signed. The two rigs being assembled at Joe Stein's yard on the Old Spanish Trail in Houston, Texas, would soon be boxed, crated and moved to Gulfports at Buffalo Bayou, put on a boat and shipped to Maracaibo. Now, while *Cerveza Sifon Regional* flowed foamily in this tropical patio, packers were working overtime, day and night, to load out the two rigs onto a Lyke's Line freighter. Near New Orleans, at the Avondale Shipyard, fitters and cutters, shapers and welders toiled around the clock to fabricate the two *drilling tenders*. They would contain the engines, pumps, mud tanks, kitchen and mess and quarters. When complete, the tenders would be towed across the Gulf of Mexico into the Caribbean and finally to dock side in Maracaibo. When hooked up to the platform rigs, they would be ready to drill through the muddy bottom of the lake and then, deep into the earth where clever men sometimes find oil. As for the platforms themselves, these flat-topped towers of steel and reinforced concrete, fabricated by Raymond Concrete Pile Company, were under construction in the yards of *Terminales Maracaibo* in Las Moroches, across the lake from Maracaibo.

Working together, Holland and Marks had the responsibility to see that the two offshore rigs would be *turning to the right*, as oil field people said, no later than 1 July 1956. Each night, long teleprinter messages went out to Los Angeles and Tulsa ordering tools, machinery, supplies, chemicals and spare parts.

Alan Prescott was lining up production and pipeline equipment, a task he knew from the Tidikelt project. His was a more speculative game, because no orders could go out until the drillers proved that the oil was there. But the effort was the same. He could plan, calculate, estimate, prepare material takeoffs, design the terminal and prepare the equipment orders. Separators. Tanks. Tubing. *Christmas trees* to sit atop the casinghead flanges. And when oil was struck, as they were certain it would be, after all, Lake Maracaibo was said to be another *Golden Lane,* then the orders would stream out with a breathtaking immediacy, for everything would be needed, as they say, *yesterday.*

On the drilling side however, they were spending money as if it were going out of style. Expenditures against the 1956 Capital and Exploratory Budget were already in the millions of dollars. And so far, not a foot of hole had been drilled.

But this humid late afternoon was no occasion to worry about the Capital and Exploratory Budget of 1956. This gathering was about Texas barbecue, Louisiana seafood, Oklahoma cheer and California luck, a time to talk about how it was back then at Coalinga, at Block 31, at Bay Marchand, Kettleman Hills, Signal Hill and East Texas. Jokes. Backslapping. Tall tales. How it was. How they all hoped it would be. Women gossiped and prepared the victuals. Men opened beer kegs. Children romped and squealed as children do on these occasions, this time in three languages.

The newcomers to this clique were little Clive Colin and his wife, Marilyn. As they enjoyed the festivity, they tried to sort out the players. They had met Holland. They knew Sally and that she had once been O'Reith's secretary. All the rest were strangers. Maxine. Magaly. Carolyn Cook. Mandy. Ines. Tuffy and Lila. Señor Torres. Ted Schaeffer, they vaguely remembered as a one time high muck-a-muck on the Calitroleum Crude Oil Committee. A blur of names. Hasty introductions. A flurry of scampering children. O'Reith's son was totally unaware that the raven-haired tot, jumping and shouting and playing with the others was his half-sister. Nobody was going to tell him.

When O'Reith arrived, he immediately saw the Cuban trio on the bandstand borrowed from *El Escondite*. Graying, but the same three cats he remembered from long ago at *El Techo Rojo,* and after it was sold to the Chinaman, the Hotel Detroit. He shook their hands and chatted with them.

It had been a grand afternoon. But now the great fiesta was winding down. The Santa Barbara barbecued brisket, the Lake Maracaibo shrimp gumbo, the arepas, the hallacas, the platanos were all finished. Maids were cleaning the tables, rolling away the depleted, sloshing beer barrels. The group turned mellow as the tropical twilight descended. Coffee and rum appeared for the adults, ice cream and cakes for the children. Garden lights flickered on. Bug burners too and frequent tiny wisps of smoke indicated that they were not alone in the equatorial gloaming. O'Reith knowing he would be called upon, was already shaping his remarks in his mind. An easy task for him, after all, he spoke regularly in Los Angeles. Indeed, Sharon Mills had been there to see that he looked good on presidential speaking occasions. Now, in faded khakis and a gray WAC fatigue cap, what he said would have to stand on its own merit.

Marks introduced O'Reith, who rose, walked to the head of the table and inserted his monocle. He smiled, waiting out the giggling applause the eyepiece evoked. He thought how much Helen would enjoy a blast like this. She was a party girl. Formal or informal, beer or champagne, it was all the same to her. She liked to be at the center of activity. Believed that for sheer entertainment, the movie crowd was not in the same league with oil field raconteurs, especially her husband. How long would it take for her to sort this gang out? Not long. Maxine might elude her quick eye. But not Monique. One look and she would know her father, if not her mother.

His thoughts gathered, he began, "Thanks to Tuffy and Lila, we celebrate tonight a drilling contract with Loffland and a concession contract with the Venezuelan Government, negotiated with Señor Rojo Torres. Rojo is with us tonight and I say to him *exito!* This great venture will succeed. All great endeavors carry with them the potential for disaster. Our job is to prevent that! Only the laughing children cannot tell if it is success or failure. We can. We have the perspective of experience. Tonight we dwell on triumph. We praise the people. Some years ago Ted Schaeffer risked his life to save an oil well. He dangled head first from a soft line to latch onto a rock bit fallen some distance and wedged in the open hole. Few men would take that risk. Alan Prescott conquered sickness and despair after returning home in 1945 from a Prisoner of War camp. Sally's stunning success was helping him to do it. Forgetting the wreckage that he made of the Luftwaffe, Holland's best night of work was putting out a fire on Lake Maracaibo. Few men have seen gas swirling up through an open blow out preventer with the bonnets off. Tuffy gets kudos for that one too although his finest hour was in the bloody waters off Iwo Jima in 1944. His grand success was marrying Lila. Made a new man out of him. Lucky Carolyn has had a string of triumphs. I say her best was finding gold on the Malheur River in Idaho. As for Mandy and Maxine, none of us can appreciate their remarkable talents. They know how to overcome bureaucratic intricacy in all its evil forms. The world thinks that Hardy's tour de force was as a battlefield commander in Europe's bleak skies. But his greatest triumph was keeping a dozen young men from courts martial. Those young men are free today and leading useful lives. Marjorie, of course, stood beside him through these trials. Without her it would have been tough going. You have been introduced to my son and his bride, daughter of Vince Blake, my drinking companion of yore. I remember Marilyn as a tot, like the ones about us today, except her face was perpetually stained with orange juice from the trees in their orchard. My son has tried to hide his triumph from his parents. But I have access to the records. His mother and I are proud to know that he won a Silver Star on the frozen battlefields of North Korea…"

Little Clive Colin, suddenly awake, arose and shouted, "Dad!" He was going to say more but the applause made him think better of it. He sat again and was silent.

O'Reith continued. "We've listened to good music this afternoon from the Cuban trio, no longer spring chickens. Their music improves as their hair grays. I asked them if their repertoire included, *The South American Way*. It did and we have someone who can sing that song. She sang it in the 3rd grade in Mineola, Texas, she sang it at many an office party in Los Angeles and she sang it at a screen test for MGM in 1942. So Sally, sing it for us here where it should be sung, along the tenth parallel, in the tropics!"

She rose, blushing, released Prescott's hand, joined O'Reith at the head of the table. She began, "Ay Ay, Ay Ay, have you ever danced in the moonlight"… The Cuban trio gave the melody a rhythm that Sally had to catch quickly. Once she had it, she put on a good show. There was plenty of applause. Sally was red faced about it all but O'Reith could see she was excited too.

The party was over and as first one then another couple said their good-byes to Tuffy and Lila, O'Reith's son came to approach his father. "He said, "Dad, I really didn't need that remark about my decoration but I do need some personal advice. Could I talk to you with your monocle out?"

O'Reith smiled. "Of course, son."

"Could I see you privately in the morning?" little Clive Colin asked, soberly.

"Come in about nine o'clock. We'll find a quiet corner in the hotel lobby."

"I'll be there, Dad."

   *   *   *

Father and son sat comfortable in the lobby diagonally across from the Mara Bar, closed at that hour. They would see anyone approaching them. O'Reith said, "Son, try me out."

"Dad, I don't need to get the stare or hear the voice. Can this be man-to-man?"

"How could it be otherwise?" O'Reith asked, in a pleasant, disarming voice.

"Dad, I'm kind of into it with a girl I met at the beer joint in Santa Monica." Little Clive Colin paused to watch it register with his father.

O'Reith asked, "Is she a looker?" Then he laughed at the perplexed expression on his son's face. He went on, "Son, old Harvey Halliday used to ask that when one of his cronies was in a fix with a woman. To find out if she was pretty enough to make up for all the trouble she was causing."

O'Reith's son relaxed. He asked, "Dad, you mean you're not upset about this?"

"Not yet. Is there more to follow? Is she giving you a hard time?" O'Reith smiled kindly.

"No. But I'm in love with her. Dad, she's only eighteen. Her name is Ellen Mackensen, a stage name. I don't know what her real name is. She wants to be an actress. Hangs around Central Casting by day and comes out to Santa Monica at night. I met her in the Beachcombers Club. She's new in town. I don't remember her from when Marilyn and I were there every night. When I was playing in the band. Dad, Marilyn is that way."

"When is the blessed event?" O'Reith asked, sympathetically.

"The doctor says November. Virginia knows. But mother doesn't. Marilyn wants to be sure before letting it out."

"Son if Virginia knows, you can be sure that your mother knows too. So what's your problem?" O'Reith asked.

"So I don't know what to do. Sometimes Marilyn gets on my nerves. I have to get away from her from time to time. I was back out to the Beachcombers Club, singing with the old combo, a song called *Too Late Now*, a favorite of mine. Jane Powell sang it in a movie. This girl came over to my table afterward. She said she liked my song. She wanted to buy me a drink. She said, "Maybe it is not too late.""

"She also liked what she saw, obviously. The way you looked that night," O'Reith added. "That's the title of a song too, at least something like that."

"Dad, I was feeling low. I needed what she had. I took her home, a little studio not far away. I mixed the drinks while she changed. When she returned, she was down to her panties and a brassiere. We had Artie Shaw's *Night Train* on the record-player. She was swinging her hips to it. M-u-r-d-e-r! Before I knew what I was getting into, I was into it."

"It seems to happen that way with some regularity," O'Reith agreed. "And not just to young people. To advise you, I have to know whom I'm talking to. 'Good Time Charlie' O'Reith? Or is it Captain Clive Colin O'Reith, ex-officer and present gentleman?"

"Both."

"Nothing like that happened to you before? When you were in the cadets?"

"Dad, if you'll remember there was a war on. They rushed us through and then onto a troop ship. Not much time to fool around. And of course, Marilyn and I were already in it pretty deep. I didn't look at another girl all the time I was in the army. I didn't have any opportunities."

"This Ellen. She know you're married?"

"No sir."

"Tell her." O'Reith's voice was still friendly but his tone was businesslike.

"She may never see me again. I don't want that to happen. Can you understand that, Dad?"

"While you were in the army, if you didn't fool around with girls, you must have had time to gamble. Ever play cards or shoot craps?"

"Yes sir."

"Well, son, that's what you're doing now," O'Reith continued. "You are gambling. Tell her you're married. She'll either say goodbye or she won't. If she shrugs, and that's where I place my bet, then ask her real name and where she's from. Find out what kind of parents you're dealing with?"

"I already know where she's from, Dad. She's a country girl from Kansas or Nebraska or someplace like that, an heiress. Oil on the family property. A cattle ranch."

"Son," O'Reith continued. "There are all kinds of women in the world. Take your mother. A first class specimen. Marilyn's mother is also first class but different. She is protective and possessive. Marilyn is a first class girl. You have to take her seriously. You know that. Even a first class man can have some big problems with first class women. If your affair with Ellen becomes common knowledge, you've got kinfolk trouble on your hands. So you want my advice. This is it. If you can't live without her, keep her on the string but undercover. Find out who she is and what kind of problems you'll have with *her* parents in the event, not unlikely, that something goes haywire. You'll remember telling me, somewhat arrogantly, that I was forcing you into a shotgun wedding with Marilyn."

"I guess I should apologize…"

"No apology required. But remember this my son, a shotgun wedding when you're already married presents some unusual complications." O'Reith smiled broadly and reached over and patted his son on the back. He said, "Son, you remember that army joke about the old bull and the young bull?"

Little Clive Colin's face suddenly brightened. "The one where the young bull has noticed a pasture full of spring cows and suggests to the old bull that they run down there and…"

"That's it, son. The old bull tells him they'll have more fun if they just walk down…"

The two men laughed. O'Reith continued, "Son, that's all the advice I can give. My grand plan is to build an international oil company. I want our company to be bigger than Calitroleum Oil Corporation. In fact I want it to be bigger than The Standard Oil Company, a tall order indeed. It would please me if you became an executive in this company. But you remember the trouble that Harvey Halliday's boy got into. He was not cut out for it. His father ruined him trying to make something out of him that he was not. So if you prefer to play in a band in a Santa Monica beer joint and surf your life away, go to it. Enjoy life. I won't hold it against you."

"So if I play around with Ellen, it's OK?"

O'Reith laughed. "Son that is definitely not what I said. It won't be play for long. Think things over. Remember that each year there is a new crop of girls provided by the good Lord in his wisdom. He did not place them on earth to become nuns, although occasionally some do. Make up your mind what you want to do. Come to see me again. When you do, I want some details about Ellen."

"Yes sir." The two men returned to the office. Little Clive Colin returned to *El Escondite*. Now he saw his father in a different light; decided he had some human blood in him after all.

The next night, there was no gaiety, no celebration, no children romping, at least not around the stone table beneath the gas lights near the dragonhead fountain in Mandy Macabra's garden. Just three men talking in the pale light as, here and there, glow-worms glowed and Cansor patrolled the paths, swinging his machete, in case a night-prowling fer-de-lance should become interested in the proceedings. All three men wore business suits. They were not armed. They were not drinking. Obregon and Fifinela stirred in the mango tree but the activity below was insufficient to attract their attention. It was truly a private meeting.

"So where do we find ourselves, Rojo?" O'Reith asked. "Is Cordero a permanent part of our establishment? Is he a present and future threat? Or is this just business as usual in the tropics?"

Torres sighed. "Business as usual for Cordero. For me it is a perilous position. I am trapped in his web. To you, he is another mouth to feed.

As long as payments are made as agreed, you have nothing to worry about. Unless, of course, there comes a *golpe de estado*."

"That's my main worry. I don't like having Cordero as a business partner but I can tolerate it. A *golpe de estado* is another matter. I want that contract published in the *Gaceta Oficial*." O'Reith said. Silence around the table. Then he resumed, "Rojo, my inclination is to seek an audience with Colonel Jimenez. Put everything on the table. Establish a transparent relationship with him. If he wants Cordero in the act, fine. But otherwise... Before I seek a meeting with the colonel, I have to know exactly your position. I don't want to betray you. Nor do I want you to be threatened by Cordero. Your usefulness to me is limited if you are under his sway. So it comes down to this, I must know if you are playing a double game before I act. I don't want to expose you. I don't want to put you against the wall. We would find another remedy. So I ask you, how will you fare if I tell the colonel exactly what has happened? If I tell him that Cordero has put himself on our payroll."

Even in the pale light, O'Reith could detect that color had drained from the face of the ministry employee. He sat silently for some moments, then began to explain. "When Cordero learned that negotiation between us was underway, he came to me and insisted that he be included. Well sir, he is a secret policeman, make no mistake about that. I had no choice. The second side-letter was his idea. I agreed. I told him that it was a reasonable expectation and that you would sign it. Then he insisted that I too, participate in the second letter. I told him it was unnecessary, that I was properly compensated and I wanted only my normal entitlement. That did not suit him. He wanted my bank account number to appear on the second letter, so that in the event of his exposure, he could denounce me as a swindler. As things stand, the Casinghead Company pays him. Then he extorts from me those funds going into my account. Colonel Jimenez knows my account number. Should he see it on a second letter, which Cordero would eagerly present to him if he wished, then I would be finished. If we assume that the colonel does not know his bank account number, then Cordero can act with impunity. When Cordero so generously gave you the unstamped copy of the second letter, it was a typical secret police trick. You may be sure he has a photocopy."

O'Reith nodded, continued, "So Cordero is unaware that the first side letter exists. Correct?" Torres continued, "Correct. Cordero has already forced me to pay him. When the contract is published, he will extort from me again. Most of the money is in the first two payments. When he has that, he can liquidate me. Or, more likely, he will discover a conspiracy in which I am involved. He will report it to the colonel and I am liquidated legally. I don't have a chance."

"You have a stronger hand than you think, Rojo," O'Reith said. "We have some time before the contract is published. Extortion is the handmaiden of treason. It takes money to mount a *golpe de estado*. The colonel will not find Cordero's ploy amusing. I can present the evidence or, if you wish, you can come with me. Rojo, your sponsor in the executive, the fellow that Hardy visited in Ciudad Bolivar, the one who gave us your name. Can't he protect you?"

"You're thinking of Señor Esteven Armas, the *Angostura* lawyer," Torres replied. "He's elderly. Plays no active role. He has a confidant on the colonel's staff. I don't know if he would help me or not. The secret police are so pervasive that we just don't know how to make such calculations. I prefer to leave him out of it. You realize how difficult it will be to see the dictator?"

"Yes, Rojo, I know that. That's my job. Overcoming obstacles."

Torres sighed, opened his fingers, put his hands palm down on the table. He said quietly, "I leave it to your discretion. This is a heavy weight over my head."

"Well I want to see the colonel. I'll go to work on it right away. In the meantime, if you're worried about your safety, why not take a vacation in France with your family, at our expense? I have a flat in Paris in the rue de Surene not far from the Madeleine. It's in the same building where we have our office. You are welcome to it."

Torres smiled, put his hands together. "Well, I thank you for the kind offer. But I don't think it is necessary. The contract will not be published for quite some months. Cordero is not so bold as to try to make it happen sooner. If I sense unusual pressure, we'll confer again. If I accept your offer, you can be sure things are perilous. Until then, I sit tight."

*   *   *

Around ten o'clock next morning, passengers and crew boarded *La Cañada Cruz*. Tarbutton in the left seat coaxed O'Reith's son in the right seat through pre-flight. Marjorie and Marilyn sat in the passenger section. O'Reith stood behind his son. They departed Maracaibo for Los Angeles via Panama, San Jose, Guatemala City, and Mexico City. It was a first for O'Reith's son. Tarbutton was showing him how to make the throttle and tab adjustments for the takeoff. In the air, O'Reith showed him how to retract the landing gear. Flying gracefully along the littoral, O'Reith said, "Son, the worst way in the world to land an airline is to cartwheel it in. That's called a Chinese Landing. Another way not to land an airline is with the wheels up. On final approach at Toucomen Field, I'll show you how to lower the gear. By the time we set this baby on the hardstand in Los Angeles, you'll have the basics under your belt. After that, it is just a matter of practice. You'll get plenty of that.

*   *   *

In Los Angeles, O'Reith and Tarbutton visited family and friends, discussed the lawsuit with Susie and the detective Philip Marlborough. On the way to San Francisco O'Reith said, "Hardy, those guys that are keeping an eye on my family. Do they send in reports?"

"Yeah, they're routine. Susie just files them."

"Is Marlborough involved in that operation?"

"No. Why?" Tarbutton asked, sensing that O'Reith had something on his mind.

"Let's ask Susie to run their reports by him. Hardy, my boy has a girl friend all of a sudden. Some kid in her teens spotted him at that joint he hangs around in Santa Monica. 'The Beachcombers'. She may be an adventuress trying to get wrapped up in some silk. Maybe just kid stuff. My boy doesn't know her real name. She calls herself Ellen Mackensen. Trying to break into the movies. I'm suspicious. Something about her name… Ask Marlborough to get a line on her."

"OK, I'll put it to him right away," Tarbutton replied.

They called on Blake. Tarbutton began his training course at SOCAL. O'Reith flew to Idlewild and then to Orly. After a conference with LeBel, it was on to Nice where Helen's limousine was waiting.

Caught up on the fundamentals, having a quiet drink together on the terrace, O'Reith said, "Helen, that lawsuit is close to the courtroom. A confrontation with the McLarssens looms. How are things in Piedras Negras?"

She shook her head in disgust. "Ace, the big fat guy, his name is Alphonse di Frangipani, I call him Big Alphonse, he had a stroke. He's finito. At first I was thrilled about it. Then Frederico brought out this second big fat guy as a substitute. I call him Big Alphonse Number 2. He's more or less the same size as number one, but he doesn't *look* like number one. At first, we shot his scenes with his face at an angle. Finally I told Frederico that it was not going to work. Now, Frederico has him wearing a mask. It's crazy. Lawson had to rewrite the script. This movie is not going anywhere. I'm about to lose heart."

"How's the money holding out?" O'Reith asked.

"I don't know. I can't get an accounting out of Frederico. All he will say is that everything is OK. Not to worry."

"How was the wedding? Grace Kelly and his nibs?"

"A musical. Pomp and Circumstance. Beautiful movie star. Handsome Prince. Fireworks. They say her daddy back in Philadelphia paid a bundle for the deal."

O'Reith smiled, asked "How much longer are you going to put up with Bolletti?"

"Ace, I want to finish this movie. Even if it is a loser, I'll have done it. I'll get him going."

"I'll be glad to have a chat with Signor Bolletti if you like," O'Reith suggested. "I have a way with guys like him. Perhaps he would be more forthcoming with me."

Helen snorted. "I can imagine that scene! Splitsville for sure! We're not to that point yet, Ace. Let's wait until after you're finished in Denver. See how it looks then."

"Alice still flashing the green light?" O'Reith asked.

"She says Mercury is in the way of Mars or something like that. Soon as the traffic in the sky clears, the movie will be back on track."

"Better ask her to let you know if they're going to collide."

They both laughed.

It was 10 May 1956. O'Reith and two SOCAL lawyers stood outside the locked door of the 4th District Court in Denver Colorado, Judge Ramon Lee Burke presiding. In about five minutes, those doors would swing open. The case of McLarssen Estate vs. Standard Oil Company of California would begin. It was actually a simple case. Was SOCAL responsible for the blowout and fire and if so was it the result of negligence? Were plaintiffs entitled to damages? But thenceforward, things were murky. Calitroleum Oil Corporation had leased the land from the John M. McLarssen Estate and had hired the Boyd and Bowen Drilling Company out of Bakersfield, California to drill the well. The drilling contract placed all responsibility for operations on the drilling contractor down to the casing point of the oil string, which was 9,000 feet. At that depth, Calitroleum would put a drilling supervisor on the rig and assume responsibility. He would supervise running of electric logs, the casing and the completion of the well. While drilling at 4,000 feet in coal measures, methane gas cut the mud, which was mostly clear water. The well kicked, began blowing gas and caught fire. The derrick collapsed and during the emergency, some McLarssen cows were burned up. Yet to be proved in a court of law was negligence on the part of the contractor. O'Reith was of the opinion that it did not matter. He believed that since Calitroleum leased the land and ordered the drilling of the well, they, and by extension SOCAL, were liable. Boyd and Bowen had offered to pay whatever damages had occurred. In all normal cases, that would have been the end of it. But this was a case of vindictiveness. The McLarssens saw a chance for revenge against Calitroleum. That it was now a case with SOCAL made no difference to them. Still, the SOCAL lawyers would defend the suit as well as they could, hoping at some point, plaintiff would settle.

While waiting for the bailiff to open the door, O'Reith and the lawyers were joined by newspaper reporters, prospective jurors, court stenographers and miscellaneous hangers-on. Then came the attorney for the plaintiff and his two star witnesses. O'Reith recognized two of the three men. Beauregard Feathermerchant, attorney for the plaintiff was the same member of Barney Donnegan's entourage that he had axed in Maracaibo in 1945. Feathermerchant was of medium build, somewhat paunchy with a plump face that seemed perpetually astonished in a pleasant sort of way, as if it had just watched the girl in red panties and no brassiere pop up out of the convention cake. He faintly resembled the movie actor Frank McHugh. O'Reith remembered his claim to fame. As a notary public for a bank in Oklahoma City he notarized Dick Tracy, Moon Mullins and other funny page personalities. As far as was known, no one else had ever done that. The other man was none other than Gimp Flagherty. O'Reith remembered him as Clyde O'Flagherty. Recognizing O'Reith, Flagherty wobbled over, extended a palsied hand said, "Well, if 't ain't Mistuh O-O-O-O'Reith. I'da knowed you anywhere, suh. I seen yore picha in the noospapuh when you wuz agoin' out there to finish off them yellerbelly Japs. Well, I sed to myself, if they's any a man can wipe them off the slate it's Mistuh, I-I-I mean jinrel, suh, Jinrel O-O-O-O'Reith"

O'Reith smiled broadly, grasped the trembling man's hand and shook it vigorously, giving him a heartfelt pat on the back at the same time. He said, "Clyde O'Flagherty. Hasn't it been a long time? When was it? It was West Texas. You were drilling for George P. Livermore in the TXL Field. Isn't that right?"

Flagherty had on preacher's black with a gray shirt, string tie and special made cowboy boots to fit his mutilated feet. His face was angular with a sharp chin. A clutch of gray whiskers grew irregularly from a deep cleft. His eyes were a watery gray and he looked a bit like John Carradine. He replied, "Yas suh, that's keerect. Exactly keerect. I-I-I wuz in better shape in them days. That wuz before I-I-I got caught in that there c-c-casing swarm and before that, that there in-in-incident at the Ace of Diamonds. Mistuh O-O-O-O'Reith, did you hear whut happint to me there?"

"Clyde, I did. Let me say I could feel for you. It was a misfortune, if a highly unusual one."

"Yas suh. It shuah wuz. I-I-I jist come out of Wilson's tailor on Highway 80 all togged-out in a brand new w-w-western outfit. Cost me f-f-fifty dollar. Had me a new b-b-b-black Stetson with a Texas brim, a s-s-sinthetic black silk shirt with pearl buttons and pearl-trimmed pockets with pointy covers. I-I-I wuz wearin' extry h-h-heavy duty coal b-b-b-black denim trousers with a calfskin belly holster. Had on new soot-colored Justin boots with four rows of stitchin'. I-I-I wuz a-rigged up to run and play. Yas suh. An I-I-I got tangled up with that East Texas derrickman. Mistuh O-O-O-O'Reith are you aback aworkin' for that C-C-Calitroleum C-C-Company? Back in the oil fields?"

"Yeah Clyde, I am. Calitroleum sold out to SOCAL. I'm here as an expert witness."

"Well, suh. Ain't that a m-m-m-mighty co-co-coincidence. That's whut I am. A expert witness fer ole Redbird. You know ole Redbird here?"

O'Reith nodded to Feathermerchant, allowed to Flagherty that he knew who he was.

"This here is C-C-Clearwater Smith, Mistuh O-O-O'Reith. He'sa driller."

O'Reith shook his hand.

"How you reckon this here case gonna come out, Mistuh O-O-O'Reith?"

"I surely don't know, Clyde. I hope we settle it soon. I'm in the oil business in Venezuela. I need to get back on the job."

"Well, I doan mind if it goes on a spell. I'm a drawin' $20/day plus expenses. G-g-good money fer a crippled up ole codger. Specially since I done lost my pushin' job with Boyd 'n' Bowen. Mistuh O-O-O'Reith, I m-m-member them C-C-Calitroleum rigs you used to run. Them fast t-t-tables. An all of them there drill collars, stalks of celery. An' 'em m-m-mud-hawgs arunnin' wide open. An 'em drillers fireballin' that pipe in the hoal acuttin' that fas' ditch. Hot dawg-a-mighty. Them wuz the days! Well suh, I wuz a called up to jine the army and I wuz lookin' forrud to it right smart. I'd a had me my accidint and I wuzn't aworkin', justa hustlin' them pool players at the Ace of Diamonds. I figured bein' a soljer with extra-light duty, mebbe aworkin' in the army p-p-pool hall. I seen pitchas of them G.I.s aplayin' p-p-pool and I cud rack the balls and keep the cue sticks neat and put out the chalk. Things like 'at. Mought even play me some pool with 'em soljers. Army wuz apayin' $50/month and I needed the m-m-money. They rounded a bunch of us and tuk us over to Midland in a school bus to the 'zamination center. There we wuz, all a-stripped down like jaybirds and a w-w-waitin' to be a-checked out. I felt kind of out of p-p-place on account of my condition. This medical sargent he wuz a fat little fucker, he come awaddlin' out of that little room, smellin' like Lysol. He had his han's on his hips an' a frown on his face. He began a-walkin' down the line alookin' us boys over, all of us nekkid. He come over to me an' he looked down and then he looked up and then he looked down agin. He called over to the medical officer, he wuz a lootenan' an' he said, 'Hey Doc, come a look at this guy, he is a medical cur-io-os-ity for sure'. It wuz me he was a lookin' at. I wuz the cur-io-os-ity. That sargent he sed, "Doc, looka' this, he's had a bad case of the clap an' it's eat the head p-p-plum' off his dick. An' it eat one of his balls off too.' That medical of-of-officer, he wuz a young guy. He come over and he looked at me in that line of nekkid boys. I wuz feelin' purty low so I said, "Lootenan', it warn't no dose of clap whut eat the head off of my dick. It wuz a blowed off by a .44 cop-cop-copperheaded bul-bul-bullet shot out of a Smith and Wesson revolver that went off half-cocked. I said Doc, I ain't never had no clap. No Vee Neeral diseases at all. I knew a feller oncet, had the blueballs, all swole up like eggplants an' purple and 'em swallered up his little filbert of a peter. Well, anyway, Mistuh O-O-O'Reith, they wouldn't take me in the army."

At the appointed hour, the bailiff opened the doors. O'Reith and the SOCAL lawyers took their places at the defendant's table. Flagherty, Smith and Feathermerchant sat at the plaintiff's table. The two McLarssens entered, sat by plaintiff's attorney.

O'Reith appraised them. Donald resembled his late brother, John. Same beefy build. Same jowled jaws, brown eyes and an overbearing expression. John's face, of course, was one he could never forget. The sister, Eileen, a more complicated study, was waif-like. Slender, with plenty of titty, she was stacked, as they said in the army. An angelic face, the beauty of youth, auburn, fluffed out hair, hazel, penetrating, eyes, altogether, made a neat-looking dish. The roughhands would say, "She could eat crackers in my bed whenever she liked." O'Reith concluded she could have been a stand-in for Jane Powell. It reminded him of the song his son told him about, *Too Late Now* from the motion picture *Royal Wedding*.

Presently O'Reith became aware that he was the object of their attention. Donald McLarssen glared at him, looked him over from top to bottom as if measuring him for a coffin. The sister seemed to be evaluating him differently, like a prospective lay. He recognized the wide-eyed stare of a hoyden. He thought, "She'd kill me quick enough if she could, but she'd want to do something else first. Looking at her, he muttered under his breath, "Sweetface, "You're one neat little black widow spider."

Judge Burke gaveled the court to order. Jury selection began and four days later the time arrived when plaintiff was allowed to present its case. Beauregard Feathermerchant called his star witness. After Flagherty was sworn in, Feathermerchant began, "Mr. Flagherty, is it correct that you were the person in charge the night the McLarssen Estate No.1 blew out and caught fire?"

"Yas suh, I wuz the t-t-toolpusher."

"Can you tell the court what happened the night of the fire?"

"Well suh, it wuz a icy night with thuh wind a b-b-blowin' right smart. We'd been awaitin' on cement from the surface p-p-pipe job and it wuz time to drill out. Roun' midnight, thereabouts. I had me a f-f-fancy-dan driller, he'sa sittin' there. Mistuh C-C-Clearwater Smith. Had a fierce reputation. Feller come up from Okeralahomer. Cl-Cl-Claimed he wuz the fastes' driller whut ever cut ditch. An' I didn' doubt him none at all. He said the secret was to keep the hoal a full of c-c-clear, c-c-clean water. Course, that Mistuh Weems, thuh drillin' sup-in-ten-dint, he wanted us to drill with that there 'drillin' fluid' an' I toal C-C-Clearwater that. He sed that 'ud jes slow us down. Well, suh. It wuz two or three o'clock in the mornin' and coal as a witches t-t-titty, abeggin' the court's pardon an' we wuz in the hoal an them plugs in the casin' wuz aternin' an' ole Cl-Cl-Clearwater, he sed, 'Gimp-boy, we'll hev to hammer them plugs out.' An' we did. Soon as we busted them plugs up, we turned the water to the hoal. Had to have them 'lectric heaters in the pits to keep 'em from afreezin'. Ole C-C-Clearwater he tuk off a drillin' and I cud see right away that we wuz a cuttin' some of that fas' ditch. I wuz athinkin' how pleased Mistuh Weems'ud be. When he come in the mornin', we wud be deep. That's whut I wuz athinkin' when here comes this p-p-plume of water aspurtin' straight up outa the hoal an' afore I knowed it, I wuz adrenched and f-f-freezin'. I jes ternd to climb down them stairs to go achange cloze an' there'us this big W-H-O-O-S-H an' it wus gas an' boy cud you smell it. Like casin'hed gasoline it wuz. I thought Wooo! Eeee! Well, I wuz 'bout froze an' had to get me some dry cloze 'cause I knowed this wuz agonna be a bad 'un. Ole C-C-Clearwater, he diden' hev sense enuf to shut off them engines an' I cud hear 'em asuckin' in that gas an' they wuz arunin' away an' BOOM! Thar she went! Big ole oranj flames ashootin' up toward the monkey board and them han's runnin' ever wichaway. Well, I'd a p-p-parked my little Studebaker seedan out at thuh end of thuh c-c-catwalk. It wuz a good runnin' little car. Blue with nice soft seats and c-c crome c-c-covers on the wheels. Had a cone up in front of the radiator made it look like a rocket. I called it my little blue devil. I'd brung a cupple new rock bits from the supply store and that's why I wuz a p-p-parked at thuh end of thuh catwalk so them han's cud fetch 'em bits up easy to the softline and snake 'em up through the veedoor. Well, I wuz a standin' in thuh door of thuh bunkhouse thinkin' bout 'em dry blue jeans an' I ternt an' lookit up in thuh derrick an' I seen that stand of 8 inch drill collars we'd lef outa thuh string. C-C-Clearwater's idea an' I knowed Mistuh Weems wud be upset 'cause he always says not to leave no tools in thuh derrick. They's hard to handle an' we had that water in thuh hoal an' C-C-Clearwater, he sed it ud be all right. I tole him Mistuh Weems ud be mad but ole C-C-Clearwater, he jes laffed, he jes sed come mornin' we'd hev such a long ditch an we'd come outa thuh hoal an' pick up them collars an' Mistuh Weems wudn't know nuthin' about it anyhow. Well, I hadda close the bunkhouse door cause I wuz afreezin'. I shucked 'em wet cloze quick as I cud and got in 'em dry jeans. When I opened thuh door an' looked out I cud see that ole derrick wuz ch-ch-cherry red an' them girts wuz sparkin' where 'em rocks comin' outa the hoal wuz a hittin' 'em. I said 'Gimp boy, you'd best move that little Studebaker car of yours. It's a too close to thuh fire.' Well, I wuz a thinkin 'bout that an' course I'm a slow mover. I lookit up there in thet there derrick an' it seemed to me them derrick legs wuz white hot an' that fahr wuz a getting stronger an abernin' blue white like a welder's torch. Them derrick legs was a bowin' out and kind of scrootchin' down like a hen over her eggs. That there stalk of collars wuz a pokin' out through them girts above the monkey board an' leanin' toward thuh catwalk which wuz natural cause it wuz on that side of the derrick. Well, I began a sidlin' my way out there an' I 'mem-'mem-'member the keys to thuh car wuz in my wet cloze so I hadda go back an' fetch 'em. An' in my condition, that tuk up some valuable time. Well, oncet I had found 'em car keys, that ole derrick wuz white as milk an' a squattin' right smart like an ole Mesican woman a makin tortillas. That stalk of collars wuz standin' straight but a beginnin' to lean out over the catwalk. I wuz about half way out there when, zing, one of 'em girts popped loose an' zing, nother'n popped an' then they wuz all a poppin' an' a zingin' an' a zangin'. That ole derrick dropped lak a sack of nails. When that derrick come down, that stalk of 8" collars, it just stood up there and teetered and tottered and awobbled lak it didn know what to do. Then, here it come, straight over the catwalk she come down like a axed pine tree. Yassuh. Well, that catwalk wuz 80 feet long and that stalk of collars was 90. White hot from bein' in that fahr. It hit that catwalk and that tip overhangin' it nipped down like a jaybird takin' hissef a drink of water an' it was limber with thuh heat an' it creased that little Studebaker right behind the steerin' wheel. The hood sprung up and 'em coil springs over the wheels, they jumped out an' fell on the groun' arollin' aroun' an a bouncin'. The tip of the collar sprang back up in the air an' come back down an' hit that little car agin. All four tires blowed out an' I cud see the ch-ch-chassy wuz a bent down touchin' the groun' an' I thought that it wus sprung an' it wud be hard to fixit that little car where it wud run as good as it did before it wuz hit.

Them tires weren't bran' new. I bought 'em in B-B-Bakersfield an' they wuz secon' han' then. But they had right smart of tread lef on 'em. I had drove that little car all the way to Williston an' thuh compny wuz a payin' me a nickel a mile an' countin' rebates from the gas stations, it wuz a good deal. Well, sir, the second time that stalk of collars come down, it didn' bounce no moar, that secont hit done used up all the bounce. Hee hee hee. Thuh upperholsteree caught afire an' 'fore too long that little car wuz a bernin' right smart. I had me a bottle of F-F-Four Roses in the glove compartment an' I thought about how good a snort of it would taste what with me still pretty coal. But while I wuz a thinkin' of it, WHOOSH, flames spurted out of the front winder an' it wuz that bottle of bourbon a blowin' up. Jes a few moar minutes an' the gas tank went WHOOSH an' tuk off a scootin' across that location. An' I said, 'Gimp boy, yore little Studebaker is finished and you better watch yore step cause Mistuh Weems is goan be one mad Mesican when he comes a drivin' up in the mornin' and sees that rig all bernt up.' I thought well, I best work through the night. Get them han's arounded up an' a doin'. I cud tidy up the lease. Pick up the dirty rags an' them ole oil cans an' pipe dope cans an' get a rake out of the tool house an' rake aroun'. I thought maybe the compny ud see I wuz in-in-interested in my job an' they'd buy me another little car 'cause without no car, I wuz up a crik. I didn' spect no noo car but maybe a second han' car, a Ford coo-pay. Sumpin' lak 'at. So I c-c-called to C-C-Clearwater but he warn't there. I figured he wuz in the b-b-bunkhouse getting' into a dry change. But I doan know whatever happint to that scamp. He wuz, well he wuz jes gone. I dint see him agin until I seen him here as a expert witness jes lak me."

O'Reith whispered to one of the SOCAL lawyers, "This story is not going to get any better. When Gimp is finished, they'll put Clearwater on the stand. We'll really be in the soup. Why don't we call a recess and settle with them? Keep this melodrama out of the newspapers."

The SOCAL lawyer said, "I'll call San Francisco and get them to agree." He rose and left the courtroom.

Flagherty continued, "Well, didn' seem lak it ud ever come, but it did, that ole sun showin' on the hoe rison an' things didn' look no better by day than they had done by night. Fahr had calmed down some. Wasn't blowin' strong lak when thuh derrick come down but it wuz still right smart of a fahr. Evy now an' then it ud WHOOSH up agin an' scear them roughnecks an' they'd run off. It wuz a koffin' an' a spittin' an wuz beginnin' to throw up some salt water too. Well suh, me and 'em han's had cleaned up right smart aroun' thet ole rig, what there wuz lef of it, picked up coke bottles an' dope buckets an' things lak 'at. Bout thet time, I lookit up an' I seen a cloud of dus' acomin' cross the country an I knowed it wus Mistuh Weems an' I figerred he 'ud be upset some an' hell to pay. I wuz gonna get ole C-C-Clearwater to 'splain about that water in the hoal but that scamp he wuz scooted. Mistuh Weems, he wuz from East Texas, a short, sawed-off red-faced buckaroo with a thick neck an' mean-lookin' red eyes. He swaggered roun' lak a little bitty bull dawg. He come up to me, a hitchin' his pants up an' he sed, 'Gimp boy, you best get to town the best way you can an' draw yore pay cause you are a run off toolpusher an' rightly you ain't much of a toolpusher anyhow. Yore rig is bernt up. You got the Stannerd Oil Compny a pissed off an' you might jes as well git!' He wuz a some torqued-up! He sed 'Gimp, thet office closes at five o'clock this evening so you got all day to walk to town.' He didn' care no mine it was a freezin' coal an' thet win' wuz ablowin' right smart straight from the north poal an thet my little car wuz a bernt up. He sed, 'Gimp boy git on down thet lease road to the highway an' hitch yoreself a ride. Git thet thum' of yours a workin'. You're lucky it ain't blowed off lak the rest of your parts.' So I sed, Mistuh Weems, this here fahr weren't no fault of mine, I hired me a driller named C-C-Clearwater Smith an' it wuz him whut done it." Mistuh Weems, he put his han's on his hips an' his face it got even redder than it already wuz an' he lookit me inna eye an' he shook his head an' he snarled, 'you f-f-fathead. Evybody knows that Smith is a no-good driller. Trubbl. Trubbl an' dubbl-trubbl. He got stuck in the Woodford Shale in Okalerahomer an' he pulled the derrick in an' he got blowed out of the hoal in Agua Dulce with thuh drill pipe asnaked out all over Jim Wells and Nueces counties. Jeereesus Keerist, Gimp boy, evybody in the oil patch knows he's wuthless.' Mistuh Weems, he stuck his little short han's in his belt in front of his belly an' he nodded his chin off in the direction of the lease road an' he said 'Git Gimp, git!'

"An I did." I felt lak I wuz ruint. I went back to Odessa, Texas an' got me a job sweepin' up in a pool hall. I wuz a workin' there when Mistuh Beauregard called me on the t-t-telephone an' said he'd pay me $20/day to work as a expert witness. That's my story. God's truth an' fore sure."

By the end of the day, the SOCAL lawyer had permission to settle the case for any amount up to $250,000, an exorbitant sum considering the insignificant damages. But the McLarssen Estate refused to settle for any amount, insisted the case go to the jury which, after further damaging testimony from Clearwater Smith, it did. After several days, the jury returned a verdict in favor of the estate and awarded it $1,500,000. SOCAL decided to appeal. There the matter rested. It was 25 May 1956.

O'Reith sat alone at the copper-topped bar in the cavernous tavern of Brown's Hotel. The SOCAL lawyers had taken a night flight to San Francisco. In the morning, he would fly to San Francisco, give Blake his view on the case. He was nursing his martini, thinking about tomorrow. It was seven p.m. and he was getting hungry. Just as he was about to ask the bartender for a menu, Eileen McLarssen sat beside him. She said, "What a shame my dear General O'Reith that the court award couldn't come from your own pocket." It was a pleasant enough voice, a clear crystalline soprano, modulated and mid-western. She spoke carefully, as if to achieve a dramatic effect. No rancor in her voice.

O'Reith ignored the barb, said, "Miss McLarssen, may I offer you a drink, out of my own pocket, of course?"

She smiled in spite of herself. "Bourbon and branch water. Can we sit at a table?"

When they were at a corner table out of the way of bar traffic in a lounge that was almost deserted, she said, "How many guesses do you need to know what I want to talk to you about?"

"Since the case is decided, at least for now it is, quite a few. What business have we together?"

"My brother and I think you are responsible for John's death. So we have that business."

O'Reith said, "I know that must weigh heavily on your mind but I think it is time for me to go. In fact I was just ready to leave when you appeared."

"But just to the dining room. You bought me a drink. Why not dinner too?"

"Why not indeed," he signaled the waiter for another menu as he rattled the ice cubes in his empty glass. He didn't need another drink but it was shaping up as a tedious evening.

"I want to talk about John. May we start now or is it indelicate?"

"Not much to discuss, Miss McLarssen."

"You were the only suspect. I suppose it is asking too much for you to admit killing him."

"You already asked that question, my dear. Remember the letter that you wrote to me? When you were much younger. Remember?"

She put her hand to her mouth. "That. Yes, but I was just a child. I was fourteen. I was in shock. I idolized John. He was my Beau Ideal. When he died…"

"Tragedy stalks us all," O'Reith said philosophically. I can understand your distress. In the course of one's life, one must suffer the loss of loved ones. Part of life. Some say it is the basis for religion. You have to accept the judgement of the grand jury. Not enough evidence to bring an indictment against me. You have to put it behind you."

"I never thought the day would come when I would see you with my own eyes. In the courtroom, I daydreamed that you were on trial for your life and that the jury found you guilty and sentenced you to die. Did it never occur to you that John had a family?"

"It occurred to me. The newspapers gave the case extensive coverage. I have a family too. I knew about you and your brother. The letter said quite a few things…"

"My brother hates you. Did you know that?"

"He glared at me often enough during the trial."

"General O'Reith, our case is strong. The appeal will fail. We'll get our money."

"Spend it wisely."

"My brother plans to use it to scandalize you, to hound you to your grave."

"Why tell me? What's the point? Anyway, it is a poor use of money. Why not use it to buy some more livestock for your ranch? Maybe even buy another 80 acres or so."

"I plan to do just that. Maybe save some for acting lessons. I'd like to become a movie star. I don't always share my brother's views. I regret sending you that letter."

"When one is young, one makes foolish mistakes. I don't hold it against you."

"I thank you for that. But could I have it back?"

"The letter?"

"Yes. I'd like to burn it," she said. "Wouldn't you want to destroy something like that?"

"It's in the file back in Los Angeles," O'Reith said. He removed his pocket diary and made a note. "I'll ask my secretary to send it to you. Would you like to give me your address?"

Suddenly she was hesitant. She thought for a moment, said, "Could I call upon her and get it?"

"Of course. We're in the Fullerton Building. Call this number and ask for Susie." O'Reith gave her the telephone number. "But it is of out of the way. We'd be glad to send it to you in North Dakota. We could send it by registered mail. It wouldn't get lost."

"If it's all the same, I'd rather have it in my hand, you know."

"As you prefer," O'Reith said.

"General O'Reith, as you mentioned, the newspapers did cover the case, the publicity that surrounded your wife, and for that matter, the entire movie industry."

O'Reith laughed. "They didn't attack John Wayne."

She was silent for a moment, thinking. Then she said, "I've seen your wife on the screen. I saw *Neon Lights*. I thought she was pretty good."

"So did the Motion Picture Academy. She won an Oscar for the role of Estelle. I'll tell her you're a fan. She's apprehensive about my being here. Worried something could happen… I'll reassure her that you mean us no harm."

She was nervous now, twisting her handkerchief into knots and looking him over pretty carefully. Her eyes were getting wider and wider. O'Reith decided she was pretty hungry and not for food. She blurted it out rapid fire. "General O'Reith, I'm a rancher and I'll put it to you straight. I need some of what you've got. Right now. How about it?"

"My child, I have to have dinner. I skipped lunch. After that, we can discuss it." It was the only answer he could think of. He knew that he could not accede to this young wanton's desires. It would complicate matters far beyond the scope of the present relationship. As hard up as he was and as much as he appreciated her desirability, at the age of forty-nine, he had learned enough about dalliance and its inevitable consequences, to know that he would have to gracefully decline. He knew further that there was no graceful way to decline a woman's invitation. No, he was resigned to the fury of a young woman scorned. He hoped she was not armed.

"I'm not a child," she told him, put off by his oblique reply. She rose with him and followed him into the dining room. They ordered steaks, well done with all the trimmings and a bottle of California Pinot Noir. Over salad, O'Reith asked, "What does your brother do?" He already knew but he was buying time.

"He's an attorney and a lay preacher. He wants to preach full time and I expect he will once we get our money. With the oil on our land, we may get more. I think you know Mr. Feathermerchant. My brother is taking him into the firm."

"Feathermerchant does not have a stellar record. He was fired from Calitropical Oil Company."

"He's changed. And as you saw, he won his case. That says a lot. He's going to get us into the oil business in Venezuela. What do you think of that?"

"Risky business."

"Beauregard is going down to Marakeebo next week. He has connections with the government. Knows how to get a concession. My brother says that he can sell it to one of the big oil companies in North Dakota. What do you think of that?"

"A better use of the money than attacking me."

"Well, he'll do that too. Beauregard says he knows something that you want kept a secret. Something that'll get you in a tangle."

Dinner was over and they were having coffee. She said, "Let's pay up and get out of here. We can go to your room."

O'Reith smiled paternally, said carefully, "Eileen, I have a daughter your age. We are on opposite sides of a dispute, yet to be resolved. What would I say to Mr. Feathermerchant in the witness box if he asked if you and I had a romantic relationship?"

"I'd never tell him." She was getting edgy. Her knuckles were white. She frantically searched her purse for cigarettes. When she found one, she rapidly tamped it down on the tabletop, eagerly allowed O'Reith to light it.

O'Reith said, "Eileen, I'm flattered by your proposition but I can't accept. We are going to say goodbye."

"Don't talk to me like that," she retorted, becoming hostile. "Nobody needs ever to know what's between us. Mister, I need it bad, real bad."

"Not from me, my child."

"Don't call me a goddamned child. I told you that before." She was agitated. O'Reith eyed her half-full cup of coffee, hoped she would not throw it in his face. It was still pretty hot. She sensed the game was over, got up, scraping her chair noisily. "OK Prunepicker. You'll get yours." She stomped out of the dining room, clacking her heels as loudly as she could.

The brother called around ten o'clock just as O'Reith was drifting off. "The Lord takes his revenge sweetly, " he intoned. He called again at eleven. "Repent sinner whilst thou hast thy breath." And at midnight, "Doom is nigh, infidel."

O'Reith got up, groggily went to the can, took a long thoughtful pee and the phone was ringing again before he finished. This time it was, "Not sleeping too good, General O'Reith. Suffer!"

In his dream, he was with Mimi Martell, doing it on the sand beneath the moon on Pismo Beach. A cool breeze was blowing in off the Pacific and he was getting cold. As he searched for his robe, he saw she had a pistol and was aiming it at him. He awoke. "Jesus," he said, "Jesus H. Christ!" It was daylight and he had overslept. He'd have to scramble to catch his plane.

*   *   *

In the office in Los Angeles he said, "Susie, Eileen McLarssen is coming in to get that foolish letter she wrote to me when she was fourteen. Call my son and let him know that. Advise him that I want him to read that letter. When she calls for it, I want him to give it to her in person."

Chapter VII

▼

Drilling

During the weeks that O'Reith shined his pant bottoms on a bench in a Denver courtroom, Holland and Prescott were taking the balmy breezes and looking at the fleecy clouds over Lake Maracaibo in springtime. Both locations had been staked. Right now, the two engineers, in khakis, wide-brimmed Panama hats, sunglasses and field boots stood on the immense deck of a *Terminales Maracaibo* derrick barge anchored up in 50 feet of water on Block 9. Beside them, similarly attired, a surveyor, sunglasses in hand, eyes glued to his theodolite, lined up the cross hairs on the *Cruz Morillo de la Cañada*. It sat atop the cathedral far away on the horizon. The surveyor took a last look to make sure they were in the right place to set the platform from which they would drill Lago Poniente No. 9-1X. At dawn, they had set the Block 16 platform. Pile drivers were securing it to the lake bottom with pre-stressed concrete pilings driven through the four hollow steel legs. This platform, like the one on Block 16 was a truncated pyramid, ninety feet long with a square drilling deck 40' by 40'. Drilling equipment would shortly be placed on it.

    The surveyor signaled the crane operator. The deck hands began attaching the wire-rope slings to the top of the platform. Within minutes it would be hanging over the side of the barge, dangling from the towering crane. Slowly it would be lowered until it rested on the lake bottom, waiting for the pile driver. The derrick barge, big as a football field, would be towed back to Maracaibo at the great speed of 3 knots to load the two drilling rigs and return to set them on the platforms. Both drilling tenders would be under tow right behind them.

Tarbutton, his 'quickie' training program under his belt, had returned to Caracas, bringing with him the detective, Philip Marlborough. He would meet Torres, get a good but surreptitious look at Cordero and visit the haunts of the *Seguridad Nacional* like the Mara Bar in the Del Lago, the Cacique Bar in the Tamanaco and of course, *La Casualidad* in *Avenida Orinoco*. Marlborough was also to interview Mandy Macabra Schaeffer and Hunter Holland. O'Reith wanted the detective to have a perfect understanding of the various personal relationships that were central to this operation. Maurice LeBel had recruited four ex-Foreign Legionnaires for surveillance duty in Caracas and Maracaibo. Torres needed protection in case of another detention attempt. These 'agents', natives of Barcelona, had lengthy police records. Long before becoming soldiers, they were experts with *arma blanca* as well as firearms. All were survivors of intense street fighting in the ghettos of Algiers and Oran. Marlborough had pronounced them harder than hand grenades. He told Tarbutton that once finished in Venezuela, he would recommend them for employment by the Los Angeles Police Department.

Holland hired Schaeffer as office assistant at the shore base. Restless from hanging around *El Escondite* with little to do, with his knowledge of drilling equipment he quickly made himself useful expediting materials and services. Over the years he had learned enough Spanish to communicate with the locals. Sally and Erma Morrow were happy. It allowed them to get away to see after the kids when necessary. Mandy was glad to have him out of her hair during the day. Schaeffer and Marks worked well together, liked to tell oil field tales over a glass of *Cerveza Zulia* at the end of the day. Altogether, it was a satisfactory arrangement. Even the cautious O'Reith smiled when he learned of it.

With McLarssen vs. SOCAL behind him and his consulting agreement expired, O'Reith called a directors meeting in Paris. Those summoned were George P. McDonough, Maurice LeBel, Hardy Tarbutton and the Widow Halliday. Invited to attend and a candidate for election to the board, was Monk Parkhurst, London banker, former Calitroleum Director and a good friend. Torres told Tarbutton that the earliest date for contract publication was mid-August. Based on this, O'Reith sent Mandy two calling cards, one as President, The Casinghead Company, and the other as General O'Reith, Commander, Eighth Far Eastern Air Force. With the two cards he asked her to line up a meeting with Colonel Marcos Perez Jimenez at least a week before contract publication. He also asked Philip Marlborough to present his assessment of political risk in Venezuela to the directors.

O'Reith passed a pleasant few weeks with Helen and his daughter. The filming of *Los Ladrones de Piedras Negras* had become more complicated. Big Alphonse had partially recovered from his stroke. He insisted upon retaking his place in the cast. He had lost weight, had a staring left eye in a half-frozen face, had a tic and limped. Shooting was suspended. A dispute broke out between Bolletti, Big Alphonse and his replacement, reluctant to be displaced. O'Reith and Helen took a Roman holiday on the Isle of Capri. He told her how he lost a night of sleep to the two McLarssens and that he expected more trouble ahead. He suggested that Helen come to Paris to hear McDonough speak. Also review her bank account problem with Monk Parkhurst, her financial advisor.

Helen was on edge about the movie. About a third of it was in the cans, most with Big Alphonse in good shape. But footage with the second hero created a discontinuity. With Big Alphonse back in the act how was Bolletti going to weave it together? The slow going meant that shooting would end late in the year. It would be the most expensive cowboy movie ever made. But encouraged by Alice Ridley astrological projections, she was resolved to see it through to the end.

*   *   *

Lago Poniente No.9-1X was programmed to test the entire geologic column from the Eocene to the Cretaceous. Verify that no gas caps existed in the Mirador or the Santa Barbara. Below those formations, the C-Series was a good bet. The Cretaceous was a shot in the dark. The La Luna, a porous lime in some places, could be an oil producer. Taking the long view, O'Reith wanted to fully evaluate Block 9 immediately. In Block 16, the first well would be 'plain vanilla' targeted to the Mirador and the Santa Barbara. If both zones were good, the well would be dually completed. Alan Prescott was the drilling foreman for Block 9. For Block 16, Holland had hired a drilling engineer from Mene Grande, named Ronald Morrow, an ex-military policeman from Enid, Oklahoma with a bull frog voice. Directing tank traffic at St. Vith for III Army in December of 1944, a German sniper shot off the first two joints of his right index finger. Morrow was a tall, heavy man with a ruddy, rectangular face and bullet gray eyes. Like many policemen, he had developed a 'dead fish' stare, which withered many a recalcitrant rig hand. But he had a sense of humor, laughed a lot, throwing his head back and roaring in his rumbling voice, showing an array of big, stained teeth. He gave orders by pointing at the work to be done with his stub of a forefinger. He resembled the actor, Aldo Ray. Morrow studied petroleum engineering at Tulsa University on the G.I. Bill of Rights. While there, he married a Tulsa girl named Erma. He learned the ropes drilling Gulf Oil Corporation leases in the Goldsmith Field. In Venezuela three years now, he was a veteran lake driller. Like all gringos, the local rig hands bestowed upon him a nickname, *El Mocho*, the stub.

The two platforms were three miles apart on an east-west line roughly parallel to 10 degrees of north latitude. A 30-knot speedboat named *La Flecha*, the arrow, reduced travel time to minutes between platforms and a half-hour to the shore base. Each tender had a single side-band short-wave radio to call the shore base. The shore base at the town of San Francisco was an hour's drive from the office in Maracaibo. Holland, Ines and the kids were in a suite of rooms at *El Escondite*. The growing oil boom, caused an acute shortage of housing in town. Holland rose at six a.m., breakfasted with the family. Then he and the children would pile into the Cadillac limousine. Cansor took the kids to school, and Holland to work.

While Prescott and Morrow worked offshore, Holland, Schaeffer, Sally Prescott and Erma Morrow worked at the base. O'Reith, when he was in town, operated out of the hotel office. With O'Reith in Europe, Holland checked the office for messages. Sometimes he would visit the adjoining offices of Halliburton Oil Well Cementers, Raymond Concrete Pile Company, Baroid Mud Company and the Charles Bottome Money Exchange Bureau where he would get whatever *bolivares* they needed for local expenses. In those days, two exchange rates existed. The official rate was 3.3 *bolivares* to the dollar. The black market rate was five. The Casinghead Company office was the last on the left, next to a side entrance that opened on to a parking lot. O'Reith kept a hired limousine standing by but usually he walked from work to his villa located in Avenida C near the Hospital Coromoto. From the office radio, at certain hours, he could raise Helen in Monte Carlo but communication was far from reliable. Most of the time he sent her cables from the ITT desk in the hotel lobby. They now had a teleprinter installed and he was trying it out with short 'hellos' when he was in town.

Now the anticipated moment was upon them. Rig up was complete. The tender was in place at Block 16. The platform fixed to the lake bed. Tools and materials were at hand. The standard derrick loomed 142 feet into the humid air. A few adventurous lake birds were already surveying nooks and corners where they might nest. Plumed diving birds sat on the railings around the crown block, looking for fish. Conductor pipe, driven in the muddy lake bottom with a diesel hammer was ready. Thirty feet below the drilling deck, a *cellar* deck of expanded steel plate had a hole in the center for the drilling tools. Welders and rig hands had hooked up the bell nipple to the conductor pipe. Wire ropes kept the conductor steady.

Assembled on the derrick floor were the players. Hunter Holland and Hardy Tarbutton, both in faded blue Air Corps coveralls; Alan Prescott and *El Mocho* Morrow in green U.S. Army fatigues; Rojo Torres, Tuffy Marks, Philip Marlborough and Stanley Ethering wore white coveralls with *Loffco* stenciled in big black letters on the back between the shoulders. Maxine, Ines, Lila Marks, Erma Morrow, Mandy and Carolyn wore blue jeans and cotton shirts of various colors. All had on field boots. On a signal from Marks, the Venezuelan driller lowered the tools until the bit was resting on the lake bottom.

The *spudding* of an oil well has often been likened to forcible sexual violation, the rape of Mother Nature. It is a common observation that the driller often gets an erection as he engages the pump and the rotary. And so it was on this occasion. A protrusion showed the driller's endowment as he waited for the nod from the Loffco Toolpusher. The observant ladies tittered. Marks looked to Prescott. Prescott looked to Holland. Holland nodded. Prescott said to Marks, "Turn her to the right!" Marks nodded to the Loffco toolpusher who touched the driller on the shoulder. The engines roared to full power, the pumps surged, the rotary table began to turn and they were drilling!

Unlike the McLarssen Estate No.1, there would be no Gimp Flaghertys or Clearwater Smiths involved in the drilling of this well. Loffland Brothers Company was the finest international drilling contractor in the world. Hard eyed drilling superintendents had long ago winnowed out the Flaghertys and the Smiths and other nincompoops of their ilk, of which there were many. This rig was no post-hole puncher looking for 50 bbl/day on the Dakota plains. This was a

National 100 Blue, rated to 15,000 feet with 4-inch drill pipe. A *big rig* and Lake Maracaibo was in the *big leagues*.

The tender was anchored up some fifty feet downwind from the platform. To descend from the derrick floor to the tender, one carefully climbed down an angled steel ladder known as a *widow-maker* because of hazards associated with bad weather. When the tender heaved and rolled, climbing the ladder was dangerous. But today was calm. The men helped the ladies down. They all assembled in the mess hall. Holland popped a cork from a champagne bottle. Prescott handed the radio operator a message to send to the office.

FOR CLIVE COLIN O'REITH
THE CASINGHEAD COMPANY
PARIS
25 JUN 56
LAGO PONIENTE NO. 16-1X SPUDDED 3 PM ATLANTIC STANDARD TIME.
REGARDS
HOLLAND

The Casinghead Company no longer a mere paper tiger, was an oil company drilling an oil well. The celebration finished, the ladies and VIPs on a Loffco speedboat headed back to the Maracaibo docks. Prescott and Marks boarded *La Flecha* for the run over to the Lago Poniente No.9-1X platform. Here too, it was time to drill ahead. This one was different from No. 16-1X. The conductor pipe was 30" in diameter rather than the 16" of Block 16. No 'plain vanilla' well, this one. They were going all the way to the bottom of the column. Blowout preventers rated to 5,000 psi instead of 3,000. Surface casing would be 13 3/8" rather than 11 ¾". Surface pipe would be set deeper. The 'long' string would be 9 5/8" rather than 7 inch. This well would require at least 90 days to drill as compared to 30 for the 'plain vanilla' one. Here they would case off everything down to and including the C-Series, somewhere below 10,000 feet. When they drilled out the shoe of the 9

5/8" casing, they would be in terra incognito, rank wildcat country, dangerous and demanding. A drilling foreman on the floor around the clock was required. Before they got to the 9 5/8" casing point, two more drilling foremen would join them. Nobody wanted a repeat of the Lago Poniente No.1X disaster. The man on duty would watch the weight indicator, listen to the pumps, check the shale shaker. He sought clues as to what kind of formations they were drilling two miles below.

* * *

On the Avensa flight back to Maiquetia, on the back of an envelope, Tarbutton estimated what The Casinghead Company had spent as of 30 JUN 56.

    Concession Costs $25,000,000
    Drilling Operations......................................900,000
    Boats, barges, Airplanes.............................200,000
    Office rental..15,000
    Payrolls and housing...................................125,000
    Communication and automobiles......................50,000
    Total Capital and Exploratory Cost $26,290,000

When the contract was published, another $20 million would be paid out. Tarbutton figured that by the time that the company was running crude oil to steel storage at Punto Fijo, around 15 Oct. 1957, total costs would exceed $150 million. On that day, 20 completed oil wells would be flowing 150,000 bopd. By contract, the company was entitled to 84% of that. It would be $195,000/day based on a crude oil price of $2.80/bbl. Two years before they broke even, if the price of oil held steady, if nothing went wrong in the government, if there were no disruptions, natural or otherwise, if...

Rojo Torres, sitting beside him in the Convair 440, watched Tarbutton figure. When the calculation was complete, he handed it over to Torres. Torres looked at it briefly, handed it back and said, "Easy money." They grinned at each other.

The team that O'Reith had assembled was in the groove, working together to make the dream come true. Carolyn Cook shuttled from rig to rig, scanning the reports, looking at the cuttings, studying the gas indicator hooked up to the return mud line. She sought clues as to where they might be on the structure, high or low. She looked for faults, discontinuities or changes in rock composition, things that might throw their rosy projections into a cocked hat. After a hurried dinner, she worked on her maps, often staying over the light table until well after midnight. So far, everything was OK, 'running high and looking good', as they said.

Prescott and Morrow looked at the same data as Cook but their concern was to keep the operation running smoothly and maintain a margin of safety in the event they unexpectedly cut a stray gas sand. The mud weight had to be high enough to control whatever pressure existed below but low enough to assure a steady drilling rate. They were vigilant. Most emergencies resulted from inexperience or carelessness. They had to be ahead of events, making sure that whatever was needed next, was on the way.

Holland took the drilling reports in the morning and again late in the afternoon, discussing potential problems, looking for deviations from the program that could cause trouble. He had a speedboat standing by, could be on either location if needed within the hour.

Schaeffer looked after material and supplies. Orders came in from the rigs by radio. He saw that material was on the next boat. He checked tools to assure they were of the correct size and up to specification. And he called out Schlumberger and Halliburton when their presence was or would soon be required. He was a veteran of many drilling campaigns, delighted to once again be useful. He was a credit to the company.

Sally and Erma kept the files up to date, typed out the messages and made the coffee. In Caracas, Tarbutton and Ethering entertained Torres and each other. Ethering was one of those rare raconteurs who composed his own material. His specialty was political jokes. His little black book was full of them; congressional, executive and even a few about the judiciary. Tarbutton controlled the local bank account and paid the bills on time.

O'Reith, in Paris, reopened the flat where he and Maxine had lived. He worked in the company office with LeBel. From Blake, he hired two ex-Calitropical geologists for Maracaibo to help Cook. She would come to Paris for the directors meetings. O'Reith wished Holland could come too but it was not practical. School was out in Maracaibo. O'Reith cabled Maxine to come to Paris for the summer. He now questioned the wisdom of the move to Maracaibo. Except for crucial meetings with government men, his team could handle things just fine. He was in their way. Perhaps they could offer their villa to Holland. Ines would jump at the chance to get out of *El Escondite,* now filled up with roisterous oil field hands. Tarbutton's financial prognostications would be the main topic of discussion at the meetings. O'Reith had already decided that if both wells now drilling were oil wells, he would pick up two more strings and drill four wells at a time instead of two. Loffland Brothers was building a new type of drilling unit called a *jack-up,* a rig without a tender. A cantilevered derrick allowed it to drill several wells from one jacked up position on the lake bottom. With an 8-well platform all of the slots would be drilled without moving. The technique was to drill one straight well and seven directional wells. Jack-ups were scarce. He could get this one because out of his own pocket, while still president of Calitroleum, he had financed construction of it. This rig was two years building and cost $2 million. He had first call on it. So he was anxiously awaiting news from Maracaibo on the two wells now drilling ahead. If both were good, he would hire the new jack-up. With luck and planning, the company could run 250,000 bopd instead of the 150,000 bopd that Tarbutton estimated. He'd have to find another rig somewhere.

Other oil companies were looking for rigs too. In the meantime, with Helen and young Helen Simpson at hand, he was in the pink.

But Helen wasn't. Bolletti had rewritten the script again for *Los Ladrones de Las Piedras Negras*. He planned a new title for it also. Rather than a tale of cattle rustling on the Mexican border, it would be a feud in the mezzogiorno between the Camorra and the Mafia. Big Alphonse, now shriveled by stroke, his vocal chords impaired and the left side of his face frozen, would be recovering from a fall down a steep hillside, thrown by his horse. Helen, no longer a practical nurse, would be a reformed bar girl who got religion and entered a nunnery, near the bottom of the hill where Big Alphonse lay unconscious. Helen would find him, nurse him back to health and fall in love with him. Garcia, the Mexican novelist, had quit in disgust and returned to Mexico City. Lawson, of Hollywood 10 notoriety was hanging around, attending Helen on the set. He was idle, had asked Bolletti for plane fare back to Los Angeles. Bolletti predicted that the revised movie would be 'in the cans' no later than Christmas 1956. It would cost a couple of million dollars. Helen, to put it mildly, was not amused.

Still she had enjoyed her husband's company. The stud service was exceptional and the squeezing was great. For O'Reith, little Helen Simpson was a true delight. It broke his heart when he had to bid her farewell.

Despite her dogged tenacity in the face of looming failure, O'Reith noticed that at night Helen snuggled into his arms more closely than he could remember since the end of the war. She slept close, body-to-body, until the dawn broke. When he turned, she turned. If he rolled, as he often did, she rolled with him. When they made love, she held him in a viselike grip. The intensity of her feeling for him seemed greater too. He could feel the tears on her cheeks at the moment of orgasm and sometimes she sobbed softly before going to sleep in his arms.

At forty-nine, he rarely slept soundly anymore; had strange, complicated dreams with no obvious meaning. He heard every sound of the night, distant sirens, barking dogs, screeching cats banging ash cans and even the trill of nightingales. This morning he was awake with the crowing cock of a farm on a French hillside. Dogs were barking all over town and pigeons rustled feathers against their bedroom windows. He stirred, unwound himself from Helen and got up. She would sleep for another hour. He bathed, dressed and walked from the casino along Boulevard Princesse Charlotte to the tennis courts of the Monte Carlo Country Club on the French line. A great stretch, soon the circulation in his game leg lifted his spirits. When he returned Helen was up, ready to order breakfast from the Hotel de Paris.

Over coffee, Helen said, "Ace, I'm sure you're keeping another woman somewhere. Not Mimi Martell. Someone much younger. Last night I dreamed that you had someone else. You'd had her for quite some long time. You were contemplating returning to her. So it is the truth. Who is she? Where is she? Why not fess up?"

"To what end, baby? To what end?" he replied, looking at her lovingly. From across the breakfast table he took her hand, continued, "Helen, when that war started, those long years ago, the genie got out of the bottle. Nothing has been the same since nor will it ever be again.

Today I am doing what I wanted to do in 1941, drilling for oil on Lake Maracaibo. Many men would consider themselves extremely successful had they climbed the corporate ladder as I did at Calitroleum. I thought it an accomplishment but an unsatisfying one. In retrospect, it could have been no other way. It was child's play. Halliday delayed modernizing the company. The war caught him standing short. When it was over he had to scramble to catch up with the majors. Men like me, like Blake, Larry Teague, men of modest talent, quickly leap-frogged his corps of aging fuglemen. What I do now is the true acid test of the oil man. Building a company from scratch, in a place like Venezuela, no place for widows and orphans, as I told Susie Briscoe. As far as the Casinghead Company is concerned, the colonel and I make the rules. Indeed, some of them are yet to be made. Vince is a great guy. But he failed his test. His overwhelming shortcoming is his inability to cope with uncertainty, particularly that induced by fickle government. He hated it that Halliday bribed politicians like milkmaids milk cows, routinely, carelessly and without a second thought. Vince believes that politicians are true servants of the people. Corrupting them is *morally* wrong. Remember when we used to play bridge with them? A renege or a trump of partner's ace would cost him a night of sleep. He's straight as an arrow. The blood in Halliday's veins had hardly turned cold before Vince strapped lobbying on my shoulders. He said he didn't understand it. He understood it. He just didn't have the stomach for it. When SOCAL flirted with us, he couldn't wait to grasp their offer. It was a chance for him to escape the burden that Halliday placed on him. Vince also worries about being caught. He was haunted by the fact that bribing those guys, whether they were petty, faceless bureaucrats or famous congressmen, would eventually catch up with him. It was wrong and he could imagine some wrathful grand jury in Washington handing down an indictment. Some benevolent, gray-haired, avuncular, senator, whom the nation adored, that if the truth about him were known, was as crooked as a pretzel would be going to jail, dragging Vince along with him. That was his nightmare. What I do, baby, requires some travel. That contributes to your suspicions which, as you admit, are based on dreams. Vince, in the final analysis, failed the leadership test as well as the acid test. I have to be a leader. I enjoy it. If that makes me attractive to a certain class of women, am I expected to wear a hair shirt? Some women circle successful men like some moths circle glowing flames. Here we are with half of our lives gone, each trying to fulfill a destiny. What are we to do? Throw in our hands? Forget crude oil? Forget motion pictures? Move to that tiny cottage in Carmel where we honeymooned so many, long years ago? Put a new roof on it? Retire to that luxurious barn at Holmby Hills? Play golf at the club every day? I don't think so. But baby, I sense your stress and distress. Your movie appears to be going down the tube. You may lose $5 million. Ponder this. Tell

Bolletti to shoot around you for a few days. Unless he's your lover and you can't do without him."

"I resent that, Ace. I've always been faithful to you. Besides, Bolleti is impotent. His dick is as limp as an oyster."

"Ha Ha.Ha," O'Reith exploded." I thought he was the essence of virility. He's married, isn't he? Got three or four bambinos?"

"She has the bambinos," Helen muttered curtly. Big Alphonse is their father. Frederico told me all about it. He's an 80% guy and he hates it."

"Helen, you know I awaited the birth of little Helen with some trepidation. For a time I was convinced that Fritz was her father. Of course, once I saw her, mere hours old, shapeless and unformed, I could tell from her dark hair and her blue eyes that she was my child. I was not only relieved but deliriously happy. Now, of course, it is clear that she is her father's daughter. Fritz came on as a man of great virility, like his idol, Joseph Goebbels. I'm not going to inquire into your relationship with him at this late hour. But at the time, I was distressed."

"Another 80 percenter, Ace. Surely you knew that. Everyone who worked with him knew he couldn't get it up. As a stud, he was a joke."

O'Reith sighed, said, "You and little Helen can come with me to Paris. Go shopping with Virginia in the rue de la Paix. Monk Parkhurst will give you a financial check-up. George will boost your spirits when he speaks at the final session. Then a dinner party at the Ritz, like old times. You and I can slip away one evening for drinks at the art deco bar in the George V. What do you say, baby?"

She got up, came around and sat in his lap, said, "Ace, as an orator, George P. McDonough is not in your class. How could I ever doubt you? I'm packing my bags right now. Allo Paree!"

He smiled at her, fondled her bottom and caressed her legs, continued, "Baby, we've got to hold on until sometime in 1957, maybe the 3rd quarter but I'm trying to speed things up. When crude oil runs to the tanks, we can reorder our priorities. Until then, your husband is totally focused on Lake Maracaibo."

"Ace, you're out of this world," Helen answered, mesmerized. That night, he pronged her heroically, unforgettably.

*   *   *

O'Reith at one end of the long, cigarette-stained table that had once belonged to Paris Petroleum Company, brought the meeting to order. It was 10 July 1956. The directors were gathered in the conference room. Behind him on the yellow wall hung Carolyn's oil field map of Lake Maracaibo. White pins marked the drilling locations in Blocks 9 and 16. Circulating around the table were the latest cables from Holland. Tarbutton, sitting on his right, presented the Capital and Exploratory Budget, expenses to date with a forecast of how much money was yet to be spent before first oil went into the tanks. Following Tarbutton, LeBel reported on the bank balances and governmental filings. Carolyn Cook reviewed the geology of the lake. Susie reported on equipment purchases and transportation expenses. Monk Parkhurst discussed the availability of funds should the company needed to borrow. Philip Marlborough brought them up to date on security measures taken in Venezuela. Vincent Blake, in a new toupee, a pencil mustache and a bow tie, doodled on a note pad at the end of the table. Sharon Mills had finished with him, some minutes before the start of the meeting. She stepped back to admire her work, clapped her hands and summoned O'Reith to see the 'new' Vince Blake. O'Reith winked at her, took her in his arms. Together they danced a little jig around the perplexed Blake, who sat in a straight-backed chair under a sheet. After lunch they were joined by Virginia and Helen, both come to hear the mellow tones of Sir George P. McDonough.

Late in the afternoon, they were all dressed to go immediately to the cocktail lounge of the Ritz for drinks. O'Reith, Blake and Tarbutton were in tuxedos. McDonough wore his trademark tropical linen, with white leather, perforated shoes and an ivory tie. Parkhurst and

Marlborough were identically dressed in navy blue pinstripes with starched white shirts and showy cufflinks. This was the first trip to Europe for Philip Christopher Marlborough. He was distantly related to John Churchill, victor of *Blenheim, Ramilles, Oudenarde* and *Malplaquet.* He planned to return via London to see his ancestor's tomb in St. Paul's and Monk Parkhurst, a notorious ladies man, had offered to show him other interesting sights. Of the ladies, all but Virginia Blake wore pantsuits; Helen in electric blue with a canary yellow shirt; Susie in white, top to bottom and Carolyn Cook in gray with shoulder epaulets. Virginia wore a matronly black cocktail dress that revealed nothing and at fifty-three, she had little to reveal.

McDonough, a Belfast boy, son of an officer in the Indian Army had been prodded into religious service. He miraculously recovered from typhus, which he contracted in Kissanpore when he was seven. His mother, a zealous Roman Catholic, to thank the Lord for his recovery, propelled him in due course to Brasenose College, Oxford for an honor degree in 14th Century Asiatic History. Thence to a Dublin seminary. He showed a remarkable affinity for languages, particularly German. Assigned as a Parish priest in an agricultural hamlet in County Clare whose chief product was onions, he was unable to bear up under the pungent breaths of his penitents. He assigned this odious chore to his gardener. A scandal arose and he was defrocked one Friday afternoon. Next Monday morning he accepted a commission in the Royal Irish Fusiliers and drifted into counter-intelligence work where he made his mark as John C. Masterman's lieutenant. When peace came in 1945, he joined Omnium Oil Producers in London with the mandate to establish a worldwide intelligence network. Helen thought that he had hung the moon and that the theater suffered from his indifference to it. She was certain he would have made a grand Shakespearean actor. When they were all seated, O'Reith said, "Ladies and gentlemen, we are to be magnificently entertained by that sage of The Club of XX, Sir George P.

McDonough. We listen to his appreciation of the world economic picture from the perspective of oil operations."

McDonough, vanity personified, expected as his right to be summoned on these occasions. He would have been hurt had O'Reith not done so. His offbeat sense of humor tended toward predictions of gloom, doom and resurrection of the capable. McDonough did not suffer fools or spies, regarded the execution of the latter as a sacred duty. In his time had shot many. He stood in awe of Mother Nature, pointed out how capricious she was in bestowing oil deposits, considered it a 'bloody shame' that much of the oil was in The Middle East and Africa. As he spoke, he digressed. His sonorous, melancholy way of speaking made him seem a prophet. When foretelling an epic struggle, no glimmer of hope appeared until victory was at hand. He usually spoke for about seven minutes. When he finished, a pin could be heard to drop even though he had, in fact, said very little. But he was inspirational and lifted all spirits, particularly Helen's.

McDonough stood in awe of Carolyn Cook, as he did of Helen and all women of accomplishment, considering it something of a rarity. He had never married, had no children of record or rumor and was regarded as a 'confirmed bachelor'. O'Reith doubted that this was true. He believed McDonough to be an ascetic, asexual and for that matter, amoral, without carnal knowledge or interest. He was all intellect, militant in the pursuit of his goals, a fanatic of the stripe of "Chinese" Gordon, whom he admired and often quoted. O'Reith likened him to Sir Arthur Conan Doyle's Professor James Moriarty, the epitome of distilled evil. But he was far from perfect in his chosen field. Once, years ago, O'Reith had taken Cook, then a slip of a girl disguised as a young man to dinner at The Club of XX, where women were not allowed. McDonough, dining with his former chief, the legendary Sir John, had been deceived, as Sir John had not. Even today, he was still a bit put off by what he referred to as O'Reith's 'caper'. He recognized her superior geological intellect and it was for that reason he invested £7.5 million in the Casinghead Company.

So now he shuffled in his chair, maneuvering his ponderous backside into position so he could push his chair back and elevate his bulk up to six ramrod-straight feet and four inches. Keeping one eye on his prospective audience, as if worried they might desert him, he slowly made his way to stand beside O'Reith, who went down the table and sat next to Blake.

Jowls sagging, his eyes darting and intent, he focused on one then the other of his small gathering, giving Helen a few extra moments of fixation. O'Reith nudged Blake as if to say, "Watch this guy operate."

That he did. With his massive back to the map on the wall, he put his huge pink hands together showing his elegantly manicured nails. He began his orotund address, "Fellow directors and charming guests, I speak to you at this meeting of the executive group of the Casinghead Company and I am supremely confidant that this is but the first of many such meetings. As you all know, or as you have been taught, the world is thought to be round, or to be more precise, spherical. I suggest to you that it is flat, flat as a pan cake…" He stopped, surveyed his audience one by one and then continued "but only at the poles." He got a good laugh. He continued in a melodic voice that became lower and lower until it was nearly bass, his words rattling the windows and shaking the yellow pencils on the table, "Not only is the world flat at the poles, it is flat, or nearly so, in other places as well. Berlin. Dresden. Leipzig. Stalingrad. London. Tokyo. Nagasaki and Hiroshima. I could name others but you see my point. Why are these places flat?

They were bombed flat by politicians. Human greed, stupidity and, above all else, arrogance, are what make politicians. Cupidity and destruction, are their hallmarks. We capitalists try to reverse the maladies that our collective politicians inflict upon us. To go further, I must tell you that also flat, or more accurately, flat broke, are the governments that created all the destruction referred to previously. Those wonderful edifices of constitutional law that staged the grand pageant that we now refer to as World War II, far larger, more destructive of capital than their previous epic, World War I." He paused, winked wickedly at Helen and in an aside, said caustically, "movie material, my dear." He let these thoughts sink in and resumed. "The national treasuries of all participants in World War II are depleted. This concerns us. Why? Because it is only from the ranks of the capitalists that these treasuries can recover. From us! Make no mistake about it. Those politicians would happily stage a third production, a melancholy trilogy. The Grand Finale. The *Gotterdammerung.* They have not yet named this new crusade but weapons are being forged for it even as we sit here planning our little affair in Venezuela. Nuclear weapons. The third opera will be Armageddon! But not right away. These governments, having no money, build their new weapons with debt. Aye, sovereign debt. Debt to be repaid with paper or TNT. We can expect to live the rest of our lives, under a crushing debt burden. It will become obvious to all humanity with the flood of paper money that it produces. We, at this table, have dedicated to this highly speculative oil venture, sums in excess of $100 million, sweat-stained dollars. Within a decade, our $100 million will have withered to peanuts. Viewed in that light, our venture is not so risky and we should all be of good cheer. Mark my words, the huge flows of fiat money will astound and confound finance ministries the world over. Bretton Woods is fated. Good for perhaps a decade, perhaps. We will look back and wonder how this world has managed to function on a gold-exchange standard. There simply is not enough gold to support the paper. Looking further out, we will see government bonds with 10% coupons and crude oil selling for $5.00/bbl. Today's world has a foundation of jelly. It will shiver and quake and much of it will come down. We may think we are risking a great deal. Risking money that would keep us in clover for the rest of our days. But it is not so. Paper assets must be converted into tangible assets. Crude oil! What is fortune, anyway? I say it is a mere chimera, a mirage, like the will-o'-the-wisp. Now you see it, now you don't. If we do not act prudently, our fortunes will vanish into air like those of Wilhelm II and Nicholas II. We are not gamblers! Nor do we speculate. We invest. But we live in a world that consists of both. We are people of sound judgement who wish to protect our envied position. In truth, this is a charity where, at the end of the day, the money we have donated, is returned to us after having worked its magic in relieving the misery of the world's masses, whose numbers increase even faster than paper money. Yes! We give those poor souls oil for their lamps. We help them hold the devils of the night at bay. And their governments will pay us for it."

As O'Reith had predicted, one could hear a pin drop.

Chapter VIII

A Call for Dynamite

Lago Poniente No.16-1X was going to make a little gem of a well. Three hundred feet of Mirador above water and a ninety-foot section of high porosity, Santa Barbara sand. Electric logs compared favorably with those from wells further to the west. No point in testing either zone. Dually completed, this well would produce 10,000 bopd. So a string of seven-inch casing was run to bottom, cemented and both zones were perforated. Perforations were scraped clean, a packer was set just above the Mirador; mud in the casing was displaced with salt water and both zones were brought in. The shut-in well showed 3,900 psi on the Mirador tubing head gauge and 2,150 psi on the Santa Barbara casing-head side-outlet gauge. Just what Doctor O'Reith ordered.

Rig and tender were moved to the next platform. Now Lago Poniente No.16-2 was drilling ahead in the 11 ¾" hole. Over at Lago Poniente No. 9-1X, an intermediate string of 9 5/8" casing was cemented at 11,250 feet. They were drilling ahead with 15 pound mud in the 8 ½" hole. Three oil zones cased off, the Santa Barbara, the Mirador and the dangerous C-Series that had brought the Lago Poniente No.1 to grief over a decade ago. The concern now was stray gas stringers in the Cogollo formation. Some had a strong content of hydrogen sulfide gas. Bad news especially as pressure was high! Holland, ready to abandon everything below the 9 5/8" casing because of the danger, thought of sending a cable to O'Reith. He needed his agreement. But O'Reith in spite of the risk, wanted the Cretaceous tested. With heavy mud in the hole, they could suddenly 'lose circulation', a common problem in wells this deep. Should that happen, the fluid level would drop rapidly, allowing high-pressure gas to enter the well bore. That would be an emergency fraught with peril. Holland ordered blow-out drills every tour with a blowout preventer inspection each time the pipe was pulled for a bit change. There was little more he could do. Prescott and Morrow, experienced engineers, knew the danger as well as he. So he left them to the tasks at hand, told them to call him for help if needed. O'Reith had cabled Holland to order an eight-well platform from Brown and Root to be built at the *Terminales Maracaibo* yard in Las Moroches. It had to fit the new jack-up so the design drawings had to be sent to the yard in Biloxi, Mississippi. The jack-up would be under tow by 1 September to arrive Lake Maracaibo on 1 October. Holland had to order equipment for three rigs instead of two. Carolyn Cook engaged an Eastman Company directional driller for the seven deviated wells. Another cable from O'Reith upset both Cook and Holland. O'Reith was looking for a 4th rig, to be drilling no later than 1 Jan 57. A four rig drilling campaign would overwhelm them all. They were stretched too thin. They were no longer supported by the entire 11th floor of the Calitroleum Tower. For this operation, there was Holland, Cook, Prescott, Sally, *El Mocho* and Erma Morrow, Ted Schaeffer and Susie back in Los Angeles. O'Reith could be a hard taskmaster. But of course, Cook and Holland had become wealthy working for him. That made it easier to bear.

 A fringe benefit of O'Reith's demanding schedule was that it left no time for dalliance. Holland became a dutiful husband. Ines had no complaints. She could do without as long as he was doing without too.

 One afternoon, Tuffy Marks said, "Hunter, my drilling superintendents was at the Bello Monte the other night. He saw *Capitan* Cordero having a drink with that guy that used to work for Calitropical during the war. That Feathermerchant guy. He was part of Barney Donnegan's entourage. They called him *Redbird* in those days. O'Reith came down here from Los Angeles right after he got out of the army and ran him off. My superintendent said the two of 'em, Cordero and Feathermerchant, were in there most every night, heads together, talking about something. This morning, Feathermerchant came in to see me. Said he represented an American independent. He was looking for tools to drill a well in the lake. That mean anything to you?"

"No, but it might to Tarbutton. He's wired into the general's private affairs. Feathermerchant was attorney for the plaintiff in McLarssen vs. SOCAL. The general was torqued up about a scandal of a long time ago. I'll tell Tarbutton what you told me. That OK with you?"

"Sure, go ahead," Marks answered. "Anything for the general."

Later that evening, Holland said to Ines, "Baby, I have to check out a strange guy at the Bello Monte for the general. Back around one."

"You're not going without me. I'll ask Mandy to look in on the kids," Ines replied, miffed.

The Bello Monte was located on Avenida 12 several blocks north of the Hotel Detroit. Although Ines hung around El Techo Rojo during its most lurid era, she never had been a lady of the night. She mixed drinks for customers and helped Maxine keep the books. Holland met Ines in late 1945 when he was smuggling a load of dynamite from Maracaibo to Tibu, Colombia for a seismic crew. Barney Donnegan, Calitropical manager at the time, sent him along the *green road* the road of *a thousand trails* as it was called then, through the high Perijas. Ines then a waif of 16 made her living selling religious trinkets, love potions and amulets under an ebony tree. Until meeting her, Holland had played the field fast and loose with conquests in Australia, England and the U.S., mostly California starlets-in-waiting. Ines changed all that. He was crazy about her. She demanded total loyalty. Threatened to kill him if he strayed; had come after him with a knife on one or two occasions when she was suspicious. She kept a daunting array of dolls, potions, rosaries, philters and black candles to keep him in line. Now twenty-six, with three children, she still had a breath-taking figure. With an oval face, luminous black eyes, she looked a bit like Dorothy Lamour. Ines loved to dance. With a red carnation in her jet-black hair, she cavorted wickedly at parties, often-raised eyebrows at the various Calitroleum functions. She was one of the few women who didn't think O'Reith was the answer to every girl's prayer. She was fond of Maxine, consulted Mandy regularly on domestic matters and was a model mother. Her children were scrubbed clean, well-dressed, polite, good students and never giggled in Mass.

To be technically accurate, O'Reith met Ines before he did Maxine, about five minutes before. At Holland's party to celebrate the extinction of the fire on the lake, Ines, tipsy and blowing in Holland's ear opened the door for him. Later, Holland introduced him to Maxine. Slowly, over a period of months, Maxine, worked her way into O'Reith's heart. She could not complain about Helen who had staked her claim many years before. Maxine enjoyed what she had won, hoped that at some point in the future she might have him exclusively.

In those days, Maracaibo was a town of 250,000 people, not crowded as it is today. The narrow side streets were congested but the main avenues were broad. Traffic moved right along. Rainfall the same amount as in San Francisco, California, fell mostly in autumn and winter, the more agreeable months of the year. City drinking water was safe although many still boiled it routinely. DDT sprayers were out regularly. In town, mosquitoes were under control. The incidence of yellow fever and malaria had dropped precipitously. But there was still plenty of typhoid, often fatal, but far, far, from the epidemic proportions of earlier decades when Maracaibo was as dangerous a place to live as New Orleans had been in the 19th Century. In summer the temperature became oppressive in late afternoon especially in streets near the center of town where the buildings cut off the lake breezes. Swimming in the lake was risky. Liver flukes and amoebas teemed. Trouble for hapless gringos. Up north of town at Santa Fe beach on the *Bahia de Tablazo*, one could enjoy the sun and the surf with relative safety, keeping an eye out for barracudas. To travel east, other than by air, one had to take the ferry across the narrows to Lagunillas. The ferries were named Carabobo, Cabimas, Casigua, Coro and Caracas. Some old and rusty, some bright, new and glittering. They all traveled at the same speed, crossing in a half-hour. Long lines of vehicles for the ferry appeared along El Milagro each morning interfering with the early traffic. Little kids sold cigarettes for a *locha* a smoke among the waiting cars and trucks. Other urchins hawked hot coffee out of thermos jugs.

The two leading hotels were the Del Lago and the Detroit. A second tier of good but less luxurious hotels included the Granada, the Peters and the Chama. The Peters, downtown near the Stalingrad Bar, served Beck's beer, imported from Germany in aluminum cans made from shot down aircraft. The Stalingrad's claim to fame was its bar with refrigerated coils of copper in pits the size of a cup on a golf course green. Each patron could lower his stein of *Cerveza Sifon Regional*, a draft beer that many believed to be the best in the world into the icy pit and it would remain cold indefinitely.

The largest, most garish bordello was the Acropolis, which stood high on a hill accessible from *Avenida Los Haticos,* which ran parallel to the lake going south. Its huge neon sign, flashing blue and red, could be seen far out into the lake, reminding hard up rig hands that, when they came in on days off, they need not be hard up any longer. Its dance floor was immense with a 1940 Wurlitzer nickelodeon that featured music by Glenn Miller and the Modernaires, Tex Beneke and Marion Hutton providing vocals for such standards as *Kalamazoo, Chatanooga Choo Choo* and *Moonlight Serenade.* Most of the girls were from Colombia. A *piece* cost the equivalent of $20 U.S. and exotic extras, more. Less spectacular and perhaps more exclusive was the Bello Monte, where Ines and Holland were going. No neon sign out front. If you didn't know where it was, you couldn't find it. Other establishments known as AAA clubs with reference to the American system of classifying baseball teams were the Tibira-Tabara, the Bambu and the La Louisiane, the latter catering to blasé elderly gentlemen. El Techo Rojo, closed at this time, had been more sophisticated, a house of assignation where each patron brought his own girl. But towards the end of its reign, when Maxine ran it for Mandy, it was a dual-purpose establishment. Through one door you could bring your own girl. Through another door, girls were provided. It was a favorite haunt of the *Seguridad Nacional*. World War II was the heyday of El Techo Rojo. After Mandy sold it, it fell on hard times, becoming first a Chinese homosexual brothel and after that, a crib for broken down harlots. Now it was being remodeled and would soon reopen, catering to American, British, and Dutch oil men brought in by the oil boom. Located at the corner of *Calle 70* and *Avenida 11*, El Techo Rojo had a definitive red tile roof.

The majority of bordello customers were single men, many of them gringo rig hands. A few married men came too, bored or thrill seeking or perhaps dissatisfied in other ways. Plenty of venereal disease existed in the houses. Scandals, suicides and a few murders were attributed to this and more than once, cries went up to close the bordellos. Many a gringo left town in a straight jacket strapped to a stretcher. American women tended to consult expensive stateside psychiatrists when their husbands strayed. Venezuelan women made short work of unfaithful mates, stabbing them to death or turning them over to the tender mercies of the local witches. Here lately a few gringo women were turning to the witches also. Telephone numbers of the really effective ones, like Mandy Macabra, passed from table to table at bridge.

Four big oil company camps existed in Maracaibo. Creole Petroleum Company, the Jersey subsidiary had a grand camp near the Hotel Del Lago. Not far away, in Bella Vista was the Shell camp. Further north, right along the lake was the Mene Grande Camp. Gulf Oil Corporation of Pittsburgh, Pennsylvania managed Mene Grande, even though it was 50% owned by Shell. The fourth and smallest camp was that operated by Richmond Exploration Company, subsidiary of The Standard Oil Company of California. It was 2 kilometers south of town on the road to Machiques. Of the four camps, it was the closest to the Acropolis. During the development of Boscan Field, Rexco provided a substantial part of its business. Single oil company employees lived in bunkhouses similar to army BOQs. Families lived in one or two bedroom bungalows. All of the camps had at least one doctor, some several. Some were capable. Some were not. Many had been trained in American hospitals, knew how to treat so-called 'social' disease. Maracaibo was a seaport. Sailors from around the world gave their diseases to the girls along with their bolivares. Chinese clap was legion as was Cuban, Turkish, Mexican and one particularly difficult to cure known as Bullhead Clap. African Blueballs was an exotic ailment but nobody really had any idea of its origin. It was not gonorrhea or syphilis. The result of infection was that the testicles expanded grossly and turned eggplant purple. It was true that no one wanted to catch the Blueballs. Many of the girls in Maracaibo, especially those from Colombia, were quite fetching. When Mandy owned El Techo Rojo, she had been particular about her clientele. Definitely unwelcome were secret policemen of the *Seguridad Nacional*. But she wouldn't allow seafaring riff-raff in either. Her place was an exception.

On beautiful *Cinco de Julio,* which ran from *Grano de Oro* airport all the way across town to El Milagro Avenue, many fine shops showed their wares, Sears Roebuck for one and Sterns Jewelers for another. Driving in from the first time, a newcomer would be dazzled by the frangi-pangi, bougainvillea and mimosa trees carefully planted along the median. Where *Cinco de Julio* crossed *Bella Vista*, the *Todos* supermarket, a creation of the Rockefellers, provided American grocery products to the public. However most of the patrons were expatriate employees of Creole Petroleum Corporation. The grocery store had more customers than the bordellos, usually from a higher social strata. The Rockefellers also supported the Hospital Coromoto, a few blocks from where Maxine lived with O'Reith. Something close to 100% of all babies born to American mothers saw their first light of day there. Radio *Ondas del Lago* reported news on the hour and played Brazilian music in between.

Holland remembered Beauregard Feathermerchant from a decade back when he was on the staff of Barney Donnegan, the Calitropical wartime manager. But working in the oil fields, he saw little of him and immediately after the Lago Poniente No.1 fire had been put out, O'Reith fired Donnegan and his entourage. Although Holland never really got to know him, he had heard plenty about him. He began as a notary public with an Oklahoma City bank. He later became a division order specialist for a crooked oil promoter. He went to prison for fraud and other offenses of a sexual nature. Something was wrong with him. It had been so long since Holland had seen Feathermerchant, he didn't know if he could recognize him. Feathermerchant usually traveled with others in the entourage, one named Donny Bob Evans and another called Billy Joe (Barefoot) Swetnam. Feathermerchant was a redhead, and on that basis, Holland thought he could spot him. Ines, unenthusiastic about leaving her children in the middle of the night, made the best of it. They departed *El Escondite* at eleven p.m. in Mandy's Cadillac, Cansor behind the wheel. Down the hill, they turned into *Los Haticos*; crossed the *Punto España* bridge, took *Milagro* up to *Cinco de Julio*. At the Hotel Detroit, they turned north and found themselves in front of the Bello Monte just before midnight. The Bello Monte was a two-story brick building with a plaster façade and a corrugated tin roof, somewhat rusted by time and rain. Once it had evidently been home to a large family, common in those early decades of the 20th Century. In the dark of night there was nothing to distinguish it from houses on either side. Holland and Ines got out of the Cadillac and went up the front stoop. Holland pushed a bell button illuminated by a hole in the wall. They were admitted without ceremony, entering the bar, dimly lit and well populated with no vacant stools or tables. They walked down the hall past what had once been a kitchen, to a screen door that opened onto steps that descended into the garden. A naked fifty-watt bulb hung just over the steps. If one were sitting in the garden gloom, one could identify a person standing under the light, especially if that person tarried to get his bearings in the dark.

The garden was a mango orchard with Chinese lanterns strung between the trees. A dozen lawn tables were spaced out between the lanterns. The Chinese lanterns were colored like the tropical fruit that they represented; orange for mango, green for papaya, yellow for banana and brown for nispero. The lanterns provided just enough light for a person to find his way. A high stone wall, with shards of broken beer bottles on top enclosed the garden. Within the cone of light above the steps sat an enormously fat crone with a box of keys on a tiny table. The tagged keys corresponded to the small cells on the second story.

Holland and Ines found a table in the gloom near the crone with the keys. A waiter in white coat, black pants and bow tie took their drink order. He placed a thin votive candle in its gaudy tin candlestick at the center of the round table, lit it, and installed its chimney. Hardly had they been served their scotch and water when the screen door opened. *Capitan* Riva Marcelo Cordero followed by a man whose hair could possibly be red. Holland remembered the face with its expression of pleasant perplexity. It was Beauregard Feathermerchant all right. The pair entered the gloom of the garden, Holland's eyes following them. At a table near the alley wall, they got their drinks and their little candle. Immediately, two girls appeared on the steps, stood for a moment and confidently went to join the secret policeman and his friend. It seemed evident from the greetings exchanged that they were not strangers. Discreet laughter flowed from their table. Holland overheard Feathermerchant boast to the girls that he would soon have a grand oil concession on the lake. He could buy them anything. The foursome quickly concluded their arrangements and rose. The two girls stopped by the crone's table gave her some money and picked up the keys. Then the four of them went inside. Once they were gone, Holland put money for the drinks on their table. He escorted Ines through the house and into the tonneau of the waiting Cadillac. They were back at *El Escondite* by two a.m.

Next morning Holland sent a message to Tarbutton in Caracas advising him of what he and Ines had seen. Tarbutton asked him to meet the evening LAV Viscount from Maiquetia. When Tarbutton stepped off the plane, Holland saw he was not alone.

Tarbutton said, "Hunter, meet Philip Marlborough from Los Angeles. You can call him Duke. He did a few odd jobs for Harvey Halliday some years ago. Susie recommended him to General O'Reith. Marlborough will help us get the goods on *Capitan* Cordero and Beauregard Feathermerchant. What they're doing could affect our drilling campaign." The three men rode in the tonneau of the Cadillac to *El Escondite*.

Marlborough said, "We've been trying to tail Cordero but each evening around nine o'clock, he disappears into the Police Quartel. All we can do is stand watch through the night. He eludes us. Must be a secret way in and out. The Quartel, the Identification Bureau and Alien Registration office were located together behind the Customs House not far from the ferry landing in old Maracaibo.

Holland suggested, "Why not tail him back from the Bello Monte?"

"It's an idea," Marlborough agreed. "Can you set me up with an English-speaking driver and a taxi?"

"I'll do better than that," Holland said. "We'll use a Ford station wagon. Our radio operator is a fine driver, knows Maracaibo like the back of his hand, speaks good English and can deal with the cops at the *Alcabalas*. He'll pick you up at *El Escondite* tonight."

"Sounds like a winner," Marlborough replied.

At the inn, Ted and Mandy were at the door. Holland said, "Ted, Mandy, like for you to meet Duke Marlborough. He's down here to snoop around for the general." With Cansor watching for snakes, the three men and Mandy sat at the stone table near the dragon head fountain. Twilight, still warm with the heat of the day, was a dangerous time. The fer-de-lances were frisky at this hour, ready to 'act up' without provocation. Ted Schaeffer brought drinks, an ice bucket and mixers. He would have stayed if invited. But he was not and dejected, slunk back inside.

Mandy said, "Mr. Marlborough, you have a pleasant voice and a handsome face. You could pass for the movie star, Dick Powell."

"You flatter me, ma'am. You can call me 'Duke'. Most everyone does."

Holland said, "Wasn't it Duke Marlborough that creamed out the frogs back in the 18th Century?"

"That's the guy all right," Marlborough answered. "Duke is a common enough nickname. Lots of 'em around. Duke Snider is a third baseman for the Brooklyn Dodgers. There's a welterweight boxer that answers to that moniker but his real name is Joe Sykes. If he didn't have a glass chin and a glass eye, he would be a pretty fair city boy boxer. Unfortunately, he's not much. Just a pug. He only won one fight. He beat the ZigZag Kid, a Mexican boy from Calexico. The Kid was famous for being light on his feet, a true punch dodger. Bell had just sounded for the first round. The Kid tags Duke Sykes on his glass jaw. His glass eye pops out as he goes to his knees. The Kid thinks it is a real eyeball and faints. Duke gets back on his feet before the count runs out. The referee declares him the winner. Hell, he never touched the Kid."

"An interesting story," Mandy interjected, not impressed. "If you don't know sir, I am a witch," she continued. "and a good friend of the general. I do as he asks. I have contacts at various levels of authority in the police, the foreign office and the executive. Should you have difficulty getting an appointment in those departments, let me know. I will assist you."

"I thank you very kindly," Marlborough said. "I try to avoid those people to the extent that I can. Most government employees look with considerable disdain on a man of my profession. Should I need to see one, I would want to have an alias, some other identity, a more respectable profession…"

"I can help you with that as well, sir," Mandy said.

Marlborough was quite curious about the Schaeffers. He had tailed Ted Schaeffer on a number of occasions when Halliday wanted to know what he was doing. He knew that Schaeffer had been in and out of trouble on several occasions, remembered Halliday telling him about his exile. Marlborough knew quite a bit about O'Reith too. While he was away at war, Halliday had hired him to look into the background of both O'Reith and Helen.

Sensing his interest, Mandy said, "Oh, Mr. Marlborough, that is, Duke, I know you must be wondering about how Theodore and I got together. Well, sir, he had been a bit of a naughty boy. General O'Reith had put him out on the lake pushing tools. Isn't that such a quaint American expression? How sir, I ask, can one push a tool? Still I know what kind of work it was. Long hours and dangerous. Theodore would come into town on his days off and somehow we met. I can't remember the details now. We fell in love and married. So here we are now just as happy and contented as those two parrots caterwauling in the mango tree. Theodore used to help around the inn but now the general has launched his drilling campaign, he works at the shore base in San Francisco. He talks to the bit peddlers and the pipe-dope salesman and people like that."

"I'm sure he must be a credit to the company," Marlborough said, just to be polite.

"Well I'm going to leave you gentlemen to discuss your affairs, "Mandy said. Rest content that Cansor will keep you safe. If you need another round of drinks, push the button under the table. So it's toodle-oo." She rose and followed the path into the inn.

Tarbutton said, "She was being modest. Her social connections include the dictator. The general uses her for getting messages to him. She's pretty sharp at fixing up phony documents too, in case you need them. And the police stay clear of her. She's the only person that I know of who has thrown Cordero out of a bordello and made it stick. None of the local police will get anywhere near her."

"She seems like a helpful sort of lady all right," Marlborough reflected.

Holland asked, "You fellows have any idea of what's going on between Cordero and Feathermerchant?"

Marlborough said, "Feathermerchant works for Donald McLarssen, brother of the congressman that got tangled up with the O'Reiths, the one that was decapitated with a machete, or so it was alleged. McLarssen is an attorney. He does title work for Amerada Petroleum Corporation in the Williston Basin. Amerada is a big player there. You heard Feathermerchant bragging about a concession on the lake. Considering that Cordero has already horned in on the contract that covers Blocks 9 and 16, he's probably trying to figure out how to pry one or both of those blocks away from The Casinghead Company. As I understand things, until the contract is published in the *Gaceta Oficial*, it is not a completed deal. Amerada is a straight company. They would not touch a tainted concession. But should McLarssen be in position to offer them a clear shot at those two blocks, my guess is they would go for it. They know foreign operations. They've worked in Mexico."

"It pretty nearly has to be something like that," Tarbutton said. "The government has made clear there will be no more concessions after this round just completed."

Marlborough refilled his glass with scotch and added a few drops of water, said, "Try this theory out. Feathermerchant offers Cordero big bucks to cancel The Casinghead Company contract. Far more than he will get if our contract is published. Further suppose Cordero will sell Torres out, rat on him and have him liquidated. Suppose Cordero has his own guy in the Ministry of Hydrocarbons – which figures, because that's how he got a line on this deal in the first place. So the dictator shoots Torres, which suits Cordero just fine because he knows too much. The contract is canceled for alleged bribery in high places. Everybody working for The Casinghead Company is declared *persona no grata* and kicked out of the country. Cordero's guy in the ministry steers Blocks 9 and 16 into Feathermerchant's hot little hands. McLarssen has his revenge on the general and Cordero is suddenly a big man on campus. Not that I'm an expert on oil and gas law in Venezuela but I know how con men think. If I were Cordero, that's how I would be thinking. Alive, Torres is a liability for Cordero. Dead, he's an asset. Why else would Cordero be talking to Feathermerchant every night? You fellows have any idea how long they've known each other. Can they trust one another?"

Holland speculated. "Could be they got acquainted back in 1944. Donnegan was involved in some funny business involving Calitropical's Macoa Concession. Feathermerchant would have helped him. Cordero was just a low-grade officer then, a mole turd, as they say. I remember that Donnegan and staff stayed at the Granada Hotel, the best in town in those days. Cordero hung around there too. In fact I think he may have been the guy who showed Donnegan where El Techo Rojo was located. Donnegan for sure wouldn't have known. That was back when Cordero used to cadge pussy. Mandy got fed up with him. Cansor threw his ass out on the street."

Marlborough sighed, took a cigarette from a pack of Lucky Strikes, tamped it down on the stone table. He lit it with a Zippo that had an embossed gold logo saying 'LAPD'. He said, "Long lost crusaders reunited to throw the infidels out of the temple. We've got our work cut out for us."

All this reminds me that I need to ask Mandy right now about the general's appointment with the dictator," Tarbutton said. "Suddenly that's crucial." Twilight was deepening into purple. Cansor turned on the gaslights and the bug burners. Soon they could hear the *psst* of incinerated mosquitoes. Tarbutton pressed the button beneath the stone table. Presently, Mandy appeared.

He asked, "Mandy, did we ever get an answer to the general's request for audience with Colonel Jimenez?"

"*El Caudillo* advised us that a meeting was inconvenient. Perhaps at a later date."

"Do we know when to expect publication of the contract? Torres told me that all of the recent awards would be published at the same time. Didn't the general ask you to try to expedite publication?" Tarbutton continued.

"The general was concerned about publication. He worried about a *golpe de estado*. After Cordero forced himself on us, the general decided to let matters run their normal course. Safety for Torres was the reason."

Tarbutton nodded. He sort of remembered that. He said, "Mandy, let me take a look at the file. Maybe we'll find a clue as to how we should proceed"

She rose, went inside and returned with a leather briefcase, thin, with no handle and tied with a wide red ribbon. She removed the carbon of the letter O'Reith had sent to the dictator. Attached to it with a paper clip was the reply. She looked further into the briefcase and saw a business card, removed it and handed it to Tarbutton who asked, "Did you send a business card with the letter?"

"The general gave me two. I sent the one showing him as president of the company," Mandy said. "I didn't understand why he gave me that one you're looking at."

Tarbutton read aloud what was printed on the card. "General Clive Colin O'Reith. Commander. Eighth Far Eastern USAAF. Tinian Island. Why that vain devil! He really thought he was going out there."

Tarbutton explained the government ruse in the summer of 1945 to convince the Japanese that the Eighth Air Force was on its way to add to their misery. It never occurred to him that O'Reith would have business cards printed up. He was pensive. Marlborough sweetened his drink. Holland smoked slowly and thoughtfully. Mandy sat looking at him, tapping her teeth with a pencil. Finally Tarbutton slapped the top of the table decisively. He said, "Mandy, let's write a second letter to the dictator. Cite the previous request and his response. Add that circumstances have worsened. The matter is now urgent. Request an audience at the dictator's earliest convenience. I'll sign it for the general. We'll enclose this card. Colonel Marcos Perez Jimenez may disdain a conversation with the President of the Casinghead Company but he'll think twice before he turns down a request from a general officer in the Army of the United States."

"I'll have the letter typed," Mandy replied. After you sign it, Cansor can take it to the Hotel Del Lago to go into their pouch for the early morning LAV flight to Maiquetia. Colonel Jimenez will have it before noon."

They all nodded in agreement. Mandy said, "Would you gentlemen like to tidy up before dinner?" They dined on arepas, platanos, and roast pork with mint dressing and Zulia beer to wash it all down. Over coffee, Tarbutton said, "Here we are, middle of August, contract still not published. Torres told me the paperwork was complete. We await the dictator's approval. O'Reith knows that. I'll cable him that we're requesting an urgent audience. Whatever he's doing in Europe is not be as important as what he has to do here."

Holland said, "Get it ready. I'll send it tonight."

Tarbutton nodded. Marlborough and Holland, with Ines for company departed *El Escondite* around eleven thirty p.m. Holland and Ines alit at the hotel. Marlborough and driver proceeded to the Bello Monte. After cabling O'Reith in Paris, Holland, worried all day about the well, radioed Prescott at Lago Poniente 9-1X. He asked, "Alan, Everything OK?" They reported 16 pound mud this morning. We're still in gas cap country. I don't like that at all."

Prescott said, "Hunter we're drilling ahead OK. Every now and then we have to circulate out some sour gas. We have 3,000 feet of open hole beneath the 9 5/8" casing. That's too much. I'm nervous as a whore in church. What do you say we set a string of seven inch?"

"Alan, I'll have to clear that with Carolyn. She's not keen on finishing up in 5-½ inch hole. I'll catch her first thing in the morning. Can you hold on until then?"

"We'll watch her the rest of the night. The seven-inch is alongside on a barge. Things get to looking worse, we'll shut her in with the rams closed until we hear from you."

"Alan, if things get too bad, go ahead and run casing. I'll explain it to Carolyn."

"Okay babe, but we'll try to keep drilling."

Holland and Ines returned to *El Escondite*. They went straight to bed. Ines fell asleep immediately. Holland tossed and turned, preoccupied with troubles on the lake. After a fitful night, he was up at five o'clock and went immediately to San Francisco. Carolyn Cook arrived at the same time. She too was worried. The two of them discussed what to do while she made a pot of coffee. They were still considering their options when the radio came to life over the spasmodic static and background noise. It was Prescott. "San Francisco base, this is Lago Poniente No.9-1X, over."

Holland rushed to the radio, said nervously, "Go ahead Alan."

"Gee Hunter I'm glad to hear your voice. We're in a fandango fix for sure out here."

"Yeah?" Holland answered anxiously. "What's going on?"

"Took a strong kick after midnight. Circulated it out OK. Gassy as hell. Got back to drilling and took another kick about two o'clock this morning. A bad one this time. Damn near unloaded a hole full of 16-pound mud. We shut the preventers. Pressure on the Bradenhead flange went up to 5,400 psi."

"Fifty-four hundred pounds on a five thousand pound flange. Jesus Christ! Is that right?"

"Roger-dodger, babe," Prescott replied. "Pressure holding steady on the Bradenhead. No leaks. Seal ring okay. We mixed a pit of 16.5 pound mud, opened the rams and began pumping again. Pipe was stuck but we could circulate. Mene Grande had just released a Halliburton cementing barge from a well in the strip. I heard 'em talking on the radio and asked them to high tail it over here. They've been on location since five o'clock. We tied one pump in on the casing side and the other on the drill pipe. The rig equipment is rated to 5,000 psi. With Halliburton we can control anything up to 10,000 psi. If we don't pop loose somewhere."

"Is the well under control now?" Holland asked.

"No. We've mixed and pumped every sack of mud on location. Still reading 5,000 psi, trending up. I've ordered mud and cement but it has to come from Las Moroches. Should be here around noon. I don't know if we can hold on that long or not." Prescott's voice was edgy.

"Alan, I'm taking the speedboat right now. I'll see you in a half hour."

"Roger, Hunter, I'll be glad to see you, Hunter. We're in bad trouble."

Holland arrived to find Prescott on the cellar deck looking at the Bradenhead. He stood silently beside him for a moment, then asked, "Everything still the same as it was?"

Prescott shook his head. "About five minutes ago, the Bradenhead jumped. Went whu-u-mp! A hell of a snap like somebody had punched in the head of a drum. Pressure between the drill pipe and the casing fell but immediately began to build up on the surface casing. We opened it up. It blew gas and black water. Sour water. Then it died. We shut it in and the pressure is coming back up now. The 9 5/8" casing is parted."

"Jesus H. Christ!" Holland exclaimed.

"Had to part above the Santa Barbara, Hunter," Prescott said. "We brought cement back up that far. So we're in two around 4,000 feet."

Holland nodded, dismally agreeing with Prescott's assessment.

"Drill pipe is still stuck," Prescott added. "That means it is not parted."

"Well that's something," Holland said. "Four hours until we get mud and cement. We've got a good breeze. Think it'll hold up?"

"Last few days it has blown like that until around noon. Then it begins to peter out. By one-thirty or so, it will be dead calm."

Just then the driller, studying the pressure gauges on the Bradenhead side-openings, waved at the two engineers. He pointed to the surface casing gauge, now back up to 5,400 psi. Prescott put it on flare. When the gas reached the tip of the vent, the Loffco toolpusher up on the derrick floor torched it off with a shot from a Very pistol.

Prescott said to Holland, "That'll burn until another slug of black water comes up and kills it. I hope that isn't too soon. We've only got four rounds of ammunition left for the pistol."

"I brought a box of cartridges," Holland said to ease his mind. "But we've got a hell of a mess on our hands," he sighed audibly.

About ten o'clock, Prescott, looked down through the steel grill at the surface of the lake. He said, "Hunter, look at that that! I see a sea turtle upside down. He's big as an automobile tire. And look! There's a dead sting ray too!" They could see gas bubbling up around the conductor pipe and the platform legs.

"Jesus, Alan!" Holland exclaimed. "I can smell it!"

Now fountains of gas spurted up everywhere. The faint odor of rotten eggs was everywhere. Dead and dying fish floated up. Big ones. Little ones. Another turtle. Eels. Sting rays. They drifted with the current northward toward the mouth of the lake. Suddenly the flare went out. A stream of black, sulfur water burst out of the flare line. Gusting. Then the gas came again. The toolpusher once more torched it off.

"Hunter if that breeze dies, that gas will come up here. We'll be dead ducks," Prescott muttered.

Holland, ashen faced, nodded, as he looked at his wristwatch. The Loffco toolpusher descended the ladder to the cellar deck. "What do you fellers think?" he asked, just as worried as they were.

"I think we had better abandon the platform and the tender," Holland said. "If we wait until the wind dies, we won't make it."

"We've got two speedboats," the toolpusher said.

"We've got a barge-load of seven inch casing tied up to the tender," Prescott added.

"And the Halliburton cementing barge," Holland added. "Put all non-essential personnel into the speedboats. If the wind drops they can take off. I don't see how the rest of us can walk away from it. I'd rather stay. Pray for mud and cement to arrive before the breeze dies…"

That's what they did. For over three hours it was gas, then water, then gas again. The faltering breeze still kept the gas away from the platform. The lake was white with dying sea creatures. Gas bubbled up everywhere. The speedboats were loaded with the cooks and off-duty crews, engines idling, ready to depart at a moment's notice. Holland, Prescott and the Loffco toolpusher remained on the cellar deck. The driller kept his eyes glued to the gauges on the Bradenhead, alert for any change in pressure. Holland scanned the horizon in the direction of Las Moroches. They were down to four shells remaining for the Very pistol. When they were gone, the game would be over. Then, far on the horizon, Holland caught a glimpse of something. He pointed to it. "See that?" he asked. "That could be our mud and cement."

And it was. A half-hour later, the new arrival was tied up to the Halliburton cementing barge. Roughnecks and roustabouts scrambled to hook up the cementing lines. Even as they scurried, the seal ring between the Bradenhead and the preventers cracked. A wispy jet of sour gas and black mist began to blow across the cellar deck. The driller unsteadily jumped back. Holland looked grimly at Prescott, signaled to the cementers to make haste, said, "Alan if we're not mixing cement within the next couple of minutes, this baby is a gone gosling. And we'll be gone with it." The smell of rotten eggs was overwhelming. A white and gray heron with a black crest crash-landed on the cellar deck, twitched, stiffened and died with his talons up. Prescott pointed down to the water surface. Other dead herons had joined the fish, turtles, eels and skates, all floating belly up. The roustabouts were divided into two crews; one cutting sacks of Quikset construction cement for the surface casing, the other Sloset cement for the drill pipe. Now they were ready. The toolpusher gave the signal. Cement dust flew downwind. The two Halliburton cementers, faces covered with red bandannas, steadily mixed and pumped. Their hair was white with cement. It caked on their bandannas. Their eyes darted from the mixing hoppers to the water in the tanks to the gauges on the manifold above them. Holland and Prescott focused on the gas hissing out of the Bradenhead flange.

The casing side took over two thousand sacks of cement before the first flicker on the gauge showed pressure was beginning to build. The leak at the seal ring stopped. A hundred pounds. Two hundred. Then five hundred. A thousand. The cementers pumped relentlessly. The roustabouts, in a cloud of cement dust, worked feverishly. With almost three thousand sacks of construction cement pumped, the casing pressure was rising rapidly now, the needle on the gauge moving steadily to the right. At 3,000 psi, the Halliburton cementer shifted to low gear. His engines lugged down and began to growl. At 3,500 psi the engines were grinding in grandma. They could pump no more. The casing side was cemented up. Gas ceased to bubble up from the lake bottom. Dead fishes floated away.

They pumped a thousand sacks into the drill pipe before getting back-pressure. But then it built up rapidly. With 1,500 sacks of Sloset cement pumped, the gauge stood at 3,500 psi. The well was dead, under control.

Holland looked at Prescott, put his arm around him. The toolpusher joined them in embrace. They were all shaking, faces pale.

* * *

It was four o'clock in the afternoon, dead calm and about 90 degrees Fahrenheit on the shady cellar deck. Prescott asked, "What do you suppose the general will have to say about this disaster?"

Holland said quietly, "He won't say a god damned thing, Alan. He'll just shrug. That's all he ever does. But he would have said plenty if we'd walked away from it. The *voice* and the *stare* and lots of other things, none of them printable. There's a bottle of scotch in the knowledge box upstairs. You fellows want a shot?"

When Halliburton was rigged down, and the barges were on their way back to Maracaibo, Holland and Prescott began to feel better. The scotch was low in the bottle. The two weary engineers slowly crossed the widow-maker down to the tender. They removed their dust-saturated khakis and showered. When he was freshly dressed, Prescott radioed for a derrick barge to move the rig and dynamiters to shoot the platform legs off. The Lago Poniente No.9-2 platform was already set. They could be drilling in a week. Holland bade Prescott goodbye, took the speed-boat to the dock, dog tired, but horny as a goat, ready for some fun with Ines.

Chapter IX

▼

Dereliction of Duty

FOR C.C. O'REITH
 THE CASINGHEAD COMPANY
 PARIS
 15 AUG 1956
 REFERENCE LAGO PONIENTE NO. 9-1X
 REGRET TO ADVISE THAT WE LOST CONTROL OF THIS WELL DURING THE NIGHT OF 14-15 AUGUST. AFTER SUCCESSFULLY CIRCULATING OUT TWO STRONG GAS KICKS, THE THIRD UNLOADED THE DRILL PIPE X 9 5/8" CASING. CLOSED PIPE RAMS. IMMEDIATELY SAW 5,400 PSI ON BRADENHEAD GAUGE, GREATER THAN RATED WORKING PRESSURE. WELL BLOWING HIGH PRESSURE SOUR GAS AND BLACK WATER. PUT CASING SIDE ON FLARE TO RELIEVE PRESSURE AND OPENED PIPE RAMS TO FIND DRILL PIPE STUCK ON BOTTOM. NINE AND FIVE-EIGHTS INCH CASING PARTED AT TEN A.M. PRESSURE ON SURFACE CASING GAUGE JUMPED TO 5,400 PSI. GAS BEGAN BUBBLING UP FROM LAKE BOTTOM AROUND PLATFORM. FORTUNATELY STIFF MORNING BREEZE KEPT GAS DOWN-WIND. SEAL RING BETWEEN BRADENHEAD FLANGE AND BOP STACK FAILED AT ONE–THIRTY P.M. WITH SOUR GAS AND

BLACK WATER BLOWING ACROSS CELLAR DECK. HALLIBURTON CEMENTERS BEGAN PUMPING AT ONE-FORTY-FIVE. KILLED CASING WITH 3,000 SACKS OF QUIKSET CEMENT. KILLED DRILL PIPE WITH 1,500 SACKS SLOSET CEMENT. FINAL SQUEEZE PRESSURE BOTH SIDES WAS 3,500 PSI. RELEASED BARGE-MOUNTED CEMENTING EQUIPMENT TO MAKE ROOM FOR DERRICK BARGE EXPECTED ON LOCATION BY MIDNIGHT. PLAN FIRST LIFT AT DAYBREAK MOVING RIG AND TENDER TO LAGO PONIENTE 9-2.

DYNAMITERS ARRIVE TOMORROW AFTERNOON TO SHOOT OFF PLATFORM LEGS AND CUT PIPE STRINGS AT MUD LINE. WILL RETURN SHOTOFF PLATFORM TO LAS MOROCHES FOR LEG LENGTHENING. MINISTRY OF HYDROCARBONS INSPECTOR WILL WITNESS BOTTOM CLEARING.

REGARDS

HOLLAND

A second cable said that Marlborough had seen Cordero and Feathermerchant together at the Bello Monte. Torres joined them. Later Cordero returned to the police Quartel. Marlborough tailed Torres to the Detroit Hotel and the next morning, from there to the airport.

O'Reith and Helen were sitting on her terrace watching the sail boats enter and leave *La Condomine*. Little Helen Simpson sat on her father's lap. He was reading to her the story of Asterix and the dolmens. Like children everywhere, she was picking up French fast. In a few weeks she could read it herself. Helen mixed his martini and as he took it, he passed to her the cable from Holland. "What do you think of *that* fiasco, baby?"

She read the message carefully. While no expert on oil well emergencies, her husband had been involved in so many of them and she had worried so often about his safety that she had no trouble grasping the dire implications. "He would have mentioned if anyone were hurt wouldn't he? Sally and Ines must have bitten their fingernails to the quick."

"Yes, he would have advised me if there had been casualties," O'Reith confirmed. "Except for a million bucks or so down the drain, we were as lucky as a dog with two dicks. We lost seven men when Lago Poniente No.1 caught fire, including two gringos."

"Would it have been different had you been there?" Helen asked.

"No. Truth is, I contributed to the calamity. I wanted to test the Cretaceous. I knew there was a risk. But I didn't expect sour gas. If they had not lost the 9 5/8" casing, they would have saved her."

"Why did the casing part?"

"A little understood phenomenon known as hydrogen sulfide embrittlement. Steels that have a high carbon content are susceptible. That's why the seal ring at the Bradenhead failed too. They're manufactured to be in tension. It snapped from the sour gas invasion. They were mere minutes away from having to abandon the location. Had they done so, it would have caught fire and, no doubt, still be burning. So we came out OK, all things considered. Guys like Holland and Prescott are rarities. It takes an iron will…"

"Sometimes I wish my little disaster could end abruptly," Helen said ruefully.

"It can. Shut it down and walk out with your cheque book."

"Not yet. I may save it. Alice Ridley says everything will be all right. I trust her."

O'Reith said, "Well, make sure she's using the star charts for 1956."

Next week O'Reith was back in Paris with Maxine. A message from Tarbutton said:

FOR CLIVE COLIN O'REITH
THE CASINGHEAD COMPANY
PARIS
23 AUG 1956

EL CAUDILLO WILL BE PLEASED TO GRANT YOU AUDIENCE ON 15 SEPTEMBER 1956 AT HIS OFFICE ON THE ISLA DE ORCHILLA. HE HAS ASKED MANDY TO COME ALONG. PLAN TO ARRIVE CARACAS TWO DAYS BEFORE MEETING. YOU MUST REPORT TO THE MILITARY AIRPORT LA CARLOTA AT EIGHT O'CLOCK IN THE MORNING FOR THE DC-3 FLIGHT TO THE ISLAND. NO FURTHER WORD ON PUBLICATION OF CONTRACT. DONNEGAN AND FEATHERMERCHANT ARE BOTH IN MARACAIBO NOW. WE ARE KEEPING THEM UNDER SURVEILLANCE AND TORRES IS OKAY. ALL OF US NERVOUS IN REGARD TO SUDDEN APPEARANCE OF DONNEGAN ALL THE MORE SO IN VIEW EXTREMELY NEGATIVE REPORT BY HYDROCARBONS INSPECTOR WITH REGARD TO LAGO PONIENTE NO.9-1X INCIDENT.

REGARDS

TARBUTTON

O'Reith recognized immediately that Tarbutton feared the negative report could influence the government to cancel the contract and give it to Donnegan. O'Reith thought that unlikely but he was just as concerned. He needed to go to Venezuela right now. He asked Maxine to begin packing.

She said, "Clive, we're settled in. Monique's school starts next week. She wants to be here with her little friends. Will it distress you if we stay? When your affairs are in order, we'll be here waiting for you."

He had to accept her logic. Once in Venezuela it would be back and forth between Caracas and Maracaibo until they had their political problems resolved. Reluctantly he made plans to travel alone. Sometimes he fell into reverie. How nice it would be if he were back in the Calitroleum Tower, in his grand penthouse office, with a view of the beautiful Pacific and all of Los Angeles. He would be reading reports from his far flung operations; making plans to put some distant oil field on production; preparing a speech for The American Petroleum

Institute. He would have aides at his beck and call. Sharon Mills just down the hall to fix his face. Susie in the outer office, his chauffeur standing by, reading the sports section of the *Los Angeles Times.* Best of all, Vince Blake waiting to join him for a long, liquid lunch at Lucey's or the Catalina Club. Helen at home in Holmby Hills with her nose in a cowboy movie script longing for a trip to Monument Valley. He could play golf at the Limejuicer Club on five minutes notice. In his mind's eye, he could see his ball dropping far down the orange tree-lined fairway on the par five hole number seven. Everything and everybody under total absolute control. He sighed. For some reason that he could not understand, it disturbed him that Helen and Maxine were both on the same continent, in the same country for all practical purposes. Not that he expected they would ever meet. Paris was at some remove from Monte Carlo. Their paths were unlikely to cross. No, it wasn't that. And after all, he had once intended to install Maxine in San Francisco; would have, if not for Blake's sensitivities. Blake, down deep inside, even with the roving eyes of middle age, still thought there was something morally wrong about keeping two women. O'Reith dismissed that kind of thinking as heresy but would agree that, as one got older, a declining libido made keeping two women increasingly impractical, especially with children involved. Too late to ponder that. He had an oil field to put on production.

He was, forty-nine years old, risking his fortune, and that of others, maybe even risking his life, on a really wild ride. He had conned Tarbutton into taking responsibilities that would have burdened a man half his age. And those two McLarssens, more dangerous than tropical snakes, out there plotting with Donnegan and Feathermerchant, sly fuglemen if ever he knew any, to ruin him. Here he was, laying behind the log in Paris, eating caviar, drinking champagne, and fooling around with the baby's mother. Tarrying. Letting things happen. Well, that had to change. Fast.

That night, sleeping next to Maxine, he flew to Berlin again. The sky was dark, full of rain clouds and smoke. The nose of the B-17 bucked in the turbulence. Flashes of cannon fire up ahead, over the target. He stood behind the two pilots, hands on the back of the bucket seats, bracing as the aircraft pitched and heaved. The pilots stared straight ahead, mindless of the threatening flak. He turned and twisted trying to get a look at their faces but in vain… They ignored him, gazed steadily ahead like hypnotized men. Then suddenly he was awake, cold and damp, feeling doomed. Maxine stirred. She took his hand, pulled him in close, caressed his backside. He took her into his arms, felt her warm smooth body. After he held her closely for some minutes, he was all right. But he didn't go back to sleep and rose with the dawn, listening to the birds singing in the cherry trees in the garden below. Once up, he showered, shaved and dressed, had a good breakfast with a steaming cup of strong, black coffee, his spirits returning. Maxine still slept. He rode the elevator down to the street, took a long constitutional, first around the Madeleine, then up and down *Boulevard Malesherbes*. He returned to a stack of papers demanding attention. When he was finished, an hour later, he climbed the spiral staircase, looked in on Maxine. She was still sleeping. He went down to the company offices. LeBel, just arrived, wanted to discuss the 'incident'. Should they call a directors meeting or merely send each one a copy of Holland's cable. They decided on the latter. The Casinghead Company was not Calitroleum Oil Corporation. No witchhunts. No search for a scapegoat.

The appointed day for his departure arrived. Maxine said goodbye. He took a TWA Constellation to Idlewild, a National Viscount to Miami and an Avensa Convair 440 to Maiquetia. Tarbutton met the flight and briefed him during the ride to Caracas. Checked in at the Tamanaco Hotel, he was whipped down. Big day tomorrow. Meetings with Torres, Tarbutton and Ethering. Mandy coming in from Maracaibo. Getting ready to go to Orchid Island.

Early at the office, he reviewed the incoming cable file. Tarbutton and Ethering arrived together. Stanley Forbes Ethering was the kind of fellow that one could never recall, next morning, if he had been to the party or not. Quiet and soft-spoken, rather shy, friendly, but in a reserved way, he was one of the small men of the world, at least vertically. Horizontally, he was wider than average, egg-shaped, bulbous, with an affable, round, pie-shaped face. His smile was more or less permanent reflecting an open personality. He usually wore a brown suit. His hair and eyes were also brown, so there was little contrast in his appearance. When he walked, he waddled like a duck. He and O'Reith had been friends since the early 1930s and always sought each other out at API conventions. Their senses of humor ran on parallel tracks. O'Reith liked to get him going with a steady stream of humorous material that made him chuckle more or less continuously, like a tea kettle bubbling on a slow fire. But today was no occasion for frivolity. The jack-up rig was on the water, scheduled to arrive on Lake Maracaibo on or about 5 October. The eight well platform was promised for a tow-out on 20 September. Casing, tubing and well heads were arriving from Los Angeles and Houston weekly.

The letter from the Hydrocarbons Minister was scathing. "Negligence. Gross dereliction of duty. Ineptitude. Carelessness. Reckless disregard for purity of the waters of Lake Maracaibo. Wanton destruction of wildlife. Flagrant disregard for human safety. Failure to evacuate personnel. Etc. Etc." O'Reith smiled at Tarbutton and Ethering, muttered in a low voice, "everything but mopery on the high seas..."

"They didn't think of it," Tarbutton said, injecting humor into a morose situation.

O'Reith read the concluding sentence aloud, "leaves us no choice but to recommend to the government that the Casinghead Company concession be canceled, assets sequestered and that all operations on Lake Maracaibo be suspended pending final judgement."

"Where does that leave us?" O'Reith asked, more to himself than to the others.

Tarbutton was silent. Ethering said, "I'll rewrite that letter. Defang it. Torres can take it in to the minister. Swap it for this condemnatory screed."

O'Reith drummed the desktop with his fingers, as he often did when perplexed. Then he got up and went to the windows to look up at the construction activity surrounding the new Hotel Humboldt on top of Mount Avila. Clouds were gathering. Soon the view would be gone. O'Reith said, "I can smooth this out when I see the colonel tomorrow. But I would like for the Ministry to soften the language of this letter. Let's call Torres. Stan, give it a quick rewrite. Make it a compliment for saving the rig. When I walk in on the dictator, I don't want to have to explain the 'incident.'"

Tarbutton telephoned. Asked the switchboard girl to put him through. The girl told him Señor Torres was engaged, couldn't come to the telephone. Tarbutton replied that he, Ethering and O'Reith were coming immediately, urgently desired a meeting with the minister. In traffic, it was a half hour taxi ride to the office of the Ministry in Santa Capilla. Ethering, seated between O'Reith and Tarbutton, rewrote the letter on a portable typewriter in his lap. Torres received them with reserve, lips tight, no color in his face, a cigarette in his fingers.

O'Reith said, "Rojo, we absolutely have to see the minister. We cannot accept the condemnation of his letter. Stan rewrote it. We must resolve this. After all, no lives were lost, not counting the fish. The equipment was not damaged. Had we abandoned the location a disaster would have occurred. The well would still be out of control, burning perhaps. Can you tell him that?"

Torres sighed, carefully flicked an ash into his tray, overflowing with stubs. With no enthusiasm he said, "Of course I can go to him. He is just down the hall. I knock on his door and his secretary lets me enter. It is my right to see him. But then what? He is furious. He will see me and say that he cannot recall or rewrite the letter. The minister is a scholar, and a poet, he will recite the Rubaiyat, 'the moving finger having writ...'" He will not change his mind. It is useless. But if you insist..."

O'Reith said, "Rojo you know there is more to this than meets the eye. This is not the first 'incident' on Lake Maracaibo. It isn't even the hundredth. What's going on here? Will he actually send a copy of it to the dictator? Will he really seek a cancellation of the contract?"

Torres made a long face, his lips compressed, his eyes sad. He took some while to reply. Then he said, "I don't know. As of today no action has been taken. Whatever the minister sends, I will see it. Still, I expect him to do it. In fact I expect to be dismissed, perhaps arrested. If not today, tomorrow. I no longer enjoy his confidence. I am in a bad position. We are all in a bad position."

O'Reith had the distinct impression that Torres was playing to an unseen audience. He wrote him a note suggesting a midnight meeting at the usual place. Torres looked at it nodded his assent. O'Reith said in a loud voice full of false confidence, "Señor Torres, we leave matters in your capable hands. Please do your best for us."

Torres smiled, nodded and showed them out.

It was eleven forty-five p.m. and O'Reith dressed in a tuxedo with a Luger in a shoulder holster, waited nervously in the lobby of the Tamanaco. Tarbutton was five minutes late, unusual for him, a model of punctuality. Another two minutes elapsed. O'Reith was just getting out of his chair to call him at home when a bellhop approached. He said, "Señor O'Reith, *una llamada telefonica.*" O'Reith followed the boy to a booth and lifted the receiver. It was Marjorie Tarbutton, frantic.

"Yeah Marjorie," he said.

"Clive, they've taken Hardy! She began crying, unable to maintain her self-control. He listened to her sob until she regained her poise. "Clive, two policemen ... They handcuffed him. They just took him away..." Her voice failed her again. She resumed her sobbing.

"How long ago, Marjorie," O'Reith asked, speaking as calmly as he could.

"Just now. Clive, they handcuffed him at gun point…" Her voice faded. She began softly crying again.

"Marjorie, get a grip on yourself. This is all part of some kind of morality play. I'm meeting with Rojo Torres in a matter of minutes. He'll help us. Hardy will be home within the hour. Sit by the telephone. Call the Etherings. See that they are okay. You'll hear from me quickly."

He returned to his room, opened his suitcase, removed a silencer for the Luger, slipped it in his pants pocket. Then he took the elevator to the lobby, glanced around, saw nobody suspicious. He went through the revolving door out into the night, muttering to himself. As he walked to *La Casualidad*, he made sure the Luger was loose in its holster. It would not be Torres whom he would face. And sure enough, it was *Capitan Riva Marcelo Cordero* who greeted him with an *embrazo* and a friendly smile. "It's been quite some long while since our last chat, my dear General O'Reith. How have you been keeping?" Mockery dripped from his unctuous tongue. "I can offer you a Johnny Walker Black. Ah but now I remember, you're a gin man. A martini then?"

O'Reith sat facing the corpulent secret policeman who was, at this hour somewhat disheveled, as if he had been smooching with an uncooperative woman. O'Reith said nothing, glared at him, as if undecided what to do. The waiter came to take their drinks order. O'Reith gave him his hardest stare, fired out at him in rapid fire Spanish, "*Telefono, Señor. Ensigida!*"

The waiter, stone faced, disappeared. Cordero opened his mouth to speak. O'Reith snapped the Luger in his face before he could utter a word. Cordero put his pudgy hands on the table where O'Reith could see them. He clamped his mouth shut, shaken. His eyes focused on the threaded muzzle of the Luger. It had no front sight. Policemen, even dumb ones, knew what that meant. O'Reith removed the silencer from his pocket. As he screwed it on the end of the Luger's barrel, he said,

"Cordero, keep your hands right where they are. When that boy brings the telephone, you can use them to call your thugs. General Tarbutton must be delivered to his wife. When that's done, we can talk."

Cordero's carotid arteries were working overtime. He said, "General O'Reith, sir, you act hastily and without thinking. Your General Tarbutton is under arrest for bribing a public official. In Venezuela, unlike in the United States, such activity is illegal. I might add that pointing a firearm at a Venezuelan officer of the law in discharge of his official duties is also illegal."

The boy knocked on the door, O'Reith put the Luger on the table and covered it with his homburg, said, "*Venga!*"

The boy came in, plugged the phone into the wall and retreated. O'Reith looked at the telephone, pushed it over to Cordero. He made an upward motion with his jaw. He said, "If Tarbutton is not home with his wife in ten minutes, you get it in the eye." Cordero's call went right through. He gave orders and was about to hang up when O'Reith interrupted, "Tell your thugs to call from Tarbutton's phone when they've delivered him."

Cordero did, hung up and put his fat hands together. He bowed to O'Reith. He said, "I know that your wife is an actress. Did she teach you the theatrics?"

The secret police Quartel was near the hippodrome. If that was where they had taken Tarbutton, he could be home in half an hour. Traffic would be light. Cordero continued, "You could put the pistol away. We could chat for a bit. Time is valuable, even at this late hour. It will take a bit longer than ten minutes."

"Yeah, Cordero, you're right," O'Reith agreed, unscrewing the silencer and returning it to his pocket. He holstered the Luger. "You're courting disaster, my friend. I went through a war with Tarbutton. He and I are as close together as the eyes on a gnat. You understand that?" Then he dialed Marjorie and told her Hardy was on his way home. "Now, Captain Cordero, he asked, "What are we to talk about?"

Color slowly returned to Cordero's face. His neck arteries were not throbbing so noticeably. He combed his hair and began, "As you are well aware, sir, the Minister of Hydrocarbons is upset about what happened to your oil well on the lake. It is certain that he will demand cancellation of the Casinghead Company concession. But he and I are old friends, from childhood. He is a reasonable man under certain circumstances. On the face of it, your company is stretched far, far too thin. You should have double the staff that you have in the country. Creole Petroleum Corporation would put a dozen men on that project. You have twice as much concession as people to attend it. We could recommend to the minister that in return for your cession of Block 9, you could continue on Block 16. With that agreement, the contract could be published immediately."

"And the government and all of its agents would return to the company all funds allocated to Block 9 and duly paid out?"

"Well sir, I don't know about that," Cordero said, as if he viewed O'Reith's suggestion as an extreme request. "That is spilt milk, as they say. But all charges against General Tarbutton would be dropped, a considerable concession by the government."

"Where's Torres?" O'Reith demanded to know in the same tone of voice he'd used on the waiter.

Cordero shrugged, muttered, "Silly question. He is under detention. Where else? He too is charged with corruption. We may charge him with treason too. It doesn't matter. I have telegraphed the executive for authority to have him shot for the dirty dog that he is."

"Where is he?" O'Reith asked again.

Cordero was positively beaming as he said, "Well beyond your reach, dear General O'Reith. I cannot produce him at pistol point. Even as we speak he is on a military plane headed for *la Isla de Orchila*. He will be shot upon arrival and buried in a military cemetery in the early morning light – with full honors, as is the custom in cases of this nature."

The telephone rang insistently. Cordero picked up the receiver. He listened, then spoke for a moment and handed it to O'Reith. It was Tarbutton. He said, "Clive?"

"Yeah Hardy, you all right?"

"Unstrung but all right."

"Ethering okay?"

"Yeah. They left him out of it."

"Hardy, I'm negotiating with Cordero. Should be finished in a bit. Take a hot shower and get a night of sleep. I'll cool off on the walk back to the hotel. See you in the office in the morning. Did our friend from Maracaibo make it in?"

"Arrived about six o'clock. In the Hotel Avila."

O'Reith hung up. He looked at Cordero. He said, "*Capitan* Cordero, our company has a board of directors. For us to do as you suggest, we'd have to have a meeting of the minds. Takes a couple of days, maybe three. Depends on how fast we can exchange cables."

"Very well, my dear general. Time is not of the essence. This matter can be delayed until you have the authority to speak for your board."

"Before I contact them, I want to know that you have rescinded the order to have Torres shot. It would be difficult for me to sign any kind of agreement with you if he were in his grave."

Cordero sighed, said, "Well sir, I'll do my best. I'll send a wire to the island immediately. I just hope we're in time. Meanwhile, General Tarbutton still faces the charges. I've released him into your custody as a personal favor. You'll have to post bond in the morning at the Quartel. Five million bolivares."

"We don't have that kind of money in the country. I'll sign for it. Take several days to get the money down here."

"Of course, after all, it is a mere formality," Cordero said generously. "When you come, bring your passport. You'll have to leave it with us until this matter is cleared up. You understand that. Regulations are to be obeyed. Actually you should turn in that weapon too. We'll keep it until you are deported if, it comes to that."

"The Luger is a war souvenir. I will not turn it in. You needn't worry. I'm not going to shoot you unless you really act up," O'Reith answered. "So it is goodnight. How do I get in touch with you when I have an answer from my directors?"

Cordero smiled, "Just call the ministry. Ask for Torres. When the girl says he's not available, give her the message. Tell her it concerns Block 9. Oh yes, my dear general, treat yourself to a good night of sleep. No need to rise early. Your appointment with the executive has been canceled. You'll find an official message to that effect under your office door in the morning. You'll also get a free copy of the *Gaceta Oficial* in the morning. You'll find it interesting reading. Goodnight sir." Cordero wasn't laughing. But he looked like he had it on his mind.

Caracas was always pleasantly cool in the early hours of the morning, even in September, but tonight, walking unhappily back to the hotel, O'Reith felt the oppressive, tropical night air. It was hazy. He could not see Mount Avila, at least not the top of it. The construction lights of the Hotel Humboldt were a blur. He pondered the events of the evening. The revelation that his appointment with the dictator had been canceled hit him in the pit of the stomach. If Cordero was that powerful, he was in real trouble. He had counted on seeing Jimenez and getting things worked out. Now he was stumped. And what would he see in the gazette tomorrow? No doubt the publication of all the other contracts. San Jacinto. Superior. Sun. Shell. Creole. Mene Grande. Phillips. But not the Casinghead Company. Cordero had forced him into the position of consulting the other directors. Although baffled, they would concur. No one of them would object because they would have no alternate solution. What had been a stall for time was now a cold reality. He had hoped, after the meeting with Jimenez tomorrow, to be rid of Cordero. It was not to be. Cordero had trumped the ace he thought he had up his sleeve.

A glum foursome sat around the conference table next morning in the office in *Altagracia*. As expected the gazette contained the notices of seven contract awards. Mandy and Ethering listened quietly as O'Reith and Tarbutton related the events of last evening. O'Reith said, "I was floored to learn that Cordero even knew of our meeting with the colonel. That he could get it canceled knocked me to my knees. Now what?" he asked.

Tarbutton was silent, recording the minutes of the meeting, as if they mattered anymore. Ethering was blank. He clearly had no idea how to proceed. But Mandy was thinking. O'Reith saw it in her face. After several minutes, she spoke. Looking at first one, then the other of the trio of men, she began. "The dictator, the Executive as they all like to call him, has an appointments secretary. A request such as ours would not come directly to his desk. In fact he would not see it at all. His secretary would advise him, perhaps show him the general's card. The dictator would agree or decline. He would have refused to see us for a second time but the card made him think twice. Now, it is a fact that forty-eight hours in advance, the Appointments Secretary shows the schedule to a senior secret police officer. This policeman has the responsibility to guarantee the safety of the Executive. He may, as a matter of routine, have asked the *Seguridad Nacional* in Maracaibo if O'Reith could be an assassin. Cordero would have seen that message. It would be a simple matter for him to suggest to the secret policeman that the visit be delayed while he looked into it. Colonel Jimenez wouldn't know anything. He would just assume his people were doing what they are supposed to do. In fact, reading the telegram, it does not say 'canceled'. It says 'postponed'. Cordero couldn't afford to take any chances with Torres so he sent him to the island. He did not request authority to have him shot. That would go straight to the colonel. Cordero could not afford for that to happen. My guess is that Torres is locked up at some low level of authority. Cordero will keep him like that until he gets what he wants. Then Torres will be released and saved for the next time.

Cordero will not have him liquidated until the game is nearly over and then quietly, with a rock bit around his ankle in the lake in deep water. So, gentlemen, I know my way around the offices of the Executive in the *Principal*. Why don't I just make my little way over there and see if I can get things back on the rails. You fellows can go to the *Seguridad Nacional* and post bail for General Tarbutton. General O'Reith, don't give them your passport. Tell them that you've lost it "

As it turned out, a cheerful, fat, gracious *Capitan* Cordero, in a freshly pressed uniform with bright brass insignia, met them at the door of the station, a highly irregular procedure, to say the least. He ceremoniously invited them into a conference room and served them coffee and cakes, an irregular gesture, at a minimum. He said, like an undertaker who has discovered that the corpse is still alive, "Gentlemen, as it turns out, it will not be necessary to post bond. The case has been reviewed at a higher level. We decided to drop all charges. We offer General Tarbutton an apology for taking him from his domicile, from his tearful wife. It was a mistake. We don't mind admitting it."

O'Reith was glad to let it go at that. That night they dined with Mandy at the Tamanaco. Boiled shrimp from the Gulf of Paria in a fiery sauce of red pepper and olive oil. Then Lobster Thermidor, platanos and fresh spinach flown up from Miami cooked in a lemon and butter sauce. They washed it down with a white Chilean Pinot Noir. Then a mango and papaya compote doused with fresh lime juice. Over coffee, Mandy explained, "My friend at the Executive telephoned police headquarters to ask about charges filed against General Tarbutton. There were none. So you two got coffee and cakes instead of an ink pad and a smudged thumb. Cordero didn't know I was behind it. He couldn't afford to look into it. That done I found the Office of the Appointments Secretary. Not an easy task, mark you. But I prevailed. The appointment is on. The colonel is still on the island. We report to *La Carlota* airport at eight o'clock. I have the permits in my purse. It is a half hour flight."

O'Reith went to bed at eleven and for once, slept the night through without waking. The telephone rang at six, Mandy. He got up looking forward to an interesting day.

     *   *   *

Ted Schaeffer awoke with a blinding headache. He was naked, on a rough mattress with no sheets, in a tiny cubicle, shuttered against the hot rays of the morning sun. Enough light came through the slats that he could see a small, knee-high altar in the corner of the room. Probably an orange crate covered with a white cloth. Two short, black guttered candles framed a calendar photograph of Jesus Christ on the cross. Above the photograph, hanging from the wall was a wooden crucifix, with a string of beads dangling from one of the cross arms. The odor of incense and cheap perfume, really cheap perfume, pervaded the cubicle. He was in a whorehouse. He had the shakes. He was nauseated. He sat up on the side of the mattress and heaved. But nothing came up. Long hours ago he had thrown up the cheap scotch that he drank with the girl. "Jesus!" he exclaimed hoarsely, "I can't even remember her name! Christ! If Mandy finds out about this, she'll snap the head off of my dick."

From his dank clothing piled on the floor, he shook out a frisky centipede that scurried off into the darkness. He opened the door and looked out. He saw a row of cribs with a bathroom at the end. He could hear water dripping. With his clothes and his shoes in his arms, he tiptoed down to the bathroom. He piled his clothes on a hamper, found his way into a shower stall and rinsed off in the tepid water. The tile floor was slippery with green slime. Gray fungi clung to the sides of the stall. He prayed that nothing venomous resided in that tiny, vertical jungle. With his bare feet, he rubbed away enough slime to get a firm footing. The falling water refreshed him but his head continued to throb mercilessly. From several damp towels on a rack, Schaeffer picked a pink one that looked pretty good. He dried off and dressed. Hands shaking, he speared a cigarette from a package of Chesterfields in his shirt pocket and lit it with his Zippo. He returned to his cell, sat on the mattress and pulled in a lungful of tobacco smoke. After a second one, his mind was clear. He got up, went to the wooden stairs at the other end of the hall and descended. From the décor, he knew that he was in the Bello Monte. The bartender in a white shirt open at the front was restocking the shelves. Schaeffer said, "*Buenos Dias, Señor.*"

The bartender nodded, handed him a bar tab for four hundred bolivares, over $100 U.S. Highway robbery, Schaeffer thought. Far more money than he had. He went through the motions of looking in his wallet. As expected, he was stone-broke. He motioned to the telephone on the bar. The bartender shoved it toward him. He called Tuffy Marks, asked him to bail him out.

As the two men were leaving the Bello Monte in a Loffland Brothers company car, Marks asked, "Ted, how in the hell did you get yourself into this fix? The shape you're in, if I take you back to *El Escondite*, Mandy'll throw you to those snakes back there in the garden."

"She's in Caracas with Tarbutton and O'Reith," Schaeffer said in a gravely voice. "High powered business, but none of mine. So you can take me home. She won't be back until late and maybe not until tomorrow. By then, I'll be OK."

"How was it?"

"How was what, Tuffy?"

"The piece. The poontang. Jesus Christ, Ted, you didn't go to the Bello Monte to get a hair cut. Was she a good lay?"

Schaeffer silently speared another Chesterfield from the pack in his shirt pocket, lit it smartly with the car lighter, said, "Tuffy, it's beginning to come back to me a little. I don't think I got any at all. We had a few drinks out there in the garden. Made a deal. She got the key from that hag out there by the back door. We went inside and up the stairs. She unlocked the room, lit the candles, got the incense pot smoking and said her little prayer. That's the drill. Then she stripped, hung her dress on a nail in the wall and rolled in beside me. I couldn't make it. My dick was as limp as a boiled noodle. She even tried to suck some life into it. No go. By then I was getting sick. I had the strangest feeling that Mandy was in the room, watching it all. I got the heebie-jeebies. I was about to throw up. She led me down the hall to the pisser and from there it kind of fades out."

"Ted you're too god damned old to be fucking around in a whorehouse. No wonder you couldn't get it up. What the hell came over you anyhow? Christ man, you're in the clover out there..." They were driving down *Los Haticos*, having crossed *Puente de España*. They were getting close to the Zangs tannery down on the lake. The smell of it was overpowering. Schaeffer felt sick again. He sat holding his breath, trying not to gag. Then they were downwind of it. Marks slowed to turn up the hill. Schaeffer lit the last of his cigarettes, wadded up the empty package and threw it out the window. He blew a plume of smoke and said, "Tuffy, she left yesterday around noon. Told me to be a good boy. Gave me a kiss and tweaked my cheek. Like I was her little kid or something. Anyhow, out there in the garden, there's a silk screen not too far from the dragonhead fountain. Near that stone table where O'Reith has midnight pow-wows with those government hands. Mandy warned me. What's behind that screen is off limits. Little Theodore is not to touch, not to look. With her gone, I figured that it was the best chance I had to sneak a peak. So I did. Guess what's there?"

"Not a clue," Marks said. His eyes were on the road as they climbed.

"It's a little cemetery. Dozen or so tiny cement monuments like cigar boxes with crucifixes on top. Spanish names and Roman numerals too small for me to make out. I went back to the house and got my glasses. One name I recognized right away. Floyd Molloy. He was in the back row. You remember him?"

"Yeah, I remember him well. He was in town running and playing the night Lago Poniente No.1 blew out. He was the toolpusher. O'Reith fired him and ordered him out of the country. But Floyd had other ideas. He just dropped out of sight. Ted, there are a lot of low-down, no-good, people in this world and Floyd is one of 'em. I was out there on that burning platform with Holland and O'Reith. We stared fiery death straight in the eye. I don't have any sympathy for him. He got whatever he deserved. Loffland Brothers was the only drilling contractor in the country in those days. Creole, Mene Grande, Shell and Richmond Exploration Company were all running their own rigs. I put the word out to our hands that Floyd was on the loose. We checked every cathouse and flop joint in town. He was gone. There was talk that a girl stabbed him to death at El Techo Rojo and that he wound up in the lake with a rock bit tied to his ankle. But no one really knew for sure. On that little tombstone, what was the date of death?"

"It's in Roman numerals. I can't read 'em. Last number is a 'V'. Isn't that five?"

"Yeah. So it is either 1945 or 1955."

"I figure it that way too. What puzzles me is that O'Reith came in to see me, this was back in the Tower, must have been late '45 or early '46. Said he'd seen Floyd and that he was OK. Said he'd gone on a retreat. Lost weight. Quit drinking. Quit smoking. Was staying out of the houses. I just can't exactly recall when it was. But Mandy knows. And if she knows, O'Reith knows too. Tuffy, those grave markers are so small? Like a god damned doll's cemetery."

"Maybe they were cremated. Nothing in the ground but their ashes."

"Yeah… That could be… You suppose that Floyd and Mandy were once…"

"Ted," Marks said soberly, "Don't get to thinking like that. There has to be a sensible explanation. Besides, look at it like this. Daylights, you're in the tall clover. Night-times, you're sleeping next to the silk. You have everything a man could want. Whatever happened to Floyd was sometime back. Forget him. Down here, friend, a guy has to roll with the punches."

Schaeffer shrugged, muttered, "Yeah Tuffy. I guess you're right." They were on the steep slope of the hill. Marks gave the car the gas. The motor began to ping as it lugged down. Marks shifted into second gear. Schaeffer continued, "Well, after I saw Floyd's name there in the garden, I kind of came apart at the seams. I got to thinking Christ, a dozen of 'em or more. Were they all with Mandy for a time? Tuffy I got down low, lower than snake shit. So I walked down the road, hailed one of those *por puesto* cabs and rode down to the Hotel Detroit. Had a couple of drinks at their outdoor bar. I guess they asked me to leave. I remember being out on *Cinco de Julio*. Sun was going down. I must have gravitated to the Bello Monte. It's just up the street…"

Marks had parked the car in front of *El Escondite* and cut the engine. "Like for me to keep you company for a while, Ted?" he asked.

"No. I'll be OK now. I'm beginning to pick up. Stomach has settled down. Couple of hours and I'll feel like having a cup of soup. We've got lots of Campbell's chicken and rice. Business is good. Every room is filled. Drillers. Toolpushers. Cementers. Bit peddlers. If Holland and Ines and those kids were out of here, we'd have that space rented too. We've got Santa Fe and Delta hands. Halliburton. Hughes Tool Company. Reed. Even several of Ned Brown's hands. Quite an assortment."

"Cansor in charge with Mandy gone?" Marks asked.

"No. That Chinese cook runs the place. Cansor drives the Caddy, mixes drinks, looks after the garden. Doesn't say much. In fact I've never heard him utter a word. Maybe he talks to Mandy. Jesus, Tuffy, she's a strange woman."

"You're sure you're okay, Ted. I'll hang around if…"

"No need for that, Tuffy. I'm going to shave, take another shower and wash up, scrub my balls and peter with creosote soap. No telling what I might have picked up. After that, a nap. Later, a bowl of soup. I'll be in the office in the morning. Come by and have a cup of coffee with me. I'll pay you what I owe you."

Marks started the car, put it in gear and rolled it down the hill. Later that afternoon, after he had cleaned up, napped and eaten, Schaeffer returned to the garden and inspected the hidden cemetery. He carefully wrote down the date cut into the cement tombstone beneath the name of his old drinking buddy. Then he surveyed the scene, made sure the silk screen was properly set and there was no evidence of his intrusion. He was still nagged by the thought that Mandy might learn of his temporary lapse. He smoked a few cigarettes, joined a game of dominoes some Delta Drilling hands were getting up in the dining room.

Chapter X

▼

Work Print

Helen O'Reith was not in the best of humor. She had arrived mid-morning on the lot at Ventimiglia. Bolletti was nowhere to be seen. He had been gone a week – to a funeral in Naples. Day after day she and Sharon Mills had driven from Monte Carlo to find the set deserted. To make matters worse, little Helen Simpson had come down with measles. She wailed mercilessly when her mother left her. This morning Helen was dressed in black bolero pants and a canary yellow jacket over a white shirt. She had on black velvet high-heeled pumps trimmed in tiny rhinestones. All around the lot she found no signs of life. She was about to return to Monte Carlo when suddenly the place became alive. Bolletti and Big Alphonse arrived in a sedan. Both were dressed formally in black morning coats, white cotton shirts with stiff wing-tip collars and black ties. The usual retinue of cameramen, gaffers and grips of varying descriptions followed. From another car, two men alit whom Helen had never seen before. One of them she thought at first glance was Eduardo Cianneli. He had a lined face, threatening nose, hooded eyes under a black felt hat with a wide, brim, tilted down at an angle. She was about to say hello to him but then realized this was a much younger man, no more than fifty. The other person looked to be an American, perhaps forty, in a navy blue pin stripe suit and fedora hat.

His face was uneasily familiar but, with everything else on her mind, she couldn't immediately place it. Seemingly from nowhere, actors and costumers and stagehands began popping up. In minutes the forlorn studio was noisily functioning. She walked across the set to confront Bolletti. She said reprovingly, "Frederico, things have gone far enough, from bad to worse. I've been lenient and forgiving but all of that is at an end. I never heard of a funeral that lasted a week. What kind of business is this? I'm taking my husband's advice and blowing the whistle on you. This affair has exceeded all limits of shabby film-making. I'm no director but I know one when I see one and you're not one. Today we are going to get this Mexican horse opera back on the railroad tracks or I'm going to Rome and file a lawsuit. I want a full accounting of all expenditures. I want to see a current bank statement. Next I want to know exactly where we stand as far as *Los Ladrones of Piedras Negras* is concerned. I need a work print. So show me a bank statement and a work print and we'll go from there."

Bolletti was nervously wringing his hands together as he always did when Helen was giving him a hard time. His head was slightly bowed. He said, "Of course, cariña. I'll call the bank today. We have the statement in the morning. We sit down and we look at it together…"

"Don't call me cariña, god dammit!" she interrupted.

"Yes, contessa, you beautiful child when you are upset."

Helen screwed up her face, glared and pointed a threatening finger at him, continued, "Well I'm goddamned sure disturbed and don't call me any pet names. I've had it with your syrupy sweetness. You're totally insincere. All sugar-water and no gin." She rubbed her fingers together, said tersely, "Work print."

Bolletti was really on edge now. He took a step back and bowed again and rubbed his pudgy hands together. He was squirming. Tiny beads of sweat formed on his tanned forehead. He said, "We sit down countess. We talk about the work print." The canvas-backed folding chair with his name stenciled on it creaked under him. He had put on some weight since the project started. With Helen sitting beside him, he began. "Tomorrow we will go to the film editors. We see the work print."

"Why not right now?" Helen said, in a demanding tone.

"Countess, we have to give them time to get it ready. Everything tomorrow. OK?"

"Bank statement tomorrow. Work print today." She was adamant. She tapped her right foot on the boards of the set.

"Just twenty-four tiny little hours, countess. That's all I ask," Bolletti implored.

Helen relented. "OK. Nine o'clock in the morning. One other thing, Frederico. This movie is not going to be about the Camorra or the Mafia. No black-markets and no revenge killings. It is going to be about cattle rustling in Piedras Negras. We're going back to the original script that we all agreed upon in Los Angeles a light year ago. No nuns and no dons. No capos. Just good gringos, or pretty good anyway and Mesicans, not so good, in fact not good at all, low down, just like Garcia wrote about them."

"Yes, countess. Of course. It will be as you say." Bolletti was breathing easier.

Helen went on, "We have our work cut out for us. How much film have we shot so far? How many feet?"

"Cariña, I don't know. Many reels. Perhaps twenty. I will go to see the editors. I find out all these things. For tomorrow."

Helen was fuming mad. "Frederico, I want to see what we've shot, what we've cut, what we've scrapped. I want to know where we are and where we're going. I'm fed up with the half-assed approach you take to important matters. Starting tomorrow, we're working together as a team."

"Yes, dear. As you say."

"Up, Frederico. We're going to see the head cameraman and tell him we want to look at the film right now. Right f—-ing now. No, I won't say that word. My husband says it and it is offensive. You know what I mean."

"Contessa, the cameramen have other things to do. They do not edit. I edit. I have assistants who cut and paste but I pass judgement. The director edits."

"Fine, Frederico, show me your work. I suspect we will both be in a state of shock."

"Perhaps. Dear, you are too impetuous. We will have a fine picture."

"It is not fine so far. Frederico, I'm tired of looking at all those fat guys. Off the payroll for them. I want them all fired. Today. Especially Big Alphonse. What kind of a hero is he? Rather I should ask, what kind of a hero was he when he was OK? I know what he is today. He's a no body. He's lame. His face is frozen. He can't speak properly, mumbles all the god damned time. Alphonse has to disappear. Frederico, I want a young guy to be the hero. Good-looking and athletic. Find a guy like that who knows how to learn his lines. Can you do that? And send a wire to Garcia. Tell him to hotfoot it back here, that we're going back to square one and he's got to help us fix the script up and drop all these f———ing diversions. Frederico, I will not say that word no matter how vexing you become. But you know! Goddammit, you know!"

"Yes, dear Helen. Oh you are so angry, so fascinating."

Helen had never learned to shoot a .45 army automatic and was upset when both her son and her daughter became expert marksmen on the 1,000-inch range at the Limejuicer Club. Now, in her present state of mind, if she had one handy, she would have gleefully shot Bolletti until all of the ammunition was used up. That is how she felt about him. She raged, "Knock all that off, Frederico. Work print. Now."

His back was to the wall. He said, "Helen, there is no work print. We are not yet to that stage. But we start immediately tomorrow." He snapped his fingers together. "Immediately tomorrow!" he repeated. "They work all night. Tomorrow you and I and Alphonse will …"

"Fuck Alphonse!" She blurted out the word she despised, then put her hand over her mouth. "Oh, you've made me say that word! It's your goddamned fault, Frederico! You made me say that!" She jumped from her chair and doused him with a glass of iced tea that the caterers had just placed on the refreshment table. Angrily she trod off to her dressing room, fighting back tears. She lay across her sofa, emotionally exhausted. Some long minutes later she heard a tapping on her door. Bolletti, she was sure. Scenes like this had occurred before. She got up, improved her face in the mirror and opened the door. Bolletti's head was bowed and his hands were wringing together in supplication. He had changed his clothing. He looked bedraggled, his usual act. She shrugged, pointed him back toward the chairs they had recently vacated and followed him. Seated, she said, "Frederico, here we are in September of 1956. We have been shooting this movie since May. We aren't getting anywhere. A movie like this should take no more than thirty days. Of course I realize that we're working together for the first time … But we have to finish this movie. I ask you now in all sincerity, when will we be finished?"

Bolletti shrugged. "And I tell you with all sincerity, I do not know. We had problems with the script. Garcia walked out. We had problems with the leading man. He had a stroke. We must find a new leading man. We must review the film we have on the reels. How can I answer you?"

"Frederico, this movie has to premiere before the middle of 1957. That is absolutely a must."

"But why, countess?"

"Because that is about the time that my husband will begin to run first oil out of Venezuela. I am not going to let him steal a march on me."

Bolletti suddenly seemed confident. "Well, Helen, we will do it if it that important. But what does the one have to do with the other?"

"Because he will do it. He's that kind of a guy. So I have to do it too. Professional pride. He and I both started our new projects at the same time. I can't permit him to get out in front of me. Besides, he doesn't think I'm up to it. So Frederico, if there is no work print, then you and I will work all night. We will edit the film. I'll call Alice Ridley. Ask her to take care of my daughter. Tonight, we have a catered evening meal. No vino. No Alphonse. Just you and I and the cutting staff. When the sun comes up out of the hills in the morning, we'll know what we have. So call the bank, order the statement and let's get to work."

It was not to be that easy. She discovered that the dailies were piled haphazardly on the several cutting-room tables. Some were mixed with film from other movies being made simultaneously by another of the co-op companies. Working through the night, Helen and Frederico separated the film, putting it in order on one table. Rum-dum from lack of sleep, Helen ordered Bolletti to form two teams of cutters, splicers and editors. Each to work twelve hours, one by day and the other by night. Helen instructed Ridley to hire a nurse to tend little Helen Simpson; advised that she would be staying in Ventimiglia for several days. She asked that a message be sent to her husband in that regard.

Helen slept on the sofa in her dressing room, woke late in the afternoon, had a sandwich and a coke and rejoined the film editors in the cutting room. She took charge of the work print. She'd seen them made many times and knew more or less what to do. The daylight team located the edge numbers of the rushes, had them in consecutive order, They started the *rough-cut*. She helped until Bolletti appeared tired and haggard. Still he pitched right in. When Helen saw that he was focused she said, "Frederico, I'm going for dinner and a nap. I'll be back around midnight. Keep the pressure on. Think work print."

He gave her a weary, if sweeping bow, said, "Yes countess," and returned to his work, coat and tie off. That was a good sign.

And so it went for five days and nights. From rough cut to *fine cut* to work print. Six months of photographic grist put through the mill in over 120 non-stop hours. Over 20,000 feet of film reduced to 3,500, forty minutes of running time. All shots of Big Alphonse No.2 were ruthlessly expunged. All Camorra or Mafia footage went to the scrap pile. Shots of Helen in a nun's habit were chopped. In the end, what remained was pretty bad. Helen ran it through the *Movieola* many times, reluctantly coming to the conclusion that of the thirty-seven minutes of true running time, another 10 would have to be cut. What was left, crowd scenes, bar room scenes, ragged children in the street and the sequence where Big Alphonse ponderously enters Piedras Negras on a sway-backed horse, could be divided into four six minute runs. She cabled Sagebrush Film Archives, Inc. in Los Angeles for a Technicolor package to include a:

1) chase along a canyon rim.

2) bar room brawl with total demolition of all furniture, the light fixtures and the mirror behind the bar.

3) corral shoot-out with snorting horses and panic-stricken women and children running for cover.

4) fat, bad-looking guy tumbling after being shot out of the bell tower of a typical adobe church on the border. He rings the bells cacaphonetically as he becomes entangled in the ropes. In all, she requested twenty minutes of running time. That, added to what they had, would give them forty-seven minutes. With the new hero, they could shoot another twenty minutes and they'd have something. She didn't know quite what it would be but it would be a western.

Returning to Monte Carlo, she was relieved to find her daughter on the mend. Messages from O'Reith were reassuring. He insisted on a daily prognostications from Alice Ridley. That miffed her. What kind of an astrological authority was he? Her domestic affairs under control, she plunged into the original Garcia-Lawson shooting script, now dog-eared and heavily annotated. She rewrote part of it and telephoned Bolletti every hour or so until, two days later, he assured her that the new hero was in the studio.

She was pleasantly surprised to meet Michelangelo Spermaceti, the new hero to replace Big Alphonse Malbecco. Spermaceti, a former soccer player, was predictably, Bolletti's cousin. Ringlets of salt and pepper framed his rugged, handsome face. He had dark, intelligent-looking eyes. About forty, he smiled a lot, seemed agile, said he could ride a horse, had nice straight legs and a flat stomach. He wore a flowery shirt, open to show his hairy chest. His tight red pants revealed a magnificent endowment. He reminded Helen of Ramon Navarro. If he could remember his lines, he would do just fine. Surely they could coax twenty minutes of decent footage out of him. With Garcia back on the job, Lawson with a second wind, if they still had money in the bank, maybe they could get this oater in the cans.

Bolletti had the bank statement. She was too preoccupied with the assessment of the new hero to get into it. She crammed it into her purse to study later. A dialogue coach began teaching Spermaceti the first of his lines. The stagehands were rearranging the set. Shooting to begin in the morning.

Helen retired to her dressing room to examine the bank statement. The legend at the top read: *Bancco Commercialli Napoli*. She'd never heard of it but that didn't mean anything. Their company name was: *Compannia de Produzzione Cinematographica de Ventimiglia*. That looked OK. In lira, they seemed to have a fortune. When she laboriously converted it into dollars, she could have spit a snake. They had spent almost three million dollars on twenty-seven minutes of usable running time. The reality of it stunned her. She crumpled up the bank statement and threw it into a corner of the room. Then, regretting it, she recovered it and tried to smooth it out. She strode out of the dressing room, found Bolletti in the cutting room and began calling him every vile expletive she had picked up in twenty years of film-making. He was a rat, a snake, a weasel, and a gnat, mole excrement. She almost called him an impotent runt but that would have been too much. Her husband would horse laugh at that. When she was out of breath, Bolletti was a quivering, cowering ruin. When it was all over, they had an understanding. Both Alphonses were stricken from the payroll along with their wives, mistresses, hairdressers and hangers-on. Gone were the bankers hours, the lavish four course lunches with countless bottles of Chianti and Amaretto. Shooting began at seven a.m. promptly, continued as long as there was light and they worked Saturdays and Sundays. Sandwiches between takes for lunch. Michelangelo Spermaceti was renamed Sixto Cigone. They shot a new five-minute beginning to establish Cigone as the hero. He was shy. Could not remember his lines. Fortunately, most of the time he just rode his horse, nothing much to say. They patched in a dummy section to represent the bar room brawl and demolition. At the end of it, a new scene showed Cigone emerging from the debris with his guns smoking. Since Cigone had no lines, this take was perfect. Next came the shoot-out at the corral, which killed off quite a few of the black hats. After that came Big Alphonse plugging what were once rustlers in the tail. Now they were remnants of a leaderless, disorganized posse. Helen was cheered that of the twenty-seven minutes they had salvaged, Big Alphonse appeared in nineteen and of that, ten minutes showed him with blazing pistols and a sneer on his face. Given the way they had originally shot it, converting Big Alphonse from good guy to bad guy was not easy but as Helen considered the various options, her enthusiasm returned. After the long sequences with Big Alphonse shooting things up, they patched in the chase. Then new footage showed Cigone knocking a Big Alphonse stand-in off his horse. Cigone wrestled Big Alphonse into submission, hog tied him and turned him over to the new posse. After a suitable trial, with a responsible-looking judge, he would be hanged, of course. Concerned about Cigone's stage fright, Helen hoped they could coach him into a creditable performance. Big Alphonse would escape as they were taking him to the gallows. Panting and wheezing, he would climb the bell tower of the church. Cigone going after him, would shoot him, and blow smoke out of his gun barrel as the bells clanged chaotically. No talking required for that sequence. To end the film, they shot new footage of Helen and Cigone happily riding off into the sunset. They were holding hands, each astride an ambling horse. As the two of them blissfully disappear, rustic music begins followed by a melodic ringing of wedding bells. Little ragged kids run along beside the horses. The old priest stands in front of the church, tears in his sad eyes, waving at them as they ride away.

Bolletti objected. Big Alphonse was under contract. He'd have a fit when he saw what had happened to him. He might sue.

Helen imagined herself to be her husband with his notorious *stare*. She let Bolletti squirm under it for a long minute and then repeated her earlier comment about what Big Alphonse could do if he felt so inclined. Riding back to Monte Carlo that night in her limousine with Sharon Mills, it occurred to her that in all the confusion of the day, she had forgotten to ask Bolletti who were the two strange men that had visited the studio. Something about them distressed her. Unnerved by the ominous facial features of the one, she was upset by the eerie familiarity of the other. Since she had to report to her husband about little Helen's measles, she would tell him about the two mystery men as well. He was pretty good at linking unrelated affairs together.

Chapter XI

▼

Orchid Island

La Isla Orchila is situate in north latitude 11.7 degrees approximately 105 miles northeast of Caracas as the crow flies, and that, more or less, was the way they were going to fly. But unlike a crow, which would find it a difficult flight over so much water, O'Reith and Mandy were to ride in a C-47, the military version of the famed workhorse DC-3. The government of Venezuela purchased this one from the Americans in 1946, as part of a *war surplus* transaction organized by the Creole Petroleum Company. The plane still had original green camouflage but with the Venezuelan flag painted on the rudder. The pilots wore snappy uniforms and were self conscious about their importance.

O'Reith had on a white, tropical linen suit and matching leather, mesh shoes. On his head was a fine-fiber Panama hat with a floppy brim, the kind that is rolled up and stored in a cigar tube. He was, of course, unarmed. It was considered bad form to call on a South American dictator with a 9mm Luger in a shoulder holster, especially one that was rigged for a silencer. He had also decided against carrying a briefcase. He had the documents in a Hotel Tamanaco envelope in his coat pocket.

Mandy Macabra Schaeffer had on a canary yellow dress with long sleeves, no décolletage and a matching kidskin belt. The dress fell well below her knees. With fine, sheer stockings and brown leather low-cuts, she looked prim and proper. She wore simple gold rings in her ears, a comb in her hair and a dab of Parure on her throat. She could have been a schoolmistress, or a hospital supervisor or a prison matron. She wore no hat and her dark auburn hair glistened in the tropical sunlight.

Together they reported to *La Carlota* airport at eight o'clock sharp. Mandy presented their travel authority to the military policeman at the gate. O'Reith showed his greenish-gray American Passport. All papers were thoroughly scrutinized. The barrier was raised. They were allowed to enter. Minutes later they were on their way. Below them, as they crossed the coastal chain of the Venezuelan Andes, ant-like workmen swung the cranes that were building the Hotel Humboldt at the summit of Mount Avila. It was scheduled to open in a couple of months. Two other passengers, both officers of the *Guardia Nacional*, sat in the rear of the aircraft, perusing the papers in their briefcases. A pretty LAV stewardess with jet black hair and red-tipped fingernails served orange juice and coffee. It would be a short flight, perhaps a half-hour.

Colonel Marcos Perez Jimenez, like most of the strong men before him, came from Tachira, a mountainous province to the south of Lake Maracaibo. He had worked his way up the military hierarchy of the army. When the peculiar alliance between the radical political party *Accion Democratica* and the Military Junta unraveled on 24 Nov. 1948, he bided his time until 2 Dec. 1952. Then he seized power. Now he was the dictator. With a powerful army, a sophisticated secret police and a docile congress, nothing stood in his way, unless it was his wife. She was said to be a woman of strong character.

He ran the country to suit himself, liquidated his enemies routinely and brought to fruition his rather ambitious architectural projects, among other things. A short, thick-bodied man, swarthy with black, slicked-down hair, in public, he had an expressionless face. He wore perfectly tailored uniforms with shiny brass ornamentation and plenty of gold braid. He, like many of that era, often rode standing in an open limousine bedecked with banners and flags, in high speed military convoys racing along the broad boulevards of Caracas, Maracay, Valencia and Maracaibo.

Among his many architectural projects was the aforementioned Hotel Humboldt which when complete would be connected to both Caracas and Maiquetia by cable car. Thus one could fly from Miami to Maiquetia, ride the cable car up to the hotel, enjoy a stunning view of Caracas by night, have a good dinner and next day, ride the cable car down to Caracas to attend business. None of this was possible today however. But what could be done today, with the dictators permission, was visit the Eden-like compound on Orchid Island, analogous to President Eisenhower's Camp David in the Catoctin Mountains of Maryland.

Flying up from Caracas, looking out the right side windows, they glimpsed the *Islas de Rochas,* perhaps the remnants of an atoll, now disintegrated into sandbars and clusters of rocks. Through the left side windows, soon appeared the triangular *La Isla Orchila.* Its hypotenuse faced north. Northwest of the island a curved, barren sandbar appeared, home only to birds and turtles. Near the sand bar, dozens of rocks broke the waves and would be considered hazards to navigation. The island, an arid low lying mass was covered with tall, thin, greenish, cacti and thorn trees. The thorn trees had small, round, white orchids nestled among tough, spike-ended leaves. At night the orchids gave off a sweet perfume but when the sun arose the odor died away. In 1956, Orchid Island had a military prison where the most dangerous political troublemakers were kept until such time as they were executed, usually not too long. Nothing like that at Camp David, as far as anyone knew. A swanky presidential retreat with every luxury known to the western hemisphere occupied the point of the island. Inside its walls one could find all the pretty girls that one could possibly kiss in a day's time. Perhaps Camp David had a facility like this too. As can be imagined, visitors to Orchid Island were few and far between and did not include the immediate family of Colonel Jimenez. The occasional South American head of state did come, informally, it must be said. Reports filtered back that almost any kind of beverage or food was available. The girls were said to be pliant and fluent in most of the modern European languages. Colonel Jimenez could not know this of course, but he would be cock of the Venezuelan walk for only about sixteen more months. It was his destiny to be deposed and to retire to Palm Springs, Florida in happy exile for a good number of years. Americans who got to know him during this passive period of his life reported that he was not too bad of a guy. He had a nice, if reticent, family. Not much is known about his ability to shoot pool or roll a bowling ball. In southern Florida, at any given time, there were always a half dozen banana republic dictators living in reasonable comfort and attracted less attention than a third baseman at spring training. But Jimenez was known to be a pretty fair Latino golfer.

On this day in September of 1956 with a subway series about three weeks ahead in New York, Colonel Marcos Perez Jimenez was still, as they said then, a really big beaver. O'Reith was under no illusions about this. As the C-47 circled the island to line up for final approach, O'Reith gazed thoughtfully out at the triangular land mass in the azure waters of the Caribbean. On the north shore he saw a long, curving beach of white sand, inviting in the early morning. Soldiers in military fatigues were setting up beach tents for bathers who were, presumably, still having breakfast. On a bluff overlooking the beach was a three-story white building trimmed in green. The building had a red, flat-tiled top, a swimming pool, a putting green, an outside bar and restaurant area all surrounded by an immense citrus orchard, oranges, lemons and limes. A flagstone cart path led through the orchard to a scenic nine hole golf course with immaculate greens and guarded by deep, fearsome sand traps. Not a place to hit your ball. Not a place for the dictator to hit *his* ball, if you were playing with him.

Along the southern coast, the beach was rocky and irregular, unattended except by sea turtles, crabs and various types of long-legged colorful birds, flamingos, perhaps. A higher bluff rose from this beach and on it was a grim two story, concrete blockhouse with barred windows. A graveled yard surrounded the blockhouse for quite some distance closed by a double barbed-wire fence with only one entrance. Elevated sentry towers stood at each corner of the yard. Manned machine-guns were at each corner of the roof. O'Reith assumed that somewhere within this forbidding structure was Torres, if he had not already been shot.

Lined up with the strip, the flaps were down, and the engines throttled back. Then the wheels touched with a screeching of tires. Puffs of blue smoke from the tires drifted across the asphalt tarmac. The DC-3 rolled to a stop. The pilots turned the plane around and taxied it back to a small station underneath the control tower. As they touched down, O'Reith spied another building some remove from the airstrip, which flew a Venezuelan flag. Smaller than both the hotel and the prison it was of one story, painted pink and brown. Escorted by armed guards, the passengers walked to olive drab Chevrolet sedans. O'Reith and Mandy got in the first one and the two officers, the second. After a short drive, all four passengers got out in front of the pink and brown building. A sign over the door read *Gobierno Militar de Venezuela*. A guard let them enter. Mandy produced their travel authority. A lieutenant seated at a desk in the foyer checked their papers. He pointed them to chairs along the wall. The two officers were allowed to pass through a door on the right with a glass panel that read *Control*. It was five minutes to the hour.

At exactly nine o'clock, an unmarked door on the left opened, an officer came out, approached O'Reith and asked him to follow. He indicated that Mandy should wait. O'Reith followed into a large, well-lighted office at which, near the far end, with potted papaya trees on both sides of his desk, sat Colonel Marcos Perez Jimenez. His impassive face gazed at O'Reith. As the subordinate helped O'Reith him into a chair, he said, "Mr. President, I come to request a clarification of our situation as regards an oil concession in Lake Maracaibo." He had thought of addressing the dictator in Spanish but decided to try him in English instead. It would be a test not only of the dictator's ability to speak English but also an indication of where he stood. If Jimenez snarled back at him in Spanish, he was really in the soup.

"It is a grave matter, my dear General O'Reith. *Asunto muy grave*," he repeated in Spanish for emphasis. "Violation of Venezuelan law. Bribery. Conspiracy. To say nothing of that 'incident' on the lake a short time back. When aliens come to our placid shores to pay our public servants to act in their behalf, we must take notice. You may be sure that Señor Torres will be punished. You sir and your employees will be declared *persona no grata* and expelled. Your oil wells will be confiscated, your contract declared null and void. And at that, you are lucky. Señor Torres and his fellow conspirators will go to the wall."

The dictator became highly agitated as he enumerated the offences of The Casinghead Company. His glasses steamed up. While the dictator was vigorously cleaning them, O'Reith let him cool off. In a while he began, "Mr. President, with your permission, let me review the negotiation, ab ovo. When we reach that point where an irregularity took place, you may interrupt and clarify matters. Is that agreed?"

Perez Jimenez was silent until he had completed polishing his glasses. He put them back on. Then he placed his small, fat-fingered hands on the green blotter on his desk and said, "You may commence, sir."

O'Reith told him of the introduction in Ciudad Bolivar and from that, the meetings with Señor Torres. He related how the negotiation had taken place in Caracas and then Maracaibo and how he thought the second side-letter agreement seemed a bit unusual but he was following what Torres suggested and sensed no danger. He omitted the meeting with Cordero.

Jimenez held up his right hand, palm out to stop O'Reith. He said, "The second letter was the irregularity sir. If there had been no second letter, we would not be facing each other on this idyllic island. The second letter was unauthorised. It made the negotiation illegal. That is why the contract must be cancelled."

"I acted in good faith," O'Reith said.

"You should have smelled a rat!"

"I did. That is why I sought an interview with you last spring. After the negotiation was complete, a third government man intruded himself upon us. As far as I am concerned, he is the rat. I asked Señor Torres for an explanation. He gave me one. I asked for and was denied a meeting with you."

"I don't give many audiences," the dictator said, softening his tone. "Running this undisciplined country takes all of my time. We have here many people we don't need. What am I supposed to do with them?"

O'Reith continued. "After the 'incident' on the lake, this same man, the rat, suggested to me that if the Casinghead Company would cede back to the government Block 9, he would arrange for it to retain Block 16. He made this suggestion two nights ago. He also told me that my audience with you originally set for yesterday had been cancelled. This disturbed me. Fortunately, *Señora* Schaeffer, was able to reset the interview."

For the first time since O'Reith entered, the dictator smiled. He said, "Remarkable woman indeed. Her born name is Macabra. Amanda Macabra. Yes, she helped me long ago. Removed a parasitic growth, a political one. I was just a young officer then serving on the Orinoco River in the east. You may continue, my dear General."

"Mr. President," O'Reith continued, "I brought with me the two side-letters. The second one contains a secret bank account number for a certain officer of the *Seguridad Nacional*. He is the man who suggested we could keep Block 16 and he would see the contract was duly published. I ask that you take these documents. Investigate as you wish. You will find that Señor Torres acted correctly. If this is the case, then I ask you to allow the publication of our contract in the *Gaceta Oficial* and that you instruct the Minister of Hydrocarbons to retract his letter to us regarding the 'incident' on the lake. And I respectfully request that you restore the liberty of your public servant, Señor Rodrigo Olimpio Torres."

"I don't know sir," the dictator countered. The second bank account may not belong to an officer of the *Seguridad Nacional*. It may belong to a Torres co-conspirator."

"Easy enough to find out," O'Reith suggested. "Our bankers in Liechtenstein will co-operate, inasmuch as it's our money that's involved"

The dictator sat a little taller behind his enormous desk. He said, "General O'Reith, I have my own methods. Leave the second letter with my adjutant. I will obtain the truth. If what you say is true, your rights will be restored, your contract published and the Minister's letter recanted. The rat you speak of, the officer of the *Seguridad Nacional,* we may as well get his name before us. It is *Capitan* Riva Cordero, and he is basically harmless to a man of your perception and power. Nevertheless, his superior in the *Seguridad Nacional* will have a word with him. He will not annoy you further."

"You're not going to liquidate him?" O'Reith blurted out, instantly realizing his mistake.

But Colonel Jimenez merely smiled, as he had earlier at the mention of Mandy Macabra. He said, "Why liquidate the scoundrel? We know him. This is not the first time he has been embroiled in a contretemps of this nature. His replacement would be cut from the same cloth. People in his line of work don't amount to much. It is the same the world over. Take your American secret service for example, the fog-shrouded Central Intelligence Agency. The very name is a joke. Oh what a romantic clique! With their maps of Eastern Europe, their tiny Geiger counters, their emergency kits with gold coins, Russians rubles, cigarettes, chocolate bars, and Swiss knives with twenty blades including a corkscrew and a fingernail clipper. So eagerly they blacken their faces, don their parachutes, and tell jokes with the pilots as the plane is taking off, drink one cup of black coffee after another during the turbulent flight to some drop zone in Croatia or Albania or Dalmatia. They smile gamely when the pilot flashes the green signal and gleefully, with full bladders and empty minds, plunge willy-nilly into the Carpathian Alps. But then what? They fall into immediate capture, betrayed by their carelessness and are never to be seen again, spend decades of their young lives in dank prisons unless, one chance in a thousand, they are exchanged for one of their equally inept Soviet counterparts. What a silly game grown men play. Not that the French are any wiser. The *Surete*, it follows in the tradition of Joseph Fouche, Napoleon's chief of police who found it much simpler to just manufacture 'intelligence' and serve it up, as if it were scrambled eggs. The French extend that to their entire government. My dear General O'Reith, those people have the world's largest bureaucracy, well perhaps the Soviet is larger, who knows for sure, but you get my meaning. The French have a gigantic government, but no governed. France is an anarchy. Only in the vineyards, cheese factories and the dining room table are they well ordered. The Germans are too abrupt to be effective spies—and their English is too precise. The Russians? Like the Italians. What can one say? Only the British have a true knack for the art of spying and, I might add, great finesse at counterintelligence. But their M.I.5 have been tainted, all to be expected when you employ perverts on sensitive missions. So all over the world, spies are of a stripe. And mine are no different. The feared *Seguridad Nacional,* they're bunglers. Minatory. Often fat. Sinister looking, contrived, I might add to bolster their cachet as 'secret' policemen. Riva Cordero is typical. He wants to extort money from your company so that he can go to Miami and fuck the Cuban whores. Well, he can just stay in Maracaibo and fuck the Colombian whores. Riva Cordero! What does he know of international finance? Does he understand the balance of payments? To ask the question of him is to answer it. So we will make it simple for him to understand. We will say to him, *Capitan* Cordero, shame on you. We need to keep the American dollars here in Venezuela to improve the lot of the poor. We give you plenty of bolivares for the *putas.* Besides, most of the time, they give it to you for nothing. We tell him to return the money that he extorted from your company. He will do it. Make no mistake about that! I'll singe the hair off of his testicles if he does not. Torres will advise you of this. While we are on the subject of Torres, it is clear to me that we will have to reorganize the Ministry of Hydrocarbons. Something is amiss there. Riva Cordero will tell us what it is. Perhaps Torres will resign soon. Could you offer him employment? He could be your government liaison man. What do you think of that?"

"Excellent idea, your highness," O'Reith said. "When I see him again, I will propose that to him."

"That may not be too long," the dictator said, laughing softly, his belly jiggling behind the desk. "Now, my dear general. You have had your moment. Could I have mine?" He smiled for the third time.

"Of course."

"Are you by any chance related to *Doña* Helen O'Reith? Of the Silver Screen?"

"Husband," O'Reith said.

Colonel Jimenez rubbed his pudgy little brown hands together as if in anticipation of a great experience. He looked at the clock ticking on the wall. It was almost ten o'clock. I could offer you a morning coffee, sir. Perhaps a scone or a biscuit too. What do you say?"

The two military men arose and Perez Jimenez led O'Reith into an immense lounge that adjoined the Spartan office. Large screened windows showed an immaculate orange orchard outside. Soft classical music greeted them, piped in through ceiling vents. They sat at a glass-topped cocktail table in a field of twelve on a spotless white tile floor. The bar itself, aligned along the common wall with the dictator's office was forty feet of polished ebony framed in polished bronze. Behind the bar was the usual mirrored bottle rack. Hundreds of bottles of bourbon, Scotch, rum, vodka, gin and exotic liqueurs of the world were displayed. The stools at the long bar had leather seats in bronze framework. A soldier in dress uniform served them coffee and cakes. Jimenez said, "On past the lounge, through that door, is a cinema. I often show movies in the evening. I have a complete set of those that feature your wife. I often watch *Las Mujeres Norteamericanos en la Guerre Mundial II*. Another favourite is *Luz Brilliante de Noche*. Was she not decorated for her role in that one?"

"Yeah," O'Reith answered. "She won an Oscar. She was Estelle in *Neon Lights*."

"Exactly," echoed the dictator, rubbing his hands together expectantly. O'Reith knew exactly how to respond. It was a story that he had told audiences, mostly men, in Europe, in Persia and in the posh watering holes of Los Angeles and San Francisco. He had it down cold. A basic biographic sketch brought to life by the many humorous experiences they had shared together. How they had met, fallen in love, married and had children; how she had returned to the world of celluloid while he was away at war; how she come to the attention of the famous American director, John Ford, and the rest was cinematic history. He always included the story of the bishop and the actress and on this occasion, the dictator interrupted him near the end of it saying, "I remember it! Yes. *"La Pequinita Pecos"*! What a wonderful bit of entertainment."

"The English title was *Pecos Lil*," O'Reith said.

The dictator laughed, snapped his fingers, repeated '*Pecos Lil!*' as if just remembering it. The soldier removed the coffee cups and cake tray. Jimenez said, "It has been my pleasure to make your acquaintance. Perhaps when it is time to cut the ribbon on your oil terminal at Punto Fijo, we can have an inauguration party. Could you induce *Pecos Lil* to attend?"

"I think I could, Colonel Jimenez. She is fond of men in uniform." He could have told him that she also liked little men but that might be pushing his luck.

Jimenez said, "General O'Reith, my guards will escort you back to the airline. I would like to say hello to Señora Schaeffer. I won't keep her long. Your problem is resolved. The contract will be properly published. We meet again at *Miraflores*. Festivities come often in the fall and your name will be on the guest list. I look forward to meeting your associate, General Tarbutton. I believe he has a distinguished military record. And Colonel Holland too. I am always comfortable in the company of brave soldiers."

When O'Reith stepped inside the C-47, he was astonished to see Rojo Torres in a window seat near the hatch. He joined him as they waited for Mandy.

"They rough you up, Rojo?" O'Reith asked.

"No. I was treated well. They told me I was to be shot. But it is a common threat. I don't take it seriously anymore."

"Colonel Jimenez said he planned to reorganize the Ministry of Hydrocarbons, suggested I offer you a job as liaison man with the government. Are you interested?"

"Of course. What choice have I?"

"Probably none," O'Reith agreed.

Mandy entered the aircraft. A soldier closed the hatch. The pilots started the engines. The flight to *La Carlota* was routine. By three o'clock, O'Reith, Tarbutton, Ethering and Mandy were seated at the long table in the office. O'Reith said, "Looks like, we have a green light. I truly expect to see our contract published right away. Torres will ask the minister to send us a retraction of the letter regarding the 'incident'. We may hear something on that later today. I'll stay here in Caracas until we know. We still have to worry about Feathermerchant. Chances are he'll have another trick up his sleeve. By the way, I 'reported' our intentions about Block 9 through Rojo. I can't imagine that we'll hear from Cordero again but the ball takes a funny hop now and then so I'm still apprehensive."

"When I get back to Maracaibo, I'll ask the detective to bring us up to date. You recall that he saw the three of them together, Feathermerchant, Torres and Cordero." Mandy said.

"I don't understand that at all." Then O'Reith snapped his fingers. "That reminds me, Mandy," he began. "Take these keys. They fit the door of our villa in Bella Vista. Give them to Ines. Tell her they can move in immediately. Maxine wants to stay in Paris so Monique can attend her regular school. Holland and Ines will be more comfortable in that flat. I'm returning to Paris. When they're settled in, Holland can operate from the office in the Del Lago.

At the Hotel Avila that afternoon, O'Reith assisted Mandy to check out. He rode with her to the airport in the Citroen that Tarbutton had rented. On the drive to Maiquetia which, in traffic, took an hour, he said, "Mandy, even with the royal welcome we received on Orchid Island this morning, things can still go wrong. Our third rig is here. A fourth rig is planned to arrive before the end of 1956. We're spending money at a furious rate. The pipeline contract has been signed. Work on the terminal at Punto Fijo begins in December. Holland has already gone out for bids on the mid-lake production station. That 'incident', what a fiasco, cost us a cool million, maybe more when all the bills are in. After your few minutes with the colonel, what do you think? Is he as good as his word? Are we finished with Cordero? Can we now trust Torres? I've always felt there was something odd underlying our relationship with him. That he's back talking to Cordero makes me even more suspicious. So?" He turned to look at her in the gathering gloom of twilight. Headlights from cars coming from the airport threw the tonneau of the limousine into chiaroscuro.

Mandy thought for some moments. When she answered, she was chose her words with care. She said, "The colonel is as good as his word. But he forgets. Others carry out his mandates. His first priority will be to chastise Cordero. An aide will rake him over the coals. He'll read him the riot act and maybe even banish him from Maracaibo. Make him the *Jefe Civil* of some backwater. Machiques. Carmelo. Some place like that. He has to keep the *Seguridad Nacional* under his thumb. As for reforming the *Ministerio de Hidrocarburos*, we should not expect that to happen right away. The bureaucracy will, as usual, stall out. The reprimand is a dead letter. Nothing further will come of that. No point wasting time and effort to get a retraction. Of great concern is the contract. We must insist upon publication. Mr. Ethering must appear at the ministry every day to speak with Torres. Keep the pressure on until we see our concession on the printed page of the *Gaceta Oficial*. I don't know if Torres can be trusted or not. They throw him in jail. They release him. They fly him off to Orchid Island, make a point of keeping him detained, then let him out again. It does seem a bit staged. But what's the game and whose game is it?"

"I'll remain in Venezuela until the contract is published," O'Reith announced. "Meanwhile, find out if Donnegan and Feathermerchant have folded their tents. They won't waste time in Maracaibo once they know their scheme to get Block 9 has come a cropper." In a flash of light from an oncoming truck, O'Reith could see that Mandy had suddenly become preoccupied. He asked, "What's troubling you, Mandy? You're miles away."

"Maracaibo in fact," she sighed. I'm concerned about Theodore. I never left him alone like this. He may get into mischief. I've cautioned him about staying out of the garden, especially around that silk screen near the fountain… You know, when the cat's away…"

"About the silk screen, Mandy, how are your little colonists getting along? Molloy still tickedy-boo?"

"No he's not. You realize, my dear general, that quite some long years have elapsed since that frivolity of mine. Well, I was just a slip of a silly girl…" Her voice trailed off. Then she resumed, "No. Mr. Molloy is not all right. None of them are. They're – well—they're gone."

O'Reith sat up, echoed her, "Gone? Gone where?"

"To their maker. They are finito. *Matica de Café*. After all, miniaturization is no passage to immortality. Age takes it toll. As does typhoid. The *guayacones* still come around, if not so often. One by one they've drifted away from me. Your Mr. Molloy was the last. We had a severe mosquito infestation last fall after the heavy rains. The *Cuerpo de Malariologia* came around with their DDT sprays. They sprayed Mr. Molloy. Alas. So behind the screen, there is no longer a colony of miniature men. No more *small boys.* Merely a tiny cemetery."

It was completely dark now. Almost to the airport, the lights of traffic headed for Caracas illuminated their faces. O'Reith said, "Mandy, I certainly hope that Ted does not discover what is behind the screen. He would be upset. He has been known to go off on some wild tangents when he receives disturbing news. You should remove the remains of those poor men to a proper cemetery, preferably a long way from *El Escondite.* You could place Molloy's remains in the *Foreigner's Cemetery* in Maracaibo. They call it *El Quadrate.*"

"You're right sir, as you usually are," the witch replied. "I'll attend that immediately."

O'Reith dozed off and on during the ride from Maiquetia back to the Hotel Tamanaco. When he was awake, he thought of all the imponderables, things that could go wrong. Finally as they entered Caracas, he sat up, took a deep breath and assured himself that, in the final analysis, he had played his cards well. Things would be just fine. He really needed to take a look at the horoscope that Alice Ridley had prepared for him earlier in the year. Just to be sure.

But it didn't work out exactly as he planned.

Chapter XII

▼

St. Theodore

FOR CLIVE COLIN O'REITH
  THE CASINGHEAD COMPANY
  APARTADO 2424
  CARACAS
  SEPTEMBER 25, 1956
  MANDY IS IN SERIOUS CONDITION AT COROMOTO HOSPITAL. SHE HAS BEEN COMATOSE LAPSING IN AND OUT OF CONSCIOUSNESS. SHE ASKS FOR MAXINE IN HER MOMENTS OF LUCIDITY. THE DOCTORS SAY SYMPTOMS ARE OF SYSTEMIC POISONING. CANSOR SAYS SHE WAS ATTACKED BY A GREEN SNAKE. TED IN BAD SHAPE TOO. DEEPLY DEPRESSED. HAS LOST WEIGHT. CLOTHES HANG ON HIM. INES AND I AND THE KIDS MOVED INTO YOUR VILLA BEFORE ALL THIS HAPPENED. INES STAYING WITH MANDY DURING THE DAY AND WE HIRED AN EXTRA NURSE TO ATTEND HER AT NIGHT. ALAN AND I HAVE TRIED TO BRING TED AROUND BUT TO NO AVAIL. HE REMAINS MOROSE, CONCERNED ABOUT MANDY AND IN A STATE OF CONTINUOUS MELANCHOLY. EVERYTHING GOING JAKE A LOO ON THE LAKE. NEW JACK UP RIG EXPECTED ON FIRST LOCATION THE FIRST OF OCTOBER.

REGARDS
HOLLAND

O'Reith handed the telegram to Tarbutton, said, "Hardy, once this show is on the road, I'm going to get a job pumping gasoline at a SOCAL service station." He reached across the desk for Tarbutton's cable pad and scratched out a message for Maxine to fly to Maracaibo as quickly as she could. Suggested she enlist Gabrielle LeBel for help with Monique. He told her that Mandy was green snake bit. It was an old vice that had returned to haunt her. A potent mixture of absinthe and ether that she drank when she was feeling low. Maxine had brought her around several times when she was so afflicted, would understand exactly what was wrong with her. Marrying Ted had stabilized Mandy, the influence of a loving husband. She began to function like a normal, exorcised witch. O'Reith calculated that Ted had peeked behind the screen while Mandy was with him in Caracas. Ted had then confronted her with it. From the inevitable contretemps, she had taken to drink. Ted would have been unable to cope with that. And when Mandy went down, so did Ted. Asking Maxine to come made it a difficult time for little Monique. But he needed a functioning Mandy. Being so hard up his eyeballs were bulging, he didn't need much of an excuse to send for Maxine anyhow. So he would go to Maracaibo. Try to help Ted. It was the 25th of September. Nothing was going on in Caracas. Despite Ethering's daily pilgrimages to the ministry, the contract had still not been published. A cable from Helen reported that little Helen Simpson was recovering from the measles but included disquieting news about the two strange men who, in her opinion, had no business at the studio. Alice Ridley remained buoyant about it all.

In Maracaibo, O'Reith took a suite at the Del Lago. Before going to see Schaeffer, he called on Mandy. Ines was with her. Mandy recognized him, although she said nothing. She smiled when he told her that Maxine was coming. After some minutes, she closed her eyes and drifted off to sleep. In a voice just above a whisper, O'Reith asked Ines, "what does it look like?"

"The worst case of the 'snake' I've ever seen, Clive. She's been here a week. Seems to be coming out of it. Too soon to tell really." Ines put her hands together and looked at the floor.

"Has she said anything except to ask for Maxine?"

"She says, "*Teodoro, pobre Teodoro, mi amor perdido, mi amor perfidio Teodoro,*"

"That's all?"

"*Mas nada.*" Ines said morosely.

"Can you bring her around?" O'Reith asked. I want her to know that I'm going to see Ted."

Ines gently caressed Mandy's face until she stirred. Then she talked to her about how she and Holland and the kids were now living in the villa. She awoke, appeared lucid. O'Reith said, "Mandy I'm going for a chat with Ted. Take him another carton of Chesterfields. He's a bit under the weather. Have you a message for him?" Mandy murmured weakly, "Ted?" He could see that she was a bit puzzled. He sat patiently, hoping she would speak. She lay in bed with her eyes upon him but with a neutral expression on her face. After some long minutes she said, "*Teodoro es finito. Matica de Café.*"

O'Reith began to get the picture. Mandy had it in her head that she had done Ted in. He said, "Mandy, Ted is definitely not finished. He's saddened by what has happened. He's in a depressed condition. Off his feed. Hunter and Alan are trying to get him straight. I'm going to see him. He'll want to visit you. I plan to bring him."

She smiled. "I'll be glad to see him," she said. "Miracles do happen, then."

O'Reith held her hand and caressed her cheek. She was weeping silently, tears running down her cheeks. She continued to smile. Ines, elated by the change that had come over the witch, followed O'Reith into the hall. He asked her, "Didn't she know that Ted was more or less, OK?"

"Less is the word," Ines said. "You are the first to mention him to her. We've all been too concerned with how she was doing. But Ted is not OK, as you will shortly discover. You may want to reconsider bringing him to see Mandy."

"Why?"

"Go take a look at him. Decide for yourself. Aside from that, thanks for the flat. It makes all the difference."

At the office he found Holland at the radio talking to *El Mocho* Morrow on the lake. When the conversation ended, he asked, "What the hell is wrong with Ted? Mandy put the shrink on him?" Holland knew about Mandy's odd brand of witchcraft. It was one of the reasons she had insisted upon being exorcised when she married Ted. Beneath those tiny tombstones that Ted had unwittingly seen behind the silk screen, lay the remains of her macabre work.

Holland grinned his wicked grin, said, "Yeah. Misfire. Close but no cigar."

"For Christ's sake, what the hell happened, Holland?"

"Just a guess, general, Holland amplified. "They got on the sauce together, something they never do, by the way. For reasons known only to Mandy, she decided the time had come to dispense with his small stud services. So she threw the switch on him. But her powers are not what they used to be. Ted is not only sadder and wiser, he's *shorter* too, six inches shorter. When you're only about five feet five, those inches matter."

In spite of the gravity of the occasion, O'Reith laughed. He said, "Well, we've always known that risk existed. With Ted's tendency to slip off, to romp and run, it doesn't come as a bolt out of the blue. Nevertheless it is a shame. After all those years of felicity, I thought there was a chance that he and Mandy might someday ride off into the sunset together."

"They may yet," Holland predicted, still with his wicked grin. He enjoyed moments like these. "They're a pair to draw to for sure," he laughed.

O'Reith was thoughtful. At last he said, "Well, I'll go see for myself."

Cansor was parked outside the office. O'Reith removed a fresh carton of Chesterfields from his bag and let the huge black man enclose him in the tonneau of the limousine. He waved at Holland in the doorway, said, "See you two for dinner tonight."

An hour later at El Escondite he met the now diminished Schaeffer wearing a blue cotton bathrobe that fell to his ankles. He asked as casually as he could, "Ted, how's-a-boy?" He handed over the cigarettes, saw that Schaeffer was twitching. His fringe of hair, once a ragged gray was now wispy white. He thought to himself, "Ted-boy, one more time through the magic hoop and you'll be a wizened elf."

Schaeffer sat down in his wicker chair. He ripped open the carton, took out a pack and quickly had a smoke in his mouth. He lit it from a packet of Hotel Granada gophers on the coffee table, sailed the packet back to its top. Blowing a long plume of smoke across the room, he began, "Clive, until I met Mandy, I never really knew anything about love. All I knew was whores. How can you fall in love with a whore, everybody's girl? The only reason to fool with them is for the physical release. Looking back, that was not so hot. Of course I knew guys that fell in love with whores, Molloy for one. But they were guys that had something wrong with 'em. They didn't have all their marbles. Making it with Mandy was such a wonderful experience. When we finished, I could just hang in there, let it slip out when it wanted to slip out and then I'd just go to sleep. No worry about being rolled. I knew I wasn't going to get a dose of clap or anything like that. No crotch crabs. After a good night of sleep I'd wake up in the morning ready to face the world. Shower, shave and get dressed. Cansor would have a plate of tropical fruit ready and a pot of steaming *Café Imperial*. Mandy would join me and… Well it was heaven on earth. I don't know exactly what came over me. She was gone. I was lonesome. I resented her going off with you. Oh I knew it was business but I missed her. Anyhow, I'd always been ticked off by the taboo on looking behind the silk screen. I'm not a kid! Hell, I'm a grown man. What was there for me not to see? Like Adam in the Garden of Eden, I was curious about the world outside. Subject to temptation. So I went to look. It turned out there was plenty for me to see. Floyd's tombstone. And all those others… I was shaken. Thought I'd go have a drink. I took a *por puesta* cab down to the ferry landing and then caught a regular cab to the Hotel Detroit. Had a couple of beers at the outside a bar where they serve Zulia on draft, 'Seafoam' they call it. Couple of Delta toolpushers came along. Had maybe another one or two. It was late afternoon. I got to thinking. I said 'Ted boy you've been married to Mandy all these years and never once got off the reservation. Maybe it's time for some strange stuff, some of that there tropical poontang. It was dark. I just moseyed up the street to the Bello Monte. That turned out to be a hell of a mistake. Next morning I had to call Tuffy to come bail me out. Mandy didn't come back that night. And I didn't sleep too good either. Next evening she took one look at me. I knew she was onto what I had done. After all, she's a witch. Why wouldn't she? She wouldn't speak to me. Just gave me the stare. This goes on for a couple of days. Clive, I got lower and lower and lower. Finally I couldn't take it any more. I went over and sat down beside her. Up close. It was the middle of the afternoon. Nothing stirring but the overhead fan. I kissed her cheek. Nothing. I tickled her under the chin, you know, the hoochy-coo. She likes that. Usually gets her going. But not this time. So I keep after her and little by little, she warms up. Smiles at me. Giggles when I go for her titties. Like old times. We fool around for quite some long time. I look up and there's Cansor with a drink tray. So Mandy and I have a drink. Something we never do that early in the afternoon. It was a funny drink. Pampero rum but really smooth. I mean S-M-E-U-U-T-H! Like that extra fine stuff they keep in a wine barrel for twenty years. But there was a little something strange in it.

Had a high, aromatic smell. Like ether. Mandy was drinking some green concoction. No telling what the hell it was. Anyhow I was so happy we were back that way again that I didn't care what we were drinking. Before long we were doing it and my dick was working just fine. Not like with that slut at the Bello Monte. We were down to the short strokes. When the magic moment came, it was the sharpest pang of joy I can remember. I was floating off, seeing the stars shoot and hearing the heavenly music. Big puffy white clouds everywhere with angels singing, plucking their harps and drinking honey. Bingo! I was, well, gone! When I woke up, the sun was down. I was alone, in our bed. The place next to me was still warm and smelling of her perfume. But she had disappeared. She'd put two small black candles on top of her vanity and lit them, between them, a doll of me with a pin in its heart. The window was open. Mosquitoes buzzed against the screen. I could hear Obregon and Fifinela banging around in the mango tree. I had a little trouble getting out of bed. I was stiff and sore and I didn't feel too good. Had a headache. Soon as I was on my feet, I sensed things were not right. In our bathroom I had to reach up to open the shower taps. I thought that Mandy had called out a plumber to raise them. When I got out, I had to stretch to get my towel off the rack. Then I saw the lavatory was higher. When I looked into the mirror, all I could see was the top of my head. I started to get the shakes. I was in a panic too. I needed a cigarette bad. Back in the bedroom, I put my shorts on. They were too big around the waist. My pants were too long. My shirt was a loose fit. Then it hit me. You know in the funny papers where the light bulb comes on for the guy with an idea. The plumber hadn't come. The towel rack had not been moved. Nobody had altered my clothing. Clive, I was not the same guy. Mandy had put the squeeze on me. There I was, holding my shorts up with my hands looking for Mandy. She was not in the house. I looked out into the garden. Not there. I stood between the kitchen and the dining room in the dim light trying to figure it out. Then I heard a noise. It was the whirring of a sewing machine. I went down the hall, took the stairs down into the basement to her sewing room. Cansor was sitting there altering my clothing. One pile was fixed. The other pile, he was still working on it. I said, Cansor, "Where's Mandy?"

He was gloomy, like he always is, maybe a little gloomier than usual. His face wasn't the bright black it usually is. Kind of gray, washed out. He said, "*Culebra Verde.*" We were not in the inn. We were in the little house where Mandy and I used to live all the time before we built *El Escondite*. You know it."

O'Reith nodded.

"I still didn't know what Cansor was talking about. He just sat there sewing and cutting, like a robot. Or a zombie. I went to the inn thinking Mandy might be there. Nobody had seen her. I found the Chinaman and asked him where she was. He was gloomy like Cansor and said, '*Hospital de Coromoto*'. So then I was really in a panic. I wanted to go to her but when I returned to Cansor and asked him to take me to see her, he just kept on sewing. I went to the clothing pile he had been sewing on and found a shirt and a pair of pants that would fit. But my shoes were too big. I couldn't keep 'em on my feet. I put them on anyway and stuffed paper behind my heels until they were tight. I was going out to catch one of those *por puesto* cabs that come along. But just then Alan drove up. He said Mandy was in real bad shape. Sally and Ines were looking after her. So I had a few drinks. I passed out. Next day Holland found me asleep on the floor. He and Alan have been looking after me since then. Everyone has been nice to me. I'm getting used to being _ well, as you see me now. I'm beginning to realize how fortunate I am at that. Christ, she could have shrunk me down to the size of a teddy bear or for that matter, a gnat. Anyhow, Alan and Sally had me over for Sunday dinner. It was a party. Tuffy and Lila. Holland and Ines. Carolyn and Magaly At first they all looked at me of out of the corner of their eyes, getting used to the new Ted Schaeffer. But soon it was OK. My spirits rose. I was having a good time. Turned out to be a nice evening. Sally left the room at one point and I heard her sobbing out in the hall.

Feeling compassion for me, Clive. Tie that! She came back drying her eyes. She hugged me and kissed me on the cheek. It was about time to go. Alan was getting ready to take me back to *El Escondite*. Sally said, 'Take care, Ted, now.' Made me feel wanted, like she really did care."

"You're a lucky guy, Ted," O'Reith said. Married to a plum of a woman – and she'll be all right, don't think she won't. She's already asking to see you. I'm going to take you there.

You *are* surrounded by real friends. Not phonies. People who like you the way you are. I'd say that you are a better man for the experience."

"Maybe better in some ways. I wish there was something I could do," Schaeffer said. "I've thought of going to the cathedral, saying a string of beads. What do you think, Clive? Would that help?"

"Ted you now find yourself diminished, unhappy and, perhaps bewildered. After all, your lot in life has been filled with difficulty. Who knows better than yourself…"

"That's for sure. I've been yoyoed up and down and around the horn."

"Ted the thing to remember is that we are all placed on God's green earth with a purpose, as a test of our character and also to learn about the Christian Way, the true path to a blissful life in the hereafter. The Chinese call it the *Tao*, the true path."

"Yeah, Clive, I remember that from catechism when I was a kid. I've strayed. No doubt about that. I was straight for awhile, after me and Mandy got married but… Still, I'm for sure not the only sinner in town. Not by a long shot."

"Ted, salvation and redemption are there waiting. Takes willpower and a little imagination."

"That's where I'm standing short. I've got willpower but not much imagination," Schaeffer said, ruefully.

"Others will help you."

"Like a priest," Schaeffer scoffed. "The ones I know are not much. Except for that Monsignor that married me and Mandy."

"In due course," O'Reith continued, "you will need the ministrations of a priest. The first step, you take alone."

"Such as?"

"Well, you can begin to attend Mass. Regularly. Sundays, holidays and holy days of obligation."

"Yeah, you know I could be doing that anyway. I'm lazy. I'll start next Sunday. What's step number two?"

"After about six months, you begin to go to Mass every day."

"That's easy. I drive right by the cathedral on the way to the office. I don't have to wait six months."

"Well, that's fine. I was thinking you'd want to ease into it. And after all, you have the balance of your life to do it."

"If it's worth doing, it's worth doing well. I'm starting tomorrow. Is that it? Confession and holy communion? Every day?"

"Well that's part of it," O'Reith continued his sense of mischief rising, sensing that he was on steady ground, "Ted, you want to go for the big gazuka."

Schaeffer's expression changed from eager enthusiasm to amiable bewilderment. He repeated absently, "The big gazuka?"

"From this point, Ted, it begins to get sticky. Imagination comes into play. I ask you. Who pays attention when you show up for Mass?"

"Why nobody. Why should any one give a damn if a little guy like me sneaks into church and kneels down at a pew. Only if you toss a twenty bolivar note into the collection plate do you get any notice."

"We'll come to the collection plate later on," O'Reith went on. "Next, Ted you get some attention by taking along your entourage. Start with that Cuban trio that Mandy's had on a string all these years. They'll do whatever she says. Those guys need to get out anyway. I'll bet you a dollar to a doughnut, not one of 'em has seen the light of day in two decades."

Schaeffer snorted, "Yeah you're right about that. Those guys are strictly night owls."

"So you build up from the Cubans," O'Reith continued. "You'll need a guy with cymbals. Another guy with a drum. And a tuba player. Wouldn't hurt a bit to have a trombonist. Maybe a sax too."

"I take those Cuban musicians to Mass?" Schaeffer asked, bewildered.

O'Reith arched his eyebrows, beamed broadly, said in his musical tenor, "Ted you don't take them. They take you. A procession. A block from church, that is, the Maracaibo Cathedral, you're out in the street. Lead guy is that Cuban trumpet player. He's hunched over, horn pointing to the ground. Behind him the cymbalist, the drummer and the tuba player, one, two, three. The trombone and the saxophone if you can line them up. Then the other two Cubans, the clarinetist and the marimba man. He'll have to put some straps on his marimba so he can hang it around his neck. All lined up. A blare from the big fat Cubano with the trumpet. He bobs up and down, blows dust off the street then points his horn to the sky and lets out a long note. E over high C. Then it's the clang of the cymbals; the thump of the drum and the ooohpah-pah of the tuba. The rasp of the trombone, the drone of the sax. The procession begins. You're on your way! The entire ensemble swings into the rhythm..."

Schaeffer's eyes were aglow. He could see it. He was enthusiastic again. He said, "I know! I know the tune! It's that army song, the one where the monkey wraps his tail around the flag pole."

"Exactly," O'Reith agreed, pleased that Ted was into the spirit of it.

Schaeffer's face clouded again. He asked, "Clive, what about the cops? They'll run us in for blocking traffic."

"Pay no attention to them. Besides, they'll think it's part of a religious ceremony. They'll blow their whistles and stop traffic until you're inside the cathedral. As you march down the street, you'll pick up street vendors, coffee-pourers, urchins, cigarette peddlers, day pimps. People like that. Lead 'em all into the cathedral. One of the Cubans, the clarinetist maybe, he seats them. After you've done that three or four times, you'll fill the pews. The priest will know who you are. So will the bishop. They will see a man of spiritual determination. At this point you begin to hit the collection plate pretty hard. One of the Cubans can hand out *lochas* and *centavos* to your retinue. Make sure they dump 'em in the collection plate. When you've got this going, after well, say a year, when the bishop sees that you are for real, hit him up for an audience with the Pope. Ask him to write a letter in your behalf. I can help you there. I have connections in the Curia. Your letter will get to the right cardinal"

"Christ Clive, wouldn't that be something, little Ted kissing the Pope's ring? My mother, bless her saintly soul, she'd be looking down from Heaven and she'd be so proud of me." His face clouded again. He started to shake, became a sober, gray, little man, his countenance deeply lined, his eyes narrowed and anxious. "Clive, what will Mandy think? I mean I don't even know if she's going to pull out of her swoon..."

"Ted, Mandy will be just fine. Ines is looking after her. The Coromoto is the best hospital in town. Maxine is coming down from Paris to hold her hand. With Ines and Maxine with her, she'll be in good shape."

"Christ, Clive, when do you suppose I can visit her? I'm worried about her so bad I've got the shakes. You think she'll even let me in? You think we can get back together again?"

"Ted, Mandy is a remarkable woman, wise in ways you and I cannot calculate. Had she wanted to, she would have finished you off. All the way off. Like going through the bug-burner. *Matica de Café*. She didn't. She just fired a shot across your bow, so to speak. If you get straight, she'll be behind you. When the time comes, we'll go to see her together."

"Christ, Clive. You're a prince. A goddamned prince."

O'Reith continued. "Before I forget, Ted, when you see the Pope, take a little ball of cotton soaked in alcohol. Palm it. Before you kiss his ring, swab it down without attracting too much attention. A lot of people kiss the Pope's ring. No telling what else they've been kissing."

"Good point," Schaeffer agreed, still somewhat shaky.

"After you've kissed the ring, tell the Pope you would like to be fitted with a hair shirt as an indication that you are a true penitent."

"What?"

"A hair shirt. In the basement of the Lateran Palace, there is a little side-room that looks like a barber shop. The Pope will make an appointment for you. Down there, you strip to the waist. Sit on a stool. Two nuns weave it on to you. They start at your wrists, work up to your shoulders, go around your neck and then down all the way to your navel. Takes two, three hours."

"How do you get it off?" an amazed Schaeffer asked.

"You don't, Ted. You have to wear it until you're beatified. Some men wear them for the rest of their lives. A good hair shirt, like you'll get in the Lateran Palace is good for some years. Tell the Pope you want a *Cilice*. That's the Cadillac of hair shirts."

"The Cadillac of hair shirts?" Schaeffer echoed mechanically, his eyes round and blank. He seemed stunned.

"Yeah," O'Reith continued. Over time, even the best of 'em wear out. An old hair shirt can get pretty tatty. But once you're blessed, you can take it off or rather, have it cut off. They say you get used to having one on and you feel undressed without one. But I don't know about that. After you get your shirt, go back to see the Pope and ask him how it looks. While you're there, ask him if he's got an extra miter around the Vatican somewhere. Tell him that if it is OK, you'd like to wear it when you go to Mass. Ask him for a white one with gold piping. After you leave the Pope, walk out to St. Peter's Square. From the entrance across the square, you'll find a shop that sells religious garb. Get yourself a nice lace surplice and an alb, red or green. Then when you get back to Maracaibo, you can go to Mass in style. You'll want to have your musical entourage in snappy uniforms. Mandy can help you with that. Or Tuffy. He's a friend of the manager of the Hotel Detroit. He can get you some bell hop outfits. Decorate 'em with little crucifixes and they'll look great. By the way, Ted, the trip to the Vatican is on me. Air fare. Hotel, even the cost of the hair shirt."

"Clive, I don't know what to say."

O'Reith rubbed his hands together, trying to create the impression that they were getting into high gear. "Ted, this part is not so easy. You have to get up a *street*."

"A *street?*" Schaeffer asked, lost. "What in the hell is a *street*."

"A widespread religious demonstration that increasingly builds in volume and emotional intensity. If you ever go out to the Middle East, you'll see right away what I mean. A sea of humanity following along behind you. Your retinue singing, chanting and shouting. But of course, your *street* will be Christians. Once you've kissed the Pope's ring, people will pay to be in your retinue. You'll have the money to work miracles. You can truly begin to do the work of the Lord."

Schaeffer once again looked forlorn, his eyes turned downward. He lit another cigarette. "Clive, what chance does a little guy like me have of working a miracle?" he asked hopelessly.

"Every chance. You can't be a saint without working miracles. Not in this day and age. It is not too difficult. Find some poor scrawny kid shaking with malaria. One whose mother has abandoned him. Plenty of 'em on the back streets of Maracaibo. You scrub him up. Put clean clothes on him. Get him inoculated. Start him on atabrine. While you're at it, better find two kids. The first one might come a cropper. You get these kids on their feet and take them to Mass. Let it be an open secret that you saved their skins. Get the priest to write another letter to the Pope. Tell him that you, Theodore Lamont Schaeffer have worked a miracle."

Schaeffer's eyes were definitely glazed over. Clive, you're pulling my leg. I won't do it."

O'Reith saw that he was carrying the little, still ailing man, too fast. He too was carried away and he didn't know why he did these things.

Schaeffer continued, "Clive, what kind of miracle would that be? A phony one. Hell, anybody can do that nowadays. I've been thinking about everything you've said. Up to the point where I kiss the Pope's ring, I'm with you. After all, my mother in heaven would like that. But I can't see me in a hair shirt. And I am definitely not going to raise that *street* you've been talking about. I'd look like a nitwit in a religious get up. Worse, the cops would throw me in the sneezer."

O'Reith shrugged, was thoughtful as Schaeffer lit another cigarette. They sat together silently while Schaeffer smoked. O'Reith detected a weakening of Schaeffer's sudden defiance. He said, "Ted I was just trying to help you get out of the hole."

"I'm in a hole all right, that's for sure, " Schaeffer agreed.

"Are you ready to go see Mandy?" O'Reith asked.

The wizened little man brightened. "Yeah, I'm ready for that!"

Chapter XIII

▼

Secret Policeman

In the tonneau of the Cadillac, riding down the hill on the dirt road that terminated at *Avenida Los Haticos*, they were on the way to see Mandy at the Hospital Coromoto. A hot, dry afternoon, clouds of dust billowed from beneath the big car. Down below the roof tiles of the Zangs Leather works glistened in the sun light. Dozens of buzzards circled endlessly above its open yards. The tannery, right on the lake, had its own dock and shipped its wares. Shoes. Belts. Bush hats. Fluffy clouds were popping up all over the lake, at about 3,000 feet. In contrast to the sunlit shore, the lake was in shadow and no doubt, the rig hands were glad of it.

Schaeffer was in a light blue, gabardine suit that Cansor had completed altering only the night before. His brand-new, black loafers fit perfectly. More than likely made just down the street at Zangs. O'Reith found them at Sears Roebuck in *Cinco de Julio*. With a quilted white tie and a new Panama hat, Schaeffer looked spiffy. Feeling expansive and still wondering about the mystery of his late drinking buddy, he said, "Clive, you remember years back after Floyd disappeared, I asked you to keep an eye out for him. One day you came down to the 10th floor of the Tower. I was a drilling superintendent then, in the old Southern

Division. You told me that you had seen Floyd and that he had taken up religion. He was leading a quiet life."

"Yeah, Ted, quite some long time back," O'Reith said. He was wearing white linen with matching shoes of pleated leather, bought in New York at Sak's Fifth Avenue. It was possible, but not likely that his shoes too, were manufactured at Zangs Tannery.

"Where was it you saw him?" Schaeffer probed.

O'Reith became wary, chose his words carefully. He said, "It was a retreat Ted, a pension, a place for people down on their luck."

"But where?" Schaeffer insisted. "Downtown? In the country? Did Mandy have anything to do with it?"

"Ted, it was around here somewhere. Back then this part of town was sand dunes and grassy patches. Pretty empty. It has built up over the years. Mandy has had that place where you all live for as long as I can remember. The pension was close by. She ran it as a charity. She told me once that doing good deeds, looking after those people made up for – well, her mischievous nature. There were a dozen or so odd fellows in that place. All stripes, all colors, all trades. They were all down too, some of 'em pretty close to being out. Mandy fed them, kept them in clean clothing and saw that their spiritual needs were met."

"You saw Floyd just the one time?"

"As a matter of fact, Ted, I saw him two or maybe three times. I can't remember exactly. That was 10 years ago. I only did it because you asked me to. Floyd was sure as hell no friend of mine."

"Did you know he had died?" Schaeffer spoke sadly.

"As a matter of coincidence Ted, I just found out about it. I rode out to Maiquetia with Mandy after we were finished in Caracas. It was late afternoon. That's a long lonely ride in traffic. I was just keeping her company. We were talking about old times. She mentioned that all of her old 'pensioners', as she called them, had gone by the boards. Typhoid. Yellow Fever. Old age. She said the place had been sold off. The new owner razed the building. She has arranged for proper burial. A private plot. She didn't want to become involved in graves registration. That would have come up if she'd taken them to a city cemetery. She also said that after you two married, she gave up all of her side activity so she could attend your needs. Uppermost in her mind was making you happy."

"She told you that, Clive?"

"Yeah."

"Well, I was going to face her down about what I saw in the garden. I could imagine all kinds of evil possibilities. When she came back from Caracas she put the stare on me right away. I was more interested in getting back in the nest than I was in finding out about Floyd. Now it makes sense. I think I'll forget it."

"Good idea," O'Reith agreed.

Schaeffer's reunion with Mandy at the hospital was tearful and joyful. Both were elevated by the experience. Maxine arrived the next day. Soon Mandy was on her feet. If she had not fully recovered her strength, her spirits were as blyth as before. Maxine galvanized her. Within days, she returned to *El Escondite.*

Whatever Maxine did for Mandy, she did much more for O'Reith. She brought Monique along. Although the child would miss a few days of school, she would have missed her mother more. O'Reith was delighted to have her in his lap again. The night of her arrival, she had been exhausted. She had flown the new DC-7C (Seven Seas) that Pan Am had put on between Orly and Idlewild. Then a Capitol Viscount to Miami and an Avensa Convair 440 to Maracaibo, over twenty-four hours of continuous travel. The next night, after spending the day in the hospital with Mandy, she was in much better shape. She and O'Reith had drinks in the Mara Bar, dinner in the Del Lago dining room and as soon as Monique fell asleep, they got down to it. She was soft and pliant and he sank deep inside her. They were together riding somewhere along the arc of the rainbow. Like a roller coaster ride, going up and down and up again and then finally they slid down the rainbow into the bliss of the grand finale. Afterwards they lay joined, clinging to one another until sleep overtook them… From the first touch of their hands, they had spoken not a word.

Too soon, Maxine and Monique returned to Paris. Mandy was almost her old self, running *El Escondite* with an iron hand. Schaeffer was again helping out during the day at the San Francisco base. O'Reith decided to return to Caracas, anxious about the contract. He wished to take Mandy along as he foresaw another meeting with the dictator. But it was a delicate period in her recuperation. He left matters as they were. One morning while Schaeffer was at San Francisco, O'Reith rode out to *El Escondite*. He and Mandy went into the garden. The grass along the path was covered with dew. Red, yellow, and green spiders with long black legs were weaving their webs in the trees. The bougainvillea were blooming. The sweet perfume of orchids in the thorn trees lingered on the morning air. Dull green cacti at the corners of the garden stood stately with their washed yellow blooms, catching the sun. Obregon and Fifinela fluttered in the mango tree. O'Reith said, "Mandy, I return to Caracas tomorrow. We are not getting anywhere with the Ministry. I plan to see the dictator again. What do you think?"

"I say let nature take its course," She responded. "The pressure is off. No more talk of cancellation. The detective left a message that said Donnegan and Feathermerchant have left town. They wouldn't do that if they were still in pursuit of Block 9. Cordero seems to be out of the picture. We should continue to remind Torres every day of our concern. But unless some negative development pops up, relax."

"I'll think about that," O'Reith said. "I don't want to hang around Caracas for nothing. I'll see Torres again. You may have to make another trip to see the dictator. Otherwise, Tarbutton can run things."

"Well, sir, I thank you for visiting me in the hospital. I was nearly a goner."

"People were concerned. Ines. And Ted…"

"Well, it was a big mistake, my leaving him alone like that. I should have asked Holland to put him out on the lake for a few days as a relief pusher. But when I returned from Caracas and looked in his eyes and saw he had been up to some mischief, I, well, — I lost control. I felt humiliated. My first thought was – well – I'll just zing that little rascal off into the land of nowhere. But as I reflected on it, I cooled off. I asked myself, 'Amanda Arxandra Macabra, suppose you do just that, zing the little imp off. Where does that leave you?' And of course, I began to soften. I thought well, Theodore is really a dear boy. And after all, I knew well enough about his proclivities… He's such a good companion. I do so enjoy those droll oil field stories from his endless repertoire. And he sleeps nice and warm and doesn't snore. Comforts me when I'm low. I decided, well, I would… You know my dear general, Japanese men are addicted to a dangerous fish delicacy. It is called *fugu*, an exotic puffer with poisonous testicles. They say that a tiny sliver of fugu testicle has an aphrodisiac effect. But too much and it is, well… *Matica de Café*. I don't know if that is true but I do know that a favorite drink of mine, I call it the green snake, makes me more excited than I usually am. Well Ted was sweet talking me and I was coming around so I asked Cansor to bring drinks. Rum for Ted and a bit of the snake for me. Alas, I overdid it. Once you get started on that stuff, you can't get off. And in my delirium, I firmly believed that I had miniaturized Ted. So I was despondent. In a state of despair to tell the truth. When you came around and told me that he was, well, OK, or nearly OK, that cheered me up. Looking back, maybe that is what he needed. An expression of my displeasure about his capricious behavior. Since then he has acted in an exemplary manner. I doubt if he will stray again."

O'Reith laughed, "I don't think he will either. Well, I'll say so long. Before I leave the country, I'll let you know." From *El Escondite* he went to the office to arrange his trip to Caracas. Holland was there, asked, "When's the next meeting of the board?"

"End of this month, why?"

"Instead of going to Caracas tomorrow, why don't we hire a photographer. Make the grand tour. Both tenders. The jack-up. The production platform. Photos for the first Casinghead Company Annual Report. Alan will be glad to see you. So will *El Mocho*. He's turning out to be a first class hand. Time you got better acquainted with him."

"You've talked me into it," O'Reith replied. Can you rearrange my travel?"

"Sure. We leave the dock at seven o'clock. I'll pick you up in front of the hotel at six-fifteen."

O'Reith said, "I'll be ready."

It was 8 Oct. 1956. A cool, fresh breeze from the north blew through the narrows. Although too early for clouds, it was a perfect tropical morning. Shorebirds were beginning to stir. They departed in the speedboat *La Flecha*. A half hour later they were in the mess hall of the tender that was anchored up against the platform drilling Lago Poniente No.9-4, the same rig that drilled the ill-fated Lago Poniente No. 9-1X. The photographer caught Holland and O'Reith having a second cup of coffee. The hole was made. *El Mocho* Morrow and the Schlumberger engineer were spread out over an empty table studying the blue-line prints of the electric logs. The photographer got that too. O'Reith looking over their shoulders, quickly saw that both the Santa Barbara and the Mirador were oil bearing. Holland joined them. Morrow said, "Hunter, what do you say we put 'em behind pipe?"

Holland nodded his agreement. Only he or Carolyn Cook could make the decision to run casing even when it was clear at a glance that the pay zones were good. The Loffland Brothers toolpusher came in. Morrow said to him, Julio, turn the mud over one more time and pull out of the hole breaking tool joints. We're going to run a string of seven inch. *Julio* was actually Jules Fontenot, a swarthy *Cajun*, from the bayou country of Louisiana. Twenty years in the oil fields, he began roughnecking right out of high school on a Texas Company steam rig. Soon he was working derricks. Over a decade of tough times he became a relief driller. Because he spoke Spanish, Loffland Brothers offered him a pushing job on the lake. Now forty, married to a Venezuelan woman, he was one of the company's top hands. They were paying him a thousand dollars a month plus living expenses.

After a quick tour of the derrick floor and the cellar deck, the two executives prepared to continue on their way. Morrow had tagged along. The three of them stood next to the speedboat, tied up to the tender. O'Reith said, "*El Mocho*," we certainly appreciate the work you're doing. Holland tells me that you're a number one drilling engineer. I met your wife Erma at the base. She and Sally are getting on just fine. You've only been with the company for a short time but your name is on the bonus list. I appreciate the good work. So until the next visit…"

The tender rig, drilling Lago Poniente No.16-6, was under the supervision of a new engineer they had hired from SOCAL. He showed them around. They paused for several minutes on the cellar deck for snapshots. Earlier that day, in the wee hours they had cemented a string of seven inch. Now twelve hours later, the blowout preventers were unbolted and hanging from the blocks. The driller had dropped the slip assembly between the Bradenhead and the casing. These circular seals with steel dies transferred the weight of the casing from the traveling block to the Bradenhead. Now, the welder had made the casing rough cut. The roughnecks were pulling the stub up through the table. Next the welder would *fine cut* the casing at the Bradenhead flange. Then they would reinstall the preventers. With the preventers bolted down, the crew would install tubing rams. After that, Schlumberger would perforate the two pay zones to a density of 16 holes per foot with a casing gun loaded with conical shaped charges. After scraping the perforation burrs, where the explosive jets had punctured the pipe, they would again remove the preventers, install a tubing head and bring the well in. The Mirador would flow through the tubing, the Santa Barbara through the casing-tubing annulus. But Holland and O'Reith did not stay to see that, which required many long hours yet. They said goodbye. As the speedboat took them to the new jack-up, cantilevered out over the first slot, Lago Poniente No. 16-7, the photographer caught it all.

Here they had finished the 15 inch hole and were cleaning out the cuttings prior to running a string of 11 ¾ inch surface pipe. Roughnecks were loosening the casing thread-protectors, cleaning and lubricating the pin ends. Down on the cellar deck, another crew was uncrating the Gray 10 inch Bradenhead which they would install on top of the surface casing.

The final stop was Production Platform No.1, set in a hundred feet of water on the north-south dividing line between Block 9 and Block 16. When complete, oil from the wells would flow to this station. After treatment, the oil would enter the 16 inch pipeline presently under construction, to be pumped to Punto Fijo. But right now, this platform, the size of a football field, with twelve tubular legs pinned to the lake bottom by reinforced concrete piles, was the scene of chaos. Tanks, separators, water knock-outs, heat exchangers, compressors and flow meters were everywhere, seemingly in disarray. Crews of fitters, welders and cutters were fabricating the station. The welders were the most visible, their torches flickering, stub ends of welding rod falling through the grates. Puffs of smoke rising from the lake where the red hot stubs hit the water. Stacks of line pipe were neatly lined up on the derrick barge. Two cranes were lifting material to the work areas. Alan Prescott and his production engineers, in sweaty khakis, stood on the deck, studying blueprints. They wore work boots, wide-brimmed Panama hats, and Ray-Ban sunglasses. O'Reith and Holland joined Prescott and his aides. "Alan, how does it look?" O'Reith asked.

"Going along pretty good, sir," Prescott answered. "We're getting into high gear. Started working around the clock a couple of days ago when we got lights rigged up. Now it's just a question of welding it all together. We'll have this baby flanged up, ready to run oil in May of

1957. Those pipeliners are clearing the right of way, say they'll be laying pipe in the next couple of weeks."

"How much time are you spending out here?" O'Reith asked.

"I come out on Monday morning and go in on Friday afternoon. Spend the weekend with Sally and the kids. My helpers are A-1. Nothing stops when I leave. They're still a little green but learning fast."

On top of one stack of four inch line pipe sat a Zenith Transoceanic Worldmaster short-wave radio. A wire from it ran across the deck up to an antenna on the top of the crane. Over the noise of the welding machines, O'Reith heard the broadcast of a baseball game. He listened for a minute and asked, "Prescott, you guys tuned in to the World Series?"

"Yes sir," Prescott answered. "That's station WRUL in New York. It's the fifth game of the series. That Yankee pitcher hasn't allowed a man on base in the first seven innings."

"Whitey Ford?" O'Reith asked.

"No sir, fellow by the name of Don Larsen. Not one of their top pitchers but he's sure putting those Dodgers down today."

Prescott continued to explain how the hook-up was progressing. By the time he had finished, the ball game was in the ninth inning. Tension in the broadcaster's voice was evident. Larsen hurled his last pitch of the afternoon. There was a stunned silence. Then a tremendous roar from the crowd. He had pitched a perfecto. O'Reith, a Yankee fan, cheered as the photographer got it on film. Before leaving, he took Prescott aside and praised his work. He concluded, "Alan, your bonus for this year will be $250,000. It'll help when those three kids need new shoes."

"Jesus H. Christ, General O'Reith," Prescott said. "That's real money! Sally'll shout halleluyah!"

O'Reith patted him on the back, said, "Alan, there's more where that came from. Stay after it but don't let your eyeballs bulge out too far. Keep Sally happy."

"Don't worry about that, sir. We're clicking along jake-a-loo."

So there it was. Wells drilling. Production Platform under construction. Pipeline starting. He hadn't been up to Punto Fijo but he knew that bulldozers were clearing the ground. Tankage was on the water. The cranes and the tank builders would appear soon. When all the smoke cleared from this operation, some twenty wells would be producing at least 150,000 bopd. All he had to do was keep everything glued together. And, of course, get the contract published. It didn't bother him in the slightest to promise Prescott a big bonus. A perfectionist, as all the contractors on the platform knew, they considered him to be a royal pain in the ass. If some connection was improperly welded; if he found a construction defect; if a piece of equipment failed to meet specification, he made them rip it out and replace it at their own cost. This production platform would be moving oil, reinjecting high pressure gas and flaring low pressure gas. A dozen or more electric motors would be running, driving pumps and machinery. At any given moment, something would be throwing sparks. An oil or a gas leak could flash into a fire that would burn the million dollar platform down to lake level in five minutes. Prescott would not let that happen. O'Reith knew that. It was worth a quarter of a million dollars to him. When he and Holland stepped off *La Flecha* at the San Francisco pier, he was tired and thirsty and ready for a hot shower and a good dinner. The LAV Viscount left Maiquetia at eight a.m. in the morning. He'd have to be up early. As they pulled up under the marquee of the Del Lago, O'Reith said, "Holland, advise me how much of a bonus for El Mocho. Whatever you think he's worth. As far as you and Carolyn are concerned, I'm putting you down for a million dollars apiece. You can tell Ines it's okay to buy a new red dress."

Holland smiled. "Easy money," he said.

"Holland, one last thing before I forget. Vince is wearing out the seat of his pants in San Francisco, wants to pay us a visit. I invited him down. Never thought he'd come. Now he's coming. I'll be in Europe. Show him around. Give him the same tour you and I took today, take him up to Punto Fijo. Let him visit one of the pipeline spreads. But first of all, introduce him to the guy that runs the Cuerpo de Ballet at the *Escuela Bella Vista*. I forget his name, Pedro something or other…"

"Urdaneta," Holland interjected. "Pedro Urdaneta."

"That's him. Anyhow," O'Reith continued. "When you meet Vince at the airport, he may look a little different. Sharon Mills gave him a going over in Paris before the directors meeting. He's sporting a toupee and all the trimmings. Basically the same old Blake but, well… Just be nonchalant about it. Vince wants to meet a girl…"

"I'll take care of it, sir." Holland said confidently. That was a chore right down his alley.

It was ten o'clock. He had dined on the terrace overlooking the lake, watching the flickering *Catatumbo lights*. Then he had gone up to his room, undressed, climbed beneath the sheets and pulled a blanket over his body listening to the drone of the air conditioner in the window, drifting off…"

He was barely asleep when the telephone rang. Riva Cordero, calling him from the *Stalingrad Bar* in old Maracaibo, "General O'Reith, he said, I have to see you immediately."

"Some other time, *Capitan* Cordero," O'Reith answered. "I have an early flight to Maiquetia tomorrow. I need my beauty rest."

"I've been translated, sir and we have an important matter to discuss," Cordero insisted.

"What do you mean, translated?" O'Reith asked, trying to decide if seeing Cordero was worth the effort.

"I'm to go to Maturin, to become *Jefe de Policia*."

"That's transferred, not translated. Anyhow, congratulations. And good night."

"General O'Reith, your contract has not yet been published. That is what I wish to discuss with you. I can see that it is done *ensigida*."

O'Reith hesitated, thought about it, sighed, said, "Okay, Cordero. I'm on my way. See you in ten minutes or so." He put on a gray seersucker suit and carefully checked his 9 mm Luger before putting it under his arm. In the elevator on the way down to the lobby he muttered, "Damn you Cordero, if this is another extortion attempt, I'm going to blow your head off."

By the time O'Reith was in the taxi outside the Del Lago, the storm that had been brewing down south began blowing through town. The wind was up, swaying the palm trees; thunder was crashing. Lightning flashed incessantly. Big raindrops blew at an angle across Milagro Avenue. Streams of muddy, reddish water flowed across the pavement from the flooded gutters. Traffic slowed. But few cars were on the streets at this hour. When they reached the turn into the narrow streets of old Maracaibo, none. He paid off the taxi under the neon sign, carefully lifted his feet above the torrent of water running down the gutter and peered into the dimly lit, cavernous interior of the *Stalingrad Bar*. In a bulky beige suit and huge brown shoes, the secret policeman was hunched over a stool, talking to the bartender. The joint was nearly empty. Other than Cordero, two elderly men played dominos in the corner under the glare of a red and white, blinking neon sign that said *Pida Cervesa Regional*. And indeed that's what Cordero, and the domino players were drinking. In this establishment, that's all that was served. *Cervesa Regional Sifon,* in the lingo, one of the finest beers in the world, not 'seafoam' as Schaeffer called it.

O'Reith touched Cordero's shoulder and beckoned to a table in the corner of the room across from the domino players. Cordero extracted his stein of beer from the refrigerated pit in the ebony bar and followed. Lightning still flickered from the lingering storm but it was moving north and the sound of thunder had diminished into a low, rolling rumble.

"Suddenly I have been dealt a bad hand, my dear General O'Reith," Cordero began.

"Chief of Police in Maturin sounds like a promotion to me. What's the complaint?" Maturin was the equivalent of a Kansas tank town.

O'Reith knew exactly what had befallen his erstwhile tormentor. Like Ted Schaeffer, he'd been exiled.

"*El Jefe Grande de la Seguridad Nacional, Teniente Coronel Ramon Arias, persona muy, muy grato del dictador* summoned me to *Miraflores*. As you gringos say it, he read me the riot act. Arias had a copy of the side-letter, determined somehow that the bank account number was mine. I had to regurgitate the money. All of it. I had to put it back into the account of Rojo Torres. Worse, Arias posted me to Maturin. You know where that is?"

"Yeah. It is a village with many oil seeps. And mud volcanoes too. I understand there is some exploration activity there even as we speak. One day it may become a great city. Like Maracaibo."

"But today it is nowhere, Cordero lamented. "What does a chief of police do in a town like that? There is only one bordello. The girls all come from Port of Spain. Black as tar. Who wants to fuck a nigger whore?"

O'Reith grinned. "There's an oil field adage saying that's the way for a fellow to change his luck."

"Alas, my luck has already changed. You're looking at a pauper. I'm strapped. I have debts. Big debts" Cordero moaned. He drank up his beer, snapped his fingers at the bartender to bring another. "You're not drinking, my dear general?"

"No. I have an early flight in the morning."

"Well, then, let's get down to it. I'm reduced to beggary. I must get my hands on some money. Quickly. Would you be amenable to a deal?" Cordero's brow was wet with sweat. He wiped it off on his sleeve.

O'Reith beamed broadly, said musically, "*Capitan* Cordero, I think I would. What do you propose?"

Cordero's face was serious. "I understand that your concession has still not been published."

"That's right. It's worrisome," O'Reith admitted.

The bartender came with Cordero's beer. He drank half the stein in one gulp. Again wiping sweat from his brow. He held up a massive hand and snapped thumb and forefinger together. Like a shot, it was heard across the room. The domino players turned and looked. "I can get it published for you just like that."

"That's interesting," O'Reith said. "Continue."

"A quarter of a million dollars in fifty dollar bills paid into my hand in Miami, Florida," Cordero said. "The contract will be published the next day. Telephone communication between Caracas and Miami is pretty good."

"How about $100,000 paid the day after I see the *Gaceta Oficial* with the name of The Casinghead Company as owner and operator of Blocks 9 and 16?"

"Small potatoes, sir. Small potatoes indeed. You're offering me a tip. *Lagniappe*," Cordero snorted bravely, pulling himself erect in his chair.

"Well, you can take it or leave, my friend," O'Reith said indifferently. "My affairs have improved somewhat since our last meeting. I can afford to be patient. It is all the same to me. I'll find someone to help me. If not you,…"

"Unhappily sir, you have grasped my testicles. I need the money immediately." Cordero spread his fingers out, idly tapped the table top, let the sweat drip off of his chin. Far in the distant north, there was still the rumble of thunder.

"Is it agreed?" O'Reith asked.

"Yes. We have to work out the details," Cordero said.

"In the airplane tomorrow," O'Reith suggested, "on the way to Maiquetia."

Cordero nodded, finished his beer. The two men shared a cab. Cordero alit at the Granada. As he was getting out, O'Reith said, "One final point, my friend. If you take my money, you become my man, not the dictator's. Not even the chief of the secret police. My man. Understood?" In the darkness underneath the dimmed marquee of the

Granada, Cordero saluted him, said, "*Si, Como no.*" O'Reith rode to the Del Lago. It was after midnight and he went back to bed.

*   *   *

In the office in Caracas the next day, O'Reith with Tarbutton and Ethering said, "Hardy, telephone Susie in Los Angeles. Ask her to line little Clive Colin up to come to Maracaibo. OK if he wants to bring Marilyn. He's to purchase and install radio equipment for the production platform and the terminal at Punto Fijo. Those dispatchers will have to communicate with tankers on the high seas."

Tarbutton nodded, made a note of it on his pad. When he had finished, O'Reith continued. "Vince will be down here in a week or two. Show him the sights here in Caracas, especially *La Casualidad*, explain its significance to him. Then, accompany him to Maracaibo. Holland will give the tow of you a guided tour of our Lake Maracaibo operations. Be a good education for you. When Vince has had enough, let me know. I'll call for a directors meeting in Paris. You and Holland in the B-17, can take the old Southern Ferry Route. Bring Ines and Carolyn and Marjorie, of course. Maybe Vince too. We'll expect a report from Holland on the status of Lake Maracaibo operations. We need to know when we'll be running first oil. If the seventeen is too crowded, some of 'em can fly commercial."

"Okay, Clive, I got all that," Tarbutton said.

O'Reith turned to Ethering, said, "Stan, I flew up to Maiquetia this morning with *Capitan* Cordero of the *Seguridad Nacional.* You know about him. We had a midnight meeting in Maracaibo last night. I agreed to pay him $100,000 in American fifty dollar bills if he can get the contract published within the next couple of days. He was desperate. There is a good chance, he'll make it. He'll be in the office this afternoon. Ask Susie to get the money out of the account at Crocker Bank.

Signal her when the published contract is in your hands. She can fly the money to Miami."

"OK."

O'Reith looked at his wristwatch, "What do you fellows say we get some lunch? Cordero will show up in the middle of the afternoon."

They had a shrimp salad with avocados on the terrace of the Tamanaco all washed down with *Cerveza Polar* in frozen mugs.

Capitan Cordero knocked on their door at four o'clock. In an official *Ministerio de Minas y Hidrocarburos* envelope, he had the galleys of an announcement. It would appear in tomorrow's *Gaceta Oficial*. O'Reith studied the grayish paper with the smell of printer's ink. It looked OK. He passed it to Ethering who could read Spanish rapidly. Ethering spread it on his desk, got out his file with the original contract. He compared the two documents, line by line. After some minutes, he said, "It's OK." Tarbutton found the copy of the *Gaceta Oficial* published some time back announcing the contracts for the other oil companies, the one that Cordero had gleefully waved under their noses. He compared the text to that of the galleys and said, "Same language. Looks good."

At the conference table with a view of Mount Avila, O'Reith said, "*Capitan* Cordero, tomorrow when the gazette is hot off the press, bring us two dozen copies. Stan will examine the announcement. If everything is in order, he travels with you to Miami. Our secretary from Los Angeles will meet you at the Miami International Airport with the money. If you need assistance opening a bank account, she will help you. That sound OK?"

"*Si Si. Si Como no!*" he announced happily. "I am grateful to you. You have saved me."

"Well, that's fine, Cordero," O'Reith continued. "You remember our little parting shot last night? You are now my guy. After you return, Stan will put you on the payroll as government liaison man. Go on over to Maturin and take your seat as Chief of Police. Round up all those colored girls in the whorehouse and ship 'em back to Trinidad. When you have your official duties under control, toddle back here to Caracas. Take a couple of days off. Get your pencil sharpened by one of these city girls, a piece of really high class poontang. Got that?"

"Pencil sharpened? Poontang? I do not catch those words, sir?" Cordero said, puzzled.

O'Reith made a circle with the thumb and forefinger of his left hand, punched through it several times with the forefinger of his right.

Cordero smiled broadly, said, "*Ah! Si. Si Si! Entiendo.*"

"O-o-o-k-a-a-y," O'Reith said in his musical tenor, smiling. "Now you're getting the hang of it. Make a little side trip to Maracaibo. Visit the Acropolis, the Tibira Tabara and the Bello Monte. High grade those Colombian girls and move them to Maturin."

"High Grade? General O'Reith, I don't catch the meaning again," Cordero said.

"It means to pick a few of your favorites." Tarbutton explained.

"Ah! Of course! I know what you mean," Cordero replied jubilantly.

"Good," O'Reith concluded. "When you've made your choice, call General Tarbutton. He and Colonel Holland will fly them over to Maturin for you. Then you can attend your official duties in dignity and comfort. Stay in touch with the Caracas office. Something might come up that would require your attention. Next year, another round of concessions may be offered. We will want our share. Understand?"

"*Si Señor*. Together we make a beautiful team." *Capitan* Riva Marcelo Cordero was a man born again, a man with a future.

O'Reith showed him to the door. He said to Ethering. "On Orchid Island, the dictator said that he was going to reorganize the Ministry. When that happens, exit Torres. I suggested that he could come to work for us. The dictator agreed. So put him on the payroll whenever he shows up. Keep an eye on Cordero. What happens tomorrow will be the acid test of his ability to work the Ministry. Right now, that's all that matters."

Ethering nodded, smiling fixedly as he did, scribbled in shorthand in his little black book. He said, "Clive, I get this worked up into something, I'll give you a copy of it. Should be a pretty good laugh. You can try it out on Larry Teague. Let me know his reaction."

O'Reith smiled, nodded.

"What else?" Tarbutton asked.

"Line me up to get out of here tomorrow to Miami, New York and Paris," O'Reith said. "Put me on one of those new DC-7s on the Idlewild to Orly leg. Maxine told me that's a s-m-o-o-o-t-h ride. Send each director a copy of the gazette. And one to Mandy, Prescott, and Morrow. Frame mine. Hang it here in the office."

"Clive, I must say I'm a bit annoyed at the thought of flying a B-17 load of whores from Maracaibo to Maturin. Since when did that get into my job description? What kind of a co-pilot will Holland be with a string of girls laughing and giggling around?'

O'Reith gave him a 'modified' stare. "Tell Holland to keep his seat belt fastened all the way through the flight."

"That's not the issue," Tarbutton said angrily. "It's flying a plane load of whores..."

O'Reith cut him off. "Hardy, you lost no sleep ordering me to dump a load of propaganda pamphlets over Leipzig. Jesus Christ! We flew right into a *gruppen* of Goering's yellow-nosed Messerschmidts. Those bastards stayed with us all the way to the target. If I could dump a load of bumwad on the krauts, you ought to be graceful about the girls. Nobody's going to be shooting at you. No one will try to hang a Mann Act rap on you. So there."

Tarbutton smiled, remembering the leaflets. "Yeah that was something wasn't it? Made a racket all the way up to Widewing. I'll get on the tickets right now. If Cordero comes through with the gazette, I'll reconsider the trip to Maturin."

Ethering, smiling listened to the two aviators talk. He put it in his black book.

O'Reith returned to the Tamanaco, took a nap and dressed for dinner. He was ready to get on down the trail, sleep next to the silk in Paris. All that talk about prostitutes and poontang stimulated his glands.

Chapter XIV

▼

Gaceta Ofical

In a window seat on the left side just behind the main hatch, O'Reith looked out at the Caribbean as the Avensa DC-6B rolled off the runway from Maiquetia. The plane banked off toward the northwest. Quickly up to 18,000 feet, before long, he spotted Port-au-Prince as they crossed the western peninsula of Haiti. Cuba was cloud-covered. Only on approach to Miami International Airport did he catch a final glimpse of the sea again. He cleared Customs and Immigration just in time to catch a Viscount turboprop destined for Idlewild. Four hours later when that airplane rolled to a stop at the National Terminal, O'Reith grabbed his bag and legged it to the Pan Am Building. He waited patiently for his flight. Off the ground at Idlewild around nine p.m. in a DC-7C, he was one of 25 passengers flying nonstop to Orly. After a double martini on the rocks while they climbed to cruising altitude, he enjoyed a shrimp cocktail in red sauce, a filet mignon, mashed potatoes and candied carrots. Cheese cake for dessert, washed down with a 1952 Pinot Noir. He flipped through *Time Magazine,* soon drifted off to sleep. Twelve hours later, three in the afternoon Paris time, refreshed but ready for a stretch, he deplaned, completed the airport formalities and taxied to his flat near the Madeleine. When he stepped into the elevator of his building, the bells of the church were ringing four o'clock.

Home from school, Monique jumped into his hovering arms just as he got the door open. Hoisting Monique, he then enfolded Maxine. A joyful reunion resulted. After thirty hours of travel since walking through the revolving door of the Tamanaco, he was pretty grimy. He needed a shave, a bath and a change of clothing.

After a shower and a splash of Old Spice, he put on a silk shirt and gray serge slacks, slipped into black loafers and dropped into a chair, Monique piling into his lap without invitation. He fondled her curls and caressed her cheeks even as he motioned to Maxine to bring him the telephone. He rang down to the office. When LeBel answered he asked, "Maurice, any news from Caracas?"

"Clive!" LeBel exclaimed. "Good to hear your voice again. Indeed, we have a message just in. I'll read it to you. 'Cordero rung the bell. Copies of gazette on my desk. He and Stan on their way to meet Susie in Miami. Also have a notification from Ministry that completion report of Lago Poniente No.9-1X reevaluated. No disciplinary action against the company forthcoming. Also have an invite for us to attend an official function at *Miraflores* during last week of November. Regards, Tarbutton.' How was your trip?"

"Couldn't be better, Maurice," O'Reith said. "Planes pretty much on time, food was excellent, no storms, no engine trouble. I slept over the Atlantic. See you in the morning. Hello to Gabrielle."

It was cloudy with the threat of mist on an autumn breeze. They bundled up, rode the elevator down, strolled past the Madeleine beyond *Place de la Concorde* across the bridge and along the Seine to the Eiffel Tower. Monique romped boisterously under the awesome tower legs. When she tired, they walked to the *Bir Hakeim* Metro station and returned home. The outing whetted his appetite. Maxine left a lamb stew simmering before they went out. After cocktails and a thorough recapitulation of his trip to Monique, sitting in his lap, the three of them made short work of the lamb.

Monique tucked in and sleeping, O'Reith and Maxine got right down to it. He was close beside her in their soft bed, feeling of what she had in abundance, chewing gently on her nipples and engaging, from time to time, in a little tongue-to-tongue communication. She was coming around so he slipped between her legs, sank it into her, plunged it actually, all the way up, or so it seemed, to her navel. Then he just let it soak while he figured out what to do. He was thinking of making an outside loop in a B-17 with a full bomb load from say, twenty thousand feet. Or maybe reclining in the nude on an air mattress in the bottom of a canoe rushing down the Rio Caroni while listening to the roar of the approaching cascades and wondering what would happen when he hit the white water. Maybe go over the Angel Falls wearing water skis, a cod-piece and a red, white and orange beach parasol.

Sometimes when he was with Maxine, he imagined she was Helen. Other times it would be Mimi Martell or Rose Ann or Elizabeth. He couldn't bring any order to this fantasy. He really didn't much care. Somewhere in this confused psychopathia sexualis, his string ran out. He and Maxine were as one, tumbled and exhausted, clinging together in the dark and drifting off somewhere... Maybe to the moon. Maybe to Neptune. Maybe to Nirvana. At any rate he was revitalized again. He shut his eyes without stretching his eyelids.

It was November the 20th, a fortnight before the dictator's function at *Miraflores*. In Monte Carlo getting reacquainted with little Helen Simpson, now fully recovered from the measles, he attended Helen in between times. Good early morning lovemaking followed by afternoon golf. Although he was not much of a salt, on Sunday O'Reith sailed a rented boat along the Riviera all the way to Port Grimeux. Little Helen Simpson was fascinated by the dolphins that popped up and down, racing the boat back to port. On the return, Helen recited her usual tale of woe about *Los Ladrones de Piedras Negras*. Back in *La Condomine*, the boat tied up, the three mariners walked the plank ashore.

In Helen's flat, after they had freshened up, having cocktails on the terrace, she, began, "Ace, I've met some dumb bunnies in this business. But that Spermaceti guy is totally witless. Even if he has only one simple line to say, he can't get it out. He's nice looking. Has a beautiful mouthful of shiny teeth. He sits tall in the saddle. Shoots straight. At least he *looks* like he shoots straight. It really doesn't make any difference since all he shoots are blanks. But when he has a line to say, he freezes. What kind of a leading man is that? What should I do?"

"Sack him. Get a new Spermaceti," O'Reith suggested.

"He's under contract."

"Surely it says in his contract that he has to speak his lines."

"Apparently Frederico overlooked that little detail," Helen said gloomily. "His contract is in Italian. We put it into English but the translation is loose. Anyhow, failure to speak his lines is not grounds for dismissal. I'm at a loss."

"Maybe Lawson could convert him into a deaf and dumb cowboy," O'Reith suggested. "Let him use sign language. In this vast world of sage brush and steers, there must be somewhere, at least one deaf and dumb cowpoke."

"You're not much help." She said forlornly. "Ace, have you ever heard of a guy named Flint Westwater?"

"No, should I have?"

"He's a stand-in for Roy Rogers. Young guy. Handsome in a thin-faced way, like John Wayne when he was young. He can ride and shoot and wrangle. More importantly, he can talk. I ran a few of his film clips through the *Movieola*. He's OK. He's available for thirty days beginning early December. That's enough to shoot twenty minutes of film. I could fly him over to be the hero. Spermaceti can be his sidekick, his role rescripted for a deaf and dumb guy."

"That makes sense, Helen. Spermaceti would make an ideal sidekick. It doesn't take much. What's the name of that fellow that sidekicks for Roy Rogers? All he ever says is 'your dang tooting'." O'Reith was getting wound up now. He could go on for a long time on this theme. He had a special place for inept people in his repertoire. He could pull the goofiest guy in the world out of it like a magician pulling a rabbit out of a hat. She cut him off at the pass.

"Gabby Hayes, Ace. And it's not 'dang tooting'. It's 'dang tootin'. When have you ever heard a genuine wrangler put the final 'g' on a participle?"

"What the hell does a wrangler do when he wrangles, Helen?"

"For Christ's sake, how the hell would I know? What does a toolpusher push when he pushes tools?" Helen asked, as if she'd just set him at bridge. Then her face clouded.

"What's the matter, baby?" O'Reith asked.

"Ace, every now and then I get the heebie jeebies thinking about those two weird guys that come around the set. Something is going there on that concerns me. I have wracked my brain trying to bring that guy's face into focus, the American. I'm certain I know him. I've seen him before. He's connected to the motion picture business one way or another."

"What about the other one, the heavy, the one that looks like Eduardo Ciannelli?"

"He's looked me over a couple of times, like he was considering a proposition but was afraid of getting slapped. I don't think he speaks English. When he talks to Frederico, it's in a guttural, sneaky voice, like he's planning something totally evil."

"Well, it doesn't have to remain a mystery. I'll find out who they are." He rubbed his chin. He said, "Baby, how would you like to meet the ultimate little guy?"

She looked at him with deep suspicion, said, "Ace, if I were not really enjoying your company after a long absence, I would be ticked. "What are you getting at? This a joke or something?"

"Come down to Caracas with me. Hardy and I have an invitation to attend a function with the dictator at *Miraflores*. He's about five feet two. Heavy, squat guy. Flat, round face. Perpetual tan. Wears horn-rimmed glasses. Full head of greasy looking dark hair. He's one of your fans. Itching to meet you. Speaks pretty fair English. Give you a chance to get away for a few days. What do you say?"

"Ace, I'm ready for that." Helen said with real enthusiasm. "Can you get me a ticket on short

notice?"

"How long has it been taking to get a call through to the States?"

"They're going through fast," Helen said. "I've been calling Rae Regan every two or three days."

O'Reith's call to Susie went through in ten minutes. He asked her to line up a visa and a health card for Helen in New York. That way she could fly with him to Maiquetia. He instructed her to send Phillip Marlborough to Ventimiglia to tail Bolletti and the two men who were making Helen feel uneasy. "I want to know who those guys are, Susie," he said." Marlborough can wire me in Caracas when he has a line on them."

Susie made notes and when she had it all, she said, "Clive, we just got a copy of Tarbutton's cable to you sent to Paris yesterday. It's about that government function. Do you have it?"

"Read it to me, Susie. Today being Sunday, I won't hear from LeBel until tomorrow."

"He says quote, we have been requested by the Executive to provide up to twenty names of company personnel who will attend function. What do you say we include family members of Ethering, Holland, Prescott, Schaeffer? Blake et ux will be joined by Follis et al as part of SOCAL delegation. All oil companies operating in Venezuela invited. Guest list to include leading diplomats posted to Caracas embassies. Attendees with military backgrounds are requested to wear grand tenue. Bring your mess jacket. Regards, Tarbutton. Unquote."

"Susie, you want to attend?" O'Reith asked.

"Maybe next time," She said. "That's too far away for me. But thanks."

He read out to her Helen's passport data for her visa application. Then he said, "Susie, can we get formal mess attire in Los Angeles?"

"Surely," she replied. "We can get a uniform for an admiral in the Chinese Navy in this town."

"Hold the line a minute, Susie." Then to Helen he said, "Baby, Holland has all his clothing in Maracaibo but my guess is that Alan has never owned a full dress uniform in his life. Could we guess at his measurements and have one made?"

"If he hasn't changed much, Sharon will have them in her little black book. She fixed him up when he married Sally." She put her hand to her mouth. "Ace, I can't go down there to that party without her."

"Run across the hall and get her passport." He returned to the mouthpiece, said, "Susie, Helen has gone to get Sharon's passport. She'll need to be fixed up for the trip too. And we'll be bringing little Helen Simpson to New York. Would you alert Rae Regan to meet the flight at Idlewild. Helen will call her in a minute. Where is my son, by the way?"

"Clive, he and Marilyn are in Maracaibo, installing radios. They better finish pdq because she is getting close to the domino line."

"Well, he knows about the Hospital Coromoto. If it happens there, it'll be OK."

"Ask Rae Regan to look through his closet at Summit Drive. Bring his mess uniform to New York. Cable Hardy to include them on the guest list. OK"

"Yes sir."

Helen was back with Sharon's passport. O'Reith gave the information to Susie.

*   *   *

It was Helen's kind of party. Lots of big dogs, really big dogs. She became reacquainted with Gwyn Follis, danced with him. Met and danced with John Loudon of Shell Trading and Transport. Met Nelson and Jay Rockefeller, whirled them around. And of course, she danced gaily with Colonel Marcos Perez Jimenez, found his company to her taste. For the occasion, she wore a white silk, gown, trimmed with tiny seed pearls that Sharon Mills had spotted in the window of Colibri on Boulevard Princesse Charlotte. With white pumps and newly platinumed hair, she out-Harlowed, Harlow. Glad to see Alan Prescott again in the dress uniform of an artillery officer, she spun him around the grand dance floor under a dozen glowing chandeliers. Holland in the uniform of an Air Corps colonel, cut in on them. Prescott returned to Sally. O'Reith and Hardy Tarbutton both sported four stars. It was a classy, brassy night. Little Clive Colin and Marilyn left early on account of her condition. Helen resisted the urge to go with them. The champagne was good. The Latin band was incomparable. During the breaks she hugged Ines and Sally. Even greeted Ted and Mandy, wondering how they got invitations. At dawn, as they were leaving, she couldn't remember when she'd had such a good time. Parties did for Helen what pussy did for her husband.

Both of the O'Reiths slept through the next day. O'Reith woke around five, dressed and called the office. Tarbutton was out but Ethering was in. O'Reith told him that he and Helen were going down to the Angel Falls for a long weekend. He asked Ethering to line Helen and Sharon Mills up to fly to Los Angeles on 4 Dec.

Then he arranged a trip to Canaima at the travel desk in the lobby. Avensa operated a lodge on the Rio Carora. It would be a DC-3 with a fuel stop at Ciudad Bolivar and a fly by of the Angel Falls.

Before she went to work for O'Reith, Sharon Mills made up movie stars at a major Hollywood studio. She knew a lot about the great outdoors. She knew Monument Valley and the back roads of Utah and was unimpressed. Sharon was a girl of the city, where people wore their finest, smelled and looked their best and didn't have to scratch fleas or swat flies while they talked. She was allergic to everything al fresco, particularly insects and crawlers. She turned down Helen's invitation to go to the falls, opted to wait for their return in the comfort of the Tamanaco.

O'Reith had been to Canaima several times over the years, used it as a retreat to get his thoughts together when he was under siege. He was a friend of Jungle Rudy, a European of unknown nationality and background who had popped up in Venezuela shortly after the end of World War II. Jungle Rudy conducted hiking and canoe tours custom fitted to his clients. He operated a deluxe camp on the Rio Caroni where the Angel Falls dropped into the canyon.

Two hours out of Maiquetia, they crossed the Orinoco and landed at Ciudad Bolivar for fuel. In the terminal lounge, they drank a syrupy demitasse of dark brown coffee. With coffee, they were served small blocks of Demarara Brown sugar with caramel oozing from the sides. Forty-five minutes after rolling off the runway at Ciudad Bolivar, they were flying by *El Salto Angel* through the canyon. Air temperature at the level of flight was above the dew point allowing a stunning view of the falls. But at the top of the mesa, the temperature was below the dew point. The origin of the falls as well as Jimmy's airplane was hidden in the swirling mist. Five minutes later they were landing at Canaima. Then a half mile walk along a dirt strip to the lodge which faced a pristine, sandy beach. A warm rivulet of crystalline water flowed into the Rio Carora, a tributary of the notorious, piranha infested, Rio Caroni whose headwaters were in the Brazilian highlands. The ice cold water of the Caroni was tea-colored. Tannin leached from the bark of fallen hardwood trees was the culprit. At Canaima, the tan waters of the Rio Carora cascaded noisily into the lagoon. In the lagoon, the line where clear water met tan water was strikingly evident.

A cluster of thatched cabañas along the lagoon guarded the lodge like pawns on a chess board. Inside the rough building was a combination bar/dining room and several rude bedrooms with basic toilet and bathing facilities attached at the end. The featured attraction of the dining room was a Zenith Transoceanic Worldmaster radio with an outside antenna. The food was simple. River-cooled Polar beer was available as well as scotch, gin and the excellent as always, Pampero rum. What little electric power there was, came from a noisy diesel generator out beyond the bathing facilities. Lighting in the cabañas was provided by Coleman lanterns and candles. O'Reith booked a room in the lodge. He had stayed in a cabaña, fascinated by the clicks, rustles and snaps from creatures dwelling in the thatches. Some of them were luminous. When sleep took its time coming, instead of counting sheep, he counted fireflies. Mosquito netting was de rigeur in the cabanas. He was pretty sure Helen would not find the nocturnal activity as interesting as he did. She would balk at the netting for sure. Not that the rooms in the lodge were comparable to the Beverly Hills Hilton but the ceiling had no residents and the windows were screened.

Swimming in the sand-bottomed lagoon was famous as long as one stayed well clear of the clattering cataracts a hundred yards downstream from the shore. A few fish darted by but no piranhas. O'Reith swam along the abrupt boundary between white and brown water, cold on the right, warm on the left. He induced Helen to have a go at it. Soon they were exhausted from the frolic in the cloudy, humid air of the Auyan Tepui.

On their third day, Jungle Rudy guided them along the Rio Carora into the moist, green highland of ancient fern and frond. Local Indians dived into pits below the rapids for the golden nuggets that accumulated there. Helen wanted a few. While waiting, she asked O'Reith to make a photo of her leaning against a huge ebony tree. As he snapped it, she put her weight against the trunk and almost fell over as the tree collapsed. Thousands of furious termites enveloped her in a whirling, whining cloud, as the grand tree, now mostly dust, crashed to the ground. O'Reith rescued her but she was shaken.

Next morning she was packed, tapping her foot and ready to go long before departure time. Flying back toward Ciudad Bolivar, she said,

"Ace, what the hell happened to Ted? What was he doing at the party anyhow? And that witch woman?"

"Ted was there because the witch woman was there, you know, husband and wife. Mandy knows the dictator from years back. She did him a favor. I don't know the details. The Schaeffers were properly invited."

"Ted has shrunk, Ace."

"Your imagination, baby," O'Reith suggested. "Been a while since you've seen him. Age takes its toll. Same old Ted."

"It is for sure not the same goddamned old Ted," Helen said carefully, trying to keep her voice level. "You think I've lost my powers of observation? Besides, I danced with the little rascal. At the Calitroleum Christmas dances, he came up to my shoulders. Now the little son-of-bitch doesn't come up much higher than my navel. For all practical purposes, he's a dwarf or a gnome or something like that."

"Big difference between a dwarf and a gnome," O'Reith said. "Just guessing, baby, he forgot to bring his elevator shoes with him. That's all."

"Humph! He doesn't need elevator shoes. He needs stilts. Ace, I've always suspected that there was something wrong with that witch woman. She's done something to him. Probably caught him standing short somewhere. She's punished him. She's fixed his wagon as they say out west."

The 'Fasten Seat Belts' sign was on. The pilots throttled the DC-3 back. They were crossing the Orinoco, lining up for the stop at Ciudad Bolivar.

Back in the Tamanaco late that afternoon, the desk-clerk handed them, along with their key, an official letter stamped with the executive seal and tied in purple ribbon. On the way to their suite, O'Reith said, "Helen I've never seen one of these letters that didn't bring bad news. You step on the colonel's toes the other night?" He was carefully untying the ribbon, using his pocket knife to slit the top. He was nervous. You suppose that bastard is canceling the concession in spite of it all?"

Helen took the letter from him, pulled out a card embossed in gold lettering. She said, "Ace, my Spanish is just fair but it looks to me like we have a invitation to play golf with *El Caudillo* and his wife tomorrow at *The Maracaibo Country Club*. Travel from *La Carlota* at eight a.m. On Tee No. 1 at noon. If we accept, I'll have to change my travel plans."

*   *   *

Colonel Marcos Perez Jimenez struck the ball squarely with his ornate, number one wood. Enviously, O'Reith watched the ball rise in a graceful long arc. It flattened out and fell far down the fairway. Hole No.1 was 445 yards from tee to green. With a good second shot, the dictator would be on in two. Helen clapped and shouted, "Bravo!" The colonel's lady smiled her approval.

O'Reith said, "Nice shot, Colonel Jimenez." As O'Reith teed up, he tried to remember the last time that he'd hit a golf ball. He'd stopped playing in the summer of 1955 when his leg began acting up. Swinging through the down stroke, as he cracked his wrists, he felt a twinge of pain where he'd had surgery. He knew right then it was going to be a long afternoon. Still he hit a fair country boy shot, not as good as the colonel's but he could be on in two.

Señora Jimenez laid one straight down the middle, a hundred and fifty yards or so. Helen drove past the 100 meter marker. She would be on in two easily. The caddies, clubs all ajangle in the bags, raced down the fairway to find the balls. Jimenez said to O'Reith, "Playing golf is more difficult than running the country. Here we have to be accurate if we wish to win. In government, you bogie every hole and are glad when you do. No such thing as par golf in politics. It's the people. Always a complaint. They say there is no work. Plenty of work. We need canecutters and gravel-makers. We have thousands of hectares of cane to be cut and plenty of machetes. We have immense stone reserves. Sledge hammers for an army. The people must be forced to work. What kind of a republic is that? And who's to blame?"

O'Reith smiled, chuckled and walked slowly beside the squatty little dictator in a khaki uniform, Ray Ban sunglasses and a white pith helmet that gleamed in the sun. When O'Reith arrived at his ball, to his surprize, he found it nicely teed up. His first thought was to object but then he realized that these caddies were not 'regulars'. They were part of the dictator's retinue. Evidently, that was the way the big dogs played golf in the tropics. With a number two wood, swung easily, he put the ball on the green. Helen and the colonel birdied the hole. O'Reith parred it. Señora Jimenez bogied. They had the course to themselves. Except for the caddies, the course was deserted, except that, here and there, trying to appear unobtrusive were policemen of the *Seguridad Nacional.* On the front nine, out of the corners of his eyes, O'Reith spotted at least a dozen. But Cordero was not one of them. After nine holes, they rested at a drink stand, downing ice-cold *Cerveza Polar.* Helen and the colonel were tied at 36, even par. O'Reith, his leg giving him hell, had shot 40. Señora Jimenez shaded him with a 38. Teeing up to begin the back nine, Colonel Jimenez said, "By the way, *Capitan* Cordero has been transferred to Maturin. He's the new chief of police, a nice little promotion."

"That's great," O'Reith replied. "A good man getting ahead."

"*Coronel* Arias had a word with him, castigated him actually. *Capitan* Cordero is, after all, a human being, like the rest of us. He has his defects. But his one strength, the quality that sets him apart from his fellows is his loyalty. I am unsure of many things, but not his fidelity. Arias doubts Cordero will be a success there but I told him not to worry. Arias asked, 'What kind of a job is that for a man of his character?' I told Arias it was a test of his character. If he does well in Maturin..."

"I'm impressed with him too, Colonel Jimenez," O'Reith said. "Perhaps someday, when you've grown tired of running the country and want to devote your time to playing golf, Cordero could be ready for a change too. I could take him on as a government relations man. After all, even with Torres, we'll need another man."

Jimenez leaned over, spoke in confidential tones to O'Reith. He said, "Why wait? Hire him now. There is nothing going on in Maturin. When you need him in Caracas, fly him in. When he does what you want, fly him back."

"Good suggestion," O'Reith agreed. "I may do just that."

"As regards my future plans," Jimenez began, "in Venezuela a military ruler rarely gets to pick the time of his retirement. Others do it for him, the ingrates. Even with all I do for those miserable fellow countrymen of mine, I can't sleep easy. One's tenure is quite unpredictable. Today one is running the country from *Miraflores*. Tomorrow one is planting a banana tree in a suburb of Havana. Or writing one's memoirs in a stuffy hotel room in Madrid. Running Venezuela is like riding an unbroken stallion bareback. One can be thrown... How would it be to live in Miami or even Coral Gables? Assuming of course that one had money."

"Not bad, Colonel Jimenez," O'Reith responded. "Climate similar to Maracaibo. Maybe a bit cooler in winter. Cost of living is low. It's easy to get around. Plenty of golf courses. As you know, many people speak Spanish. Dade County has a Spanish language newspaper. Maybe a radio station too."

"That's not good," Jimenez retorted. "Spanish-speaking people don't need newspapers. I don't allow them myself. A radio is all right, if the news is properly reported. Most of the time our radios play music. Should someday I find myself a *guest* in Florida, do you suppose we could get up another game?"

"Of course," O'Reith answered. "It's my time to treat. But let's hope that day is far away."

Jimenez laughed a small laugh. "Yes, we agree on that." In fact the little dictator had about a year left. He probably knew it too.

Helen could have beat the colonel by at least two strokes. But on the par five tenth, she let a putt get away and another on the par five, 18th.

So the colonel won the game, Helen one back. O'Reith, limping, was four over as was the colonel's lady. Altogether, O'Reith considered the outing a success. Helen's dropping those two strokes was worth at least a million. She knew it too. Jimenez was pleased as the cat who ate the canary. He would be telling it around the officers club that he'd played golf with the famous Helen Huntington O'Reith and actually outscored her.

Next day Helen, Sharon Mills and Marilyn departed. An Avensa Convair 440 to Miami, and then an American Airlines DC-7 to LA. She had come to a meeting of the minds with Flint Westwater. Susie helped her work out a contract. So when she arrived, she signed him up, visited with Rae Regan, retrieved little Helen Simpson and returned to Monte Carlo. O'Reith remained in Caracas to find out what Marlborough had on his mind. Then he joined Holland for a trip to Tyler, Texas to ink the contract with Delta. Then he was going back to Paris. The Directors Meeting was on the calendar for 17 December. The Casinghead Company Christmas party was slated for 22 December in Maracaibo. He was invited to a SOCAL party in San Francisco on Christmas Eve. All were important events. So he was resigned to a Christmas of 1956 in Los Angeles with Rae Regan, little Clive Colin and their families. Not a bad holiday but he would prefer being with Maxine. If not her, Helen. It was a bit hard to take. Two women and not be able to hold either of them on the merriest day of the year. Well, he reflected, it would not happen again. He would reorder his priorities once the crude oil was running to steel storage. Of course, he genuinely enjoyed the company of his two older children. An introduction to grandfatherhood loomed. How would that be? He told his son to cease work and join Marilyn for as long as was required.

With Cordero on their payroll, it no longer made sense to keep him under surveillance. He was no threat, even to the colored whores in Maturin. When Cordero tried to deport them to Trinidad, he unleashed a tiny but furious storm not only from the girls, but from the various merchants who depended on their trade.

"I'll just run all of this by you the way I put it together," Marlborough began. "Stop me if I carry you along too fast, okay?"

"Shoot," O'Reith said.

"It would be far too much to expect that your wife's activity in Italy would escape the attention of *The Yellow Peril* and *The Hollywood Reporter*. All of the relevant clips are in the file. You can pursue them at your leisure. We all understand that Donald McLarssen is vindictive. He has enough money to cause trouble. Both Donnegan and Feathermerchant have scores to settle. Clear so far?" Marlborough asked.

"Indeed,"O'Reith replied.

"So, if McLarssen reads the papers, he knows that your wife is making a movie in Ventimiglia with Frederico Bolletti." Marlborough paused for a minute as if trying to decide if he should add something he hadn't planned to. Then he went on.

"The American that your wife spotted is Donald McLarssen. He looks like his brother John. That is why he seems so eerily familiar to Helen." Marlborough paused again.

O'Reith was studying his face carefully now. Something was bothering the detective. He said, "Duke, I hired you on Susie's recommendation. She said that you had worked for Mr. Halliday. I always assumed that Halliday had delved into my private affairs. When Helen was in trouble with John McLarssen, I worried that I might lose my job. If you were the guy that Halliday hired to pry into my business, don't let it distract you from the matter at hand. I wouldn't hold that against you. Neither would Helen."

"It was on my mind, General O'Reith," Marlborough confessed. "I know things about you that I'm sure you wouldn't want exposed. McLarssen may discover some of those things too. But not from me."

O'Reith smiled, asked, "Parkhurst show you a good time in London?"

"Yeah, he did," Marlborough replied, with a big grin. "London ladies are pretty stylish, in a class by themselves. I finish this job, I'm going back. Give 'em another whirl."

"Let's get on with it," O'Reith said. "I can already spot soft points in my armor. What's next?"

"John Ford referred me to an Italian investigator in Naples," Marlborough continued. "I figured he was OK, hired him to check those birds out. The clan name is Malbecco. Bolletti's mother was a Malbecco. Big Alphonse is his cousin. The AMG was after him for awhile in connection with black market activity in Naples. Big Alphonse No. 2 is another cousin. He *worked* for the AMG. That is why they never pinned anything on Big Alphonse. Both have records as petty criminals and were suspects in several extortion cases. The guy that looks like Eduardo Ciannelli is named Orgoglio. Ugo Orgoglio. He got started as a secret policeman for Mussolini. When the war ended, he hopped a boat for Bolivia and stayed down there until 1951. He is another cousin. He was a suspect in the same extortion cases that involved the two Alphonses. In Italy guys of this stripe never go to jail for anything and I might add, rarely in the good old USA. If all of this is not enough to put you off your feed, while I was snooping around in Ventimiglia, guess who joins the party. None other than Donnegan and Feathermerchant. Maybe they came over to make a golf foursome but somehow I don't think so."

"I can write the script," O'Reith interrupted. "But since you've come this far, go on."

"There's more for sure," Marlborough continued. "Bolletti is an expert at getting money out of women. He doesn't have a criminal record, but he is a known associate of criminals, mostly family members. My investigator says that it is a certainty that he was deeply involved in the black market. His movies reflect a certain expertise in that regard. In a suit filed in Rome, he is charged with embezzlement by a woman in St. Moritz. Still pending."

"Duke, have you made plans for Christmas?"

"I'm too poor to make plans for anything," Marlborough said, laughing.

"O-o-o-k-a-a-y then," O'Reith said. "This afternoon with Tarbutton, go over the bodyguard situation. What we did may be amateurish. Make changes as required. Take a plane to Paris. Check out rue de Surene. See that Maxine is protected properly. Helen is back in Monte Carlo. When you're finished in Paris, go see her. Tell her that she has two choices. She can throw in the towel and return to Los Angeles. Or she can continue with her movie project with the realization that she is under heavy surveillance. Tell her that Bolleti is no good. Observe the look in her eyes when you recite Bolletti's defects. She likes him, tends to be defensive. Avoid calling him a 'little guy' or a 'runt' or a 'dwarf'. That gets her going. OK? She relies on her astrologer, a woman named Alice Ridley, who used to write for the *Yellow Peril*. Be cautious. Don't get her pissed off."

"Yes sir."

"Susie paying your invoices on time?" O'Reith asked.

"No complaints."

"Tarbutton will help you with travel plans. If you need an advance,… If you need French Francs or Italian Lira, LeBel will get them for you. Keep me informed. I have a heavy travel schedule. We can confer again in Paris at our Directors Meeting. Keep us out of trouble."

After the hour with Marlborough, O'Reith's imagination began to run away. He could visualize everything from abduction to rape to murder. Not just Helen. Little Helen Simpson was even more vulnerable. Even with a dozen bodyguards, things could go wrong. He put in a call to Rae Regan, fretted during the hour it took for the call to go through; said he just wanted to know if she'd heard from her mother. She reassured him that all was well.

At dinner that evening with the Tarbuttons, he found it difficult to be attentive; excused himself at an early hour and slept uneasily. Up early, he was on the way to the office by eight o'clock. Traffic was heavy. The taxi crawled along. He was booked on the noon flight to Maracaibo. He put in another call to Rae Regan even though it would be an early hour in Los Angeles. But by ten thirty the call had not gone through so he canceled it and took the limousine for Maiquetia.

Holland met him at *Grano de Oro*, rode with him to the Del Lago. After O'Reith checked in, they went to the office. Holland took the afternoon radio reports. At his villa, Ines was cooking. The kids, home from school, were larking around. O'Reith discussed the forthcoming Directors Meeting at which Holland would present the situation on Lake Maracaibo. Today was 10 Dec. 56. On the 14th, they were to sign a contract with Delta Drilling in Tyler, Texas for the second jack up rig.

O'Reith asked, "Holland, do we have a contract lawyer lined up?"

"Pop Stevens," Holland answered. "He's flying from Bakersfield. We'll meet him at Love Field."

"How's he doing," O'Reith asked. Stevens, a Superior Oil Company contract lawyer for most of his career, had been stricken with Valley Fever in the 1930s. He had it so bad the doctors had inserted a tube in his right lung to drain off the fluid. Now he was over it, to the extent that anyone ever gets over Valley Fever. Retired from Superior, he was seventy, had a good, if limited, law practice and traveled up and down the valley routinely. This would be his first trip to Texas in thirty years. Drilling contracts were his specialty. There was nobody better in the business.

"He's doing okay for a broke-down old geezer," Holland replied. "At least that what Susie says. She lined him up for us."

"I'll be glad to see him again," O'Reith said. "We ink the Delta deal on the fourteenth, Pop can take the papers back to LA. You and I fly to La Guardia in the afternoon. Take the Pan Am daylight flight to Paris next morning. Leaves Idlewild around nine o'clock. Odd arrival in Paris but it fits our plans pretty neatly. We finish up there on the 18th. You can return to Venezuela. I'll be back in Maracaibo for the Christmas party.

Catch a plane for San Francisco the next morning. Attend the Standard Oil party that night. Return to Los Angeles to see in the new year with the kids.

And that's the way it happened.

Chapter XV

Tyler, Texas

At ten o'clock in the morning, they boarded a Pan Am DC-6B at *Grano de Oro* destined for *Toucomen Airport* in Panama City. From there, it was a milk run to San Jose, Guatemala City, Mexico City and then Houston. Arriving Hobby Airport late, they spent the night at the Rice Hotel. Up at six, breakfast in the coffee shop, returned to Hobby to meet Rush Johnson, a maritime insurance specialist. He greeted them at the Braniff counter. Their Lockheed Electra turboprop departed promptly at ten. Holland and O'Reith sat together, to discuss the forthcoming negotiation. Both knew and admired the feisty Joe Zeppa, President of Delta. But they didn't have the long, trouble-tested relationship with Delta that they had with Loffland Brothers. The contract with Delta would have more disclaimers, more boilerplate and far fewer uncertainties, the stuff of arbitration. By eleven-thirty, the Electra was on final approach for a landing at Love Field. Pop Stevens met them at the gate, was introduced to Johnson. Holland picked up the keys to a sedan at the National Car Rental counter. On Northwest Highway, they began the 100 mile drive to Tyler.

    At Terrell, they turned on to Texas 64 which went through Wills Point and Canton, of flea market fame, then and now. Around two o'clock in the afternoon, they pulled into the Delta Drilling Company parking lot.

Tyler, Texas, with a population of 45,000 souls, mostly Baptists, hard-shelled ones at that, was in the East Texas Piney Woods country, a beautiful, well-watered part of the world as both Alan and Sally Prescott would enthusiastically testify. About 25 miles south of Mineola, where they had been born and raised, in those days and still today, Tyler was famous for its rose gardens and its celebrated Azalea Trails. The Chamber of Commerce proclaimed it to be a "modern metropolis with all the warmth and hospitality of a small town." At the city limits sign, Rush Johnson told the legend thought to have originated in the depths of the depression, when prohibition was in full swing. A traveling salesman on his first trip to Tyler pulled up to a man reading a newspaper on a street corner. He asked, "Buddy, where can a man get a drink in this burg?"

"Anywhere except the First National Bank and the First Baptist Church." was his reply.

If anything, in the fading days of 1956, it was more difficult to find a drinking place in this remarkable little city that would, in years to come, be considered among the top ten places to live in the United States. That, no doubt, would come as a great surprise to the ghosts of Union soldiers, prisoners of war, who were penned up in Tyler stockades during the great American Civil War. But Joe Zeppa, aware of the requirements of his new customers from California, had cocktails and lunch lined up at his private suite in the Blackstone Hotel, just across the street from his office. Zeppa, whose reputation for astute trading matched that of the late Harvey Halliday, greeted his guests profusely. He introduced them to his executives. Then promptly escorted them across the street to as luscious a spread as you could find at Laserre in Paris or The Savoy in London. Tyler being a long way from the Top of the Mark, O'Reith watched the bar tender make his martini carefully. Holland sipped a single-malt Scotch called Laphraoig, a whiskey he remembered fondly from the Officers Open Mess at Boxsted in 1944. Rush Johnson, a chain smoker, drank Jack Daniels with a few drops of water. His low raspy voice reflected this addiction to the weed. His flushed, deeply lined face was that of a man who had lived a hard life. Pop Stevens was a gin drinker. At his age, and in declining health, he could only tolerate one drink a day, which he usually had at home with his wife of forty years. But he was away from home. The situation called for conviviality so he, like O'Reith, had a dry martini on the rocks with a twist. The Delta executives were, for the most part, bourbon drinkers.

In the oil fields, contract negotiation was then and is today, an art form. The negotiators talk about: (1) the old times and tell war stories if they have any to tell, and these did; (2) a really bad fire where the derrick was down in a minute or two, (3) college football games, particularly ones in which their fondly remembered alma maters won the game; (4) notable scandals of a sexual nature, particularly when a white politician, a governor or a senator had 'gone down on a colored whore', and that in the Rice Hotel, or, more probably, at the notorious *Chicken Ranch* in La Grange, witnessed by a dozen or more drunken bit peddlers, Aggies, or, improbably, Texas University Teasippers; not that anyone knew if these things were true, nor would they care. The tale-spinning spaced out the time, allowed for thinking before ink met paper. At some point among these digressions, the essence of the contract came into focus. Paper work was then dispatched with celerity.

Joe Zeppa, a man of short stature, the kind that Helen O'Reith liked, or said she liked, had mannerisms that were similar to those of Colonel Jimenez. Zeppa was more jovial, at least with his customers, more animated and he radiated vitality. Even knowing that the man would drive a hard bargain, O'Reith found his company entertaining.

Most of the work had already been done through cable and telegraph exchanges. Pop Stevens had laid out the necessary boiler plate. Rush Johnson estimated costs for the ocean tow enumerated the types of insurance required. The disclaimers related to wreck removal, confiscation, war risk and the many forms of force majeure were all agreed. The only open matters were the day rates. Delta, no newcomer to Venezuela, had three land rigs working for Richmond Exploration Company in Boscan Field. Operating costs were known. By four o'clock that afternoon, well watered and well fed, the oil field executives had a contract. The Casinghead Company would pay for the tow of the new jack-up from the Mississippi shipyard to Lake Maracaibo. The rental rate would allow Delta to recover one fourth of the construction cost per year. The term of the contract was one year with renewal options. If the company did not renew it, they would pay one half of the cost to tow it back to Bay St. Louis, Mississippi.

By eight o'clock that night, Holland and O'Reith were on an American Airlines DC-7 headed for New York, booked into the Waldorf Astoria. Next morning at nine o'clock they would be two of sixty passengers aboard Pan American's special DC-7C daytime flight to Paris, a novelty in those years.

The directors of the Casinghead Company met at ten o'clock in the morning at that same cigarette-stained conference table as before. On the pith-board was Holland's map of Lake Maracaibo showing the oil wells, the demarcation lines of Blocks 9 and 16, the location of the two 8-well platforms, Production Platform No.1, the pipeline right-of-way and the terminal at Punto Fijo on the *Paraguana* Peninsula.

O'Reith, at the head of the table, stood in front of the map. On his right sat Tarbutton, on his left Holland. Next to Tarbutton sat McDonough and across from him, Parkhurst. LeBel next to Parkhurst and across from him, Cook. Susie, overwhelmed by material and equipment requirements, did not attend. Vincent Blake sat at the end of the table doodling on a yellow legal pad. Coats and hat were piled on the empty seats. O'Reith welcomed the directors, read the agenda and turned the proceedings over to Holland. Interest was keen. All of them had their fortunes on the line.

Gently whipping a swagger stick of World War II vintage, Holland began. "Everyone wants to hear where we stand now. But let me dispose of the unpleasant business first. We lost Lago Poniente No.9-1X to Hydrogen Sulfide gas. There were no mistakes made. No one can be faulted. There were no casualties, except for a few fish and birds. We lost a million and a half dollars. Should we again test the Cretaceous, we will need special tools. That can wait until the field is on production. When we have a little extra money in the bank."

"Amen to that!" they all muttered together.

Holland continued. "We have now completed three wells in Block 9 and seven in Block 16. These ten wells can produce 100,000 BOPD. Drilling continues with three rigs and a fourth coming. *El Mocho* Morrow, our Drilling Superintendent has eight drilling engineers under his supervision. Alan Prescott, our Production Superintendent has two production engineers helping him. We need a terminal superintendent, expect to have one at Punto Fijo by the end of January 1957. By the end of the year we will have thirteen completed wells and by the end of the first quarter of 1957, twenty-two. Moving down structure, the pays thins in both blocks but it is still plenty good. We'll go on the line with around 200,000 BOPD. The crude oil has been assayed at 31 degrees API and designated *Tia Juana Light* by the Ministry of Hydrocarbons, a marker crude, known around the world. Production Platform No.1 has been set. Fabrication of equipment is in progress."

He pointed out the tiny blue lines on the map that represented the flow lines from the wells to the production platform. He continued, "High pressure oil will flow from the well heads, across the cellar deck, down the platform leg to the lake bottom and then across to the production platform. There, the oil will go through two stages of separation, one high pressure, one low pressure." With his swagger stick he traced two red lines. "These," he continued, "represent gas and natural gas liquids return lines. One goes to each of the of the platforms for reinjection into the C-series, below the main pay zones. We do this with a triple completion on the eighth well of each platform. The Santa Barbara and the Mirador will produce oil as usual. But this well will be deeper, with a liner and a second string of tubing for the return gas. Triple completions are uncommon but the technology exists. We plan to use it. We will save these valuable hydrocarbons. At a later date, build a natural gasoline plant."

Holland continued, "The pipeline right-of-way was cleared last October. Houston Construction Company is laying a sixteen inch line to be ready by 31 March 1957. Brown and Root will complete the terminal at Punto Fijo 30 April 1957. The location has been cleared and graded. Cement pads for the tanks poured. The pier is underway. Dredging is in progress. We are putting up twelve fifty-thousand barrel tanks for a steel storage capacity of 600,000 barrels. We expect to run oil on 1 May 1957. Questions?" There were. The morning passed as he answered them.

To conclude all business in one day, Fauchon, just down the street, catered lunch. They dined on a salad of lettuce, heart of palm and pickled artichoke with vinaigrette. Then merlot filet in lemon and butter with minced chives and steamed rice with dill. Apple turnover topped with whipped cream came last. The wine, an unpedigreed white called Estandon, was delicious. Coffee, Cognac and Calvados ended the meal. By two o'clock, the caterers had cleared the wreckage away. O'Reith stood and received the reports of LeBel, Tarbutton and Parkhurst. LeBel recited the bank balances and government filings. Parkhurst had little to say. But Tarbutton gave an estimable account of their quest for legitimacy. He proudly passed out to each director his personal copy of the *Gaceta Oficial* dated 15 Nov. 1956. Applause and laughter for Tarbutton's adventures with *Capitan* Riva Marcelo Cordero. Carolyn Cook described a possible Cretaceous test in the lake, a 'hope for 1959' as she phrased it. No one showed any interest. Once again Sir George P. McDonough had the floor. O'Reith said, "George give us your estimation of the Suez Crisis." It was a shot in the dark.

A pleased expression on his pink, plump face, in his trademark white linen, McDonough lumbered his way to the head of the table saying, "Clive, by Jove sir, you're a bit of a clairvoyant. I hadn't told a soul what I planned to say."

"I didn't think you'd be able to resist a hot potato like that." O'Reith joked.

"Lady and gentlemen of the company," Sir George began, "In their infinite wisdom, our governments, Whitehall, Quay d'Orsai, and Washington, DC, have managed to block a great waterway. East of Suez once meant a pleasant voyage on that placid body of water, between two great land masses, the Mediterranean, a sea between Europe and Africa, as the name connotes. Since November the first, our former friends in Egypt have sealed off the Suez Canal with block ships. Now, East of Suez means a long, tedious voyage around the Cape of Good Hope in seas more often stormy than not. The South Atlantic is famous for its hostility. What folly brought this great fiasco about? Modern statesmen. Men of little vision. Men of no vision. We live in an era of great statesmen. President Gamal Nasser is a splendid example. Surrounded by advisers of the *jeunesse doree* who know nothing and tell him what he wishes to hear, he stumbles blindly into a war with England and France whose statesmen have many talents but perception is not one of them. Nasser, a populist, an opportunist and, as we see, a thrill-seeker, could hardly wait to get his sweaty hands on the Suez Canal. The American Government, with a wooden-headed secretary of state named John Foster Dulles didn't know he was ahead of the game. Mr. Dulles had to interfere in an affair that was none of his business. All this roiled by Israel showing its muscle. Our governments, mine and Monk's and Maurice, couldn't resist plunging headlong into the contretemps, provoking the anger of the government of Clive, Carolyn and Vince and Hunter. What a mess! On this very day, newspapers in London proclaim the reimposition of petrol rationing. Of course, the price goes up too. What other way would it be? As we sit here, the Suez Canal has been shut tight as a drum head for seven weeks. Will it soon reopen? To ask the question is to answer it. Why are we, two Englishmen, five Americans, and a Frenchman concerned about this masterpiece of folly? Because it may happen in Venezuela. Without putting you all to sleep over this dreadful affair, just let me say that water has a way of provoking trouble. A sea. An ocean. A river. A canal. A lake? Let me give you an example. On the thirty-first of May 1847, a dispute arose between the Sublime Porte of the Ottoman Empire and the Persian Shah over the frontier, in the legendary Shatt-al-Arab. The Porte insisted on the low water mark on the Persian side. The Persians, logically enough, insisted that the thalweg should be the boundary. For those of you not acquainted with riverine terminology, the thalweg is the deep channel, usually in the center of the line of flow. How long did this contretemps last? Until 1937, when the moribund League of nations decreed that for eight kilometers, near Abadan, the thalweg was the frontier. Ninety long years to solve such a simple problem!" McDonough continued but, interesting as it was, his speech lacked the sparkle that would have been there with Helen O'Reith to hear it.

Le Bel lined up a banquet at the Prince de Galles in the Hotel George V, a soup to nuts affair. Pistachios from Persia. Fish soup. A salad of endive, artichoke and black olives with oil and vinegar. Roast pork loin in mustard sauce attended by new potatoes and baby carrots with mint was the main course. Vin rouge, vin blanc and champagne to suit each preference. Creme caramel and the usual array of liquors. Coffee, cigars and cigarettes. They began at eight o'clock and were finished by ten thirty.

From the George V, O'Reith and Blake shared a cab to the Hotel Meurice in rue de Rivoli. Blake alit, said, "Clive, I had a good time in Venezuela. Should have taken a trip down there long ago. Holland introduced me to the director of the Corps de Ballet there at Bella Vista, fellow by the name of Urdaneta. Great guy."

"How'd that go?"

"Just right. Clive, I'm going back soon. I may get an apartment in Maracaibo. Think you could give me an assist?"

"That's an easy one. Space is tight. But two blocks of new flats are going up on *Cinco de Julio*. They're leasing now for March occupancy. We took four of them on speculation. You're welcome to one. Two bedrooms, two bathrooms with modern kitchens. Sally could help with furniture. You'll find everything you need just down the street at Sears Roebuck."

"Ask Sally to fix one up for me," Blake said.

"OK, we'll expect you." O'Reith said. "And remember that around the end of April we inaugurate the terminal at Punto Fijo."

"I'll be there. By the way, Larry is getting restless. At SOCAL every project has a couple of committees to go along with it. He's used to being a one man band. Make a couple of phone calls to M.W. Kellogg or R.L. Parsons, design a refinery on the back of an envelope and call for the bulldozers. Can't do it that way at SOCAL."

"He had better learn to like it," O'Reith said. "Where else can he get that kind of money?"

"Yeah, that's right," Blake agreed. "Another thing, Clive, SOCAL wants to sell the tower."

"No kidding?"

"That's right," Blake added. "The only SOCAL man that's ever been inside it is the custodian. It sits there locked up just like it was the day the sale closed. If you were there, you could occupy your old office. It hasn't moved an inch."

"Auction?"

"Probably."

Blake closed the taxi door. O'Reith said, "Vince take care on the way home, say hello to Virginia. Hello to Larry. You heard Holland say we needed a terminal superintendent. How about asking Larry to find one for us?"

"I'll do it, pal," Blake said.

"See you in San Francisco for the Christmas party, Vince. Have you heard what they named the baby?"

"Virginia-Helen. With a hyphen. Everybody OK."

O'Reith nodded, let the cab move on.

Maxine was waiting up for him. She had declined an invitation to the banquet, preferred staying home with Monique and Gabrielle LeBel. Gabrielle had just left when O'Reith came in. They piled into bed and got down to it. Afterwards, he lay awake for a long time, holding Maxine close, lamenting that he had to travel again tomorrow. O'Reith hated being pressed for time. He so much enjoyed being with Maxine. But as hard as he had tried, they had been apart most of the year.

Tomorrow he had to go to Monte Carlo to see Helen. Maxine always left him whipped down, drained of vital juices, a limp-dick commando. Of course, with Helen he could always rise to a command performance but it was a hell of a way to operate. As it turned out, Helen was not in a romantic mood. She wanted to talk. That suited O'Reith fine.

On her terrace in the late afternoon they were having drinks. She had just returned from Ventimiglia. Dinner was on the way from the Hotel de Paris. O'Reith said, "You missed an oration of quality. Would have been even better with you there."

"McDonough?" she asked. "I wanted to hear him but my business is not in great shape. What did he talk about? Crises in the Middle East?"

"Suez closure," O'Reith explained. "He was running hard on statesmen in general, Gamal Nasser in particular."

"Nasser is my kind of guy," Helen said, smiling wickedly. "The Sonny Tufts of The Near East. If he were my leading man, he'd be a Mexican cowboy. I understand he doesn't drink. In my book that's a plus."

"Proper Moslem." O'Reith changed the subject. "What did you think of Phillip Marlborough's news? You like what he had to say?"

"I'm frightened. I was frightened already. I'm still thinking about it. Ace, this kid I hired in Los Angeles, Flint Westwater. He's not too bad. Remembers his lines. Looks and acts like a cowpuncher. In thirty days, if

I can keep Frederico out of it, I can finish *Los Ladrones de Piedras Negras*. Spermaceti is a pain. He can't get it through his dense skull that he's strictly a supernumerary. He's dragging his heels. Not a famous sidekick. Still we're making progress. Marlborough gave it to me straight about the surveillance that you set up. I thank you for that."

"What else could I do?"

"Lot's of men wouldn't."

"It's fine with me if you throw the hand in. Even at this late date. I'd rather see you write it off, go back to Los Angeles. Figure out another approach."

"Ace, *you* never pull the plug on your projects. Some of 'em are dangerous as hell."

"Not the same thing, baby. For sure not the same thing. McLarssen wants revenge. He'll do his damnedest to get it. The son-of-a-bitch is prowling around in our affairs. If he pulls something off in Italy, we sure as hell can't count on any help. Italian policemen can't even help Italians. We are sitting ducks. Your safety depends on those bodyguards. Alice Ridley could take little Helen Simpson back to Los Angeles to her stay with her sister…"

"I've considered that too. She was annoyed about being dumped on Rae Regan when we went to Venezuela. She wants to be with her mother. Rae Regan doesn't want her underfoot. I need Alice at my side."

"Helen, I'm worried the ball could take a crazy hop." He clinched his chin. Lines stood out on his face. His eyes went cold.

"Ace, I'm worried about my five million clams. Four million of it is already down the tube. If I can get this film finished and into distribution, maybe I can get some of that back."

O'Reith snorted. "Baby, you earned five million dollars when you missed that putt on the 16th hole of the Maracaibo Country Club. If you'd beat the dictator… Well, I don't like to think about it. His admiration for the great movie actress Helen O'Reith would have vanished before your ball hit the bottom of the cup. Piss on the five million."

"Clive!"

O'Reith briskly rubbed his hands together, smiled his 'this is what we're going to do' smile. They were eyeball to eyeball. He asked, "What is the status of the film you've shot? How much is processed?"

"Edited?"

"Yeah, you know what I mean."

"We have a work print, a fine cut of everything we shot before Big Alphonse took his dive. I pushed that through when I found out that Frederico never looked at the dailies. We worked around the clock for two weeks to get that far. We don't have a film editor. Frederico said he would do that when filming was complete. But I blew the whistle on him. I wanted an idea of what the movie would look like. That's how I found out what a hole we were in. Well, every horse opera that I've been in has a chase at the end, a bar-room brawl in the middle and a shoot-out at the corral near the beginning. Just to be different, I decided to put a shot off the campanile scene in it too. All of these are pretty common. I bought twenty minutes of running time from a film library in Los Angeles. Four sequences. With a work print of each sequence included in the package. Twenty grand worth of canned footage. Two reels arrived today. They are in the flat in Monte Carlo. The work prints look great. If we shoot and edit ten more minutes of running time with my new leading man, we'll be finished. Has to be in the can by the middle of January. Flint has another commitment."

"Have you made a final negative of the early footage, the shots with Big Alphonse?"

"The negative cutter is doing that now. It's slow work. Tedious. She has to wear gloves and that splicing cement gives you a headache if you stay around it too long. Ventilation is not great in our cutting room. Then there's the sound track... But she stays after it. Works late. She'll finish by the end of December, at least she will if the holidays don't ruin us."

O'Reith digested all she had said, thought about it, said, "So as soon as she finishes the old stuff she can go right to work on the new scenes with Westwater?"

"Yeah."

"By the end of January, you could have it in the cans."

"That's right."

"That girl, the negative cutter, who does she work for?" O'Reith asked, rubbing his nose.

"The studio. I guess she works for the studio, Ace. I really don't know. Why?"

"You get along with her?"

"Yes. She's nice."

"Married?"

"With a couple of bambinos. Ace, what the hell are you getting at?"

"The film company itself," O'Reith probed, relentlessly. "Is it an Italian company? How much of it do you own?"

"It is an Italian company. Keeling and Keeling in Los Angeles drew up the statutes. Plenty of boilerplate in the charter. They insisted that I own 51% which Frederico raised hell about but he agreed to it."

"So when the shooting and editing is complete, or even almost complete, if the girl would help, you could load the film reels into the limousine…Cut a fast trail back to Monte Carlo. Catch a plane out of Nice and be in Los Angeles with everything twenty-four hours later."

"Probably be some pissed off Eye-Ties, "Helen said, simpering. "But I could do it. You better believe it Bob. I could do it."

O'Reith grinned wickedly. "Helen, give that girl a nice Christmas present. A purse maybe, full of Lira. Tell her there is more where that came from. Tomorrow call Amos Keeling and make sure you're within your rights. If you own fifty-one percent, you control the company. No reason why you can't market the movie. Jack will help you locate an honest distributor. I'll advise Marlborough of the plan. If you do this fast enough, Bolletti won't know you're doing it. You'll have your movie made. You'll know a hell of a lot more about the business than you did. With a little helpful hyperbole from *The Hollywood Reporter*, we may even get some of our money back."

Next day on the plane to Paris, as he thought about it, what he'd suggested to Helen was a plan far from perfect. He was still nervous about it. But at least she had an escape. At the office, he called Marlborough, suggested, he keep a watchful eye on developments. He said so long to Maxine and caught a TWA flight to New York with connections to Miami and points south.

The Christmas party in Maracaibo was at a restaurant called Rincon's. Grilled steak and roasted chickens on a grand patio with seesaws, swings and slides for the kids. Tuffy Marks and Lila arranged everything. Even with the holidays upon them, tension was high and no one could relax. Wells were being drilled, three at a time. Platform construction was in high gear. The pipeline was being laid apace. At the terminal site near Punto Fijo, bulldozers groaned through the night under glaring spotlights. Jack-booted tank-builders with heavy gloves and hard hats labored under the crane booms to hoist steel plate into place on skeletal structures atop the concrete pads. Dredges jetted silt and sludge from the tidal waters adjacent to the long loading piers that jutted out into the Gulf of Venezuela. All of the men at the party knew that tomorrow they would be back on the job, traveling back and forth between the work sites and up to the *Paraguana* Peninsula. O'Reith, appointed Santa Claus, sweltered in his red suit as he handed out gifts to the squealing children, who tried to climb him as if he were a Christmas tree. As the party ended, while getting out of his Santa Clause suit and removing the cotton beard, Schaeffer pulled him aside and said, "Clive, I've talked to Mandy about putting in to be a saint. She thinks I ought to go for it. She said she'll help me. She thinks we can wire around the hair shirt. If we can't, that Cuban clarinet player can wear it. She says he needs to wear one anyway. Cheaper too. He wouldn't need a Cilice. An ordinary horse hair shirt is good enough for him. What do you think?"

"Great idea. Listen to Mandy, she'll see you get there, won't throw you any curves. That's a good idea about the clarinetist. Ted, you'll have to get on the church calendar. We'll try to get your birthday or your baptism day or for that matter, it could be the day you and Mandy got married. I can help you with that when you go to see the Pope."

"How long after I get on the calendar does it take to become a saint?" Schaeffer asked. He was enthusiastic.

"Oh, say a couple of hundred years," O'Reith speculated. Maybe even five hundred. But hell, Ted, you'll have all the time in the world. So don't worry about it."

"Jesus Christ, Clive! I never thought it would take that long!"

"Well, there are ways of speeding things up," O'Reith said. "We'll get into that next time I'm down this way. Have you talked to Mandy about getting up a *street*?"

"I talked to her about the miracles," Schaeffer said, his face becoming apprehensive. He didn't wish to displease O'Reith but this was important. "Finding some little sick kid and giving him some shots to cure him... Well, that's not my way. Mandy said it was sinical. She said it would be far better to set up a little house for maybe a couple dozen of 'em. You know, like an orphanage. That could really do some good. With our experience running the inn, it would be easy to manage it. Who knows? Maybe one of those ragged urchins would amount to something one of these days. Become President of Venezuela. Maybe even a Pope someday. We're making good money in this boom. Not an empty room since last March. So we can finance it. What do you think about that idea?"

"Ted, it is a hell of a lot better than the one I had," O'Reith said emphatically. "Many people complain about the way the world turns. Not one of them knows how to run it. That's a wonderful approach. Whatever you and Mandy put into the project, the company will match it. I don't know of a better use for oil money. Harvey Halliday would agree!"

Schaeffer smiled, said, "He would at that, wouldn't he? Christ, Clive, I would like to think that Harvey could see his way clear to forgive me for..."

O'Reith patted the small man on the back, said, "Ted, he will. He will for sure."

"One other thing, Clive. About raising a *street*. Just how important is that?"

"You have to do it, Ted," O'Reith replied using his magisterial voice. "You've got to have an organization to carry the ball forward after you've checked out."

"Checked out?"

"After you've gone to see your mother and Harvey and for that matter, Floyd." O'Reith said.

"You reckon Floyd made it?" Schaeffer asked, more to himself than to O'Reith.

"Why wouldn't he, Ted. He had plenty of time to reflect on his transgressions. Time to atone..."

"Yeah, I guess you're right," Schaeffer said, indifferently. His mind was thinking about his own salvation.

O'Reith could see that he had lost him again, decided to save the *street* issue for another day.

Holland took him to the airport the next morning for the Pan Am DC-6B milk run up through Central America. He arrived late in LA and taxied to Holmby Hills. At nine o'clock the next morning he was in the office of Dr. Max Parkinson, who declining a job with SOCAL, had set up a practice in the Fullerton Building two floors above Susie's office. He specialized in industrial accidents. O'Reith wanted another look at his leg. Ever since the game of golf with the dictator, he had twinges of pain after being on his feet for an hour or so. "Max, can you do anything about it?" he asked. "It's just a nuisance so far. But I'm afraid it's going to start giving me hell again. I'm out of shape. Been living in airplanes and hotel rooms and not eating right. What do you say?"

"I say that you need to settle down in one place, Clive," Dr. Parkinson told him. "Globe trotting is a quick road to the scrap heap, at least the way you do it. Establish a healthy routine."

"Easier said than done, Max," O'Reith replied. "Maybe when we get crude oil running next spring. What about my leg? What about right now?"

"Well, you pulled a ligament loose when you swung at that golf ball," Parkinson said scornfully. "Happens to professional athletes all the time, including the famous golfers of our day. In your case, you've lost some muscle as a result of two surgeries. We could operate again. Might help some. Might not. You could wear an elastic sleeve when you play. Or go on a hiking expedition. That might help. Might not. Plenty of pain killers on the market. Want to pop pills? Or get injections? Clive, you are no longer a schoolboy. You're pushing fifty. You ache when you overexert. Don't overexert. When you play golf, ride a cart. If you don't want to ride a cart, walk slowly. Rest when the going gets tough. Stay out of the rough. Avoid sand traps."

"It's like that, eh?"

Parkinson nodded.

O'Reith sighed, "O-o-o-k-a-a-y, Doc. What do I owe you?"

"You owe me a half hour of time when you come back from San Francisco. I have a few questions about how it would be to live in South America."

"Call Susie and set it up. I'll be back Christmas day."

Alone at the party in Maracaibo seemed natural. Without Helen at the Standard Oil party, he felt ill at ease. They functioned as one at affairs like these. This blast, at the Sheraton Palace Hotel in San Francisco was one of many SOCAL parties taking place around the world. Parties in Houston, Taft, New Orleans, Maracaibo, Tehran, London, Jakarta, Dhahran, Bahrain and many tiny outposts of the great oil company. This one was the Big Dogs party. He had barely surrendered his homburg hat and his black, camel skin topcoat, than he spied through the grand entrance to the Crystal Ballroom, Gwyn Follis, T.S. Petersen, Vince Blake, Ken Crandall, Gage Lund and Otto Miller. They were at the head of the receiving line. Larry Teague was there too, looking nifty as always in his finely fitted tuxedo. O'Reith stepped briskly forward to greet the oil executives and their wives. He was immediately engulfed in questions about Helen. "When would *Los Ladrones of Piedras Negras* premiere? Where, Hollywood or Rome? Who was Sixto Cigone? What did he look like? Was 'she in over her head' as claimed by the *Hollywood Reporter?* Was it true that the cowboys and Indians wore opulent costumes designed in Rome by Dalmain? Were the sets as baroque as the paper observed?"

By midnight, after dancing with all of the women, his leg was aching. His throat was dry from exposure to perfume and cosmetics. Still he was in his natural element, even without Helen to lubricate it. He'd said a lot of 'hellos' that needed to be said, filled in a few blanks about their lives and kept his connections for another time. Before saying goodnight, he had a last flute of Pommery Greno to wet his whistle. With only a single martini before dinner, he had skipped the wine altogether. Blake had laid the champagne on with him in mind. It would be a shame to leave without tasting it. As he drank, he made the rounds, saying so long to the SOCAL big dogs and their wives. Retrieving his hat and coat in the cloakroom, Larry Teague approached. They had chatted briefly earlier in the evening. O'Reith had danced with his pretty and animated wife, Lucille. O'Reith had great respect for Teague. The little man was vain, often arrogant. His coats were fashionably padded to square his shoulders. He wore elevator shoes and heavy gold rings on his fingers. He preened for committee meetings but he was not the only one who did that. Larry Teague knew refining and marketing from A to Z. He was decisive. Once his vision of a project was clear, he had the bulldozers moving and the welding torches blazing. He relentlessly pursued good jokes and recognized O'Reith as a master raconteur. He was not going to let O'Reith leave without something. Teague scorned

Blake's jokes as tepid, often pointless and lacking in originality. By contrast, when O'Reith told a joke, it was rich in irony, had at least one double entendre and was invariably biological. Teague said, "Clive, before you get out of here, how about a quick lesson in anatomy?"

O'Reith smiled, got a midnight twinkle in his eye and in his musical tenor, said, "Larry, there's an army joke that's not too bad. These three guys are caught in the draft. They show up for their physical examinations. You know the army way. The draftees strip down to the buff and then the army doc asks them embarrassing questions. An exercise in intimidation. The army doctor asked the first guy of three before him, 'What do you do in civil life?' This raw recruit said, 'Doc, I'm a coke-sacker. I sack coke at the coke works.' The doctor asked the second guy, 'What do you do, buddy?' The second guy said, 'I work in a sock factory. I tuck socks for the sock boxes.' The doctor asked the third guy, 'and you, Mac. What do you do?' The third guy was kind of funny looking and he lisped, 'Doc, these other two guys have got me so confused, I don't know exactly what I do do.'"

The little refining executive doubled with laughter, got out a notebook from his vest pocket and made notes so he could retell it. He said, "Clive, once you get to running crude oil, if you decide to get into the refining business, don't do anything without telling me. I could have some ideas."

"Stay in touch with Vince, Larry. He'll always know what is going on. And thanks by the way for putting us on to a terminals superintendent. Holland said he was going to hire him."

To clear his head, O'Reith walked from the Sheraton Palace to the Mark Hopkins. Early next morning he called Pacific Western, to confirm his seat on their noon flight to Los Angeles. He planned a quiet holiday with his Rae Regan and her family. Drop in for a drink with his son and Marilyn. Inspect the new addition to the clan, Virginia-Helen. He would visit Susie and little Briscoe. Find out what was on Parkinson's mind. He needed a gringo medic for Maracaibo. Maybe

Max was interested. He wouldn't be allowed to hang out a shingle, only Venezuelans could do that. As the DC-4 lined up to land, he fondly eyed the Calitroleum Tower until it dipped out of sight behind the Fullerton Building. As the plane touched the runway, he made a mental note to ask Susie to line up a chat with Phillip Marlborough. He wanted to be sure they had an air tight guard in Monte Carlo and Ventimiglia.

Chapter XVI

▼

1957

It was New Year's eve 1956 at Holmby Hills. O'Reith was baby-sitting Rae Regan's three children. She and her husband were swinging at the Palladium. O'Reith telephoned Maxine, then Helen, then Blake, his son and Marilyn and finally Susie, wished them all the best for 1957. By ten o'clock the kids were down. Reading from his briefcase, he nursed a snifter of five star Martell. At eleven, yawning, he looked in on the sleeping children. Then to bed and before the first siren sounded, he was asleep. Tomorrow would be soon enough to check out 1957.

New year's day was a drag. The Limejuicer club was closed. Rae Regan and her husband slept in. The maid got the children up and going. O'Reith played with them on the lawn until they were all tired. That afternoon he visited his son, daughter-in-law and the new baby, wishing he were in Paris with Maxine or in Monte Carlo with Helen or for that matter, out on Lake Maracaibo setting a string of pipe. Not that he had anything against grandfatherhood. In short, he was bored. But next morning, he was on the golf course at nine. Life was pleasant. That afternoon he drove over to the Summit Drive bungalow. His son and Marilyn had taken the baby to San Bernadino with the Blakes. He parked in the driveway, let himself in. In his study, he removed an army .45 automatic from its cosmoline packing. He cleaned it. Put a pair of ancient earplugs in his pocket. At the Limejuicers club, he shot bulls on the thousand inch range until he used up his ammunition. Shooting below par, he resolved to see an oculist for new distance glasses.

The next day, 3 Jan 57, in the Fullerton Building at nine o'clock, he shared a cup of coffee with Susie while reading the messages that had arrived during the holidays. The first was a telegram from The Standard Oil Company of California.

GENERAL CLIVE COLIN O'REITH
THE CASINGHEAD COMPANY
875 THE FULLERTON BUILDING
LOS ANGELES 12, CALIFORNIA
28 DEC 1956
WITH REFERENCE TO DISCUSSIONS BETWEEN YOURSELF AND OUR MR. LAWRENCE TEAGUE, WE NOTIFY YOU OF THE INTENTION OF OUR SUBSIDIARY, RICHMOND OIL REFINING COMPANY OF NASSAU TO BEGIN LIFTING 150,000 BOPD OF 31 DEGREE TIA JUANA LIGHT CRUDE OIL FROM YOUR TERMINAL AT PUNTO FIJO COMMENCING ON OR ABOUT 1 MAY 1957. WE ARE TODAY FORWARDING SUGGESTED CONTRACT TERMS TO YOUR OFFICE IN CARACAS, VENEZUELA. WE ENVISION AN EVERGREEN CONTRACT WITH PROVISIONS FOR ADDITIONAL LIFTINGS AS AVAILS PERMIT. PROPOSAL TO CONTAIN USUAL PROVISIONS REGARDING GRAVITY VARIATIONS, SULPHUR AND METALS CONTENT AND STANDARD FORCE MAJEURE PROVISIONS FOR VENEZUELA. WE WILL NEED THE FREQUENCIES OF YOUR MARINE RADIOS IN PUNTO FIJO AND WOULD APPRECIATE RECEIVING THIS INFORMATION ON A TIMELY BASIS.
REGARDS
POSTLEWAITHE
CRUDE OIL LIFTINGS COORDINATOR
THE STANDARD OIL BUILDING

SAN FRANCISCO 6, CALIFORNIA

"Susie, that's good news!" O'Reith said jubilantly. " Larry. must have told Postlewaithe a good joke. Vince is involved too. It's great news. We don't have to tender on the open market. No brokerage fees, no commissions."

She smiled and passed him a cable from Tarbutton. "What do you think of this one?" she asked.

GENERAL CLIVE COLIN O'REITH
THE CASING HEAD COMPANY
875 FULLERTON BUILDING
LOS ANGELES 12, CALIFORNIA
27 DEC 1956
ATTENDED SHELL DE VENEZUELA CHRISTMAS PARTY CONVERSATION WITH LAUGHTON VAN METER, THEIR REFINERY MANAGER IN CARDON. HE EXPRESSED AN INTEREST IN BUYING A LIQUID NATURAL GAS STREAM IF WE WOULD DELIVER IT AT PUNTO FIJO. HE SAID IT IS A SIMPLE AND INEXPENSIVE MATTER TO RUN A 6 INCH LINE TO THEIR REFINERY. ON OUR SIDE, THIS WOULD ENTAIL DOUBLING THE PRESENT 16 INCH CRUDE LINE WITH A PRODUCTS LINE FOR A HIGH PRESSURE MIXTURE OF BUTANE, PROPANE AND PENTANES PLUS. SHOULD WE AGREE TO SELL THIS STREAM TO SHELL, THEN THE PLANNED TRIPLE COMPLETIONS SHOULD BE REDESIGNED SO THAT WE CAN TAKE FROM THE C-SERIES AND ADD THIS LIGHT HYDROCARBON STREAM TO THE LNG STREAM FROM SECOND STAGE SEPARATION OF MIRADOR AND SANTA BARBARA CRUDE STREAMS. SUBSTANTIAL WORK REQUIRED TO DO THIS BUT IT APPEARS TO BE ATTRACTIVE. BY COPY THIS CABLE I REQUESTED HOLLAND TO MAKE AN ECONOMIC ANALYSIS AND REVERT WITH FEASIBILITY.
REGARDS
HARDY

"Life can get complicated in a hurry," O'Reith said.

"Well I surely don't understand all that," Susie said, pouring their second cup.

"It's pretty simple, Susie," O'Reith said. "The crude oil from both the Mirador and the Santa Barbara contains propane and butane. Going through the stages of separation, we either refrigerate it, compress it and find a place to sell it, or we do something else with it. We can either burn it or, as we planned, reinject it into the C-series, to use at a later date. Right now, we're set up to reinject it. To sell it, we'll have to lay a second pipeline alongside the crude oil line, bring it ashore at Punto Fijo and reship it to Shell at Cardon. Can we can make money doing it? Holland will have to figure that out."

"Cable from him on that subject in this stack," Susie said. She fished it out.

GENERAL CLIVE COLIN O'REITH
THE CASINGHEAD COMPANY
875 THE FULLERTON BUILDING
LOS ANGELES 12, CALIFORNIA
1 JAN 1957
BASED ON PRICES QUOTED BY SHELL AND ASSUMING NORMAL INVESTMENT FOR SECOND PIPELINE TO CARRY PRODUCTS STREAM, IT APPEARS WE CAN MAKE PROFIT OF AROUND ELEVEN CENTS A BARREL OVER A CONTRACT PERIOD OF THREE YEARS. HAVE ADVISED TARBUTTON IN CARACAS. AWAIT YOUR DECISION TO ORDER LINE PIPE AND NEGOTIATE AN EXTENSION OF PIPELAY CONTRACT WITH HOUSTON CONTRACTING COMPANY.
REGARDS
HOLLAND

"So what do we do, Clive?" Susie asked.

He grinned at her cagily. "We call Larry Teague in San Francisco."

Susie put the call through and motioned that Teague was coming to the telephone.

"Larry boy, how you are?" O'Reith asked in his most musical of tenors. "All the best for fifty seven and years beyond."

"I'm standing tall, Clive, "Teague responded. "Same to you for the new year."

"Larry to thank you for the telegram from Bob Postlewaithe. Saves us a hell of a lot of running around."

"Well, Clive we need the crude."

"Larry, babe. Let me try something out on you?" O'Reith asked.

"Shoot."

O'Reith read him the cables from Tarbutton and Holland. He said, "Larry, I'm out of my element. We considered setting a gasoline plant on a platform in the lake but put it on the back burner. Now that may make more sense than pumping a stream of high pressure product from the lake to Punto Fijo. What do you think?"

"Let's get together and talk about it, Clive," Teague said. "How long you in town?"

"I had planned to fly to Paris on Thursday, but ... Larry, can you slip away? Come down here and see me tomorrow? Two or three things on my mind... I heard a new biological the other day at the club. Not too bad of a joke."

"You could tell it to me over the phone," Teague suggested.

"Some sweet young operator might report us to the Texas Department of Pure Food and Candy Confections. You better come on down..."

Teague laughed uproariously, said, "What say ten o'clock in the morning in your office?"

"Susie'll have the coffee pot a perking."

Little Clive Colin reported promptly at nine-thirty. Susie showed him in. O'Reith motioned him to a chair and handed him the telegram from SOCAL. After reading it through, he said, "Dad, I'll send them the frequencies this morning."

O'Reith nodded, his face became sober, as he began speaking his voice edged lower. It was not *the voice* but it was one his son instantly recognized as carrying an extra authority. Words to be listened to with care; words to be remembered. O'Reith said, "Son, it's time you got additional exposure to the business. At some point you will have to assume a position of greater authority so we might just as well start now. Larry Teague tipped us to a guy to become Terminals Manager in Punto Fijo. He's sixty or so, has a few good years left. You could be his understudy. While you're at it, you could spend a day or so each week with Hunter Holland. Get an education about lake operations. Before you know it, you'd be checked out. Looking on down the road, the first responsible position in either terminals or crude production, you'd be ready. What do you think?"

"Live in Venezuela?"

"Punto Fijo. The camp is almost complete. Nice area. Close to Cardon. You and Marilyn could get away once in a while. Clean sandy beaches. Just right for surfing."

"Dad, I've flown over that water. It's shark infested."

"Not all the time, " O'Reith continued. "Anyhow, kick it around with Marilyn and see what she thinks. No hurry. You can let me know, well, say tomorrow afternoon."

"Tomorrow! What kind of a 'no hurry' is that?" Little Clive Colin appeared outraged.

O'Reith asked, "You still fooling around with Ellen?"

"A little," his son admitted.

"Larry Teague coming in the morning. You're invited to join us. Golf at the club. Let me know then. By the way, do you have your pilot's license yet?"

"Yes sir. Single engines, daylight only."

"Well that's a start. Get some four engine time in Venezuela. Hardy and Hunter will help you. We're hiring six pilots and three aviation mechanics to keep those two B-17s in service. We'll have a tarmac strip at Punto Fijo. Fly back and forth to *Grano de Oro*. If you need to go to Caracas, that too. Get in some cabin time on Sundays."

"Sundays! Jesus Christ, Dad. I haven't yet agreed to go down there. What kind of surfing could we get in if I have to fly on Sundays?"

"Well, it could be every other Sunday." O'Reith suggested in tones suggesting flexibility but no alternative. "So fill Marilyn in." O'Reith looked at his wall calendar, brand new, a gift from the Rigid Wrench Company. A Varga Girl with pursed lips in a scanty, red two piece bathing suit smiled at them. He said, "Son, it's the third. Try being down there on the first of February. That'll give you time to get your business in shape. The camp will be finished. May have a rough edge or two but nothing serious..."

"A rough edge or two! Dad would you live in a raw refinery camp where you had to boil the drinking water?"

O'Reith waved a hand in dismissal. "Not a refinery son. A terminal. You need the experience. How's your golf game by the way?"

"Not too bad."

"Good. On the tee at two o'clock tomorrow afternoon. Just a threesome, you and I and Larry. Work out something with that girl. Come to see her every six weeks or so."

His son nodded, smiled weakly.

Susie announced the arrival of Dr. Max Parkinson. O'Reith rose, cordially shook his son's hand, patted him on the back. The two of them greeted the medical man. As his son was leaving, Susie entered and asked, "Max, Coffee?"

"Thanks Susie," he answered, "but no. I'm down to a cup at breakfast and that's it for the day. Drink more than that, I get the shakes."

O'Reith waved him to the sofa, said, "Max, what's on your mind?"

"Clive, when Calitroleum merged into SOCAL, I lost my way for a while. They offered me a job in Alaska. I'm as adventurous as anyone. I'm just not an ice and snow man. So I turned it down."

"How are you doing now?" O'Reith asked.

"Just fair," the medico responded. "Money is okay. But I rarely get a night of sleep. That's OK when you're young but… Industrial accidents have a way of happening in the middle of the night, or during an earthquake or after a flash flood. Things like that. I have to scramble. I go to bed at night knowing that the phone will ring before daylight."

O'Reith nodded, sifted through the doctor's comments quickly, said, "Max, Venezuelan law requires all medicos to have a local license which, in effect, keeps foreigners from practicing medicine. But the company is entitled to a Safety Director, which, right now, we don't have. No reason it can't be you. What do you know about tropical medicine?"

Parkinson laughed. "A lot more than I did ten days ago. When Susie called to say you were coming in, I took a crash course at the UCLA library. All doctors have a basic knowledge of typhoid and malaria and yellow fever."

O'Reith added. "There's amebic dysentery and bilhartzia. A fly down there drills through your shirt and lays an egg in your back. Egg grows into a *gusano*, that's a worm. Makes a boil. The locals force the worm out with the tip of a lighted cigarette. But it's kind of dangerous. Blood poisoning. The biggest problem is infection. A minor cut becomes a major inflammation. Of course, everything responds to treatment… Then there is the usual assortment of spiders, snakes, scorpions, centipedes and a few insects that remain unidentified."

"Living conditions? Women get along OK?"

"O-o-o-k-a-a-y, Max. Simple but comfortable. Food is cheap and plentiful. Beef tastes odd at first but you get used to it. Women soak lettuce and tomatoes in permanganate to kill off the amoebas. Fruit is first class. Mangos. Papayas. Bananas. Nisperos. Good restaurants. European chefs. Excellent Chinese restaurants. As good as you find here."

"Houses comfortable?"

"It would be a brand new furnished flat on the main drag coming in from the airport. We leased four. Building to be complete the first of March. We're hiring new hands."

"How's Holland doing?"

"Great. Couldn't make it without him."

"Ines?"

"Three kids to look after. Holland under her thumb. He's resigned to a life with out any side openings. But he's a short timer in Venezuela. Once we get crude oil running, Alan Prescott will take over. Holland will move to Paris to help me."

"Prescott's OK? Sally?"

"Both of 'em right as rain. Couple of great kids. In fact, Max, we've got a wonderful bunch of people. You know most of 'em. It'll be like old times..."

"You mean I've already got the job?"

"Sure," O'Reith said. "I was going to strap it on you anyhow. We're standing short. Susie will get you a visa. Other formalities. Give yourself the required shots. Pay the same as Calitroleum. Company picks up living expenses in Maracaibo. Stock option. The usual. Office and a clinic in Maracaibo. Infirmary up at Punto Fijo. Couple of Venezuelan doctors to look after the day-to-day aches and pains. Your guys. Of course if we have a crown accident or a bad fire..."

"I understand. When do you want me down there?"

"When you're ready. Soon as you wind up your affairs."

"How about the first of March?"

"That's fine."

Susie announced Phillip Marlborough. O'Reith said goodbye to Parkinson, greeted the detective. It was eleven o'clock. O'Reith said, "Duke, I've had to cut out lunch time drinking. My metabolism can't keep up with it. But Susie's got a jug of pretty fair country boy scotch back there. How about a shot? Stagger those rats gnawing away in the woodwork."

"Ye-a-a-h, General O'Reith. I would like a little nip. We've got some talking to do and my throat'll get as dry as yesterday's toast."

O'Reith pressed his intercom button, said, "Susie, Duke wants to wet his whistle. Think you could pump him up a finger or two of that divine northern nectar?"

"On the way, sir," she said cheerfully.

O'Reith began, "Duke, I've done my damnedest to convince Helen she's skiing down Mount Blanc with nothing on but her brassiere and a pair of pink tissue-paper panties. She's scared but she refuses to throw her hand in. She's determined to finish that sagebrush saga of the Texas border. I got into it with her. Showed her an exit. She thinks she can get it into the cans by the end of January. I told her to play it cagey with Bolletti. Apparently he doesn't watch things carefully anyhow. I told her to sneak everything out of the studio when it's finished. Just pile the reels and the work print and whatever else she needs into the trunk of her limousine and head west and I mean really west, like Los Angeles. That's all well and good. But! I worry that Bolletti and company will smell a rat, realize she's going to take a powder on 'em and alert his pal, Donald McLarssen that the string is running out. He could urge him to do something. Are we set up strong enough to protect her and, importantly, little Helen Simpson?"

Susie brought a tray with a bottle of Haig's Pinch, a bucket of ice, two glasses, some bottled water and a seltzer siphon. She poured Marlborough a generous dollop of the whiskey, some water for O'Reith. Marlborough looked up at Susie, made a pistol with his thumb and forefinger, pointed it at the siphon, wriggled his thumb and said, "psst."

Susie smiled, jolted the scotch, looked at him with arched eyebrows. He fired again and she jolted the scotch again. He said, "Thanks." Then turning to O'Reith he began, "There's a limit to what we can do, the old law of diminishing returns." He raised the glass and quaffed off an inch of it. "Pretty fair drinking whiskey," he continued. "The flat in Monte Carlo is covered. Studio covered. Both of 'em, twenty-four hours a day. We tail the limousine back and forth between Ventimiglia and Monte Carlo. Best guards money can buy. If he starts off toward Rome or Nice, we're right on her tail. If something looks funny, we come in close and ride her bumper. Can anything go wrong? Sure it can. We don't know their game. Don't even know if they have a game. But we know McLarssen. He's trouble. He'll make a move. We're ready. But..."

"If they were onto the tail," O'Reith speculated, "They'd have ways of breaking it..."

Marlborough pulled down on his drink, livened it up out of the bottle Susie had left behind, worked a cigarette out of his shirt pocket package and, nodding to O'Reith, lit it with a gopher match from a Beverly Wilshire packet. He blew three quick, perfect smoke rings, one after the other. When he had expelled the rest of the smoke from his lungs, he said, "I'll notify our people that we expect trouble anytime from now to the end of the month. Helen should give us a clue just before she blows. That way we'd be ready to block 'em if they tried to follow her."

"That's a great idea," O'Reith said. "I'll call her tonight. Duke I never did get around to asking you if there was anything significant to that meeting where Torres met Feathermerchant, the night that you tailed Cordero... Remember?"

"As I see it, Cordero and Torres are together. I can't imagine what they would have had in common with Feathermerchant. I've thought about it. Does Torres have any information that would be useful to Feathermerchant? I don't mean about the contract. Any personal information?"

"I don't know Duke. I'll think on that and get back to you. Could be he knows something. Maybe about Maxine... I just don't know."

The telephone rang as Marlborough departed. It was Blake in San Francisco. He said, "Clive, Larry was just on the line. Said he had a golf date with you tomorrow. You and him and my son-in-law. What's wrong with making it a foursome?"

"Nothing. I didn't think golf was your game."

"Well, it is now. You can't operate out of 225 Bush Street if you don't play golf. Besides, lots of things on my mind. After the game, I'll stay over and we'll talk."

"Sure Vince. One thing we better talk about right now. I know you never did trust Larry. You thought he was trying to put a knife in your back. But things have suddenly become complicated on Lake Maracaibo. We've got a chance to sell a stream of LNG. I don't know anything about that part of the business. Larry does. If he wants to run it, I'm in the mood to hook him up. That going to piss you off?"

"Of course not, Clive. He can't do me in now. And who knows, I could have been wrong about him in the first place."

O'Reith laughed. "See you tomorrow, babe," he ended the conversation and hung up. He quickly concluded his business with the detective.

O'Reith was just as comfortable on a tee box at a golf course as he was on a derrick floor, or for that matter, flying an airplane or having a drink in a cocktail lounge. It was cloudy at the Limejuicer Club, an afternoon with the temperature in the 70s with the sun peaking through here and there, splotches of bright green on the shadowed fairways. A light breeze off the Pacific stirred the faintly aromatic odor of oranges. His son won the toss, was waggling his behind, standing over the ball, getting ready to drive. Teague and Blake off to the side, limbered up, twisting and turning, drivers hooked under their armpits. O'Reith waited patiently. To hit last, he reminded himself to be careful, to swing gracefully through the shot and not to twist his bad leg. After all, this was recreation, not heroics. 'What a wonderful course!' he thought, looking down the long undulating fairway, framed by orange trees, heavy with fruit. No.1 was straight but narrow, four hundred and forty yards from the white balls to the center of the green. He had played this course hundreds of times over the years, couldn't remember exactly when he began but it was when he was a young man, single, and under his mother's tutelage. He could remember how attentive Helen was their first game together. In her white silk ankle-length skirt, curls tucked into a saucy tam-o'-shanter, she was easily the most elegant creature on the course. They had been regular players for years. Suddenly it came to him that this was home. Not just the golf course. Everything. Holmby Hills. Lucey's. Hollywood Boulevard. The Catalina Club. The Palomar Ballroom. Rae Regan and her family. Even The Calitroleum Tower. At No. 14 tee box, which was on a rise, if the clouds were not too low, he'd be able to see LA in the distance. He knew what the rest of the world had to offer. Paris. London. Rome. They had their charms. Biarritz. St. Moritz. Monte Carlo. Cali. All had their dash. Compared to Los Angeles, nothing extra. He deeply yearned to give up his meandering ways. Move back to Holmby hills with Helen. Vegetate.

Blake was saying, "Clive, your time. Give it a good swat. No mulligans today." Teague and Blake were both looking at him curiously.

O'Reith smiled at them shyly and pulled himself back into the real world. He drove, watched his ball describe a long, steady arc and drop a couple of hundred yards down field, about twenty feet from an orange tree. He joined the others, already walking rapidly. The caddies were far ahead of them. Blake was saying, "Clive, if it were me, I'd set two more eight-well platforms and put both those jack-ups to work drilling the C-Series. That's 45 degree oil. Blend it with the second stage of separation off the Mirador and the Santa Barbara. Lay a twelve inch products line instead of a six inch."

Jolted back into the problems of the day, said, "Larry, that make sense to you?"

"Yeah it does but I'd like to have accurate offtake information," the little refining executive said, his voice reflecting uncertainty. Can we cable down there for an estimate of what sixteen C-Series wells will produce? Didn't you tell me you'd cut the pay twice?"

"Three times actually, if you count the well we had to abandon. Susie'll get us some good numbers in a couple of days." It occurred to him at that moment that he would not be going back to Europe any time soon. He would not be seeing Maxine. Nor Helen. Nor the kids. His affairs were becoming more pressing by the day. At the turn he had hired Teague, to be on the job no later than 1 February. His job would begin at the main offtake valve on Production Platform No.1. O'Reith's son would be his assistant, working out of Caracas. His training program in the Production Department was shelved. So was surfing. So was getting in some four engine time in the B-17. O'Reith was encouraged that his son was the only one to shoot par on the front nine. Teague was next with a 37. Blake shot a 40 and he, himself, 41. Not a famous front nine.

Behind the hole number plaque on No.16, a clump of Key Lime trees were bearing. The yellowish, hickory-nut sized citrus were prized by fanciers of a 'Key Lime Pie'. Edward G. Robinson had suggested planting them, inspired by the movie *Key Largo*. They were special. Did wonders for a gin lime or a rum punch. O'Reith slipped four of them into his golf bag as he waited his turn. Clouds were piling up against the foothills.

At the 19th hole, drinking Lucky Lager on tap, at a window table facing the putting green, Teague said, "You know, instead of a products line back to the terminal, maybe we should set another platform and building a natural gasoline plant on it."

O'Reith, drinking club soda on the rocks, looking out at the neatly trimmed lemon trees that circled the putting green, said, "Larry, I'll shoot the information up to you as soon as it comes in. You can make the decision. We begin running crude oil on or about 1 May. Everything else is secondary to that."

That evening before dinner at Holmby Hills with the Blakes, his son, Marilyn, Rae Regan and Clifford, O'Reith brought out the Key Limes, showed Rae Regan how to cut them into eight slices for the gin-limes. He mixed them in tall, frosted glasses. Outside it began to mist. Tiny drops clung to the panes of the big French windows. Hollywood Caterers of Beverly Hills arrived with barbecued beef, chicken, hot sausages, cole slaw, baked beans and of course, pecan pie.

Blake holding hands with Virginia, said, "Clive, I'm going to resign from Standard Oil. I don't do diddly. Read the Oil & Gas Journal. Make a speech now and then. Bend a few paper clips. Play wastebasket pool. A great life but I'm bored. Virginia is tired of San Francisco. I never was fond of it. She wants to be able to drive to San Berdoo on the weekends. Can you plug me in somewhere? I still know a little about drilling and production. Shoe horn me in to an alcove in the Fullerton Building?"

O'Reith regretted talking everybody into drinking gin-limes. He'd been in the mood for a martini. But he couldn't gracefully drum up enthusiasm for the new drink without having one himself. Now he was glad he did. It had just the right tang, far better than the last one he'd had in a hotel bar in Panama City. The gin was superb, the Rose's Lime juice was fruity. The shaved ice made it a heavenly concoction. In a mellow mood he said, "Whenever you're ready, Vince. So much going on and so few people working, you'll earn your keep the first day. When do you want to start?"

"No later than February first. I don't want that goddamned refining midget to have any seniority over me."

They all laughed. O'Reith said, "O-o-o-k-a-a-y, then, I'll tell Susie in the morning. She'll enjoy your company again after such a long absence. Vince, once we get on the line, we'll have a directors meeting. Reorganize the company. Run it from LA. If I set Holland up, would you be disturbed?"

"Hell no. He's probably the only guy that knows what to do down there."

"You'd be vice chairman," O'Reith said, watching Blake's face closely.

"Lobbying?" Blake asked cagily.

"I hadn't thought of that exactly, Vince," O'Reith said, his eyes dancing mischievously. "But since you brought it up, it's a possibility."

Blake horselaughed. "Why didn't I keep my mouth shut?"

On Saturday, 12 January, looking down at the fleecy clouds from his window seat of the Pan American DC-6B as they crossed the Chihuahua desert, O'Reith looked forward to being back in Maracaibo. Soon the pilot would let down for Mexico City. Then *Aurora* Airport in Guatemala, *Toucomen* at Panama, by midnight, he would be on the ground at *Grano de Oro*.

*   *   *

Yawning, he went through customs and immigration and into his waiting limousine for the ride to the Hotel Del lago. Sunday he was up early for a golf date with Holland, Prescott, and a Houston Contracting Company executive. After the milk run through Central America, walking the fairways was a delight. His leg behaved. He shot a decent score for a change.

Monday morning with Holland on board the speedboat *La Flecha*, they began 'the grand tour'. On Block 9, at the eight-well platform, *El Mocho* Morrow from the cellar deck observed the welder make the fine cut of the seven inch. This last well would be a triple completion. Morrow wriggling his stub of a forefinger at the drilling engineer, said, "Mack, when you get nippled up, run in and feel easy for those plugs. When you find 'em, drill with 10,000 pounds and a slow table. Take it easy. Couple days ago a Jersey foreman ran too hard, parted the string, got gas in his eye." Morrow turned to his visitors, continued, "In half an hour we'll have the preventers bolted up. We'll drill out with the bit on a tubing string. Should be in the C-Series four or five days from now. You fellows want to hang around?"

"Like to, *El Mocho*," O'Reith purred, "but this is our last chance to see the entire operation before we're hooked up. Seems that we're in good shape out here."

"Yes sir, we're doing fine," Morrow replied. "I'm nervous about the completion however. I've never done a triple."

"Specialists coming out of Long Beach to hold your hand, *El Mocho*," Holland said. "Only difference between a double and a triple is that you'll be running two strings of tubing. Spaghetti they call it. The tubing head has two holes, one for each string. Nothing to worry about. Just take your time. Use two completion engineers. Let them spell each other and get some sleep. Can't have rumdum hands on the floor when you're making a triple."

Next stop was Production Platform No.1. The speedboat tied up to the flow line manifold. The production foreman was testing the flow lines that began at the wells, ran across the lake bed and came up at the platform. Each line was tested hydraulically at flowing well head pressure. Nobody wanted to see oil bubbling up from the lake bottom. Not only would it be expensive to fix but if spotted by the hydrocarbons inspector, they would get a stiff fine for pollution. Today, everything seemed quite orderly. None of the chaos O'Reith had seen on his last inspection. Each item of machinery was in its place. The great stacks of line pipe were now part of the installation. Workers flanged up the first stage separator, a great, shiny, cylindrical tank that towered above them. Into it the high pressure crude oil would be jetted against baffles to knock out the propane, butane and higher fractions. After a second stage of separation these would be called the LNG stream. These gases, exiting at the top of the tank, refrigerated into liquid, would be pumped to the products line. From the smaller second stage separator a flare line rose high into the air. Running along it to its tip was a copper wire with an igniter at its end. Once production started, the dry gases, ethane and methane, would flow to the top of the flare line and be torched off. A side outlet at this stage led the LNG stream to the refrigeration unit and the compressor. Far from the production equipment at the end of the platform, stood three prefabricated camp buildings for the crews. Each crew worked two weeks and were off one week; two production foremen, two assistants, a gang of sixteen roustabouts and two welders. O'Reith, Holland and Prescott lunched in the mess hall with some of the workers. Everything here OK. Over coffee, O'Reith advised Holland and Prescott that Larry Teague would be joining the company, to live in Caracas and run the pipeline and the terminal.

Holland said, "Jesus Christ, General. I thought I'd seen the last of that poison dwarf. What the hell is going on here?"

"You're speaking of your loyal lieutenant, my boy," O'Reith said casually. He always enjoyed these moments.

"What!"

"Larry is your guy. Or, I should say, one of your guys. Come May we're going to reorganize the company. You will be in Los Angeles as president of the company. Larry will look after the downstream. Hardy will remain in Caracas as President of the Tropical Oil Company, wholly owned subsidiary of The Casinghead Company. Stan Ethering will be General Counsel in Los Angeles. Riva Cordero will replace him."

"Riva Cordero!" Holland snorted.

"I fixed it with the colonel. Logical, once you think about it. A rat for the rats. Vince is joining us as my aide. Susie will run the Purchasing Department. Alan will manage the Production Department from Los Angeles."

"Sally is ready for that," Prescott said with relief in his voice. "She wants to raise those kids as gringos."

So on to Punto Fijo, following the pipeline. They spent the night at the Houston Contracting Company construction barge, half way along the line. After that, a day of hiking around among the tanks at the terminal. Late on Sunday night, 20 January 1957, the two weary oil men climbed out of *La Flecha* at the San Francisco dock and headed for downtown Maracaibo. Both exhausted from sixteen hour days on the lake, after inspecting the results of a one hundred million dollar expenditure. At Holland's villa, they drank Pampero rum while Ines cooked. Holland's three children, full of questions, swarmed over him in his easy chair. They inspected his shirt pockets, wanted to know if he had brought them anything. He gave them oddments picked up from the production platform. A zinc tee. An ell. A tiny copper tubing valve. Useless things that kids love. O'Reith and Holland were thoroughly tanned. The Lake Maracaibo sun had done its work. After dinner, O'Reith said goodbye. He walked to the hotel, happy to stretch his legs without stepping into a mud hole. By ten o'clock, he was asleep.

At the office next morning, a Pan Am pilot delivered a letter from Susie. In it was a clipping from *The Hollywood Reporter,* 15 January 1957

LOS LADRONES DE PIEDRAS NEGRAS BREAKS NEW GROUND IN OATER GENRE! By Hedda Hopper

Flint Westwater, just back from Ventimiglia, Italy, says that Helen O'Reith's first-lunge-out-of-the-directorial-chute is a solid gold production. She has broken new ground and risen to a higher level of cowpokery in this lavish sage brush saga. Westwater, her new leading man, replaced the much touted Sixto Cigone. The latter, according to Westwater, is tongue-tied. Yet he performs magnificently as a mute sidekick. Alphonse di Frangipani, one of the famous Malbeccos, has done for the western what Sydney Greenstreet did for the film noir. Horse operas will never be the same. This movie introduces Sixto Cigone, a new Italian actor of exciting dimension whose only drawback is his inability to remember his lines. A silent actor in a Technicolor venue, he moves across the screen like a whirlwind, an action-packed dynamo of thespian authenticity. Helen O'Reith, as always, brings her magic presence to the camera in the role of Señora Elena, the frontier medico's unsung assistant. In collaboration with the Genius of Naples, Frederico Bolletti, she has delivered to the world, a motion picture that is truly different in every way; a one-of-a-kind 'mule-blaster', to quote Westwater. This is the one the cinematic universe has been waiting for. *Los Ladrones de Piedras Negras* filmed on two continents will be released in five languages. Westwater says the film is in the can and should be out no later than 1 March 1957. So don't miss this bustling drama of the Mexican border from the novel by Alberto Garcia, filmed in Ventimiglia, Hollywood, and Monument Valley.

Susie noted in the margin, "Copy sent to Phillip Marlborough."

"Now what?" O'Reith asked himself, audibly. "Helen forgot to warn Westwater."

Holland arrived as O'Reith was worrying said, "We have a dinner invitation."

"Yeah?" O'Reith answered vacantly. "Where?"

"Mandy's place. Not the inn. The house next to the garden. A Venezuelan dinner cooked by her own hands. You and I and Ines and Alan and Sally."

"What's the occasion?"

"I don't know, exactly," Holland replied with some mirth. "Something to do with Ted's 'religious' experience."

O'Reith sighed. "I should learn to keep my mouth shut. I led him off on that tangent. Looks like he's hooked."

"It'll do him good," Holland said, dismissing it. "Mandy's a good cook – when it's for friends."

"Great!" O'Reith said. "I'm always ready for home cooking. What's on the agenda for today?"

"Delta drilling superintendent coming in a half hour. Carolyn wants to show us her maps on the C-Series at ten. Prescott reports on the flow line tests at ten-thirty. Tuffy coming in at eleven. Needs help with a faulty generator. It shut down the jack up light plant. Brown and Root *jefes* taking us to lunch. This afternoon, we're on our own."

"That suits me." O'Reith said. I should stay here to keep this project in high gear but I'm worried about Helen. I plan to strap all this on your broad shoulders. I'm going to Monte Carlo. Take a gander at this blurb out of *The Hollywood Reporter*."

Holland noted Susie's reference and asked, "Think that'll get back to McLarssen?"

"Marlborough thinks it will." O'Reith was glum.

By the end of the day he had recovered his good cheer and eagerly awaited that first blessed martini at Mandy's place. With a drink in his hand and Ted was telling about his latest adventure, he would be OK. Their troublesome decisions made, he had decided to fly to Europe the next morning. Holland drove, Ines beside him, O'Reith in the back with the kids. At Mandy's front door, they were greeted by the aroma of succulent roast pork. It would be a nice evening. With the roast, seasoned with thyme and sage, she served *arepas, platanos* and a mixture of mangos, papayas, bananas and pineapple. Six voracious children, assured there would be no leftovers. Over coffee, Schaeffer announced that he and Mandy were building an orphanage down the street, to be called *Puesto Tranquilidad*. To open for business early in the summer. It was to be their future. They would attend the needs of the abandoned children of Maracaibo, of which there were more than a few. Schaeffer's little speech drew applause from the adults, the children being asleep in their chairs. The Chinese cook and his helpers began to clean up. Ines, Sally and Mandy sat around talking. Holland and Prescott got up a game of gin rummy. Schaeffer said, "Clive, I've been going to Mass regular now. Couple more months and I'll bring the Cubans into the act. When Mandy says it's time. Everything going jake-a-loo. I want to ask you more about getting up a *street*."

"Shoot, Ted," O'Reith said beaming broadly. This was a game he enjoyed.

"What happens if I skip that?"

O'Reith shrugged, his smile turning dour. "Forget about sainthood."

"Why?"

"Ted, as I explained before, your *street* carries on for you after... Think of it as if you were running for governor or for congress. There's a differences of course. Yours is a celestial, rather than a political campaign. Think of your *street* as a committee. Political candidates organize committees that function long after the candidate himself has given up, starts delivering mail or picking up trash or, often, gone to jail. Norman Thomas comes to mind. First running in 1928 he was still on the ballot in 1948 – twenty years later. Finally he gave it up but his campaign committee rolls along as if it were eternal."

"I never thought much of him," Schaeffer said. "Too radical. Another guy that didn't amount to much was Harold Stassen."

"But he raised huge sums of money, Ted. Running for high political office is a form of beggary. One seeks alms to win an office to steal with legitimacy, an elevated art form indeed."

"What happens to all that money?" Schaeffer pondered.

"It disappears," O'Reith said with a laugh. "Well, that's what a *street* is for, Ted. You need a following. Raise money to lobby the Vatican. Of course it is early in the game yet. We can discuss it further as the scene unfolds."

"Clive, I know this is really looking a long way ahead, but say a fellow makes it, becomes a saint. Can he then put in to be an angel?"

"Interesting question, Ted. I don't have the answer to it," O'Reith replied. "McDonough knows a bit about that. I'll ask him."

And so the evening ended. They piled into Holland's station wagon, O'Reith in the back seat with children all over him. At the hotel, he said goodnight. But his worries returned. Not sleepy, he walked through the lobby past the music and chatter of the Mara Bar out the back door past the cabañas and down to the sandy beach at the lake shore. Lake water lapped softly against the sand at his feet. In the south where the Catatumbo Lights often flickered, darkness and stars in the heavens above greeted his eyes. No storms pounding the distant mountains at this early hour. Rio Catatumbo, a grand current that tumbled down from the Andes to fill the lake got its water from moist trade winds blown against the Andes. O'Reith speculated that much of the radio interference could be attributed to the magnificent electrical display that accompanied the storms, as frequent here as the Aurora Borealis was in the higher latitudes of North America. Cooled by the gentle night breezes, still not sleepy, worries about Helen pressing, he retraced his steps, went through the lobby again. The Mara Bar was quieter, beginning to empty out. He walked all the way to the end of the long corridor and unlocked the door of the Casinghead Company office. He turned on the lights and sat at his desk. At seven that evening when they locked up to go see Mandy, the radio loudspeaker was warbling, crackling, hissing, squawking and occasionally clattering out the echo of some vagrant teleprinter signal. When they first opened the office, a radio operator was on duty around the clock. But reception was poor between late afternoon and midnight so he had been dismissed. O'Reith was alone. Now at almost three o'clock in the morning, Atlantic Standard Time, the loudspeaker was quiescent, as if it had been sedated. Only the hum of the carrier wave, an occasional short outburst of cackles, warbles and hoo-hoo-hoos broke the silence.

He was trying to make up his mind about the gasoline plant, a decision of some financial import. It looked promising. To be in operation by the summer, when demand was high, work would have to begin now, an eleventh hour, vexing oil field decision. Pondering the pros and cons, bouncing the eraser of his pencil against his yellow legal pad, he thought he heard his name above the background noise of the radio. It sounded like Helen.

He quickly arose, walked to the radio, sat, and put his ear to the loudspeaker. He took the microphone in hand. Now he heard it clearly, "Maracaibo, this is Monte Carlo. Maracaibo, this is Monte Carlo, over." There was a hoo-hoo-hoo and a squawk and then he could hear her again, "Maracaibo, this is Monte Carlo..."

He pressed the microphone button, watched the power needle swing around. He said, "Helen, I can hear you. Go ahead."

"Ace, I didn't expect to catch you! Why it must be three o'clock in the morning! Has there been an accident?"

"Helen, everything is okay. Had dinner with the Schaeffers. Holland dropped me off at the hotel. I couldn't sleep."

"Ace, I have my film. Five reels of it. I'm all packed. We're going to Nice in a few minutes. I'll be in Paris this afternoon. Susie said you would be in Los Angeles in a week or so. Rae Regan is fixing up our suite at Holmby hills. It will be like old times. Ace, the bell is ringing. It must be my chauffeur for the bags. Stand by a minute while I let him in."

He listened, waiting for her to return. But she did not. He tried again, "Helen, come back. Helen, come back."

But she did not return. He sat there with his ear to the loudspeaker waiting for her to respond.

Next morning, Holland found O'Reith asleep with his head in his arms on the radio table, waiting…

Chapter XVII

▼

Abduction

January 21, 1957 began well for Helen. She was up betimes, saw little Helen Simpson off to school and was in Ventimiglia by ten o'clock. Except for a bit of sleight-of-hand, she didn't need to be there at all. But today was the day the girl in the cutting room, Josefa, her bribed accomplice was going to complete the release print and help her load the several reels of film into her limousine. As Helen worked daily with her in the cutting room, nothing would suggest that today was different from other days. Big Alphonse was long gone. Sixto Cigone was 'on call' in case additional shooting was required, a pretext inasmuch as it was all over. Helen planned never to set eyes on him again. Bolletti, more than likely, would appear around noon, walk around the studio and depart for lunch, not to return until tomorrow. Helen believed that the only reason he came at all was to see that she was still piddling around. Helen realized that there were still several hundred thousand dollars in the bank. She considered it to be her money. But she didn't know how to get it in her hands without a stir. Both her husband and the detective cautioned her not to make one. She was to concentrate on getting her movie out of Italy and into California for placement into distribution.

A cable just in from Marlborough notified her that Flint Westwater had revealed all to Hedda Hopper. It had appeared in *The Hollywood*

Reporter. But she discounted what effect, if any, it might have here in Italy. That the detective was en route from Los Angeles with new warnings was also shrugged away. After all, when she left the studio in Ventimiglia tonight, she was well, g-o-n-e. Everything went as planned. Bolletti came and went with barely a tip of his hat. The studio was deserted. By five o'clock, her limousine loaded with the reels of film plus a now badly smudged work print, Helen tipped Josefa generously, thanked her and waved goodbye as she departed.

Back in Monte Carlo, the chauffeur helped her bring the film upstairs. She packed it in a suitcase, changed clothes, called Alice Ridley and Sharon Mills to join her for a drink and whiled away the minutes with her daughter. Over cocktails, Helen revealed her plans. Alice and Sharon were to close down the flat, call the movers and liquidate the lease. That done, they were to fly to Los Angeles. She ordered dinner from the Hotel de Paris. By ten o'clock, little Helen Simpson was asleep in bed. Helen was reading *Nice-Matin*. The telephone rang. Bolletti. "Cariña," he began, "I have exciting news. Our wonderful production, our movie, *Los Ladrones de Piedras Negras,* has caught the eye of the industry. I just learned that an extremely favorable article has appeared in *The Hollywood Reporter*."

"Maybe we will make our fortunes at last, Frederico," Helen said, worried and suspicious because he rarely called her in Monte Carlo. Never this late in the evening. She felt her pulse coming up. "I appreciate the call, Frederico. It is late. We can discuss it further tomorrow. Let me say good night."

"But I have other news as well, cariña," Bolletti insisted. "This is not too good, I fear. From the same newspaper. By Hedda Hopper. Do you know her, cariña?"

"Everybody knows her, Frederico. She is a gossip columnist. What she says is not to be taken seriously."

Bolletti was not to be stopped. He continued, "This woman, this Hedda Hopper, says that your husband plans to divorce you. It seems he has another woman in Paris."

"Standard Hollywood garbage, Frederico. To be ignored. Now I must say goodnight." She was worried. Her pulse was racing and her hands were getting sweaty.

"Cariña, I know this woman in Paris. I know her name. Where she lives. I take you to see her." He was matter-of-fact about it.

"Tomorrow, Frederico. It is late." She was shaking, sat down in her easy chair with the lamp on the end table throwing an oval of light around her. She could hear the clock ticking on the wall.

"Very well, countess. Tomorrow," Bolletti replied. He seemed saddened. "I see you at the studio at ten o'clock. Bring our film. We look at it together in the *Movieola*. Then we go to Paris..."

At the telephone, she sat quietly trying to regain her poise. What to do? So he knew. Josefa had told him The ticking clock in the shadow on the opposite wall said, ten-thirty. Four-thirty in the afternoon in New York. One-thirty in Los Angeles. She put in a call to the office, waited patiently for it to go through. In ten minutes, Susie was on the line. Helen said, "Susie I have a cable from the Phillip Marlborough saying he is coming but no ETA. When can I expect him?"

"He left here yesterday on a TWA flight to New York. They had engine trouble and landed in Saint Louis. Arriving Idlewild, the plane to Paris had already departed. He's in the air right now. Should be in Paris tomorrow. He'll call you from Orly."

"Any news from Venezuela?" Helen asked.

"Routine messages from Holland. The general plans to be back here around the first of February. Has a meeting with Max. Another with Larry Teague. That's it."

"Thanks Susie," Helen said. When the connection was broken she placed a call to Rae Regan. That one too, went through in minutes. Helen asked her if she read *The Hollywood Reporter* regularly. Was there anything of interest? Rae Regan told her that there was an occasional report on her movie project. Westwater gave Hedda Hopper a glowing account of *Los Ladrones de Piedras Negras.* The usual scandals. Normal unsupported gossip. Nothing that involved Helen nor anyone in the family. Hedda Hopper had asked, 'Where is the dashing General O'Reith?' But there was no suggestion that he was anywhere in particular. He was just gone. Helen thanked her, told her she was on the way home. So Bolletti was lying. Or he was trying to make something out of the reference to her husband being invisible. Besides, how could he possibly know whether or not her husband had a mistress in Paris? He said he knew her name... She took a deep breath, got up, carefully checked the front door, double locked it. She locked the door to her terrace too, something she never did. Only the most daring cat burglar could enter that way. Little Helen Simpson was quietly sleeping. She finished packing, checked her airline tickets, her passport and her money. Everything OK. It was a few minutes after eleven, five thirty in Maracaibo. Would she be able to raise the office? She went into her bedroom, closed the door, pulled back the curtains that shielded the radio. For fifteen minutes no response. Nothing doing. Communication was almost impossible at that hour. Something to do with the *Catatumbo Lights,* or so her husband believed anyhow. She disrobed and turned in.

*   *   *

Next morning, up at six, she roused her daughter, fixed breakfast and finished packing. She put on a confederate gray pant suit with a white poplin shirt that had long sleeves and frills around the cuffs. Her shoes were gray low heels, with a single strap, made for ease of travel. The chauffeur would appear at eight to drive them to Nice. Their flight to Paris was scheduled for ten-thirty. Just before the chauffeur was due to arrive, she tried again to raise Maracaibo. She could leave a message for O'Reith. To her great surprise, O'Reith himself answered. She told him she had her film and was about to depart for Nice. The bell rang. She asked him to standby while she let the chauffeur in. But it was not the chauffeur. It was Bolletti and Orgoglio was with him. He had a black pistol in his hand.

Bolletti said, "Cariña, you're packed for a trip. How convenient. We don't have to wait. The chauffeur can come immediately." He turned to Orgoglio, said "Ugo, ask the chauffeur to come up." Then to Helen he said, "The film, countess. Where is it?"

Too terrified to speak, Helen pointed to the suitcase. Bolletti hoisted it up on the sofa, tried to open it. It was locked. He held out his hand to her, a snarl on his face. Without a word she removed the keys from her purse and handed them over to him. He unlocked the suitcase, briefly examined the reels, saw the rolled up work print and said "Aha!" He relocked the suitcase, put the keys in his pocket and took her purse, deftly removing her money, passport and air line tickets He tossed empty purse on the floor. Enraged, Helen kicked him in the groin. She said between her teeth, "You cocksucker. You filthy cocksucker."

Bolletti staggered, fell to his knees. As he tried to recover, she kicked him again, in the face. He reeled. She was about to kick him the third time when the chauffeur appeared. Pistol in hand, Orgoglio said ominously, "You should be more thoughtful, madam. Try to restrain yourself. This is business. No one will be hurt. Now fetch your daughter and we will be on our way."

Bolletti groaning, stammered, "You pay cariña. You pay."

Orgoglio, holding the pistol with the muzzle pointed at the floor, said to Bolletti. "She pays Rico. But with money. Do not damage the merchandise."

Followed by Orgoglio, Helen went to little Helen Simpson's room where the maid was combing her hair in preparation for their departure. Helen took her daughter's hand and said, "OK sweetie, we're on our way."

The chauffeur, pale and shaking, led the way to the elevator.

Holland awakened O'Reith, listened to his story, said, "General , go up to your room. Shower and shave. Take a nap perhaps. If Helen called home, we'll have some messages pretty quick. When you're refreshed and your mind is clear, we'll decide how to proceed." He helped O'Reith to his feet and walked with him back to the lobby of the hotel, waited at the elevators until his chief had gone up.

Around ten o'clock, O'Reith returned to the office. Holland was on the radio taking the morning report from Prescott, quite lengthy now with four rigs drilling, the production platform fabrication, the laying of the pipeline and the terminal construction, work on the loading pier and progress of the dredge. O'Reith listened to Prescott's voice, distorted by the radio, but he was only vaguely interested, couldn't get his mind off of Helen. The teleprinter in the corner began to clack. O'Reith read the messages as they came in.

GENERAL CLIVE COLIN O'REITH
THE CASINGHEAD COMPANY
MARACAIBO
JANUARY 22, 1957
JUST ARRIVED ORLY. CALLED OUR AGENT IN MONTE CARLO. HELEN RETURNED TO VENTIMIGLIA THIS MORNING IN COMPANY WITH DAUGHTER AND BOLLETTI. LIMOUSINE ESCORTED FRONT AND BACK BY TWO STUDIO LAMBORGHINIS. ORGOGLIO SPOTTED IN LEAD CAR. ALL THREE VEHICLES ENTERED STUDIO AND GATE WAS CLOSED BEHIND THEM. GUARD POSTED INSIDE. OUR AGENT STANDING WATCH. I TELEPHONED LEBEL TO RECRUIT ADDITIONAL AGENTS IMMEDIATELY AS WE ARE STRETCHED TOO THIN. LEBEL SAID AN AMERICAN DESCRIBED AS HAVING REDDISH HAIR CAME BY THE OFFICE LAST WEEK ASKING FOR YOU. MAN REFUSED TO GIVE NAME BUT DESCRIPTION SOUNDS LIKE FEATHER-MERCHANT. HOW WOULD HE HAVE OBTAINED OFFICE

ADDRESS? FLYING TO NICE WITHIN THE HOUR AND WILL REVERT.

REGARDS

MARLBOROUGH

ORLY 1500 HOURS GMT PLUS 1

The next message was from Susie.

THE CASINGHEAD COMPANY

MARACAIBO

FOR O'REITH

HELEN CALLED YESTERDAY TO SAY SHE WAS ON HER WAY TO LOS ANGELES. RAE REGAN JUST CALLED AT SEVEN O'CLOCK, WORRIED, HAD SPOKEN TO HER MOTHER YESTERDAY BUT NOTHING FURTHER. SHE IS EXPECTING A CALL FROM HER WHEN SHE ARRIVES IDLEWILD. TWA REPORTS ALL FLIGHTS FROM EUROPE ON SCHEDULE WITH NO DELAYS. DONALD MCLARSSEN TELEPHONED YESTERDAY. SAID HE WOULD BE IN THE NEGRESCO HOTEL IN NICE ON FRIDAY AND WOULD LIKE TO SEE YOU. ADVISE.

REGARDS

SUSIE

Holland had finished taking the reports. O'Reith ripped the two messages off the teleprinter and handed them to him. Holland quickly digested their content. He jerked up the telephone, dialed aircraft maintenance at *Grano de Oro*. When their maintenance engineer was on the line, he told him to prepare one of the B-17s for a flight to Europe. He asked how long it would take, listened to the response, and said, "OK, get after it." To O'Reith he said, "Take off at four o'clock sir. Be at the airport at three. Go on up and pack. I'll pick you up under the marquee. We'll have lunch with Ines and be on our way." Without waiting for a response, he returned to the radio and raised Prescott again. He said "Alan, the General and I are headed for Europe. You're in charge. Send us a report every morning."

As O'Reith disappeared down the hall, still somewhat in a daze, not thinking correctly, on his way to his room, Holland went to the teleprinter. Hunting and pecking, sent a message to Tarbutton in Caracas.

The two oil men sat silently in the rear seat of Holland's white Ford station-wagon. O'Reith's suitcase was in front on the seat next to the driver. Holland's several bags were in the cargo space behind them. The driver turned off *El Milagro* into *Cinco de Julio* and in ten minutes they were getting out at the passenger terminal at *Grano de Oro*. O'Reith, carrying his bag, walked up the concrete stairs. Holland was beside him, one bag in each hand. Behind them the driver brought Holland's third bag. Both men in khakis, Panama hats and black field boots. Inside the terminal, they turned to the right, went down the hall to the desk with a black and white sign over it that said 'Oil Company Control'. Holland signed them in. The Customs and Immigration inspector checked their passports and waved them through. They went down a ramp and out into the bright afternoon sunlight to the hot concrete perimeter of the airport. They would be taking off to the south on Runway No.1 crossing over the hippodrome. *La Cañada Cruz* was parked between an Avensa Convair and an LAV Viscount. The main exit hatch in front of the tail was open and a one-step aluminum ladder was hooked over the bottom lip of the hatch. The flight engineer went ahead of them, took their bags as they passed them to him. Holland dismissed their driver. The three men walked forward through the waist, the radio room, the galley that had once been the bomb bays, into the cabin. Holland nudged O'Reith into the left-hand seat. They quickly ran through the preflight check. O'Reith flipped the master switch and turned on the ignition. Holland started the engines. O'Reith signaled through the side window to the maintenance engineer to pull the wheel chocks. He said to Holland, "Tail wheel." Holland unlocked it, carefully checked all instruments as O'Reith pulled the B-17 out from between the two commercial airliners. Clear of them, he gave No.1 engine extra throttle and turned the airplane until it was lined up parallel to the runway. He slowly, slowly taxied all the way out to the end of the runway, some 4,800 feet. With just enough room to turn the aircraft around, he braked and said to Holland, "Engine run-up."

Holland said, "Brakes set."

O'Reith glanced at the throttles. All four were set at 1,000 rpm. He set the trim tabs at zero, ran the throttles up to 1,500 rpm and checked out the turbo-superchargers. He ran the propellers through 'low' and 'high' rpm and brought them back to 'high'. He waited for the propellers to change pitch and drop rpm.

Holland was watching the gauges, said, "No red lights. All four turning 1,100 rpm."

O'Reith returned the propeller controls to 'high' and shut off the turbo controls. He began running the engines up one at a time. Magnetos checked okay. Holland's eyes were on the instruments. O'Reith looked out at the engine nacelles. Both men checking for rough running. The engines were OK, purring along. Holland released the brakes. O'Reith turned the B-17 around, lining it up for take-off. The tower gave them the OK. Grasping all four throttles, O'Reith led them forward. The plane began rolling, gradually increasing power as they picked up speed. At 115 mph with still a bit of runway left, he pulled back on the column. They were airborne. He nodded to Holland who braked the wheels. Then he hit the landing gear switch. Both men's eyes were on the control panel. O'Reith said, "Left up."

Holland said, "Right up." The flight engineer came forward to tell them the tail wheel was up. O'Reith set all four engines at 2,300 rpm at 35" manifold pressure, brought the airspeed up to 150 mph and began the climb to 12,000 feet, their cruising altitude for this short leg of the flight. By six o'clock, they were on the ground at Maiquetia topping up the tanks with triptane. They considered a northern route through New York, Iceland and London but decided against it. North Atlantic storms were fearsome and unpredictable. Icing could be severe. The southern route was longer but the weather should be good all the way. Tarbutton joined them. He and Holland, put the final touches to the flight plan which was:

Maiquetia to Cayenne	1,000 miles and flying time of 5 hours.
Cayenne to Dakar	2,550 miles and flying time of 12 hours.
Dakar to Rabat	1,400 miles and flying time of 6 hours.
Rabat to Nice	850 miles and flying time of 4 hours.

With two hours on the ground for each refueling and twenty-seven hours in the air made a total of thirty-three hours from Maiquetia to Nice. The next one thousand mile leg took them to Cayenne in French Guyana, an all night airport. Loaded lightly, as it now was, the B-17 could make it to Dakar in one pass but with red lights showing on the gas gauges. O'Reith was game for it but cooler heads prevailed. So it was Cayenne and then Dakar, 2,500 miles further, and across the Atlantic. Holland sat on a small swiveled, pull-out stool right behind the pilot's chair. Next to it, at a small metal table bolted to the floor, with slide rule, map of the central Atlantic, and a set of star charts, he navigated the aircraft. Stars were coming out between the scattered cumulus clouds, a purple evening. Holland completed his dead reckoning calculations by flashlight. As long as the light held, O'Reith flew the coast line, trending south. Through the top hatch in the radio room, Holland checked the stars with a sextant. Shortly after midnight they picked up the Cayenne beam. O'Reith nudged Tarbutton to prepare for landing. Holland tapped O'Reith on the shoulder, beckoned to him to give up his seat. O'Reith wearily trudged his way back to the half bed in the waist. He was finished for the day. He knew it. He slept through the landing, the refueling and the take-off at three o'clock in the morning. Tarbutton slept in his seat. Holland used to long hours, stayed alert. His chart strapped to his knee under an instrument panel light, he was on his way to Dakar. When the sun came up on the central Atlantic the next morning, O'Reith was up with it. He washed his face and came forward to relieve Holland. As he clicked the seat belt buckle, Tarbutton stirred.

The flight engineer brought black coffee. After two hours at the controls, O'Reith realized he had to keep correcting his course by putting more power on the two left engines. On the panel, the oil pressure on No.1 was down a few pounds. But the temperature was OK. Now the engine was running rough. He tried a different mix setting. The flight engineer came forward and said, "Sir, I can see an oil stain coming back off of number one nacelle." O'Reith glanced again at the oil temperature gauge. It was up about five degrees. Oil pressure was dropping too. He closed the propeller feathering switch for No.1, chopped the throttle, set the mixture to 'idle cut off' and cut off the fuel. The propeller slowed, began to windmill and then feathered out. Tarbutton turned the ignition switch off. Their cruising speed fell off immediately from 220 to 180 mph.

Tarbutton looked over, said, "More power, Clive?"

O'Reith said, "As badly as I want to cross this ocean, I'd rather run with the engine rpm down. We lose two..?"

"I agree," Tarbutton said.

So instead of twelve hours, this leg took sixteen hours. Landing at Dakar at around ten o'clock that night they found a copper tubing flange had vibrated loose causing the oil leak that had shut down No.1. It was a simple repair but they were on the ground until daylight. Six hours later they were in Rabat. After refueling, they crossed the Mediterranean and lined up for a landing at Nice. It was five o'clock in the afternoon on Thursday, January 24, 1957. Le Bel had arranged for hangaring and maintenance. With *La Cañada Cruz* chocked up on the hardstand in the long-stay parking area, the four weary crewmen hailed a taxi and went straight to the Hotel Negresco. LeBel met them with a grave face. Beside him stood a haggard Phillip Marlborough. Before LeBel spoke a word, O'Reith knew that Maxine as well as Helen had been taken.

The abduction of Maxine and Monique had been merest child's play. Beauregard Feathermerchant had called Maxine around seven o'clock in the evening. He represented himself to be a consular officer at the American Embassy. He had a message from Maracaibo that her husband had been badly burned at a fire in Lake Maracaibo. He was being flown to Hollywood West Hospital in Los Angeles. If Maxine wished to go to him, the American Embassy would issue an emergency visa. All she had to do was bring her passport to the consular section. Normally closed at this hour, an officer would admit her and issue the visa without delay. She could catch a flight the next day. Maxine grabbed Monique, rushed out of the house and in to the Madeleine Metro station. Marlborough's agent on duty was hard pressed to keep up with her. He saw her come out of the Iena Metro station in a rush to the American Embassy. Just as she was on the grounds, a black Chrysler Limousine with an American flag on the front bumper rolled up to her. A man with a knife in his hand alit, seized the child and forced Maxine into the car which sped away. The agent hurried to telephone LeBel but nothing could be done.

The five men were assembled in O'Reith's suite. The travelers showered and changed clothes. Now they sat at a cocktail table, drinking. O'Reith had downed his first martini in one belt. Now on his second one, he listened to Marlborough.

"McLarssen has not checked in yet," he began. "We're watching the desk around the clock. Alice Ridley and Sharon Mills are in a state of shock but they're holding up. Nurse with them. Waiting on instructions. I told them to sit tight. We put three more men at the studio in Ventimiglia. Front gate is still locked. At night we see lights in some of the rooms. Our agents have scouted the place. Doesn't appear to be any other exits. However the back of the studio abuts a tangle of shops with narrow streets and alleys. Hard to figure it out at short notice. Helen and her daughter are probably being kept in the studio. But we can't be sure of anything. One choice would be to break in. Shoot it out with them. Pretty risky. Better choice is to sit tight until tomorrow morning. When the general asks for McLarssen at the desk, my guess is that he won't show. But somebody will. Maybe Orgoglio. He'll demand the money."

"What about Maxine and Monique?" O'Reith asked plaintively, a man lost.

Marlborough shook his head. "They could be anywhere. Our guy didn't get close enough to recognize the thug with the knife. But Clive, spare yourself that worry. You can't think straight about this. But I can. This is a big league abduction for big time money. Those thugs figure they're holding four aces."

Holland was sitting on the floor with his suitcases. As Marlborough talked, he assembled a Thompson sub-machine gun from its components. He looked up at Marlborough and asked, "So how do we cue this up?"

O'Reith became alert. He asked, "Holland, where in the hell did you get that jack-hammer?"

Holland smiled wickedly. "Borrowed it from *El Mocho*. With two canisters of ammunition. He liberated it from III Army in 1945. General Patton would turn over in his grave and spit a snake if he knew about it."

O'Reith smiled thinly but it quickly faded. He became morose again. His countenance was gray, his once crystalline blue eyes faded, both by age and by anxiety. Beneath them, were yellow-black pouches. His features were swollen and puffy. He could not concentrate. The long journey across the Atlantic had sapped him.

Marlborough said, "General, to get things back where we want them requires a team effort. Are you up to it?"

O'Reith sat up straight, recognizing the wisdom of the detective's words. "Okay, Duke, I'm paying attention. You're calling the shots."

Marlborough continued, his cigarette dangling, his head tilted upward to keep the smoke out of his eyes, "Let's think ahead. General, tomorrow, somebody is going to put the squeeze on you for a great sum of money. There is but one reply. Tell the guy that the only way he will see a dime is when all four females are together, where you can see them, in one place, unharmed. Has to be a hotel lobby. The guy is going to demand that you transfer money to a Swiss bank account. Refuse. No advance payments. Any other stance puts Helen, Maxine and the children at great risk."

"I can see that, all right," O'Reith acknowledged.

"Clive, would you like for me to be at your side when you ask for McLarssen?" LeBel asked.

Marlborough intervened. "Maurice, there's a good chance those thugs don't know your face. Looking on down the road, we've got to have a back-up plan. Better for the team if you remain anonymous. The general will be alone tomorrow. We'll have him under surveillance. But nothing is going to happen. They're after money." He became thoughtful, as if an idea had just come to him. He continued, "Maurice, that big fat guy at the directors meeting, the one that likes to talk, always dresses in white linen, didn't you say he was an ex-spy or something?"

"Sir George P. McDonough? He was a counter-intelligence man. A spy shooter."

"Yeah," Marlborough replied, snapping his fingers. "McDonough. I remember now. Can you give him a ring? No need to keep anything a secret from him is there?"

LeBel nodded, said, "He can be useful. I'll just use the telephone in the next room." He returned some minutes later and said, "McDonough is coming to Paris in the morning. He'll call Monk Parkhurst too. Helpful if we have to raise money in a hurry."

O'Reith said, "Once I know how much they want, I suppose I can get it in Liechtenstein."

"Monk can go with you," LeBel said. "You'll have to negotiate for it. He can get you a better deal than if you try it alone."

O'Reith nodded, sat silently listening. The sub-machine gun snapped loudly as Holland affixed a drum of ammunition to it. They agreed that Tarbutton would keep O'Reith company in Nice and copilot the B-17 to

Paris if it came to that. Marlborough, Holland, LeBel would catch the early flight to Paris, meet McDonough and Parkhurst to develop a strategy to cope with events subsequent to the turning over of the ransom money to whoever and wherever that might be. Holland took the tommy gun apart and returned its components to the suitcases. It had been over ten years since he'd hammered some no good bastard down with a machine-gun. And as the Texas Chile hawker said, "That was too long."

Chapter XVIII

▼

High Noon at the Hotel Negresco

When O'Reith awoke the next morning, his spirits had improved. After more than forty hours of cat napping in a cockpit, the full night of sleep in a soft bed renewed him. He ordered up bacon and eggs. More than the reinvigoration, he was strengthened to know that he had a good, solid team. Remarkably, they sprung up overnight, like a tropical mushroom. In his anxiety, it had never occurred to him that LeBel and McDonough and Parkhurst, all battle-tested veterans with extraordinary skills, would step forward so rapidly. And Marlborough. What a gem! Exactly the leadership demanded by this extremely dangerous situation. O'Reith had dealt with some rough characters over the years. But Marlborough had been tested in LA by the most sophisticated criminals of the Western Hemisphere.

O'Reith was no stranger to snake-eyes in all their many varieties. When he picked up the telephone at noon and asked the operator for Donald McLarssen, he knew he was embarking upon one of the greatest gambles of his life. Everything he loved was on the line. He heard a hissing voice with an Italian accent say, "My dear General O'Reith. You are to be admired for your punctuality. Please come to my suite? I'm on the third floor in the corner with a splendid view of the *Promenade des Anglais.* Come. We can have a café on the terrace."

The sinister Ugo Orgoglio was dressed like a diplomat, in a morning suit, with a red carnation in his lapel. His English was precise, if raspy, like a man recovering from influenza. He opened the door for O'Reith, stood aside to let him enter, closed it again and escorted him out to the terrace. They sat in wrought iron chairs painted white at a round, wrought iron table with a glass top. The chairs had padded seats of white leather. On the table top was a pot of black coffee, cube sugar wrapped in white paper, a pitcher of cream, cups and spoons and a wicker basket of croissants.

O'Reith sat, refused coffee with a shake of his head, looked at his foe and waited. Orgoglio began, "Now sir, we might just as well get straight to the pith of the matter. We hold four beautiful creatures that you would like to have back in your domicile, or is it a menagerie?"

O'Reith ignored the remark. "I'm listening," he said.

"Today is Friday, January 25th, . We shall meet again Saturday after next." Orgoglio consulted his pocket diary. "That will be on February 2nd. Now sir, the money. It must be in bills of denomination $100 or smaller. Forty million dollars. I imagine it will fill a suitcase. But we will spare you that. The money can be wire transferred to our Zurich account. I will give you the instructions presently."

O'Reith pulled his Luger and pointed it at the man's face. "I might just as well kill you right now. I will not transfer money to your account. I want to see my people."

Orgoglio looked at the muzzle of the gun but was not impressed. "You can put that away, my dear general. We can continue this discussion like civilized men. Besides, I was merely trying to save you the embarrassment of having both of them in the same place at the same time."

O'Reith held the muzzle of the Luger steady, pointed at the man with tiny, ophidian eyes seated across the glass table. He said in the *voice,* "I'll give you the money. Probably not in $100 bills. Maybe in $1,000s. Maybe in $5,000s. Maybe in $10,000s. Depends on what I can raise on short notice. But I only deliver when I see the four faces that I recognize as being mine. And if you have ill-used them, I will hound you to your grave."

"No need for theatrics, sir. You need have no fear, my dear General. We are gentlemen. No harm will attend your dears. If you are prepared to accept the awkward situation of having them all together, then so be it." Orgoglio smiled, ignoring the threat of the pistol. "But surely you can raise some amount in smaller bills. What do you Americans call it? Carrying around money? Yes, let's say that in addition to the 40 million in gilt-edge, we get $250,000 in denominations of $20s, $50s and $100s. Dear Frederico Bolletti has earned that anyhow. Talk about ill-treatment. Your wife, my dear general, can be a virago. Well, then sir, it is settled. I leave you to get the wherewithal assembled. Have it ready on the first Saturday in February. No need for you to cool your heels in this provincial town. Go to Paris. Attend your affairs. Get the money ready. We will determine a suitable rendezvous. I will telephone you the day before we close, say twenty-four hours notice." Orgoglio arose, still ignoring O'Reith's weapon.

O'Reith kept him covered until he was out of his suite and into the hall.

Following the meeting with Orgoglio, O'Reith called Tarbutton. They roused the flight engineer and asked him to prepare *La Cañada Cruz* for a flight to LeBourget. O'Reith and Tarbutton lunched on sole filets in lemon sauce with string beans and rice. While they ate, O'Reith described the meeting with Orgoglio.

They got a call for a three o'clock takeoff. The forecast was not too good. With a north wind blowing across the runway, both pilots struggled to keep the aircraft level during taking off. Within minutes the tower advised of snow and ice all the way up to 20,000 feet. Sure enough they needed deicers immediately. On oxygen at 12,000 feet, they wrestled the controls all the way up to 30,000 feet and never did break clear. But the deicers worked OK and late in the afternoon with LeBourget on the compass radio, they swung around into the traffic pattern for an instrument landing in marginal visibility. They were late. O'Reith weary, his leg giving him hell had no desire to sleep in his flat with Maxine abducted. So they went to the George V, had dinner and straight to bed.

Next morning, Saturday, January 26th, they met in the offices of The Casinghead Company at the cigarette-stained conference table. Marlborough was sitting in O'Reith's chair, his pork pie hat pushed back at an angle, showing his thinning brown hair. A cigarette dangled from his lower lip with the smoke curling up toward the ceiling. The handle of a Police Positive Colt 38 protruded from the coat of his blue pinstripe suit. He wore a maroon tie with tiny white dolphins in javelin down formation. On his right in khakis, sat Holland tight-lipped. He was bare-headed, wearing a regulation webbed pistol-belt with an Army .45 hanging from it. Over his shirt he had on a scruffy, brown leather A-4 jacket, the elastic long gone from the cuffs. Chafed imprints of eagles were still faintly visible on the epaulets. He wore reading glasses, a Lucky Strike in his lips, and with a yellow pencil, worked his way through a stack of cables from Maracaibo. Across from Holland also in pinstripes, sat Monk Parkhurst, wearing rimless spectacles, with a memo in front of him on Linen Bank stationery. He was smoking a Panatela, turning it between puffs and looking at the tip to make sure it burned evenly. A Webley .44 with a brown, pleated-leather cord dangling from the bottom of the handle was stuck in his belt. His face, though lined, was a friendly face. When he blew out a plume of smoke, it was if he were praying for something nice to happen. LeBel, unarmed, in a gray suit and a white, rough cotton shirt sat next to him, methodically smoking a Gitane, gazing at nothing. His diary was open in front of him with a blue and gold fountain pen on top of it. The ponderous McDonough, frowning as he often did, in white linen despite the cold, faced LeBel. He was such a large man it would be difficult to tell if he was armed or not. Attentive, he had a pencil in his hand and a yellow pad in front of him. O'Reith sat at the end of the table, opposite Marlborough in the seat that Blake took at directors meetings. Tarbutton sat beside him. Both men wore midnight blue suits, O'Reith with a white silk shirt and a black bow tie, Tarbutton in a starched, white cotton shirt with silver cuff links embossed Eighth USAAF and an ivory tie. O'Reith carried a 9mm Luger in a shoulder holster; Tarbutton an Army .45 in a chamois-skin belly-button holster. Their briefcases were propped against the leg of the table.

Their hats were piled on the far end of the table. Two homburgs, Parkhurst's bowler, Holland's Panama, LeBel's gray and white checkered beret and on top of the heap, McDonough's taupe deerstalker. O'Reith pondered what appeared to be a bullet hole through the crown. McDonough saw him peering at it, said, "It isn't a bullet hole, Clive, it's an arrow hole. It's my biretta that has the bullet hole, from when I was on sabbatical as Father Mendel at La Roche-Guyon in 1944. Sir John sent me over to 'brush up on my Nietzsche' as he put it." He smiled his most dangerous smile. O'Reith smiled back.

Marlborough began, "Without Maurice we would be totally in the dark. He has helped us get the cooperation of the *Surete*. We've had a look at the arrival card of Donnegan, Feathermerchant, Evans and Swetnam. Feathermerchant arrived on 10 January and said he would be staying at the Hotel Raspail. He never checked in there. Donnegan, Evans and Swetnam all arrived together from new York on a TWA flight on the 23rd. They said they would stay at the Hotel Horset in rue de Sevres. They are not there. In fact, they are all in Ventimiglia. Our agents saw them arrive by taxi..."

"What about Maxine and Monique?" O'Reith interrupted.

"I'm getting to that, General," Marlborough answered patiently. "The taxi carrying Evans and Swetnam arrived in the middle of the afternoon yesterday. Stopped at the locked gate, was there several minutes until it was opened and then went in. Our guys got a good look. Just the two of 'em. The cab with Feathermerchant arrived late at night on the 23rd. The only reason we know it was him was that our man picked the cab up at a stop light on the road coming east from Nice. A street light on the corner showed Feathermerchant sitting close to the right rear window, looking out. We made him positively. A woman, or at least what looked like a woman, sat on the other side. We couldn't identify her. Our man thought he could see a child's head resting on the woman's lap. Remember this was in the dark. It's hard to be certain. But they are trained to look for details. They knew that Maxine and Monique had been taken. And that makes sense. Get them all together. Easier to control. Donnegan arrived in Ventimiglia in a taxi about eight o'clock this morning. Two other guys with him. One looked like he might be McLarssen. The other, maybe Orgoglio. They were evidently expected because the gate swung open a couple of minutes before they showed. They went right in and the gate immediately behind them. This is good news. We know where they are. We know what they want. We've doubled our lookouts. They have automobiles at their disposal. Any departure from that studio, we'll be on their tail. None of that means we've got the problem under control. We have no idea where the transaction will take place or what the circumstances will be. We have the option of trying to take them in the studio. But it is plenty risky. Might not come out right. No cooperation from the Italian police. The toughest part of this play is the fact that it is in Italy."

McDonough, rubbing his chin as he listened to Marlborough, said, "Let's refuse to meet with them in Italy. If Orgoglio calls and says Rome or Milan or, for that matter, even Ventimiglia, we say nothing doing. Tell 'em France or Germany or Spain or Switzerland but not Italy."

O'Reith looked at Marlborough, asked, "What do you think, Duke?"

"I don't think they'll want to do it in Italy," he said. "Like throwing raw meat into a pool of sharks. Too many other of their own kind that would like to grab a share of it. Must be a dozen people involved in that operation. They all know what's going on. I think Orgoglio'll go for either France or Switzerland. I say France for no other reason than the banks are open on Saturday morning. They get their money, put it in the bank and they're gone. Home free."

"He's right," LeBel said. "In the south of France there are many small private banks, some with strong Italian ties." He lit another Gitane, blew a plume of gray smoke across the table, continued, "Bolletti would arrange for an armored car or maybe they would simply do a bank-to-bank transfer. Bolletti would know how to do that. Yes, I think Duke is close to the mark."

Marlborough said, "We can operate on that theory." He turned to Parkhurst. "Your turn Monk."

"Clive, I've had a word with BIL," he began. "We can borrow $10 million based on your custodial account. They'll lend 50% of the value at 4% interest. In London, from Helen's account at our bank, over which you have signature authority, we can line up another $10 million at the Lombard rate plus half a percent. After a rather heated discussion with our board, Linen Bank agrees to lend you $20 million. Security for that loan will be your shareholding in The Casinghead Company. That one was a sticky wicket. Our chaps think it is a hell of a risk. But for old time's sake, they'll go along. The carrying around money they want, we can get that from the account in Liechtenstein that covers Maxine's expenses. So we're set. You and I fly to London on Monday morning. The BIL bankers will join us in the conference room of the Linen Bank. We'll sign the papers. The money can be delivered by armored car to the office here. Should have it by the end of the day on Wednesday. Let's see. That'll be the… the 30th. Plenty of time for the Saturday transaction."

"Clive," LeBel said, " we can store the cash in your office on the third floor. We'll have men down here, up there and a couple on the roof."

"Put me on guard duty, Maurice," Holland said. "Right there in the room with the money."

They all smiled. They knew he was itching for a good blood-letting. He was that kind of a guy.

The meeting ended. Tarbutton and O'Reith went up to O'Reith's flat. Marlborough said to Holland, "Next Monday while Parkhurst and the general are in London, the rest of us, could get together here and talk about what we'll do at the moment of truth. The general doesn't need to be in that meeting. It could unsettle him. There's a good chance Bolletti, Orgoglio et al, will have some kind of a trick to play once they get their hands on the money. We have to be prepared for funny business."

"I'll speak to the others," Holland said.

Tarbutton and O'Reith rode the elevator up to the top of the building. O'Reith opened the door with his key, said. "This won't take long Hardy. Have a seat. I just wanted you to keep me company. I can't stand this place by myself."

"Of course, Clive. I understand."

In the kitchen closet, O'Reith turned on the overhead light and reached up to a shelf at head level. He took down a frayed olive drab face towel that was wrapped around an oblong object. He put it out on a newspaper on the mail table in the parlor and opened it. It was an army .45. The towel was oil stained where the muzzle, the trigger ring and the hammer touched it. "Hardy, they issued this piece to me when I was commissioned a second lieutenant in 1927. All I've ever shot with it were rats. The barrel went bad some years back. I'm going to put a new one in it. Just take a minute." He quickly disassembled the pistol, installed the new barrel, reassembled it, removed the clip and ejected three cartridges which he wrapped in newspaper and tossed into the waste basket. "Ten years old, Hardy. I don't trust 'em." He left the gun on the towel and fetched a can of machine oil from Maxine's sewing room. He expertly lubricated all moving parts and returned the clip to the magazine. He wrapped the pistol in newspaper and shoved it into his belt. "Wish I had a holster for this. Maybe LeBel can find one. Let's go."

"What are you going to use for ammunition? Tarbutton asked.

"Holland's got two canisters for that sub-machine gun. He can spare me seven rounds. All I'll need…"

O'Reith locked up; they rode the elevator down to the ground floor landing and took a taxi to the George V for lunch.

A short year ago, right after the merger, he had been a fabulously wealthy man. There was nothing he could not buy. Why, he had cash and securities to the value of $200 million! A mansion in Holmby Hills. A bungalow on Summit Drive. A four story building in rue de Surene. Prime Paris real estate. Airplanes. Limousines. He lacked nothing. Now, on this damp, drizzling morning in the conference room of The Linen Bank on Oxford Street, in London, he had signed pledges that, if called, would reduce his fortune by over $190 million. He'd sunk $150 million into The Casinghead Company. He didn't draw a salary. He had no expense account. What he spent came out of his own pocket. He spent a million dollars a year. Bodyguards. Real Estate Taxes. Two families. He ate the best. Drank the best. Played golf at the finest course in the world. On the flight back to Paris alone, for Parkhurst had his own affairs to attend, he couldn't help but wonder how he had fallen so far so quickly. He thought about Ted Schaeffer, kidding him along. Trying to get him to do better. Well, he himself was certainly not doing better. Everything going down the drain before his eyes. Looming disaster was, of course, nothing new. He'd stared death down more than once. From the smoking cockpit of a battle-damaged B-17 with a fire in the Tokyos. From the soot-covered cellar deck of a roaring fire in the middle of the lake. In those instances he coldly and analytically assayed his chances. Now he was heartsick. As a result, he found it difficult to think straight. He simply could not contemplate a world without Helen, without Maxine, without those two little girls he adored. Like an automaton, he got off the plane at Orly, went through Customs and Immigration. Cheered momentarily when Tarbutton greeted him in the arrivals lounge, he quickly lapsed back into melancholia. Tarbutton whisked him to the George V for a restorative martini and a good meal. LeBel met them there. Gleefully advised O'Reith that a Foreign Legion tailor was coming on Friday, a grizzled veteran of desert warfare who had mended many a bullet torn uniform on the battlefield.

Late Wednesday afternoon, a Thomas Cook armored car arrived with the money. Holland, sub-machine gun at the ready, stood over the heavy canvas bag as they ascended to the third floor. Once inside, the Cook guards unlocked the bag. Most of the bills were gilt-edged. Madison and Chase. Five thousands and ten thousands. With a few Clevelands to round it off to $40 million. Plus the small change, a quarter of a million in fifties and hundreds. LeBel provided an attaché case, black and battered but with heavy hinges and a solid grip. O'Reith was surprized when the banded bills fit into it with room to spare.

On Friday morning, the telephone rang as O'Reith was having breakfast. Gabrielle LeBel at the office said that a call had come. He asked her to ring them back. Tell them he was at the hotel. Breakfast finished, he was drinking coffee when the call came. It was Orgoglio. He said, "General O'Reith, I trust your day is beginning well. Soon we will have this unpleasant business behind us. We will be able to jest about it. Talk about what could have happened and didn't. How it was a well planned, well executed operation and everyone was a winner. Are you ready to complete the transaction?"

"I am."

"Splendid. Please bring the money to me in Biarritz. Be in the lobby of the Hotel du Palais at eleven o'clock in the morning. At eleven-thirty you will be summoned to the telephone at the desk to receive further instructions."

"You understand Signor Orgoglio that I must see my loved ones or there will be no exchange," O'Reith stressed.

"Impossible," Orgogolio replied. "You must put the money into the hands of my agent. When that is done, your dears will be released and you shall shortly see them."

"No deal."

His heart pounding, O'Reith listened for some long, long moments. Then Orgoglio began to speak again. "All right, General O'Reith. It shall be as you say. You will receive your instructions. If you follow them to the letter, you will see your dears. You will then bring the money to me. I will, of course, examine it. If it is as we have discussed, I will signal for their release. You will be able to join them momentarily. There may be some embarrassment for you. But that is your own doing. As a matter of personal interest, when all this is a distant memory, perhaps you could tell me what happens when wife meets mistress under such extenuating circumstances."

"So it is Saturday morning in Biarritz at the Hotel du Palais," O'Reith said.

"Exactly. Good morning to you sir," Orgoglio said in his raspy voice.

O'Reith called Gabrielle to assemble the team. The tailor was just finishing as the others entered the conference room. Chairs scraped the floor. Matches flared. Cigarettes and cigars filled the room with smoke. LeBel opened a window even though it was quite cold. The tailor's sewing kit was open at the end of the cigarette-stained table, his scissors beside it. The holster cut from a white cotton towel would absorb the gun oil, prevent it from staining the pants. A quick job by an experienced hand. The tailor expertly enfolded the automatic in the towel, basted it in outline, removed the weapon, quadrupled the basting. Trimmed it into the desired shape. Finally he attached it inside the trousers with four big brown, bone buttons. He whispered 'voila'. As the tailor departed, O'Reith, putting on his pants, repeated to the assembled men his recent conversation with Orgoglio. He inserted the .45 in the new holster and zipped up his fly. The butt of the piece covered his navel. The muzzle was an inch and a half above the family jewels. In front of a mirror on the door, he took a profile look, put on his coat, took another look and satisfied with his appearance, sat down in the chair across from Marlborough. Remembering the unfortunate Gimp Flagherty, with a faint smile, he double checked the pistol's safety catch.

Marlborough began, "How are we going to move the money from Paris to Biarritz? Do we send it by armored car or take it with us on the plane? How are we going to protect the general when he gets the signal from Orgoglio? I favor sending the money by unmarked armored car. The general checks into the Hotel du Palais with an attaché case filled with newspapers. When he gets the word, we'll exchange the money for the newspaper. Any suggestions?"

Tarbutton said, "Let's fly to Toulouse in the B-17, with the money. Clive takes a taxi to Biarritz with the newspapers. Holland guards the money in a Toulouse hotel room while the rest of us go to Biarritz. Find out where Orgoglio and his gang are holed up. When that's known, or if the clock runs out, Holland takes a cab to Biarritz. Once Clive knows where to take the cash, we'll bring it to his room at the hotel, exchange briefcases and follow him to the delivery point."

"That sounds OK to me," Marlborough said. "We're dealing with a good-sized gang. Abducting two women and two children takes organization. I have fresh reports from Ventimiglia? Movement at the studio. Late last night, two automobiles departed through the main gate. The side windows were covered. Our men couldn't see much. We tailed them with two cars. After they crossed into France, on the Grand Corniche with the gas pedals to the floorboards, a couple of police cars cut our guys off. Phony French police. They ticketed our guys for speeding and let them go. Well, they'd lost that one so they went back toward Ventimiglia. At Menton, coming in the opposite direction a caravan of movie vehicles passed them. Two trucks with movie gear. Another truck with a cabin on a low-boy. The truck cabs had the studio name on the doors. Same thing on the cabin. One of our men is tailing the caravan. One man still in Ventimiglia. Nothing stirring at the studio. After the caravan left, the lights were turned off inside. Once we get to Toulouse, I'll call him again. My guess is that Helen, Maxine and the kids were in the cars, en route to Biarritz. The rest of the gang is in the caravan. We spot that, we'll know where they are. Let's hope our guys don't lose them."

"We fly to Toulouse?" O'Reith asked.

Nods of assent went around the table. Chairs scraped the floor. Men with long faces donned hats and overcoats. O'Reith leading, they filed out of the room.

*   *   *

Landing at Toulouse around five o'clock, Tarbutton accompanied O'Reith, to keep his morale up. From the airport, LeBel called the Hotel du Palais, reserved O'Reith's room. Then he called the Plaza Hotel to reserve rooms for the rest of them. O'Reith was ready to go. Marlborough said, "General O'Reith, you will not know where we are. But we will know where you are. Follow instructions to the letter. You will have the money in time to meet the delivery deadline. We will force Orgoglio to live up to his end of the bargain. Helen and Maxine and those kids will be escorted out of danger as fast as automobiles can travel. Don't even think about that part of it. After you see them and you are satisfied that they are OK, do your duty. Keep in mind that we are stronger than they are, far stronger. We have experience that they lack. We are determined to prevail. OK?"

O'Reith nodded. "He had given enough speeches on rainy tarmacs with dew dripping from cold B-17s to recognize a pep talk when he heard one."

LeBel said, "Clive, I asked Gabrielle to come down on a commercial flight from Paris. It is due now. She'll be with us..."

Marlborough said, "Sharon Mills and Alice Ridley are already in Biarritz, General. I spoke with them this morning after we heard from you."

O'Reith and Tarbutton departed immediately. Holland, the submachine gun wrapped in newspapers under his arm, waved them off.

The road to Biarritz was narrow. They went through Auch, Orthez and Bayonne. Around ten o'clock, O'Reith alit at the marquee of the Hotel du Palais. He was in a corner suite on the fourth floor above the semicircular dining room called *La Villa Eugenie*, famed for its Basque cuisine. From his terrace with a wrought iron railing, he could see the ocean below him, Pointe St. Martin to the north and the casino to the south, all marginally visible in the misty gloom. It was cold so he didn't stay long. Tarbutton came along to see the layout. Satisfied, he said, "Clive, I'm on my way, I'll call from the Plaza."

O'Reith was awaiting room service when Tarbutton called. Told him that Holland, Parkhurst and McDonough had arrived right behind him. LeBel and Marlborough were coming with Gabrielle, expected within the hour. Their agents from Ventimiglia arrived. So far, so good.

O'Reith, in bed, turned and tossed, distracted by the lighthouse flare that crossed his window every minute or two. At seven, he arose and ordered breakfast. Waiting on the terrace, he watched the angry Atlantic waves roll in, hammering relentlessly at the concrete seawall. Soon, chilled, he came inside to eat his croissant. He waited beside the telephone. The call came at eleven o'clock on the dot. "A good morning to you again, my dear General O'Reith," Orgoglio began in impeccable English. "I trust you slept well. Sir, things are on schedule. We await your presence. The transaction will take place in the Hotel Miramar, just up the street. A five minute stroll. But we prefer that you take a taxi. Who knows what could happen to an unarmed man carrying such a large quantity of money? At the marquee, you will see a policeman in uniform standing beside the doorman. There is a concern about Algerian terrorists in the land these days but not to worry. The policeman will wish to see the contents of the attaché case. You may show him the money sir. He will allow you to enter the hotel through the revolving doors. As you come in, your little family will be in the lobby, in perfect condition, waiting as if to catch a taxi to the airport. You pause only long enough to satisfy yourself. They will not be looking in your direction but seemingly, at each other. Your wife and your daughter will be on the right. Across the central square on the left you will see your mistress and her child. Then sir, turn to the left, skirt the lobby come all the way around, until the desk is on your left. You will see the entry into the bar. I believe it is called *bar de la plage.* Yes, the bar of the beach. I will be sitting there alone at a corner table. This is not the high season. Should there be a guest of the hotel in the bar, we will pay him no attention. You will join me, open the attaché case so the top prevents the bartender from seeing its contents. I will examine it, test it, and if all is in order, then the affair is ended. You may walk out into the lobby and join your loved ones. Is all that clear, my dear general?"

"Yes."

"Very well, you should leave immediately. I await you."

No sooner had he hung up than there was a single rap on his door. One of Tarbutton's men. O'Reith recognized him immediately as an ex-paratrooper out of the 82nd Airborne Division that they had interviewed in the Fullerton Building. The man said nothing, held out to O'Reith an attaché case identical to the one on his bed. He took it, motioned the man inside and gave him the case full of newsprint. When the courier retreated into the hall, O'Reith snapped open the case and took a last quick look at Messrs. Madison, Cleveland and Chase. He riffled through the piles and marked them all present and accounted for, at least for the next few minutes.

Chapter XIX

▼

Melee at the Miramar

For all of its reputation as a balmy, sub-tropical paradise, Biarritz can be frigid in January. This morning a foggy, fresh wind was blowing in off the Atlantic. Gray cotton-topped waves crashed across the beach. O'Reith had on his newly altered midnight blue business suit, a white silk shirt and a black bow tie. He was unarmed except for the Model 1911 Army .45 with the new barrel, which pressed against his stomach. Despite the obvious dangers attendant thereto, he cocked it and slipped the safety off. He didn't relish the idea of having the ready-to-shoot piece aimed at the tip of his penis but he might not get another chance to get set. If he pulled it, he would be shooting it within a second. Over his suit he put on a heavy, alpaca overcoat that fell to his ankles. Designed for north European winters, it had a wide, stiff collar that could be turned up to protect the face against howling winds. He donned his homburg hat, picked up the attaché case with the money and walked down the hall to the staircase. Presently he was crossing the grand lobby. As he approached the revolving doors, the doorman gave them a starting push. Outside, the doorman closed him in to the first cab in the rank. O'Reith tipped him and settled gingerly back into the cushions, nudging the pistol to lay along the line of his leg, aimed more or less at the driver's backside. He told the cab driver where he wanted to go. The taxi, crunching gravel, slowly wended its way to the wrought-iron gate, made a broad U-turn, into the Avenue de l'Imperatrice. Going up the hill, the driver had hardly shifted into second gear before turning into rue Louison Bobet. The Hotel Miramar loomed. In the parking lot on the right, O'Reith saw two studio trucks from Ventimiglia. Further up was the cabin, still on the low-boy trailer. On the side of it in large black letters was stenciled: Compannia de Produzzione Cinematographica de Ventimiglia. A steel ladder lead to an open door in the cabin. Near the fringe of the vast lawn that stretched all the way to the Avenue de l'Imperatrice, two cameramen were adjusting their tripods. A worker was placing the cameras atop them, setting up to shoot the entrance to the hotel. Blue-frocked workmen were unloading the trucks, carefully arranging the lights, decorations, and scenery. Clearly the hotel was to be a backdrop for a motion picture scene.

A seven story hotel, it was of a color somewhere between yellow and dun. The outer rooms on the sixth floor were terraced. Three arcades loomed over the grand colonnaded entry. On the central gable high above an electric sign read: M I R A M A R. Beyond that, the right wing of the hotel continued, at last ending beneath a similar gable which gave the building its asymmetrical but distinguished appearance. The dull color of the hotel was livened up by the beige and red trimming on the terrace ironwork.

As the cab pulled into the arched entry, O'Reith spotted the policeman, chatting with the doorman. He alit, paid off the cab. The policeman's nodded him into a nook where the entry abutted the hotel proper. Bracing the attaché case against the stone wall, he snapped it open and let the policeman inspect it. Then he closed it, pulled his hat down low over his forehead, turned up the collar of his greatcoat and pushed through the revolving door, centered between two tall French windows in stone frames.

Immediately he was in a vast, colonnaded lobby with a short, cylindrical projection descending from the ceiling. Beneath it was a square central area with no furniture. Beyond that were several round wooden tables with hotel stationery in vertical pigeon-holes. Heavily padded easy chairs filled the lobby. On his right was Helen in a gray pantsuit sitting stiffly upright in a straight-back chair at one of the tables. Little Helen Simpson in a blue pinafore sat beside her. Next to her sat a small, lumpy man in a morning suit. He appeared to be reading *L'Express*. O'Reith thought him to be Bolletti. Another, younger man, rather handsome, sat in an adjacent chair. His dark hair was slicked down. In gray pants and a white coat with shoes to match, he was just sitting there, a vacant expression on his face.

Across the central empty square, some distance away in an easy chair, sat Maxine in a brown flowered dress with white lilacs made in Bogota. O'Reith remembered it as a gift from Ines. Monique, in a green, corduroy smock with straps over her shoulders, sat in Maxine's lap. Next to her, O'Reith recognized Beauregard Feathermerchant in a brown business suit. A folded newspaper in his lap covered one of his hands. His hair now was mostly gray but still with a bit of the red that had given him his nickname. In the next cluster of tables, closer but on the other side of the rug leading into the left wing, O'Reith spotted two more Americans whom he took to be Swetnam and Evans. They too, had newspapers covering their hands. Sitting beside them, a deeply tanned, portly Arab sat, a spotlessly white robe engulfing him, his head covered with a pristine mantle edged in three rows of golden piping. The Sultan of Morocco? Or the Sultan of Swat? His suitcases, marked in Arabic sat near him on the floor. He was waiting for his limousine. Straight ahead, at the long, ivory check-in desk, O'Reith observed a huge man, in white linen, a Panama hat atwirl in his hand. He was discussing his bill with the desk clerk.

Following instructions, O'Reith skirted the central area of the lobby, walked quickly around the perimeter, unbuttoning his greatcoat and folding down his collar as he went. He saw the entrance to *Le Bar de la Plage*. Entering it, on his right, was the paneled hardwood bar with brass railing, a mirrored backdrop and bottles of liquor. On the lowest shelf were glasses turned upside down, reflecting light from the chandelier. Four metal stools with backrests faced the bar, two of them occupied. At the far end of the bar, near an octagonal seascape featuring a pastel mermaid preening herself in a mirror, a waiter attended his trays. A swarthy, heavy-set man at the bar, wore black pants and a white coat, his shirt unbuttoned at the top. He was hunched over reading the sports page of *Sud Ouest*. Two empty stools separated him from a thin wizened officer of the Foreign Legion, his dazzling white kepi beside him on the bar, his array of medals reflected by the mirror. In the corner across from the seascape at a dark, wooden table sat a man with a cruel, deeply lined, menacing face. Orgoglio. His sinister face looked up at O'Reith and smiled. His small, dark eyes were dancing behind the thick lenses of his glasses. His falcon beak of a nose twitched in gleeful anticipation. This was his lucky day! He was dressed in black, with a white cotton shirt and a thin black tie, clipped to his shirt, that showed all the way around the collar.

O'Reith came to the table where Orgoglio sat smiling, noiselessly pulled back the chair and placing the attaché case on the table, joined him. Orgoglio said, "Well General O'Reith, you are right on time. I always respect a man who is punctual. A good quality in business. You know these last few days I have had to educate myself about so-called gilt-edge American money. We have no historic continuity in Italy. Imagine those interesting American men of history. Salmon P. Chase. Stephen Grover Cleveland and of course the great James Madison, one of the founders of the nation. Could any one of them have ever imagined himself gracing such bills of great denomination? A banker at the casino in Monte Carlo, who is an expert on these high-powered bank notes gave me a rudimentary financial education. I got the feel of the paper, the smell of the ink. I held them up to the light, examined the gold edging. I feel quite up to the task of appraisal. Well, shall we begin?"

O'Reith snapped open the case with the lid blocking the view of the bartender. Orgoglio took his little black diary from an inside coat pocket. He opened it and quickly noted the number of packets and the denominations. He counted the packets expertly. Riffled several of them to satisfy himself it was all money and no ballast. His tests completed, he finished his computation and returned his little book to its place. At random he held some of the bank notes up to the light. Satisfied, he left the inspected bills loose on top of the packets and closed the case. "Everything seems to be in order," he remarked, removing his glasses and cleaning them with a handkerchief.

"We're finished then." O'Reith said.

Orgoglio smiled cruelly, said. "If only it were so. Actually we have one more hurdle ahead of us. The gentleman you see at the end of the bar is coming to collect the attaché case. The gentlemen in the lobby have already escorted your dears back to the cars. Even as we speak, they are on their way back to Ventimiglia, a vacation. You and I go to Los Angeles where, I am advised, you have about $10 million dollars in the Crocker Bank. We wish to have that money transferred to one of our accounts. Then, and only then, my dear General O'Reith, will you have your little 'family' back." He was gloating and enjoying it.

As the swarthy man at the end of the bar left his stool, the old legionnaire shot him once through the temples with a 9 mm Luger that had a silencer attached to the muzzle. It sounded as if a fly had been swatted. The bartender dived. Even before the swarthy man had fallen to the floor, even before O'Reith could jerk his .45 to clear the table top, the Frenchman had pivoted on his stool and fired again. The shot was louder this time. A tiny dark spot appeared at Orgoglio's left temple. He stiffened, sighed and slumped in his chair.

The Frenchman, his white kepi on his head, expertly lifted Orgoglio's billfold and pocket diary, motioning to O'Reith to search the Mexican-looking guy. O'Reith patted the heavy man down, got his billfold and papers. The Frenchman said, "Clive, we'll just be on our way now. Bring the attaché case. We have miles to travel."

O'Reith recognized the voice of LeBel, his face heavily made up by Sharon Mills no doubt. LeBel removed a smoke bomb from his tunic, lit the fuse and set it on top of the bar. In seconds a dense black plume jetted from the top of the bomb and began obscuring the ceiling. By the time they were out of the bar, the chandelier had vanished in the expanding blanket of smoke. From the lobby came the rattle of a machine gun, several short bursts and then silence. O'Reith, deeply worried, followed LeBel. In the now deserted square of the lobby, four smoke bombs poured out acrid, sooty vapors. The air smelled of burnt nitrocellulose. Underlying that was the stench of excrement. Empty .45 cartridge cases covered the parquet. A row of gunned-down bodies sprawled against the riddled chairs. The wall behind was bullet-torn with chips of plaster and red brick fallen to the floor. Backs were shot off of several expensive-looking chairs. Smoke was now just above their heads. O'Reith, his handkerchief over his face, followed LeBel out through the revolving door. Standing where the doorman had once stood, was Marlborough, impatient and looking at his wrist watch. Beside him, still in his sheik get-up, was Holland, smoking a Lucky Strike, the Thompson sub-machine gun under his arm. Marlborough said, "General we better get going. This place will be alive with cops pdq."

LeBel winked at them, said "We have about five minutes."

Marlborough pushed O'Reith into the back seat of a taxi, LeBel beside him. "Toulouse Airport", he said to the taxi driver. As they rolled along, LeBel said, "The instant you entered the bar, our team covered the Orgoglio gang. By the way, your son was on the same plane as Gabrielle. He was helpful this morning. Monk, George, and your son escorted Helen and little Helen to one taxi. When they were gone,

Hardy escorted Maxine and Monique to another. I assume that Hunter and Duke liquidated the gang, gleefully, I imagine."

"So where is Helen going?" O'Reith asked.

"Back to Monte Carlo," LeBel said. "Alice Ridley and Sharon Mills are with her."

"Sharon did a good job on your face, Maurice," O'Reith said. "I was taken in until you spoke. Of course when you plugged that Mexican-looking guy, I figured it was you."

"We started at seven o'clock this morning in Sharon's suite," LeBel explained. "She had some extra chairs sent up but not enough. We had to rotate. Hunter called it a game of 'musical chairs'. I didn't catch the meaning."

"Child's game, Maurice," O'Reith said. "Music plays. Little kids dance around and sing. Music stops, little kids, laughing, giggling and squealing, run to claim the chairs. One fewer chair than kids. One without a seat is the goat. Silly game. Most kids games are. Fun for the adoring mother's to watch, at least until one of the little kids gets fed up and starts to howl. Sharon must have worked pretty fast to get you guys all fixed up in time for the grand finale."

"Duke located the studio trucks last night in the Miramar parking lot. We assumed that was where the action would be," LeBel amplified. "He explained to Sharon what we needed. She was all set up for us this morning, ran an assembly line. By ten o'clock we were done. Hunter and George were in the lobby at ten-thirty. I was in the bar at the same hour, alone for some minutes. The Mexican-looking guy, as you call him, came in first. Shortly after, Orgoglio. Helen and Little Helen appeared at ten-forty-five, passed in front of the bar, Bolletti ahead and that other man, whomever he was, behind. At about five minutes to the hour Maxine and Monique came down, passed by the bar, guarded by Feathermerchant and company. I suppose that by then, we were all assembled but of course, I was not in position to see. Once I saw the women and the children, I was convinced we would make it."

"So we're going to Toulouse. What then?"

"Duke and Hunter will be right behind us. We take the B-17 back to Paris."

"I suppose I can call Helen in the morning," O'Reith said, thinking out loud. "What was the idea of hustling them away so fast?"

LeBel laughed. "Zut! Who could predict how *that affair* would end! We wanted them out of harm's way while Orgoglio was preoccupied, counting his money. That was the only time we felt we could be sure of."

O'Reith nodded.

Of course it was a joyful reunion at Toulouse Airport. O'Reith swept Maxine and Monique into his arms at the same time. Tears filled all eyes. On the flight back to Paris, after they got up to altitude, O'Reith took over the right hand seat. Holland retired to the waist to disassemble the sub-machine gun. He laid the parts out on newspapers, cleaned and oiled them, then packed them away in the suitcases where they would remain until the aircraft was back in Venezuela.

From LeBourget, O'Reith, Maxine and Monique took a taxi to their flat in rue de Surene, the attaché case with the money across his knees. Marlborough, Holland and Tarbutton went to the Hotel Meurice in rue de Rivoli. LeBel and Gabrielle went home. The men agreed to meet in the morning at the office of The Casinghead Company at nine o'clock.

In their flat, Maxine cooked a pot of pasta and uncorked a bottle of red wine. O'Reith unloaded the .45, returned it to the shelf in the closet. He changed into slacks and a fresh silk shirt. He mixed drinks while the pasta cooked. They ate it with tomato sauce and Parmesan cheese. Monique had to settle for canned milk.

Once Monique was asleep, O'Reith and Maxine showered together and went to bed. He was so frazzled, he couldn't remember when he'd last had a piece, was surprized his eyeballs were not bulging. But in spite of her kisses and tender caresses, he couldn't get it up. Worn and exhausted, he was a limp-dick commando. But at dawn with a frigid wind whipping around the building, snuggled in close to Maxine, both of them in the nude, he awoke refreshed and ready to go. She was ready too. So they went, with the saints ringing the bells, the angels singing the hymns and all the saved souls of nineteen hundred and fifty six years of Christianity chanting the Anvil Chorus.

Their idyll barely over, the telephone rang. Monk Parkhurst calling from Monte Carlo. He said, "I say Clive, but I'm frightfully concerned about all that lolly. We're paying almost five thousand dollars a day in interest charges. I called Lombard Street just now for a Thomas Cook armored car to come round and pick it up. The ticket number is triple six, triple nine, triple four. Got that?"

"Yeah, do I give them a ring?"

"No. They'll be at the office within the hour."

"I'll be waiting for them. Monk, thanks."

"Don't mention it, Clive. They'll head straight for the Calais ferry. The money will be in our coffers right as rain by the close of the day. We'll wire a credit to BIL and stop the interest charges instanter."

"Where are you staying, Monk?" O'Reith asked.

"I'm in the Hotel de Paris near the casino, just a hop a skip and a jump from Helen's place. All is well. Tedious trip across France but we made it safe and none the worse. I'm flying to London as soon as I can get out. George will hang about until Helen gets properly sorted out. Rum go in Biarritz, eh what?"

"Indeed. I thank you for that too."

Parkhurst laughed a long rattling British laugh. "Hah! Hah! Hah!," he began. "Done with the greatest of pleasure, old boy. Haven't had such a time since Gold beach. George had a romp too. Said it was more fun than when he was the Vicar of La Roche-Guyon. How long are you in Paris?"

"Depends on Helen. Decisions piling up on us in Venezuela. We're stretched thin. I'll call you tomorrow. Let you know where we stand."

"Well, take care, old boy. I'm off. See you at the next directors meeting if not before."

O'Reith left Maxine sleeping, showered, dressed and went down to the office, called Helen. When she answered, he purred, "Say baby, I could get used to that voice. Did you sleep well?"

"Yeah I'm OK. Relieved. Alice and Sharon are with me. Little Clive Colin is still asleep I was sure glad to see him yesterday, even with an automatic pistol in his hand. Ace, he shot one of those thugs!"

"Runs in the family. Monk called a minute ago. Said you had a long trip but that all was well. What next?"

"My five reels of film are in Ventimiglia. I'm not leaving here without them. Ace, I know there was a dust up in the Miramar yesterday after I was escorted out? I nearly jumped out of my skin when Holland popped out of that sheik-suit and pointed a Tommy gun at those guys. But his voice was sweet music. He said, 'Helen, grab little Helen and get the hell out of here!' Which I did. Where were you?"

"I was in the bar with Orgoglio. I saw you when I came into the lobby but I couldn't tarry. I saw that Arab too. Had no idea it was Holland. George was at the desk. That put my mind at ease, partly anyway. Tell Sharon she's in line for a bonus. I don't know about Alice. As a prognosticator, she's not so hot. Helen, we're getting together here in the office in a few minutes. Donald McLarssen and Barney Donnegan are absent and unaccounted for. They must be frustrated as hell. Marlborough has to sort that out. I don't have the details on the melee. I'll call you back when I know. How's that?"

"OK. I need some help. That's for sure. George said I could count on him."

"You'll need more than George. Turn your film recovery operation over to Marlborough. He can fly down to Nice today. Tell him what he needs to know and then let him do it."

"I'll go for that, Ace. I'm ready to get the hell out of town."

"Okay, baby. I'll call you back in a bit."

"Clive, when you were in the lobby of the Miramar yesterday, did you see another woman? A blonde in a print dress? She had a little black-haired girl in her lap."

"Baby, I only had eyes for you," O'Reith purred in his most convincing tones. But he could tell by the tone of her voice when she said goodbye that there was more to be heard from her on that subject.

He really didn't have to go to Monte Carlo. It would be so easy to plead the pressure of business in Venezuela. But that would not be right and he knew it. So he began preparing for a difficult conversation. He smiled as he hung up. He deemed the matter with Maxine well within his control. Still, if he could go back to late 1945, when he got himself into this, he would surely do it all quite differently. Content in the belief that the Good Lord took care of his faithful subjects he mused, "After all, tomorrow will be another day, sure to be better than many a yesterday."

Holland, LeBel and Tarbutton arrived together. In the conference room, Holland read the accumulated cables from Los Angeles, Caracas and Maracaibo. Marlborough had been on the telephone with his agents. Gabrielle LeBel arrived with a basket of croissants and a jar of peach preserves. She made a pot of coffee. Everyone had breakfast. She took croissants and a peach preserves to Holland.

O'Reith told Marlborough that Helen needed help recovering her film. They joined Holland. He put the cables aside. The meeting was short. Holland and Tarbutton would depart for Maiquetia immediately in the B-17 via Nice. Marlborough and O'Reith would deplane there for Monte Carlo. When Marlborough had completed his assignment in Ventimiglia, he would fly to Caracas. They would decide what to do about Torres and Cordero. O'Reith believed they had supplied information to the late Beauregard Feathermerchant. Both were still probably on Donald McLarssen's payroll. LeBel said he would strengthen security arrangements for Maxine and Monique. Holland said he had shot four men in the lobby. Three of them he recognized; Feathermerchant, Evans and Swetnan. The fourth, a younger man speaking in Italian to a fifth member of the gang had slicked down hair. These two were guarding Helen and little Helen Simpson. The younger man flashed a gun. Little Clive Colin shot him out of hand. The small rotund man, Bolletti was cut in two by machine-gun fire. McDonough had killed the phony policeman. Parkhurst had accounted for the two cameramen and three drivers. As near as they could calculate, it was a clean sweep. Gabrielle announced the arrival of the Thomas Cook truck. Holland put the money in the hands of the driver. With a .45 automatic in his hand, escorted him to the armored car.

O'Reith telephoned Helen, to say they were on their way, went up to say goodbye to Maxine, promising to return in a day or so. He hugged and kissed Monique. Packed an overnight bag. They departed LeBourget at noon and by five o'clock that afternoon, O'Reith and Marlborough were in Helen's limousine. In Monte Carlo, little Clive Colin, Sharon Mills and Alice Ridley were all waiting in Helen's flat. When the hugging and kissing came to its inevitable end, with everybody listening intently, Helen told Marlborough how Bolletti had removed the suitcase with the five reels of film. She presumed he had taken it back to the cutting room. She sketched out the layout of the studio, described the marks on the reels and explained to Marlborough that she needed the work print too. Additional editing could be required once she had the film back in Los Angeles. Marlborough promised a report and left. As did the others. They knew that Helen was ready for some privacy with her husband.

She was immediately in his arms. They were caressing one another and within minutes were stripped and getting down to it. He couldn't remember when she had been so ready for him. He still had a round or two left in his pistol. It was not the majestic heavenly experience of the early morning in Paris but, how could he complain? When they had worn it out, they showered together, she mixed the drinks. They ordered dinner from the Hotel de Paris.

Over martinis, Helen told O'Reith that Spermaceti, stiff as a board right now in a Biarritz mortuary, would presently become immortal as Sixto Cigone in *Los Ladrones of Piedras Negras*. "It's always that way, Ace. When one of the actors expires just before a film goes into distribution, he immediately steals the spotlight, no matter how obscure his role."

"He didn't merely expire, baby. Your son shot half of his handsome face off."

Helen put her hand over her mouth, "I hate that it was little Clive Colin who shot him. He wasn't too bad of a guy! As for Bolletti, no love lost."

O'Reith shrugged, explained that Holland and Tarbutton, were somewhere over Africa enroute to Venezuela. He had to meet them within days. Teague and Parkinson would be joining the company in Venezuela. He told her that Blake was joining too. He would work out of the Fullerton building. Virginia would be back in their place just down the street from the Holmby Hills mansion. He had to go over the books in Paris with LeBel. They had overspent the budget. Parkhurst would help with further financing. O'Reith said he would soon join her in LA. Neither he nor Helen wanted to return to Holmby Hills. Rae Regan was comfortable there. They were content to leave her undisturbed. Susie wanted to dispose of the penthouse in Long Beach where she had lived with Harvey Halliday in the last few years of his life. Helen remembered it from the time they had cocktails with Halliday when he was running for Congress, reminded O'Reith of the occasion. O'Reith said, "Baby when you get back, call Susie and take a look at the place. Maybe that's where we belong." Helen agreed.

The next morning O'Reith said to little Clive Colin, "Son, would you like to fly to Maiquetia with me?"

"Sure, when?"

"Day after tomorrow?"

"OK."

O'Reith called Gabrielle in Paris and asked her to book them together on the TWA flight to Idlewild, then down to Miami and on in to Maiquetia. He said to his son, "I'll meet you at Orly."

*   *   *

Father and son were having drinks at 25,000 feet on the TWA Super-Constellation as it cleared the English channel and pointed its nose in the direction of North America. O'Reith was having a dry martini on the rocks and little Clive Colin, scotch and soda. O'Reith asked, "Son, were you surprized when Susie called you about that letter from Ellen Mackensen?"

"Yeah, I was. I couldn't imagine how it involved me. I drove down to the Fullerton Building wondering what the hell it was all about."

"How did it go when she came to pick it up?"

"We just looked at each other for a few minutes. Even after I read the letter, I found it hard to believe that the two were the same person. Anyhow, I passed it to her. She snatched it out of my hand. She stuck her tongue out at me, turned and walked out."

"That should have been the end of things." O'Reith said.

"Well maybe so but it was not exactly that way. She called me that afternoon. Apologized. Wanted to get together so she could explain things."

"What then?"

"We had a few drinks in a club downtown near Global Marine's office. She really didn't want to explain anything. She wanted some personal service."

O'Reith said nothing, sipped his martini.

"Well, Dad, I was hard up," his son said, in an attempt to justify what he had done.

"How's Marilyn? She had an easy time of it, I hear."

"She's fine. Not thrilled about living in Caracas. But of course with Dr. Max close at hand, it is a bit easier. She trusts him. Dad, how did you know that Ellen Mackensen and Eileen McLarssen were one and the same?"

"Just a suspicion. Marlborough confirmed it in a couple of weeks." Did you see her again after the great apology?"

"Couple times. I've been on the road, as you know. We parted friends. She asked me if mother could help her get into movies. I put her off. Imagine me asking mom something like that. Your stare is fierce. Mother's would kill a hippopotamus."

"We haven't seen the last of sweet little Ellen," O'Reith said. "She still has cards to play."

"What makes you think that?"

"Her brother is on the loose somewhere. Donnegan with him. No doubt sore as hell their scheme backfired. I don't know Ellen's involvement in all this but at some point, she'll pop out of the cake."

Chapter XX

Oil in The Tanks

In early April, Lago Poniente was drilled up. The wells were hooked up, ready to produce 175,000 bopd. All connections were tested tight and free of leaks. The separators, heat exchangers, refrigeration equipment, and compressors were all in place and tested to their working pressures and temperatures. Ready to run crude oil. The sixteen inch pipeline to Punto Fijo was laid. Houston Construction Company was pigging the line to push out construction debris. Completion promised for end April. The six inch insulated products line was being laid parallel to the main crude oil line. This line, promised ready by 30 April, would transport the propane, butane and natural gasoline, chilled by refrigeration and pumped at high pressure first to Punto Fijo where it would be metered in the Casinghead Company Terminal and then to Cardon where the stream would be fractionated by Shell de Venezuela. The propane and butane would be bottled for local consumption. The gasoline would become part of the feedstock for the Shell gasoline plant.

At Punto Fijo, the terminal area was cleared, leveled, paved and fenced. Twelve 50,000 barrel steel storage tanks were nearly erected. Shipping pumps were hooked up as well as a booster refrigeration plant for the LNG stream. Dehydration equipment was tied in, meter runs were installed. The camp was complete with hot water and electricity.

Two water wells had been drilled. The light plant was running. They worked around the clock under high overhead electroliers with clusters of 250 watt lamps that illuminated the terminal. Two fifty men crews, fitters, welders, shapers, and roustabouts rotated on twelve hour shifts. Dredging, a slow business, continued at the tanker loading pier.

Down on the south end of Block 9, where it abutted Block 19, pile drivers were securing a second production platform in 110 feet of water. Two derrick barges and a dozen smaller ones ponderously moved back and forth between the shore base and the work sites, bringing material and equipment.

Larry Teague, on bachelor status in a flat in the *Las Mercedes* district of Caracas, commuted by air to Punto Fijo and Maracaibo as required. O'Reith's son was his aide. Dr. Max Parkinson now living in one of the new flats in *Cinco de Julio,* established industrial safety standards for company operations. All workers, gringos as well as locals, had to wear steel-toed shoes and hard hats at hazardous locations. Weekly, Dr. Parkinson conducted a short arm inspection at Punto Fijo, treating venereal disease as it turned up. It turned up with some regularity. Since construction had begun, a string of brothels had sprung up like tropical mushrooms all around the site. The fence could keep the girls out but it couldn't keep the workers in.

In Ventimiglia, Marlborough discovered that a nightwatchman was on duty in the padlocked studio. This complicated the recovery of Helen's film. After studying the layout and the guard's routine, one dark night Marlborough climbed the fence. He torched off a sound stage. While the nightwatchman was calling the fire department, Marlborough twisted the lock off of the cutting room door. With a flashlight he quickly found what he looked for. By the time the firemen arrived, he was back over the fence on the way to Monte Carlo.

Helen quickly reached an agreement with Susie to buy the Long Beach penthouse. The same day Marlborough's cable arrived. She shouted gleefully at his news, awaited his arrival eagerly.

After delivering the goods to Helen, Marlborough took the Pan Am DC-6 milk run to Venezuela. He arrived in Caracas on the first of April. From the office the view of the Hotel Humboldt atop Mount Avila was magnificent. Marlborough was impressed. O'Reith said, "What's the latest on McLarssen and Donnegan?"

"They're in Omaha, Nebraska, banging the Bible, drumming up crowds at night and passing the hat. Business as usual."

"The sister?"

"Hanging around Central Casting. Trying to break into the movies," Marlborough said cynically. He tamped a Lucky Strike down on O'Reith's desk, put it in his mouth and lit it with a Zippo.

O'Reith said, "Duke, after that business in Biarritz, you're in pretty deep. My feeling is that you'll never have to face a grand jury. But you've run long risks in my behalf. I'm not content to let McLarssen get out of this. Not that I'm particularly vindictive. I am pissed off purple at him. I'm going to liquidate him. You don't need to be involved. It could get you into big trouble on down the line."

Marlborough shrugged. He said, "It's up to you general. I need the money. Be glad to help."

Tarbutton said, "What about *Señores* Torres and Cordero?"

"I was going to get into that, Hardy," O'Reith said. "Duke, we probably know as much as we're ever going to know about those two. They are in a different category. To liquidate them, I would clear it first with *El Caudillo*. But faithless as they are, they can be useful to us. So I'm at a loss there."

Marlborough said, "Cordero has the stronger personality of the two. With him on the company payroll, he'll be loyal, or as loyal as those kind of guys ever are. Torres strikes me as a guy without much strength of character. He goes with the wind. He does whatever they tell him to do."

O'Reith said. "Cordero knows Donnegan pretty well. Goes back to when they were plotting against Calitropical Oil Company right after the war. He may know McLarssen too. I'd like to lure both of those guys down here. Put the squeeze on them. Cordero could help us. You recall that McLarssen once did and maybe still does title work for Amerada Petroleum Corporation on their Nesson Anticline leases in North Dakota. Amerada might back him if he were trying to get a clean Block. Like Block 19 to the south. No secret that the Mirador and the Santa Barbara are likely to be productive. I'd like to get that block. Cordero might even do the job for us. I don't know... He often talked of having Torres shot. But he never shot him. He talked about chasing all those colored whores out of Maturin. I understand they are still there. He's their most frequent, if not their best paying customer. McLarssen's religious convictions could keep him out of a whorehouse. Donnegan's seen the inside of plenty of 'em. If we could get them inside one of those places, in a town like Maturin, well those girls are not so squeamish... They all carry knives. I'm just thinking out loud." The three men sat silently, looking at one another. Marlborough finished his cigarette, lit another one from the glowing tip of the stub, dropped the stub in the ashtray, let it burn itself out. O'Reith drummed the top of his desk with his fingers. Tarbutton had a worried look on his face.

Tarbutton said, "We could visit *Capitan* Cordero in Maturin. Spring it on him."

"Hardy, Maturin has its charms, among them, world class mud volcanoes. But one thing that Cordero and I have in common is that we don't like Maturin. I have not the slightest hankering to meet with him in some odious backwater bordello full of black whores. Get a message to him. Ask him to visit us here in Caracas, *ensigida*."

The meeting was arranged for 10 April 1957 at *La Casualidad*. The usual hour. The two oil men and the detective were admitted routinely by the young man in the gray liqui-liqui. They followed the usual path, skirting the dancers in the shadowy cabaret. Cordero awaited them. There were handshakes, *abrazos* and introductions. The waiter brought drinks. Johnny Walker Black and Coca Cola for Cordero. Scotch and water for Marlborough. Mineral water for O'Reith and Tarbutton. O'Reith got down to it at once, said, "Cordero, in France we had a run in with your friend, Beauregard Feathermerchant. Somehow he got information about my private affairs, where I live, things like that. You met with him pretty regularly in Maracaibo at the Bello Monte. What did you talk about? Oil? Girls?"

"Well of course we talk about the girls," Cordero answered. "After all, what kind of a place is the Bello Monte if not for the girls?"

"Oil?"

"Yes. That too. Block 9. Other blocks sometimes."

"Block 19?"

"We did talk about Block 19. Yes sir. We did do that." Cordero sipped his drink.

"When you were talking about oil, did the name of Barney Donnegan come up?"

"Naturally. He is the *jefe*. Feathermerchant reported everything to him."

"The name McLarssen ever come up?" O'Reith probed.

"Yes. He came to Maracaibo. We met with him, *Señor* Feathermerchant and I. Torres was there too. But not in the Bello Monte. We met in the lobby of the Hotel Detroit. He said he represented an American independent oil company with money to invest in Venezuela. When it was clear that he could not get Block 9, we talked about Block 19. He knows that your company, that is, our company was successful in the south of Block 9."

O'Reith's eyes narrowed. Cordero became uncomfortable. He squirmed. O'Reith said, "Cordero, did you tell them anything about me at that meeting?

"I don't know of your affairs, my dear general," Cordero answered. Torres told him. You had offered him a vacation in Paris once, for his health. Feathermerchant asked him where in Paris. Torres gave him an address from his little diary."

The memory of the meeting in Mandy's garden came back to O'Reith. The night Torres said that Cordero was going to shoot him. After a few moments, O'Reith said, "I want those two guys in Caracas, Donnegan and McLarssen, and then... Well... *Matica de Café.*" Cordero jumped, sat straight up. From his shirt pocket he took a *Barinitas* wrapped in tinfoil. Unwrapping it carefully, his eyebrows went up and down nervously. He cut the tip off the cigar, put it in his mouth. Marlborough lit it for him with his Zippo. When it was burning evenly, Cordero inhaled a lungful of smoke, blew it across the table and shrugged. Mesmerized by the intensity of O'Reith's steady stare, he said, "Well. Why not?" Cordero lifted his right hand and snapped thumb and forefinger together. It was quite audible. Not the first time O'Reith had seen him do that. Cordero added, "Like that?"

O'Reith nodded. No one spoke. Cordero smoked as he pondered the proposal. Finally he asked, "How do we manage this?"

O'Reith laughed, said, "I was looking to you for a suggestion."

"Getting them into the country is not difficult," Cordero said. "Torres can send them an official ministerial letter, inviting them to discuss Block 19. Of course the Minister of Hydrocarbons won't know anything about it."

"Then what?" O'Reith asked.

"Give me time dear General O'Reith," Cordero said. "This one is not so easy. We have to be careful. Capital punishment is forbidden in this country. I must consider other options. If they rise to our bait. When we know they are coming, we meet again. Determine the next move."

"Capital punishment was not forbidden when it came to Torres?" O'Reith remarked.

Cordero smiled. He said, "It never happened though."

O'Reith nodded. "Before we adjourn, my friend," O'Reith continued. "What's your view about the sense of the country? I hear there is unrest. Uneasiness. Fear of a *golpe*. What do you think?"

Cordero shrugged, put his hands together, rubbed them. "It is true there have been disturbances. In Maracaibo the women want all the houses moved out of town. They say it is an effrontery to common decency to have the Bello Monte next to a private dwelling. The Club Louisiana is more notorious. It is located next to a girl's school. Yes. We see evidence of ferment. But the colonel is strong. Quite strong. I don't think he will be toppled. The country would be ruined if he were."

The next morning, to his great astonishment, Tarbutton got a registered letter notifying him that his application to join the *Valle Ariba* Golf Club was approved. If he would present the letter, his *cedula*, and pay the required fees, he would receive his membership card. The club facilities would be immediately at his disposal. The waiting period at this exclusive golf club was around three years. His sudden acceptance after a matter of mere months was remarkable. Gleefully he shoved the letter under O'Reith's nose. His eyes lit up. He rubbed his hands together. He said, "Well... This calls for a celebration. What do you say we get up a foursome and let out a little shaft? Try out the course."

Tarbutton said, "Good idea. You and I. Stan. What do we do for a fourth?"

O'Reith arched his eyebrows, grinned, said, "Not to worry." He picked up the telephone and asked the operator to put him through to *Miraflores*. With almost no delay, Colonel Marcos Perez Jimenez came on the line. O'Reith explained that by some miraculous means, General Tarbutton's application to join *Valle Ariba* had been approved. Would the colonel care to join them for an inaugural round? The acceptance was immediate; the date and the time fixed. Laughter from both O'Reith and the telephone were audible.

"Clive, sometimes I think you put too much exuberance into your speech. I give you high marks for your command of the language but you were laying it on thick. One should spread fertilizer economically."

"Tut tut, Hardy. Widewing oratory," O'Reith said, dismissively. "I learned it from you. After all, your new membership removes many,

many obstacles. It becomes immeasurably easy for us to do what we have to do. Now I give *you* some news. Vince joined the company. He's already at work in the Fullerton Building. At your old desk. But he won't be there long. He doesn't know this yet but he's to become our lobbyist in Washington, DC He won't live there. Virginia wants to live in Los Angeles. But he'll commute. Stan will move to Los Angeles to become General Counsel. You can tell him. He may object, say he has no experience in corporate law. But it is already decided. I would like for you to remain here for another year as President and Chief Executive Officer. We'll have a few kinks to iron out once we begin running oil. You're just the man for it, all the more so with that new club membership. While we're playing golf, I'm going to sound the colonel out about Cordero. He can replace Stan. His connections with the Ministry of Mines and Hydrocarbons are invaluable. He knows his way around the police, the army, the Ministry of Labor and Communications, the Ministry of Public Works and Sanitation and The Treasury. He has that touch. He can make things happen. Of course, you know that snake like the back of your hand. He acts up…Well."

"For a minute, Clive, I thought that you'd forgotten what kind of a guy he is," Tarbutton replied, not enthusiastic about having Cordero as an aide.

O'Reith shrugged, said "He's a thug. Maybe one cut above a thug. In Venezuela, in this time, in this situation, in this administration, I don't hold that to be a liability. Besides I need your help in liquidating those two tormentors of mine. You'll have to make sure Cordero does the necessary when it is time to do the necessary."

Tarbutton let out a long sigh. He said, "I don't relish that. Clive, as a favor to you, I'll stay here. Caracas is not a bad place. Marjorie is quite taken with it. The club is the icing on the cake. I'm not enthusiastic about what has to be done with McLarssen and Donnegan. You could change your mind… I was never enthusiastic about heavy strategic bombing either. But there it was. When this is done, at the end of the day, when we find a suitable replacement, I'd like to return to Los Angeles. Resume my previous role of personal adviser and estate counselor."

O'Reith patted him gently on the back, said, "That's a deal, Hardy. Now let's brief Stan on how to play golf with the colonel. He's a quick learner. Played with lots of congressmen around DC"

Tarbutton laughed. "That's right. He beats the colonel and where are we then?"

"Santo Domingo Prison," O'Reith said, laughing. From his briefcase he removed the score card he had marked when playing with the dictator in Maracaibo last November. "Stan can study this. He can come in a couple strokes behind Jimenez. Somehow I don't think you and I have to fudge our scores."

O'Reith always waited until the fourth hole before bringing up a business proposition, no matter with whom he was playing. It took him that long to assess the person's frame of mind. This April morning on the fourth fairway of the delightful *Valle Ariba* Golf Course, with fleecy white clouds softening the sun's rays, Colonel Jimenez was clicking right along with two birdies and a par, fully confident of his ability to compete with these gringos. In an expansive mood and as he sized up his second shot, O'Reith said, "Colonel Jimenez, you remember some time back I asked you if I could speak to *Capitan* Cordero about joining our company?"

"Yes I do," the dictator said. "You could do a lot worse than Cordero. He's a stout fellow. No doubt of it. No doubt at all."

"We're going on the line in just a matter of days," O'Reith continued. "We'll have quite a bit of business with the government. All kinds of permits. Matters of public safety. Transportation. Compliance with edicts from the Minister of Hydrocarbons. That sort of thing. No one could address those matters with greater acumen that *Capitan* Cordero. With your blessing, I propose that he become our Vice President in charge of Government Relations."

"Excellent idea. He's being wasted in Maturin. And that reminds me. I was going to offer you *Señor* Rojo Olimpio Torres but I've changed my mind on that. He fits in well at the Ministry of Mines and Hydrocarbons. I'll leave him in his present position. Make the changes at higher levels of authority."

"Well, then," O'Reith said, "*Capitan* Cordero can resign his police commission and join us in Caracas in time to participate in the inauguration of the Punto Fijo Terminal."

Colonel Jimenez made a brilliant seven iron shot. The ball fell a few meters short of the green but rolled within centimeters of the pin. "Bravo colonel," O'Reith said.

Jimenez smiled his appreciation, thrilled by his great shot. "Excellent plan with regard to Cordero," he said. "There's no requirement that he resign his commission. We just let him 'double the dip'. You know that phrase, General O'Reith. I think it is an Americanism. Something to do with ice cream in a cone. You know I am a graduate of The General Staff College at Fort Leavenworth, Kansas. I picked up quite a bit of army slang there. Like 'short arm inspection' for example. A good one! When *Capitan* Cordero joins you, he will *need* one of those."

The two old soldiers laughed and slapped each other on the back. Tears ran down their cheeks. Jimenez continued, "You know General O'Reith, I may have mentioned to you that we use what we call the 'electric whore'. Not often. Just from time to time. Juan Peron gave me two of them. He said they burn out if they're used frequently. That's Buenos Aires for you. Ours has been running like a top for quite some time. If you'd like to have the other one, you're welcome to it. Quite effective in getting to the truth when you need to have it right away. When you're running a country, everything you need is right away. You can understand that."

After nine holes, the colonel led Ethering by one stroke. Tarbutton and O'Reith were four strokes back, unlikely to catch up. On the 16th, Jimenez hit another one of his electrifying drives that whizzed and whistled down the fairway. The three Americans applauded The colonel was elevated with joy. Smiling and twirling his driver like a drum majorette her baton, he gleefully accepted his accolades, squealing with mirth. Even the caddies cheered. He said, "You know, my dear general, if I should one day give up the practice of statecraft, I would like to be a club pro in America, perhaps in Florida. Teach young people how to hit the ball, young ladies in particular. Help them with their swing."

"You shouldn't rule it out," O'Reith replied without levity.

"I'd have to take English lessons," Jimenez said, as much to himself as to O'Reith. "Of course, I learned a great deal at Fort Leavenworth but not enough. That reminds me that I've had it in my memory to ask you the precise meaning of the phrase, 'to have someone by the balls'. I asked Colonel Arias about that the other day. He was with me in Kansas. He said he thought it meant the same as our expression which translates roughly into 'to press the peter'."

"Colonel Jimenez," O'Reith explained. "When you have someone 'by the balls', it means he is checkmated."

"Aha!" the colonel exclaimed. "You grasp them, then?"

"That's it," O'Reith said.

"That one, I must remember!" the colonel said. He was glowing with his new English phrases.

The game over, Colonel Jimenez had finished two strokes ahead of Ethering, three ahead of Tarbutton and four ahead of a limping O'Reith. In a military limousine, the foursome returned to *Miraflores*. Over drinks in the dictator's private bar, discussing the terminal inauguration, Jimenez asked if Helen O'Reith would be present. He beamed broadly when O'Reith told him that Helen was excited about coming.

Some days after the outing with the dictator, *Capitan* Cordero, summoned by telegram, presented himself. Awaiting him were O'Reith, Tarbutton and Marlborough. O'Reith said, "Cordero, we played golf with the colonel the other day. I proposed to him that you join us here in Caracas in the new post of Vice President of Government Relations.

He thought that was a splendid idea. So the job is yours. You can return to Maturin, pack your bags and come immediately. We expect to inaugurate the oil terminal at Punto Fijo in ten days and, of course, we would like for you to be there. It will be a gala affair with government dignitaries, the directors of our company and their ladies. The colonel has graciously offered an army band."

Cordero smiled, flashed his teeth, including the gold one in front. He bowed slightly and said, "General O'Reith you will find me to be a faithful, devoted servant, around the clock, twenty-four hours per day."

Tarbutton asked the girl to bring drinks. There was a clinking of glasses. Cigars and cigarettes were ignited. Good cheer flowed in the office whose window looked out at Mount Avila and the stately, round Hotel Humboldt. Cordero said, "To tell you the truth, sir, I can hardly wait to leave that stinking place. Those mud volcanoes vent their sulfur gas around the clock. Day and night. And indoors, the cheap perfume and the sweat of the whores. An odor worse than that of the volcanoes. Only when it rains are we free of them. Luckily that happens almost every day. But then, we are then plagued by mosquitoes. Yes sir. I am ready to say, *'Adios Muchachas'* to the girls of Maturin."

"You'll need a new suit of clothes for the office and of course, a new *liqui-liqui* for Punto Fijo." O'Reith advised.

"I will arrange that today sir," Cordero said, blowing smoke across the room. "I am affluent. I know an excellent tailor. I buy the best. I will glisten like the dew-covered orchid in the sun's rays at dawn."

O'Reith rubbed his hands together as if to dismiss all previous business. With his most severe face, he looked into Cordero's eyes and said, "O-o-o-k-a-a-y. Now, in the matter of *Señores* Donnegan and McLarssen, where do we stand?"

Cordero's eyebrows arched. He rolled his cigar to even the glowing coal. His face became long, somber and seriously contemplative to match that of his master. The bags under his eyes diminished, losing their oily luster. Silent for some moments, suddenly he became animated, as if he had just seen the burning bush and knew the revelation was nigh. He began, "There is a town called Ocumare del Tuy, perhaps five thousand souls, just big enough to have its own police Quartel. I know the *jefe de policia*. In fact he is my cousin. More importantly, he owes me money. This town is a scant fifty kilometers south of Caracas. By fast car, one can drive there in less than an hour. The road is good. With myself in the car, sitting beside the driver, we flash right through the *Alcabalas*. They do not stop automobiles with secret policemen in the front seat. From Ocumare del Tuy, a dirt road, passable during the dry months, as we have now, goes to the village of Quiripital, where the vast sugar cane plantations begin. That valley is well watered sir, by the *Rio de Cura* and the *Rio de Taguay*. A fertile valley where the cane thrives. But, as the economists say, those great cane fields are *labor intensive*. They need many *peons* to cut the cane and move it to the presses where the juice runs into vats and is fermented to produce rum. We have some splendid rums in Venezuela, gentlemen. I bring you a case of Ron Pampero next time I go down there to that valley."

"I know Ron Pampero," O'Reith said. "It is a good rum. Nothing better in the market anywhere in the world."

"Well then," Cordero continued. "We solve the problem of those two gringos and contribute to the production of rum. By extension, that helps the economy of the nation as a whole which is a solid solution."

"I don't quite follow you," O'Reith said, lines showing on his fifty-year old face.

"In this country we don't have indentured labor. We have penal labor," Cordero explained. "The government hires out convicts, murderers, rapists, arsonists, extortioners and the odd extremist I must confess. These unfortunate souls work in the cane fields. Regrettably I must advise you that some of these men are not convicts. They are mere 'suspects', charged with a crime and in detention while their case works its way up through our rather antiquated juridical system. It isn't just Venezuela. Colombia. Panama. Peru. They're all the same. Honduras, now there's a place... All the same. Often the wait is a matter of months. Sometimes, years. Some cases never come to trial. Justice can be slow. That is its nature. So... These gringos can arrive at Maiquetia late in the afternoon. By the time they reach their hotel it is dark. Just as they are about to register, they are arrested. The charge is attempted bribery of a government official with regard to fraudulently obtaining an oil concession. We know, the four of us, that they are guilty of this heinous and traitorous act. They are taken to the police car where sits that famous officer of the Maturin Secret Police, *Capitan* Riva Marcelo Cordero, who escorts them apace to the jail in Ocumare del Tuy. Booked immediately, the ink is not dry on their thumbs when they are back in the car racing down that dusty, dirt road in the middle of the night, in chains now, to be delivered to the superintendent of caneries for Valle del Tuy. They can be there for quite some long time. No one will know who they are nor where they came from."

Marlborough's face was beaming, fascinated by Cordero's elegant solution to a vexing problem. Cordero, excited by his presentation, wiped sweat from his brow with his huge handkerchief. Marlborough lighted a cigarette and said, "I like it. It's a marvelous idea. Instead of *Matica de Cafè*, we have *Matica de Caño*."

O'Reith asked, "When are they coming?"

"This week. I must call Torres. He has to confirm the meeting."

O'Reith said, "Cordero, accept no postponements. Before the first of May, I want those guys in knee pants and sandals, sombreros on their heads out in the tropical sun, cutting sugar cane with their machetes."

"It shall be that way, sir," Cordero responded with solemnity.

Marlborough smiled.

*   *   *

So the great occasion was upon them. The leading personalities had arrived. The dedication area, near the master valve on the incoming production manifold was festooned with flowers. Between two of the huge steel storage tanks a banner pronounced: PROGRESS IN VENEZUELA. THE LIFEBLOOD OF THE NATION FLOWS INTO THE TANKS.

One cuts a ribbon to open a road or a bridge or the entrance to a grand edifice, perhaps. To open an oil installation, one turns a valve. On this day however, four hands will rotate the wagon-wheel-like handle of the Incoming Crude Oil Master Valve situate at the intimidatingly massive manifold where the sixteen inch pipeline emerges from the Gulf of Venezuela. From this manifold, lesser valves that control the flow of oil to the several 50,000 barrel tanks are already open, a preliminary requirement for the ceremony. Two of the four gloved hands that will grasp the big wheel belong to Colonel Marcos Perez Jimenez, President of the Republic of Venezuela. The other two are those of Helen Huntington O'Reith, Oscar winner, mother of three, motion picture director and wife of the oil magnate.

The venue for this dedication is the concrete quadrangle, freshly limed, between the pipeline connection and the steel storage tanks, some hundred yards in the distance. The celebrants are assembled in a semicircle beneath a crepe paper awning that keeps the noon day sun at bay. Decorated in red, blue and yellow bunting, with white stars on the blue, the awning oscillates in the gulf breeze. Beneath the bunting are festoons of flowers, with red, blue and yellow blossoms. How could it be otherwise? These are the colors of the Republic. At right angles, a second awning, similarly decorated, shades the army musicians who sit at attention on fold-up chairs. Quietly, or as quietly as possible, they tune their instruments. Everyone waits for the great moment.

The principals of this drama at the manifold, laugh and make small talk. These two have developed a rapport. They like each other. Colonel Jimenez, squatty, dumpy, swarthy, beads of sweat on his forehead, is decked out in the finery of his magnificently tailored uniform with heavy, Sam Browne belt and gleaming brass buckles. His ample chest is overwhelmed by the multiplicity of awards and decorations, gold, bronze and silver medals all adangle from bright rainbow-like ribbands. His brass tunic buttons, half-dollar sized are polished like astronomical mirrors. They flash the rays of the sun to dance on the silvery manifold. The colonel's glittering, tan boots, which reach his knees also reflect the sun. He wears horn-rimmed glasses. An ornate cap with a tall crown and a shiny black bill adorned with gold tracery sits heavily on his head.

Beside the dictator is the famous American movie star, Helen O'Reith. Insouciant, a strikingly slender blonde, hair in a fresh cut page-boy coif, she wears a new outfit from Saks Fifth Avenue, a white pantsuit, trimmed in green piping. On her head sits a matching pill box hat, similarly trimmed, a fluff of green cotton at its center. Her pumps, Nile green, show no toes. As these two talk, each has one gloved hand on the wheel. They stand ready to do their duty.

Some small space, perhaps a dozen strides, separates the principals from the directors of the Casinghead Company, their wives, children, in-laws, girlfriends and invited guests. On the far left stands Sir George Portland McDonough, erect, massive and dignified. He wears white linen, a Panama hat and banker's ventilated shoes. Sir George has had a remarkable career. Failed priest in County Clare, wartime genius of counter-intelligence, once Vicar of the diocese of La Roche-Guyon where in that dark fall and winter of 1943-44, he was confessor to the high command of Field Marshal Rommel's Seventh Army. His dangerous work greatly improved the odds of survival of the oil magnate. He is a Knight of the Order of St. John's, Lecturer in Oriental History at King's College, Oxford, recent Minister and Plenipotentiary to the Throne of the Golden Peacock in Tehran and raconteur of note. Next to Sir George stands Mother Amanda Macabra Schaeffer, simpering in a maroon shift that falls well below her knees and exquisitely sets off her svelte figure. Her reputation as a dangerous witch extends from the muddy marshes of the Orinoco Delta to the towering, snow-covered peaks of the high Perijas. Some years ago, she minimized a blackmailer's threat against the oil magnate. As a *religiosa*, and *Madre Superior* of an orphanage in Maracaibo, she is less renowned, but gaining recognition. Her husband, the diminutive *Padre Teodoro*, is at her side, his wispy white hair curling out from under his black biretta. Once a member of the powerful Crude Oil Committee of the Calitroleum Oil Corporation, now he is a self-ordained man of the cloth and perhaps of God as well. When Alan Prescott returned from Hammelburg Prison in 1945 in deep depression, Schaeffer, demoted down to obscurity on the tenth floor of the tower, helped Sally bring him around. Now they are good friends. Today dressed in pastoral black, with a white cotton shirt , a Roman collar and tiny black shoes, he is something of an ecclesiastical curiosity. Still, as shepherd of the orphanage, he does good work. In the heat of a tropical springtime, he is happy not to be wearing a hair shirt, which at some point in the future, he may have to do. Next to him, Maxine deMoustier, often known by other names, wears a simple rose-colored dress with a cloth belt and low cut canvas slippers, good for walking in the city. Once she was the elegant 'Miss Maxine' of the exotic *El Techo Rojo.* Today she lives quietly with her daughter in Paris. She is gentle, caring, attentive to the needs of her daughter as well as her lover, the oil magnate. Escorting Maxine, is Monkton Albert Parkhurst, KCB, MC DSM, DSO, VC, tall, arrow-straight and distinguished in tropical white, he is a banker and a banker's son. Once a brigadier of Marines, he is no stranger to wind-swept sandy lands. He was with Montgomery in the rearguard at Dunkirk. With him again on bullet-swept Gold Beach, directing Tommy Atkins, water dripping from his pants, into his proper lane, for the advance up the cliffs, across France over the Rhine River and points east. Somewhere in those shifting Normandy dunes are the long-ago fragmented bones of Parkhurst's left leg, shot off below the knee. Beside him, stands Colonel Maurice André LeBel. Graduate of the *Ecole Militar*, a *genie civil,* officer of the Armee of Marechal LeClerc, confidante of *Le Grand Charles,* wounded at Bir Hakeim, he has only one good eye. LeBel helped the oil magnate change his name to

Capitaine Gerard Chameleon de Troisetoiles so that he could marry Georgina Marie de Cahors d'Ampere, (nee deMoustier) at a side altar in the Madeleine. In tropical white, and a pith helmet of the sort favored in black Africa, he holds hand with his wife Gabrielle, a *Pied Noir* and a linguist. She wears an open-necked yellow blouse and pale blue slacks with cork-soled sandals. Beside her is Colonel Hunter Hawke Holland. On 18 March 1945, when he was Fighter Command Executive Officer for the day, he threw a cordon of P-47s around the oil magnate's battle-damaged B-17 coming back from Berlin on two engines. He holds hands with Ines, his wife of a dozen years, mother of his three children and protectress of his manliness. Even today, after all these years of marriage, she still thinks the hole in the head of his penis is a birth defect. She wears a white silk blouse, a magenta skirt and low heels. Hidden in the folds of her skirt is a stiletto. Except for the guards at the gate, she may be the only armed person at this ceremony. In her hair is a red carnation. She has seed pearls in her ear lobes. She stands close to her husband, often squeezes his hand and from time to time, flashes him a wanton smile. Next to Ines stands Carolyn Ann Cook, Chief Exploration Geologist of the company, a graduate of UCLA. Without her, the company wouldn't amount to much. She wears a no-nonsense manila pantsuit and penny loafers with her head wrapped in a large flowery silk scarf. Her friend, Magaly, is at her side in a yellow blouse, red toreador pants and a black sombrero with dangling tassels. Black Justin cowboy boots with Cuban heels cover her feet.

In the second rank of luminaries, stands General Hardy Harold Tarbutton. When the oil magnate was a field grade officer in those bitter days a decade ago, Tarbutton coped with his moodiness; cajoled him out his depressions; sent him down into *The Smoke* to relieve excessive pressure on his optic membrane; kept him from ditching in Lake Constance; gave him a seat at his bridge table; taught him the fundamentals of combat command; promoted him; and set him up to return home as a decorated hero of high rank. In tropical white he stands beside Marjorie, his wife. She has on a long-sleeved pink dress of light material and wears a golf cap with *Valle Ariba* embroidered in red letters on its crown patch. Next stands Susan Briscoe Halliday in a white business suit from I.Magnin in San Francisco, with a matching tam o'shanter and low cut white leather shoes. A platinum blonde with an hourglass figure, she is not unnoticed. Once a lowly stenographer on the tenth floor of the Calitroleum Tower, she is now an heiress and officer of the company. In her ears are silver squares. She has a diaphanous scarf around her neck. Days ago, she sold her Long Beach penthouse to Helen O'Reith. Sharon Mills and Alice Ridley are next in the line followed by little Clive Colin and Marilyn, and the Thorneberrys. At the end, Alan and Sally Prescott hold hands. Madly in love since they discovered what each other had, in the dark, school auditorium in the winter of 1931, they look in each other's eyes. He may have a kraut doctor's platinum disc in his skull, but he has nothing but love in his heart for Sally. He often thinks of this when Ted Schaeffer talks about becoming a saint. Sally is the one person at this gathering who knows the truth about the hole in Holland's penis. Squeezed between the Prescotts, the diminutive Erma Morrow, glows in the presence of these extraordinary people who have allowed her humble person to attend this momentous event. Also present are Stanley and Merle Ethering. Both wear white. He smiles, listens carefully to the conversation around him, unobtrusively makes shorthand notes in a tiny black notebook. He has briefed the oil magnate on the personalities of the Venezuelan ministers, given him some carefully constructed jests for use at the cocktail party to follow the inauguration. Ethering of course, fully understands the danger of springing an indelicate or poorly conceived bit of humor on a scheming politician. It would be like walking in a mine field. In this man's hands, whiskey, hired women and jokes are diplomatic tools with which he extracts the malignancy from threatening legislation. He would prepare the oil magnate for whatever bad political patches that loomed ahead.

On the Venezuelan side, to the right of the company luminaries, stand the important government personalities, the Minister of Mines and Hydrocarbons; of Public Works and Sanitation; of Justice, what little there is of it; of Agriculture; of Labor and Communication; of Development. Manuel Egaña, Raul Leoni, Juan Perez, Faustus Urribi, Sixto Sulbaran, Pedro Tagliafero. Among these eminent functionaries, in his magnificent new liqui-liqui stands Riva Marcelo Cordero, technically a member of the company. Today he stands with his compatriots. Everyone agrees that it is completely proper. Only a few Venezuelan ladies appear at this affair. Oil installations are old hat to ministerial wives. Latin women tend to avoid commercial functions. But three mature *señoras* stand patiently with their husbands, shifting their weight from one foot to another, unobtrusively, studying what the American women are wearing. Garbed in the latest Miami summer fashions, elegant gold coin bracelets glittering, these ladies all wear wide-brimmed hats with feathers.

Two steps behind Madame O'Reith, at parade rest in a sparkling white liqui liqui, the oil magnate's shoes are freshly polished and free of oil stains. On his head is his fine-fibered Panama hat. His monocle in place, he is beside Vincent Barkett Blake, Vice Chairman of the company. This rough, tough footballer of days long past has been the force behind the oil magnate. He has nurtured him, protected him from the wrath of the founder of the Calitroleum Corporation, sheltered him when cruel corporate winds blew in the Great Depression. Vincent Blake converted a bronc driller into an oil field executive. He wonders how they managed to remain friends. He wears a tropical white business suit expertly fitted to him by Sharon Mills. With her discriminating eyes, she has made his face up too as she has also made up Helen, Alice Ridley, Sally and Susan, and of course, the oil magnate. Virginia Blake, who attended her own make-up, stands beside her husband. She is a Daughter of the Golden West, a pianist of some skill, an excellent cook, and a Methodist Church matron. She wears a simple print dress, of soft pastel colors, elegantly and properly fitted. Lawrence Teague is not in this august gathering. He is minding the store, nervously making the rounds of the tanks, the vents, the flare lines, the transfer pumps and all of the other equipment that is part of a modern oil terminal. He wears a white coverall with the letters SOCAL in red on the back. An aluminum hard hat covers his head. Steel-toed shoes protect his feet. His superintendents stand ready to cope with trouble wherever it may occur. Something will go wrong. Something always goes wrong. But they don't know what it is. A valve will stick. A tank will leak. A key instrument will fail.

Unknown to nearly all of the big shots waiting for the dramatic moment, the company is already running a hydrocarbon stream to market. It is the LNG stream. For now, we leave this refining executive and his lieutenants to their chores.

We note that the attorney, Beauregard Feathermerchant, his two assistants, Donny Bob Evans and Country Boy Swetnam will not attend this function. They are buried in paupers graves in Ventimiglia, Italy, nor are they lamented as far as we can tell. Of course, neither Barney Q. Donnegan nor Donald McLarssen can attend. Both of them, in brown knee-length peasants trousers, leather-thonged, cork-soled sandals on their feet and broad straw hats on their heads, cut the sweet sugar cane in the sweltering *Valle del Tuy*.

Crude oil locked up in the rock pores far beneath the surface of the earth, or in our instance, far below the bed of Lake Maracaibo, is an entirely different substance from the crude oil, designated 31° *Tia Juana Light*, that has been flowing since eight o'clock yesterday morning into the sixteen inch pipeline. The oil in the earth contains dissolved dry gases, methane and ethane. It also contains butane, propane and pentane, heavy gases which liquefy readily if compressed and refrigerated. When passed through the several stages of separation, the ethane and methane will be burned off at the tip of the flare line. There is no use for it. At night these flares illuminate the waters of Lake Maracaibo for mile after mile after mile. The propane, butane and pentane flashes out of the boiling hot crude oil in the first stage of separation and is immediately refrigerated, compressed and pumped into the six inch NGL pipeline, destined for Punto Fijo, thence to the Shell de Venezuela refinery at Cardon. So the volume of liquid processed at Production Platform No.1 is the sum of the Tia Juana Light and the NGL. In this case, 210,000 bopd of which 35,000 bopd of NGL flows in the six inch pipeline and will race ahead in the much smaller line and beat the *Tia Juana Light* to the terminal by a long margin. Like the tortoise and the hare except this time the hare wins.

Thus the notables at the pipeline manifold will presently inaugurate an operation that began some days ago in Lake Maracaibo. Those oil wells, some completed months ago, were left full of brine. In these last few days, *El Mocho* Morrow and his gangs of roustabouts, have swabbed in the tubing sides with rubber cups on wire lines and aerated the casing sides with acetylene. Since eight o'clock yesterday, the wells have been on production, flowing unseparated rock oil to Production Platform No.1. If drilling the wells, fabricating the production platform and laying the pipeline is a complicated, time-consuming operation, putting the oil on production is no simple matter either.

The pipeline from Production Platform No.1 runs almost due north up the narrows of the lake for a distance of 110 kilometers. Just north of the town of El Tablazo, in the Gulf of Venezuela it turns to the northeast. Then it runs along the bottom of the gulf for another 150 kilometers until it emerges into the manifold where the crowd is now gathered. A barrel of oil travels 260 kilometers before it enjoys the luxury of sloshing around in a 50,000 barrel tank.

Alan Prescott is the Production Superintendent for the Lago Poniente Field. Why is he not on the job? Yesterday, when the wells went on production, he was. He and Morrow stood together watching as, one by one, the needles of forty-four gauges flicked up from zero to well head pressure. For the Mirador, 3,900 psi. For the Santa Barbara, 2,150.

At that point, the master valve was opened and the flow of crude oil began. Similarly, the master valve on NGL line was opened.

     *   *   *

Today Morrow is in charge. At the instrument panel on the production platform he reads the pressure and temperature gauges. All of the wells are flowing properly. Both crude oil and NGL go into the pipelines. Originally, the two pipelines were filled with water to prevent their collapse from hydrostatic pressure. Today the smaller line is full of NGL. Indeed some of it has already arrived in Cardon. Into the main pipeline, because of the festivities planned at the other end, a red dye has been injected. Some few minutes before the oil arrives, white water will turn red, a signal for the band to get ready. The celebrants are curious about this stream of white water gushing from an open manifold valve. It cascades into the shallow waters of the gulf. Has something gone terribly wrong? Instead of an oil field is it a water field? Not to worry. What they see is completely normal. A roustabout attends this flow. He knows what to do when the red water appears. He sees it! He signals his foreman who signals the leader of the band, a bemedaled *Capitan* of music. Drops of oil appear in the red water. The roustabout closes the dump valve. Simultaneously, the band strikes up the Venezuelan National Anthem. The clang of cymbals fills the air, then the blare of trumpets and the oom-pah-pah of the tubas. Next the rasp of the trombones and the drone of the saxophones. Helen O'Reith and Colonel Marcos Perez Jimenez, both smiling, both attentive to the cheers from behind them, vigorously open the master valve. Crude oil flows noisily into steel storage!

 Corks pop from champagne bottles. Servants in white mess uniforms bring trays. Flutes of mellow liquid are poured. The dictator proposes a toast. The air fills with '*oles*'. The celebration begins. The band plays *The Winchester Cathedral March*. Crude oil swooshes into the tanks behind them, splashing against the baffles. It gurgles, rumbles and resounds as it waits for the tanker which will come on the morrow to take it to SOCAL's refinery in El Segundo, California.

In the noise and confusion of the celebration, Helen pulls her husband aside and whispers in his ear, "Ace you better be careful, the colonel is definitely my kind of guy."

After lunch, the assembled dignitaries climb aboard aircraft for the flight to the military *Aeropuerto la Carlota* in downtown Caracas. The Casinghead Company has provided two B-17s, *La Cañada Cruz* and *L'Ame de Paris*. The government has provided two C-47s, more than enough room for these important personalities. In Caracas they motor to *Miraflores*, for a special preview of the movie, *Los Ladrones de Piedras Negras* in the grand ballroom.

In the dark dress circle with Helen, the dictator and his wife, as the film credits go by on the enormous silver screen, it is not lost on the oil magnate that the first showing of *Los Ladrones de Piedras Negras* occurs on the same day that first oil flows into the terminal at Punto Fijo. Nor is it lost on him that the dictator seems far more interested in the movie than he is in the oil. He is even more taken with the beautiful blonde heroine, this Nordic Sif of the Golden Hair, who sits beside him stroking his ego shamelessly and with effortless skill.

The oil magnate is also aware that another genie has been let out of the bottle on this beautiful tropical day. This morning, Helen's eyes examined the luminaries with the relentless acuity that was her hallmark. More than once, her eyes lingered on Maxine. For over a decade, except for these last few months, the oil magnate has kept these two a continent apart, the one working diligently in the Western Hemisphere, the other living tranquilly in Paris. Now within five short months, the two of them have twice been in the same place at the same time. That first time, each with a small daughter, they sat poised and proper across the lobby from one another in the Hotel Miramar in Biarritz. Then their hearts hammered. Both fearful for the lives of their lovely children. Terrorized by cruel men with sharp knives who had threatened to cut their throats if they raised a cry. Both waited apprehensively for an uncertain deliverance.

Back there in the dark beside Monk Parkhurst, Maxine would for the first time, see Helen on the screen. Of course she knew her to be a famous actress. Indeed, until Biarritz, she had never seen her in the flesh. Tonight, she was a projection on the screen. Looking below the screen now, she sees the oil magnate's silhouette beside Helen in the gloom. What could she be thinking? For O'Reith, life would never be exactly the same again.

As western movies went, this one was not too bad. The oil magnate has seen them by the dozens. When he was a little boy and again when his son was a little boy, the famous cowboy stars were omnipresent. On the screen and many of them in the flesh. Johnny Mack Brown astride 'Reno'. Tom Mix riding 'Tony'. Roy Rogers on 'Trigger'. Bill 'Hopalong Cassidy' Boyd doing his best to stay atop 'Topper'. He recalls 'ole' Gene Autry riding 'Champion' down Main Street in Houston, Texas to kick off a rodeo, and that, not too long ago. Charles Starret. Bob Steele of 'Three Mesquiteer' fame. Hoot McCoy. He'd seen them all. Their sidekicks too, Smiley Burnett, Gabby Hayes and Andy Clyde.

Western heroines were mares of a different stripe. Few women specialized in this genre. If there was a stereotype it was Helen. Close to her would be Dale Evans who in fact, was more of a canary than an actress. Jean Arthur was stellar in *Shane*. Marlene Dietrich had performed famously in *Destry Rides Again*. Vera Hruba Ralston was notable as was Clare Trevor and Jennifer Holt. But for sheer variety of looks and personality, it was a cowpokes world.

The oil magnate fully comprehends the theory of the oater. The good guys, usually, but not always, wearing white hats, rally to reduce the oppressive, villainous bad guys in dusty black hats, come to terrorize the frontier. The hero's hat is blindingly, brilliantly white without a speck of dust from brim to crown. Pretty consistently, the bad guys wear black dark clothing and pretty consistently, they are dirty low down dogs. Their leader needs a shave in the worst way. He could use some drops for his evil red eyes. They are 'Mesicans' or white renegades or sometimes, treacherous red Indians.

The movie begins with the discovery of malfeasance; a robbed bank, the safe often flashily blown open; a rustled herd of cattle mooing in the moonlight; an embezzled mining syndicate where the villains took not only the gold but also the dynamite. Then comes the bar room brawl with total destruction, the mirror behind the bar, spectacularly so. It is here that the hero first confronts the villain and brings him low, but not for long. Later there is the shoot-out at the corral. Hundreds of rounds of ammunition are fired from six-shooters only rarely seen to be reloaded. And, it seems, scores of cowpokes shot to the ground, often dying in melodramatic ballet-like contortions only to rise again miraculously from the straw-strewn dirt. Magically, they leap upon their horses. Gallop out across the prairie; the bad guys fleeing, the good in hot pursuit. The chase begins. Steeds of incalculable stamina race at high speed along the canyon rim for an eternity. Until the hero catches up with the villain. Somehow, he tackles him from the back of his horse. Still wearing their hats, the two antagonists wrestle on the hot caliche scrabble of the burning desert. Clouds of dust rise from the scuffle in the moonlight. A monumental fisticuffs engagement ensues. As the sun rises, the villain is subdued. In the fadeout, the hero and heroine hold hands, as they ride off into the sunset. Fiddle music and the clop of the hooves of contented horses fill the cinema. All this in say, fifty-five minutes.

Helen has done better. Or Helen and Bolletti have done better. The costumes of extraordinary design and quality, fit perfectly. The volume of burnt gunpowder has been reduced to a believable level. Of course, an expert like the oil magnate, can detect a few oddities. The bar room brawl, the chase, the shoot-out are scenes he has seen before down to the tiniest detail. The bell tower scene he remembers so well he can name the picture in which it first appeared. But these are small potatoes. This audience gives it a splendid review. Clapping, shouting and hissing at the robbers as only South Americans can do with authenticity. The minister's wives, who callously eschewed the inauguration at Punto Fijo were among the first to fill the seats for this premiere of *Los Ladrones de Piedras Negras*. That this edition of the film has dubbed in Spanish with Italian subtitles adds to its appeal.

A reception follows the movie. Drinks, more drinks and finally the ball. Around three o'clock in the morning the revelers are off to bed. Helen and Clive O'Reith to the Tamanaco. Maxine, Mandy and Ted to the Hotel Avila. During the course of the evening, with Maxine (among many others) in his arms on the dance floor, he contemplated the idea of a 'double header' but it was a fleeting thought. He no longer had the seminal stamina for such high jinx. In this particular situation the logistics were prohibitive. Anyhow, tomorrow is already here. A few winks and they have to be up. Helen is booked on the LAV Super-Constellation to Idlewild. She has an appointment with her agent in Manhattan to begin negotiation for the distribution of *Los Ladrones de Piedras Negras*. Nothing will keep her from that. Her husband will escort her to Maiquetia, see her off and wait there for passengers bound for Maracaibo in the *La Cañada Cruz*. But at this moment they have heroically completed the act of love and, still together, the oil magnate is falling asleep. She stirs and asks, "Ace, that woman with Monk. She looked so familiar. But I can't place her. Who is she?"

The oil magnate has gone to sleep.

* * *

Helen and her entourage are in the air on the way to Idlewild. It is the afternoon of 2 May 1957. O'Reith, is also in the air, on the B-17, destined for *Grano de Oro*. The pilot, General Hardy H. Tarbutton will fly them over the Punto Fijo terminal. The oil magnate wants to see the Standard Oil Tanker, MV 'D.G. Schofield' which tied up at the pier last night. She is loading a cargo of *Tia Juana Light*. Ted Schaeffer, in black pastoral garb, sits beside him, silently, patiently, not wishing to disturb this absorbed man who, with a No.2, yellow Mirado pencil, calculates on the back of an envelope. O'Reith estimates that at $3.00/bbl, the company will today earn about a half million dollars after allowances for royalty, operating expenses and taxes. Soon that figure will rise to $700,000 per day as more wells are brought on stream. So earning say, $2 million every three days, the entire investment, which is not yet precisely known, but believed to be $150 million, will be recovered in the weeks just before the Christmas holidays. What better time to recover it? The directors will applaud. Tell him he did a good job just as they sent laudatory notes to him in Punto Fijo yesterday. All that to be expected. He returns the envelope to an inside pocket of his white coat, closes his eyes. To Schaeffer's chagrin, naps. A half hour later the voice of the co-pilot, Colonel Hunter H. Holland, announces from the loudspeaker that they are over Punto Fijo. The tanker can be seen on the right hand side of the aircraft. O'Reith stirs, looks out. Schaeffer unbuckles his seat belt and leans over O'Reith. He wants to see it too. So do all the other passengers; Mandy; Maxine; the Prescotts; Erma Morrow and Ines. While looking down, the oil magnate reflects that if he were a Standard Oil hired executive, during these last seventeen months, since the project began, he would have earned about $150,000. Maybe a bonus. Some small stock participation. Say $200,000 all told. Perhaps a pat on the back. Perhaps not. His accomplishment was par for the course. Nothing extra. As it is, until today, he earned nothing and will continue to earn nothing for the next 200 or so days. Only when the certified public accountants, Price Waterhouse for the company, a Venezuelan, a British, or maybe even another American firm for the government, agree and attest that on or about 10 December 1957, the Lago Poniente oil project is paid out. An important date for both sides, overnight, the government revenue jumps from 16%, the royalty, to 50%, the so-called '50/50 split'. Beyond that date, of course, the oil magnate has an income, a good one. A stream of regular dividends will cheer the others too, warm their hearts and line their pockets.

Now, as Pinto Fijo, the tanker and the terminal recede from view, Schaeffer becomes bold enough to break the oil magnate's train of thought. He says, "Clive, I'm ready to see the Pope."

O'Reith smiles, nods, says, "I'll advise the nuncio to put you on the calendar."

"If only I could take Mandy along," Schaeffer adds wistfully. "But she'll have to stay and look after the kids."

"How many have you got now, Ted?" the oil magnate asks.

"Twenty-four boys and a dozen girls. Trying to even that out but there are more boys than girls on the street. The building is already crowded. We must build a second one. Girls in one, boys in the other. When are you coming for a look-see?"

"Could be tomorrow, Ted. I was going to ask you about it. Maxine would like to see it too."

"Well, sure thing, Clive," Schaeffer answers. O'Reith can tell by the tone of his voice that there is something else on his mind. After a minute, Schaeffer goes on, "Clive, I know this isn't any of my business, but what is Maxine to you?" He reddens, as if he has violated another taboo, like looking behind the Japanese screen in the garden.

"Ted, she's my girl friend," The oil magnate answers.

"I kind of figured that. And you such a straight guy. I asked Mandy about her, two, three times. She won't tell me anything. Just looks at me that way. Looks to me like you should be wearing a hair shirt too."

O'Reith had that speculative look in his eyes. He said, "Don't have time, Ted. You put a big offshore oil field on the line, it takes from you. Drains you."

"Clive, you're pushing me toward sainthood. Why not go that route yourself? For a guy like you, it ought to be a snap."

"Ted. You want to be a saint. I have another agenda. Now, back to your trip to Rome. I understand that Mandy can't go with you. My son could accompany you. I'm going to suggest to him that he and Marilyn take their lovely daughter to be blessed by the Pope. What do you think of that?"

Schaeffer's voice dropped an octave, as if he were trying to make it more mellifluous. He said, "I think that's marvelous. Lots of kids born with a silver spoon in their mouths but how many get sprinkled by the Big Gazuka Himself?"

"Exactly."

"Clive, it's a comfort that they will be with me. My only foreign travel is Venezuela. I'd be lost in Rome without somebody to show me the ropes."

"It's settled then," O'Reith said. "When I hear from the nuncio, I'll cable you the details."

Their visit to Maracaibo was a moving experience. Maxine saw the offshore oil installation. Then the orphanage. She and O'Reith were impressed by the scrubbed, nicely dressed children residing there. One evening they dined at their old hangout, the Hong Kong restaurant, famous for Cantonese cuisine. They drove by the corner of Calle 70 and Avenida 11 where El Techo Rojo was being redecorated. Workers in brown jumpers cleaned, scraped and painted, bringing it back to its once glossy appearance.

Then they flew to Maiquetia on the Avensa Convair 440. To Idlewild on the LAV Super-Constellation. Then another one just like it painted with the TWA colors to Orly.

Monique was beside herself as the limousine stopped at her school. Her father and her mother came to the classroom. She hopped from her seat, ran to her father and jumped into his arms, squealing, giggling and babbling in her tiny French voice. After a week of strict governess under heavy guard, she was elated to be with loving parents again. At their place in rue de Surene they alit. O'Reith turned her up over his shoulder. Playfully patting her tiny bottom, he rode her up to the fourth floor. Monique giggling, Maxine smiling and O'Reith laughing.

Chapter XXI

▼

The Casinghead Tower

It is summer in Los Angeles, late August in fact. The oil magnate is fifty and a half years old. His metabolism has slowed. A drink of gin takes more time to burn up. Sexual arousal takes longer. Less longer to discharge. He still has a healthy appetite. He indulges himself if it does not affect his waist line. Even with half a century of years behind him, he is vain, vain, vain.

Back in his old office on the 39th floor of the penthouse, he sits at his coffee table, awaiting the imminent arrival of his ebony-topped desk from the Fullerton Building. Before the day is over he will sit behind it. All of his cherished pictures hang where they hung before the merger, with some new additions. A wedding photograph of his son and Marilyn. A portrait of a placid Maxine with Monique sitting blissfully in her lap, crafted in oil by the celebrated Breton portraitist, Claud de Quattrebarbes. Unlike all the other pictures on the walls, this one is fitted with a drape that can cover it in an instant should circumstance dictate. On the far wall hangs a photograph of the Punto Fijo ceremony. A joyful Helen and a smiling Colonel Perez Jimenez open the master valve. Behind him, on the 'wailing' wall, is a photograph made by Colonel Holland from the deck of *La Flecha*. It shows, hanging in wire rope slings, from the crane of a *Terminales Maracaibo* derrick barge, the dynamited-off platform from which they drilled the fated Lago Poniente No.9-1X. Next to it, a photograph of the Hotel Miramar with all the glass shot out of the revolving door. Dense black smoke billows out therefrom.

O'Reith is back where he is, because a week ago Vincent Blake reached agreement with Standard Oil to buy the Calitroleum Tower, saving it from the auction block. Now, unchanged in any way, still with its old furniture and fixings, it has become *The Casinghead Tower* as proclaimed by the art nouveau sign above the great tower clock. Anyone driving along Sepulveda Boulevard can verify this. Even in the great, modern California metropolis, a thirty-nine story building catches the eye.

So the two old friends are back where they have wanted to be. His morning has been filled with appointments. Sharon Mills nipped in at eight-fifty for a quick dust-off, to brush his tuxedo, to check the angle of his monocle, to see that his face was right for the summer morning's light, to file a hangnail. Carolyn Cook in at nine to discuss a wildcat in Sumatra, running low and looking bad. Tarbutton at ten to nominate Monk Parkhurst to replace him in Caracas. Parkhurst retiring from Linen Bank, wants to run out his days in the tropics. At ten-thirty Max Parkinson looked at his leg. At eleven, Holland presented a repressurizing plan for the Mirador zone in Lago Poniente field. Ines came along. She had on a stiff, maroon sheathe of taffeta that rustled when she walked. At twenty-eight, still a stunner with flashing black eyes, pouting lips and inviting smile. She had a red carnation in her jet black hair.

O'Reith asked, "Ines, when you were a child up there in the Colombian Perijas selling those philters, were they, well, popular?"

"Yes, I sold a dozen or so every day. Good money it was." Holland, sitting beside her, seemed a bit at sea.

"Could I ask you, what was the principal ingredient?" O'Reith continued.

"Caño."

"Caño?" He repeated. "Just that?"

Ines smiled wickedly at him, said "*Mas nada Señor.* That's all that was required. It was cheap. Delivered a powerful jolt. One thought one was getting something."

"Just caño. No eye of newt? No wart of frog? No snake semen?"

"Caño."

"And it worked?" O'Reith probed. He could be relentless when he sought the truth.

"If one followed the instructions, it worked fine," Ines said.

"Which were?"

"Find a pretty young girl. Give her a piece of candy. Drink the philter and proceed," Ines said, bubbling now, finding it difficult to keep a straight face. The three of them laughed. He watched them off affectionately.

So what to do? Get a pretty young girl? Or build a huge international petroleum empire? O'Reith knew men who were trying to do both. But he didn't think that would work for him. He missed a lot during those long months when he was propelling Lago Poniente Field into production. Hundreds of pieces. Well, maybe not hundreds, scores.

In between his meetings he has spoken by telephone with Helen, about a script called *The Golden Lane,* to be the '*Last Remake of Boom Town*'. She seeks his professional advice. He promises to give it tonight over cocktails.

He speaks to his son about the forthcoming trip to Rome where 'Father Ted' will kiss the Pope's ring and baby Virginia-Helen will receive his blessing. Whichever one of the children who thought of Virginia and Helen linked with a hyphen should consider a political career. Then he remembers a girl of decades past who dropped her last name on her way to dancing fame. Helen, no doubt would quickly recall *her.* He tells little Clive Colin that the business in Rome has been thoroughly arranged by George P. McDonough, a personal friend of Pope Pius XII. Those two shared many a dangerous wartime secret; saved many a doomed refugee. For the eminent Pius XII to let a small oddity of a Ted Schaeffer kiss his ring was nothing. Nor did it matter that tiny Virginia-Helen was Episcopalian-Methodist without a drop of Roman Catholic blood in her veins. It would be all the same to Pius XII. He would sprinkle little Virginia-Helen and send her on her way, a special child of the Church.

Now, after an executive pee, a pre-luncheon facial from Sharon Mills and a quick look at this afternoon's schedule, it was down the hall to meet Blake at the elevator landing. Soon seated in the executive dining room, they order tuna salad and a bottle of mineral water. As they wait, O'Reith says, "Vince, some unexpected good news from Maracaibo this morning. *El Mocho* cabled Holland that they found another pay zone down south on Block 16. Carolyn is trying to figure out what formation it is. Icotea, maybe. It's high gravity crude, 45º API. Gasoline grade."

"That's a coincidence, Clive," Blake rejoined. "You remember Bill Palmerston? Stanford man. Worked for Standard Oil. Then went into the refining business for himself. He calls his company 'San Diego Oil & Refining'. He owns a little tea kettle refinery on the outskirts of town. He bought some pretty good Oceanic production in the lower San Joaquin from an independent a few years back. High gravity oil too. Palmerston ran a little pipeline from Wheeler's Ridge all the way down to San Diego. His wells are beginning to decline. A couple of 'em on the edge of the field went to water. He's scratching his head, trying to figure out where he's going to get feed stock. You suppose we could run *Tia Juana Light* through his refinery? Maybe add a couple of second-hand fractionation towers. Standard Oil has some they want to get rid of. We'd have to rebuild 'em. Make sure they pass inspection... Maybe put in extra storage tanks. His little refinery is close to the water. Maybe build a short pier..."

"It's a thought," O'Reith said.

"Palmerston's got a couple of gas stations too. One in San Diego and one in Oxnard. We could have a drink with Bill. Kick some ideas around," Blake continued. "If we were to come up with anything, I could catch a plane to Caracas. Go over with Larry. Maybe go on down to Maracaibo for a few days. Visit Morrow. Tour the lake."

"What's her name?"

"Pilar."

"Venezuelan?"

"Yeah, but her parents are Italian. From Genoa. Her daddy was a fighter pilot in the Italian Air Force during the war. Captured in Libya. Got a job flying for Shell after the war. Retired now."

"Lots of Italians in Maracaibo, Vince. They hang around the *Plaza de la Republica.* Many of the waiters in the top restaurants are Italian. Take her to the *La Bologna.* Pasta place right off the plaza. First class. If you tire of spaghetti and meat sauce, just around the block is a steak house called *Mi Vaquita.* Santa Barbara beef. Flavorful and tender. Spell Santa Barbara: R-O-C-K-E-F-E-L-L-E-R. One of John D.'s boys set up a model ranch around Maracay some years back. Gave it the same tedious attention that he gave Creole Petroleum Corporation. Vince, have a good time down there. When you're feeling pensive, think about how we need to set up in Washington, DC. If we go into refining and marketing, we require a lobbying organization. You wouldn't have to move to Washington. Hire a couple of men who know their way around. Maybe go there once a week. Something like that."

"Clive!"

"Think about it, Vince. You were the leading critic of Halliday's system. It's a chance for you to lobby the way you have always wanted to. Get acquainted with the lovable Congress of the United States?"

"You have me there all right. Clive it was disgraceful the way Johnny Knobles would interrupt a Crude Oil Committee meeting to get a briefcase full of $50 bills out of the safe. He'd toss them in his little black bag, wave at us and off he went to Washington. He thought nothing of walking up beside a congressman right there under the dome of the capitol, shaking his hand, patting him on the back and dropping $250 into his coat pocket. He'd tell the poor guy to go buy himself a piece of tail and a couple of bottles of beer. How crass! How crude! How would you like to be treated like that?"

"I'd get used to it," O'Reith answered. "Vince, whatever you think about Knobles, and I detested him, he learned on the job. Do you remember the *Spruce Goose*?"

"The Howard Hughes folly," Blake responded, smiling. "It's still with us. Hangared up over in Long Beach."

The *Spruce Goose* was the name given derisively to an experimental amphibious aircraft built for the U.S. Government during World War II that cost far more that estimated. It was, for some time, a *cause celebre* with frequent mention in the *Los Angeles Times, The Yellow Peril* and back east in the *Washington Post* and *The New York Times*.

"Vince it was a wooden airplane with eight engines. Preflight check took an hour." O'Reith said with a broad grin on his face. "Hughes figured he'd have to testify to congress about what a failure it was. So he flew it across the harbor, maybe a mile. That was late 1947. Sure enough they got after him for cost overruns. Hughes, if nothing else, was a movie magnate. He knew what you could accomplish with an airplane full of Hollywood starlets. He'd fly them up there. Throw a party for the congressmen who were going to give him the third degree. Worked like a charm. The hearings never got anywhere. Knobles picked up on that. Over the next few years, until age and dissolute living caught up with him, he honed the technique to perfection. Then Stan came along. He courted the key congressmen that had an impact on our business. He found out if they liked baseball or football or golf. Did they patronize the arts? That kind of stuff. He learned their booze preferences. He had 'gin' men and 'bourbon' men and 'scotch' men and 'vodka' men. Lots of 'vodka' men. Many of those birds thought that vodka couldn't be detected. No boozer's breath. After a few belts, chew some cardamon seeds. Smelled like you'd been in church where the padre was burning incense. So Stan could provide both the girls and the booze. In an unobtrusive way, that was progress."

"He was effective," Blake said. "But it didn't really take off until you were in charge of it."

"Aha! Pal!" How did I get that wonderful opportunity? Halliday died and his body hadn't cooled off before you dumped that job on me. Remember that, babe?"

"I didn't force it on you. You didn't complain."

"I suggested to Stan that he hire some congressional staffers that had lost their jobs after the 1948 elections. When he delivered booze, he also delivered draft legislation. He picked up on that. Not only did he draft bills, his staffers bird-dogged them right up to the oval office. Stan Ethering has made more federal law than most congressmen."

"Why not plug him back in?" Blake suggested.

"Because I want him to be the corporation attorney. He knows how business works in this country. He knows how to write contracts that will stand up under attack from government lawyers. No sir. Stan stays where he is. Vince, lobbying has evolved from a shady beginning. Think how you can improve it. I'll give you a tip. Stan had a subtle form of bribery. He called it his 'Send A Congressman's Kid to College'. He had a woman working for him, Nancy Nelligan, not a bad looking piece. She knew all the colleges in the country. On speaking terms with their deans of admission. Kept 'em oiled up no doubt. Stan would ask the congressman where he wanted his kid to go. Yale. Harvard. Smith. Colgate. Bryn Mawr. Anywhere. Nancy did the rest. Got the kid enrolled. Paid the tuition. New wardrobe. Carrying around money. Think about that, Vince. Compared to fighting a federal antitrust suit or a restraint of trade case, the cost of that program was peanuts."

They left the dining room silently. Blake was off balance but he didn't refuse outright. O'Reith took that as a good sign. As the two men got out of the elevator on the 39th floor, Blake said, "Clive, did it ever occur to you that some of those guys are honest?"

"When you figure out who they are, make a list of 'em. Send a copy to Stan. Another to Diogenes."

Waiting for him in his office was Phillip Marlborough. O'Reith motioned him to a sofa. O'Reith said, "Duke I asked you to drop by so I could thank you again for the expert advice as well as sticking your neck out a time or two."

"A pleasure general," Marlborough replied. He lit a Lucky Strike, inhaled deeply. "I needed the money. Earning it was both educational and entertaining. If you get in hot water again, give me a jingle." Marlborough produced a brand new business card from his coat pocket with his name in gothic letters and a Police Positive 38 Revolver in silhouette.

"Duke," O'Reith continued. "Couple of things. First, I want to put you on a retainer. We've got office space we'll never fill. If you want a free place with phone and teleprinter, it's yours. Discuss it with Susie. Now, as you are well aware, that McLarssen girl is right here in Los Angeles. She's sweet on my boy. He likes her back. Potential for big trouble. I'd appreciate it if you'd keep an eye on her. Make sure she doesn't have any funny looking boy friends. Nothing we can do about her fooling around with little Clive Colin. I've spoken to him and he knows the risk. If she starts to act up, alert me."

"Yes sir," Marlborough replied. "Personally I think she's harmless. She wants to get into the movies. Just a couple of kids fooling around. As long as they are discreet, I doubt anything will come of it. What about you-know-who? Our friends down South America way?"

"I asked Cordero to go down to *Valle del Tuy* every once in a while and check with that cane master. I don't have much confidence in Cordero. While you're ogling Eileen, watch her mail box too. She might get a letter from Venezuela..."

"I've got you faded, general."

O'Reith arose, Marlborough behind him. They went into the hall and to the elevator landing. Down to Susie's office on the 38th floor. O'Reith said, "Duke, this was my office when Halliday was still alive. Wonderful view of Santa Monica and the airport." Susie, smiling, met them at the door. She hugged Marlborough playfully. O'Reith got the idea that there was more between them than business. He hoped so. They'd make a neat twosome.

His appointments for the day over, at two o'clock in the afternoon with the temperature in the street near a hundred degrees but at a comfortable seventy where he was, O'Reith turned to the papers atop the cigarette-stained conference table that LeBel sent from Paris. On each side are eight chairs. But only the oil magnate sits at this table, usually in the afternoon. Every morning Sally puts there the cables, memos and letters. This is central intelligence. Everything comes here for his attention. Playing card-sized placards identify the content of each stack. Maracaibo. Caracas. Paris. California. Refining. Exploration. Production. And so on...

Diligently, and quickly, O'Reith reads each document, annotates it for action. He goes on to the next pile. If uninterrupted, by five-thirty, as the cocktail hour approaches, he will be finished. But late this afternoon, a few minutes after four, Sally tells him he has a visitor, a young lady named Ellen Mae. He marks his place with a worn .50 caliber machine-gun casing.

O'Reith says, "Ask her to wait five minutes until Sharon can touch me up"

Expertly, Sharon Mills banishes the afternoon shadows beneath the oil magnate's eyes. She restores the inkiness of his hair, trims his mustache, moistens his cheeks with rose water and blots them dry. She paints out a few brown spots on his chin and throat. Adjusts his monocle. In three minutes she has him fixed up. While she worked, Sally returned.

O'Reith says, "Show her in, Sally."

And so the slender, winsome girl, with poise and presence, follows Sally. She does not swivel her hips, nor does she slink, or jiggle. Dressed in widow's weeds, her knees just visible above the hem of the quite basic, black dress, she wears net hose, seamed in the back and a black felt cloche with a dotted veil that comes down to her chin. She appears chaste, virtuous and at the same time, fetching. One of Marlborough's competitors would describe her as 'a girl that had what you needed when you needed it, whatever it was you needed'. The oil magnate would agree with that assessment. He rises from the straight-backed chair where he always sits for Sharon Mills, smiles. When the mourning girl extends her hand, he touches it and beckons her to the sofa, where, earlier in the day, Marlborough sat. He says, "Do sit down, child."

If she is annoyed by this salutation, she conceals it. As she sits and adjusts her bottom, her eyes dart from one to the other of the several pictures on the 'wailing' wall. She takes them all in but her eyes linger on the eerie, cabinless, B-17, blithely cruising through a smoky, flak-filled sky, moments before its plunge to earth. Painted on its fuselage are the words: *Okie from...*

"Okie from where?" she asks.

"Okie from Fenoki," O'Reith says. "A mythical place in southern Oklahoma, in an area called *Little Dixie*."

"Why that?" the girl asks further.

The oil magnate replies. "Air crews often named their planes in mysterious ways."

"Such an arresting moment. Such high drama," she continues. "To think of those poor boys..." Without asking his permission, she rises, approaches the great, enlarged snapshot. She studies it in detail.

O'Reith, still sitting says, "It is unique in the annals of Air Corps photography."

"Does it have a special meaning for you?" she continues relentlessly, as if she must know why the picture is on the wall. She reoccupies her place on the sofa, beside the oil magnate.

"My wing-ship," O'Reith answers. "On the bomb run at Berlin, the last one of the war. In the spring of 1945." He does not tell her that the aircraft commander of that fated maidenhead, unpainted and untested, was First Lieutenant Clive Colin Martell, the boy he and Mimi Martell made on a pink and rose towel on the wind swept sands of Pismo Beach that damp evening under the stars in August of 1925. Then he was fresh off the desolate Afghan plains. His blood was as hot as the winds off the Pacific Ocean were cold. He does not tell her that this precocious boy was raised by Mimi's parents on a farm near Hugo, Oklahoma, in the Bible Belt. He does not tell her that he paid the boys expenses, saw him properly educated at Oklahoma State University. He does not tell her that the boy became an Army Air Corps pilot. He doesn't tell her that, willy-nilly, some desk-bound staff officer at 2nd Air Force Headquarters in Salt Lake City, Utah assigned *Okie from Fenoki* to the ETO and that it came into a group under his command. He does not tell her that on the eve of battle, he summoned the nineteen year old boy to his office where he stood him at ease and explained to him who he was. Tomorrow, they were to be comrades in arms in a deadly air battle.

Thinking of those long ago events, he awaits her next words. She begins, "I am in mourning because my brother has disappeared. I fear I will never see him again. He went to Venezuela with Mr. Donnegan to get an oil concession. I have heard nothing from him since last April… Some evil has befallen him."

"That's unfortunate," O'Reith responds. His voice is sympathetic.

"I hurt so much I have decided to become a nun. I have applied for admission at St. Elizabeth. They are full up for the fall but they'll take me next spring."

"Where is it?" O'Reith asks. "He knows many colleges in the United States but not this one.

"It's at Convent Station, New Jersey, founded in 1899. It has a fine reputation."

"Well, I hope you will find peace there."

She looks down at the floor, lifts her veil. She asks, "General O'Reith would you mind if I smoke?"

"Of course not, my child," he says with warmth. The ash tray on the coffee table is full of cigarette stubs left by Marlborough. O'Reith gets up, empties them into a wastebasket, returns just in time to light her *English Oval* cigarette with the desk lighter. He is careful not to singe her lifted veil.

She inhales deeply, blows a cloud of smoke out across the room and asks, "Would you be shocked if I told you that I was having an affair with your son?"

"No. Should I?"

"Well, with the tragedy in my family, for which I hold you partly responsible, I think you would be somewhat stunned."

"Well, I'm not."

"He's a nice boy but I will be candid with you. I'm using him. He goes often to Venezuela. I've asked him to inquire about my brother."

"Well, that's natural enough."

"I've also asked him to use his influence with his mother to get me a screen test. What do you think are my chances?"

"With his mother, not good. Not good at all."

"But I feel that I know her. I've seen everyone of her pictures, even the one made in Italy with the big fat guy. It was such a moving experience. Helen O'Reith is so worldly. So sophisticated. She would understand that a girl of my background could have an affair with a boy of your son's background."

"She might. But I wouldn't bet more than pocket change on it."

"She would see my need even as she saw her own need." There was urgency in her voice.

"That, my dear," O'Reith said sternly, "would be a dangerous extrapolation."

"I offered myself to you once and you spurned the opportunity. You missed a chance to have me as your lover, your mistress. Your son is of a different make up. He didn't hesitate. And even if I use him, I love him."

"Well that's something. He's nearer your age. Has a long lead in his pencil. Much longer than mine."

She blushed, put out her cigarette carefully, keeping the debris inside the ashtray. When the red began to fade from her cheeks, she looked up, blurted out, "Oh. I bet your lead is long enough. And that's *everything* in a love affair. I wouldn't mind giving you another shot at it." She struggled to restrain a giggle.

"I bet you wouldn't at that," the oil magnate replied. He was beginning to see this scenario.

"General O'Reith, if your son cannot help me, can *you* help me to get a screen test?"

"I might. I once helped a young actress. Wouldn't a movie career interfere with your religious ambitions?"

"Oh No! Not at all! Not in any way!" Her mouth, red and inviting makes a perfect circle.

"Do you think you could play the role of a young person who has had a vision? A girl who has seen the Holy Ghost high in the sky, a girl who then finds herself possessed of miraculous power?"

"Oh, I could! I could!"

O'Reith rose, walked to Sally's door, said, "Sally, can you get Bill Perlberg on the line for me? If he's not at TCF here in town, he'll be at his office in New York."

O'Reith returned to the sofa. Eileen McLarssen, also known as Ellen Mackensen, and more recently as Ellen Mae, had her cloche off, abandoned on the coffee table. She had lit another cigarette. Her face now seemed older. She began puffing anxiously, waited expectantly for the telephone call to come through.

When it did, the oil magnate purred into the receiver, "Bill, babe, how you are?" He listens as the movie magnate makes small talk, asking about Helen, *Los Ladrones de Piedras Negras,* about how things were going in the oil fields of Venezuela and points west. The pleasantries finished, O'Reith says, "Bill, I saw something in *The Hollywood Reporter* the other day. A rumor that you were casting for the last remake of *The Song of Bernadette*. Any truth to that?"

Over the long distance connection, the oil magnate hears a chuckle and then an admission that maybe in fact, it is on the Perlberg mind. He is encouraged to continue. "Bill, you know I'm not a movie expert. But living with Helen, a certain amount of grease paint gets on my collar from time to time. In my office a young girl sits across from me, an ingenue if ever I saw one. I've been acquainted with her for a couple of years. She just might pass a screen test for the role of Bernadette."

Over the telephone, Perlberg asks, "How old is she?"

"Nineteen, maybe twenty. A looker. Classy."

"Any bad news in her background?"

"A little, nothing you couldn't wire around."

"Scandal?"

"Her name is Eileen McLarssen. She's the brother of that guy that Helen got tangled up with back in 1948. You remember all that."

"Yeah, that could be a plus." Perlberg said. "Well, hell, let's give her a crack at it. Ask her to call Harry Cohn. I'll get something to him on the wire right now. Come see me soon. Bring Helen."

O'Reith said goodbye, hung up, and asked Sally to get Cohn on the line. Like many motion picture moguls, Harry Cohn was a despot, in the same class as Harvey Halliday, Harry Collier, Charles deGaulle, Stalin and Colonel Marcos Perez Jimenez. O'Reith handled him deftly, tactfully related to him the substance of the teleconversation with Perlberg. In five minutes, the screen test was arranged, the day and the hour appointed.

Ellen Mae was around the desk, in his lap with her lips glued to his in something less than the time it took the West Texas derrickman to blow Gimp Flagherty's hat off of his head. After some long minutes, the oil magnate disengaged from the actress. She was a good kisser all right.

"One other thing, General O'Reith," Ellen Mae began. "That poor, unfortunate man who testified in our behalf at the trial. Mr. Flagherty.

Could you help me locate him? I want to assist him. He needs speech therapy and plastic surgery. The least I can do…"

O'Reith said, "He spends most of his time in Odessa, Texas. Try the telephone directory. If not there, leave a message for him in The Ace of Diamonds, a beer joint. Sometimes he works as casual labor doping tool joints for Sharp Drilling Company in their pipe yard. Sally will help you."

"I'll try that," Ellen Mae said.

As she floated off, O'Reith summoned Sharon for emergency battle damage repair.

It is five fifteen. O'Reith is thirsty. Helen expects him. He summons Cook and Holland. The three of them work rapidly disposing of the remaining papers on the long table. In five minutes, they are done. Sally takes the papers. O'Reith calls Maxine. He talks to Monique. Then he tells her mother that he will be on his way to Paris day after tomorrow. Maxine allows that she is ready to see him again.

For the oil magnate, removing his monocle and pulling loose his tie as he rides the elevator down to the parking lot where his Cadillac limousine is purring in idle, it has been one of those really mellow days. Everything just clicked along, famously. As Parkhurst would say, 'everything tickedy-boo.' Even the interruption, which at first caused him some anxiety, had turned out just fine. The dull ache in his leg seemed insignificant in the overall scheme of things. He still had a few bad patches to get through in the coming days. While in Paris he had to talk LeBel out of retiring. The Frenchman, Treasurer and Secretary of the company, wanted to lead a more leisurely life in the south, near Port Grimeux, on the Mediterranean. He was thinking of moving there with Gabrielle, a girl of the sunny south. O'Reith wanted him to stay on at least another year, until he find a suitable replacement for that sensitive post. He remembered the chat with Holland and Ines. What a gem of a woman she was. A tiny but essential cog in the great clockwork of the Casinghead Company. Holland, with the sharpest mind of anyone that

O'Reith knew, could solve a complex mathematical problem in his head with lightning speed. He was a superb pilot, an accurate navigator, a driller in a class by himself. But inside him ticked the time bomb of self destruction. He was capable of mayhem and assault if unfettered. Ines kept his psychopathic volcano quiescent. Even if she had to take a stiletto to him once in a while; keep a close watch on him and let him out of her sight only under carefully controlled circumstances, she saved him from certain ruin. Holland knew that. So did O'Reith. Carolyn was a genius of a different species. Like McDonough, she was analytic, a puzzle solver. From mounds of seismic data that O'Reith could never fathom, Carolyn could quickly come up with a drillable prospect. But she had a fear of inadequacy. O'Reith had taken advantage of that, more than once. He worked her down to skin and bones in Venezuela, reduced her to a jaundiced, trembling wreck. And he did it again in the Tidikelt. She let him get away with it because she wanted to please him. He couldn't do that now. Magaly had entered the picture, kept Carolyn's ego in balance. Now she was her own person.

The other members of the team were odd too. But the show stayed on the road. Money was rolling in. As the limousine rolled south on Sepulveda Boulevard, heading for Long Beach, he thought about how pleasant it would be to tell Helen about Eileen McLarssen. Not that he would tell her the full story.

So Helen looks inviting in a canary yellow pantsuit, yellow suede shoes and a scarf over her hair. She has silver triangles in her ears and a drop or two of Chanel No.5 behind them. From the penthouse terrace, it is absolutely balmy with just enough of a breeze off the ocean to keep them comfortable. The view is spectacular, breathtaking.

Here lately, the oil magnate has taken a fancy to Pampero rum. Riva Cordero sends a couple of cases from time to time. But this evening Helen has mixed a pitcher of martinis made with Booth's High and Dry gin, her favorite, graced with Noilly Prat vermouth. She twists a meticulously cut, thin rectangle of lemon peel. Drops it into his glass; pours his drink and lowers a large ice cube into it, careful not to make a splash.

Helen touches his glass with her own and icy gin wets four lips. After the divine first sip they talk about *The Golden Lane*. It will be based on the life of the English oil baron, Sir Weetman Pearson. O'Reith reluctantly agrees to be her technical consultant. When he rattles the ice cube in his empty glass, she refills it and says, "Another jolt Ace. Stun those rats gnawing in the woodwork.

He knows he shouldn't but he drinks up. She continues, "Ace, Monk is my personal financial adviser, isn't he?" She looks him full in his face, searching the depths of his eyes. He notices this. And something in her voice catches his attention too. He sees her red lips compressed. He watches her wet them with her pink tongue, expectantly, like a robin in the field with its eye on a worm hole. Her mouth is slightly open, her white teeth glisten.

Yes, he is quite concerned. He downs a double jolt of his martini, braces himself. His adrenaline is flowing. He flies a battle-damaged B-17. Instrument panel red lights glow ominously. Hydraulic fluid sloshes around his feet. The wet English wind whistles through the blown out cockpit windows. He'll have to bring it in with the wheels up…

She says, "Ace, I've figured out who that woman is. It took me awhile. You know the one. She was with Monk at Punto Fijo. Remember that I asked you about her and you dissembled, as you do so well. I give you an A+ for *savoire faire*. I didn't recognize her then because she didn't have that cute little black-haired kid with her, like she did when she sat across the lobby from me in the Hotel Miramar. Monk will level with me, won't he? If he doesn't I could get a new financial guy. Couldn't I, Ace?"

The end.

Epilogue

The Tarbuttons awakened that January morning of 1958 to a cacophony of car horns honking in the streets, a demonstration strictly forbidden by the dictator in Caracas as well as throughout the nation. Only on a rural road to encourage movement by a sluggish animal, was the honking of vehicle horns permitted. This morning church bells were ringing too. Aclang all over the city and not to summon the faithful. Rushing to the bedroom window in their pajamas, they saw throngs of people milling and dancing in the street, some singing, some jumping up and down, everyone excited. Taxi cabs blocked the street. Their drivers had ripped off the white plastic roof lights. The pavement was littered with them. These lights were manufactured by a company controlled by guess who? Colonel Marcos Perez Jimenez. As a compulsory purchase for a poor cab owner, they were symbols of oppression.

These two Americans, like many others in Caracas and Maracaibo, and indeed in all of the oil producing regions of the land, were witnesses to a *golpe de estado*. Rumored for months, the Tarbuttons stocked their larder with staples as had every expatriate in the country. Fresh milk might be unavailable for several days. Fresh meat would be hard to find but the Tarbuttons would live through this political crisis in relative comfort. The electricity would stay on. The water would run. The telephones would work, more or less. Occasionally, arm in arm, they would go to the street during daylight hours for bread, eggs and fresh fruit. A curfew, announced by stern, hard-voiced, commentators on the over-modulated *Radio Avila* in Caracas and *Radio Ondas del Lago* in

Maracaibo was called in Spanish, a *toque de queda*. And if one had business abroad in the dark hours, one needed a *salvoconducto*. In Caracas, of course, an oil company executive would rarely go out at night. But in the oil fields across the land, drillers, engineers, geologists and workers of all types were lined up at provincial offices to be photographed and get their safe conduct passes.

On Radio Avila that morning, the newscastress spoke so rapidly that the Tarbuttons could only catch the drift of the events that had overtaken them as well as the distressed Colonel Jimenez. The colonel was gone. He had flown away from La Carlota. That was a fact. But where was he? He was in Havana. Panama. Madrid. Bogota. San Jose. He was in Miami. And that is where he was or at least that was where he was going. He made it OK, stayed there for quite some long time, tired of it, moved to Coral Gables, there for over a decade, until diplomatic pressure by a democratic Venezuelan Government finally forced the American State Department to order his deportation. Then only after assurances that he would not be hanged by his heels.

When Colonel Jimenez departed, ex-Capitain Riva Marcelo Cordero got the idea that perhaps he should go somewhere too. And he did. He went to Maiquetia International Airport and probably would have gone a good deal further but recognized by someone in the crowd milling around the departure lounge, he was apprehended, beaten, stabbed and eventually hanged from a light post. For some days, his lifeless body, in a soiled and bloody liqui-liqui, the same garment he wore at the Punto Fijo ceremony, lay in a dirty ditch on the road to La Guaira. Eventually he, with others of his ilk, was buried by a clean-up crew of the Department of Sanitation, a division of the Ministry of Public Works. The exact location of his grave is no longer known. His fate was shared by many of his colleagues as they ran for cover in cities like Caracas, Maracaibo, Maracay, even smaller hamlets like Maturin. In fact the *Seguridad Nacional* was the first institution of the old order to be liquidated. It was done quite informally. No paper discharges. No gold watches. No mustering out payments. Few, if any, of the rank and file of this notorious corps were ever put on trial – for anything.

As it turned out, Tarbutton did not miss Cordero. His services were no longer required. The new Minister of Mines and Hydrocarbons was none other than Juan Pablo Alfonso, a correct and honorable man whom he had met in Mexico City. He was a friend of the oil magnate.

Rojo Olimpio Torres, and many like him, came out of the short period of chaos in far better condition than ex-*Capitan* Cordero. Torres quietly put in his small hours at the Ministry of Mines and Hydrocarbons. When the hue and cry tapered off, with his family just as quietly, he flew away to San Jose, Costa Rica. With plenty of money and a yen for the good life, he enjoyed for the rest of his days the pleasures of the capital's excellent restaurants, the opera, the ballet and the famed brass bands. He was never prosecuted by anyone for anything.

Barney Quigley Donnegan died with his sandals on. Never a robust man and he was no spring chicken either, the rigors of cane-cutting were too much for him. What with the poisonous snakes, scorpions, centipedes, fire ants, screw worms and other pests of the cane fields, he died. The only person who could say what he died of, never did.

That person was one Donald McLarssen, who awoke that same morning as the Tarbuttons, to find the cane master gone and the premises deserted. Authority had vanished. The penal servants, convicted or otherwise, were free. McLarssen, toughened by his austere life style, wandered around for some days until he spotted the derrick of a drilling rig towering up over the abandoned fields. It was his luck that the rig belonged to Loffland Brothers. It was drilling a deep Cretaceous test for the Casinghead Company on newly acquired acreage in central Venezuela. The toolpusher recognized a fellow gringo, took him in, tended his many insect bites, gave him the luxury of a hot shower, his first in over a year, and fed him a solid meal. By radio, he asked the Maracaibo office what should be done with this poor creature, whose color was a dark tan, and who was mere skin and bones, and barely lucid. In the end he was sent there. His name and condition was reported back to Los Angeles by cable, one of many documents that found its way to the cigarette-stained conference table. O'Reith read it with interest. He advised *El Mocho* Morrow to turn the fellow over to Father Ted and Mother Mandy, whom, he believed, would be able to address both the physical and spiritual needs of Donald McLarssen. In due course, McLarssen recovered some, but not all, of his faculties. He joined Father Ted in the administration of the orphanage called, *Puesto Tranquilidad*. Later he became the leader of Father Ted's *street*.

By this time, of course, Father Ted had already seen Pope Pius XII. He did not kiss his ring. Apparently nobody ever kisses the Pope's ring. In fact, the pope doesn't wear it, merely uses it to seal documents of high ecclesiastical import. So Father Ted did not wipe it off with a cotton swab soaked in alcohol as the oil magnate had advised him to do. In fact, this was a bit of a sore point with him. He planned to tell the oil magnate that to have done that would have been a breach of ecclesiastic etiquette and perhaps protocol as well. Nor did he try to cadge a miter from the Pope. What nerve that would have taken? Bad advice. He did, however, get himself fitted with a Cilice, the Cadillac of hair shirts. But he only wore it for a couple of hours. It itched. Little Clive Colin found a tailor who cut the Cilice in the back, removed it from Father Ted's chafed shoulders, and resewed it with a cleverly concealed zipper. Thus, if pressed to appear in it, as he thought possible by this oil magnate of the bad advice, Father Ted could do so. In this little conspiracy Father Ted swore O'Reith's son to secrecy.

Ellen Mae passed her screen test and rose to stardom as the peasant girl of vision in *The Last Remake of The Song of Bernadette*. She was nominated for, but unluckily did not win an Oscar for her fine performance. Still, her career was launched. Her friendship with the oil magnate's son endured. In fact, little Clive Colin, without his father's knowledge (he thought), arranged a trip for Ellen Mae to Maracaibo to see her brother, and for other matters of a private nature.

It is a common observation that men who like war, like women. The oil magnate did not really enjoy war. But he had been forced into one. He survived it. On the whole, he had no regrets about that experience. That it had changed him is clear. It is another observation that men who can face death on the battlefield can face life living with women. And this, the oil magnate did with considerable gusto. He liked the smell of fine French perfume; the slippery feel of silk. Without qualification he enjoyed the company of a woman, in bed or at a cocktail party. He had some tense moments with one of his women as he had leisure moments of ecstasy with both of them. Nosing around in titties with pink nipples. Kissing soft, red lips. Touching pink tongues. Running it in the hole, feeling for bottom. He couldn't 'turn it to the right', but he could circulate and he could certainly drill ahead. That was enough.

As a seasoned executive, he could quickly assimilate, digest and consolidate critical information. Then come to some logical conclusion which would lead, inevitably, to a decision. One of his two women had pressured him to end the relationship with the other woman. She had hoped to exert even stronger pressure on the oil magnate. She gave her financial adviser the third degree about his consort at the Punto Fijo inauguration. But he was not forthcoming in this matter. He, like the oil magnate, was capable of great dissimulation.

So, how this issue would be resolved was not clear. The oil magnate, seeing it as a question requiring delicate and subtle handling, had so far, not acted in any meaningful way. The contretemps between the oil magnate and his wife was, in the words of Dr. Parkinson, 'in remission.' The oil magnate agreed that, in principle, some atonement on his part, could possibly be expected at some future time. He had thought it through quite carefully and when the time came, he would do what had to be done. But not just yet.

About the Author

Linton Morrell is in the autumn of his life. After service in the Army Air Corps, he studied petroleum engineering at The University of Texas. Following a career in international oil operations, he has become a novelist. His first novel, published in London in 1999 is titled: STEEL STORAGE. He lives in Biarritz.

Glossary

AFCE	Automatic Flight Control Equipment
API	American Petroleum Institute. Sets Standards for the American Petroleum Industry and by extension, the international industry. For example a crude oil having a density of 27 degrees API can be given a reference price anywhere in the world without further assay.
Alcabala	Police checkpoint in Venezuela during the Military Junta days.
AMG	Allied Military Government
Angel	Air Corps slang. Thousand Feet of Altitude
Barinita	Cheap cigar from Barinas, Venezuela
BIL	English abbreviation for Bank in Liechtenstein
Bird Dog	To follow something carefully like a piece of legislation through congress.
Blue-line	A photocopying process to print electric logs.
Bopd	Barrels oil per Day
BOQ	Bachelor Officer Quarters
Box end	Female threaded connection, drill pipe, tubing or casing

Boul Mich	First Class (Boulevard St. Michel)
Blowout Preventer	Device to close in a drilling well, has two or three cavities for the rams. Sits atop the Bradenhead. Used in emergency well control.
Bullhead	To pump against pressure directly into the wellhead side-outlet, the tubing head or drill pipe.
Cajun	A person of French extraction who lives in Louisiana. Corruption of the word 'Acadian'.
Caño	Raw white rum usually 150 proof.
Casing swarm	A rig accident that occurs when casing is stacked improperly on the racks. Similar to a cattle stampede.
Casing stub	Junk pipe cut from landing joint in a string of casing.
Cedula	Venezuelan Identity card.
Cutting Ditch	Drilling ahead. Also called 'making hole'.
Cue one up	Pool hall slang to start a game of pool or billiards.
Charnel House	Central slaughter house in downtown Maracaibo, a noxious landmark.
Chinese Landing	Air Corps slang. Landing with one wing low usually because one or more engines are out. Frequently catastrophic.
Christmas Tree	The final assembly of valves, nipples and gauges at the top of an oil well. The tubing head which sits atop the Casinghead (Bradenhead) once the Blowout preventers are removed.

COC	New York Stock Exchange symbol for The Calitroleum Oil Corporation.
Crown Block	Set of sheaves at top of the derrick. Drilling line and traveling equipment hang from the crown block.
CB	Ciudad Bolivar, once Angostura, Venezuela.
Crown Accident	Catastrophic event caused by driller pulling the traveling equipment into the crown, breaking the line and dropping tools onto the derrick floor. Sometimes the derrick is pulled in.
Crude Avails	Developed crude oil production ready at the well head or in steel storage.
Deck of Bikes	A deck of Bicycle (trademark) playing cards.
Derrickman	Crew member who hooks elevators around tool joints during trips. A step up from roughneck on the way to becoming a driller.
Doctor it up	To change data, maliciously or fraudulently or with an intent to deceive.
Driller	Supervises drilling crew. Operates drawworks during trips. If he's good, he will become a toolpusher.
Elevator Shoes	Worn by a short leading man to be as tall as the leading lady. Popular in the 1940s. Worn by many men in other walks of life who wished to appear taller.
Edge Water	Water encroachment into an oil well from the periphery of the field, often happens to a well low on structure.

Exito	A toast. Spanish for 'Success!'
Faded	A poker term. I see. By extension, I understand.
Finca	A farm in a rural area in Venezuela.
Fireballing	Running drill pipe or tubing into the hole at a dangerous speed. By extension, reckless behavior.
Frogsticker	A stiletto, favored by Latin women to kill off an unfaithful lover.
Gang Pusher	Foreman of a gang of roustabouts on a workover rig or a pipeline.
Grano de Oro	Maracaibo Airport in this era. Now university grounds.
High Sign	To signal, hand held high, from a distance or above a deafening noise.
Hollywood 10	Ten creative film industry persons subpoenaed to appear before the House Committee on Un-American Activities in 1947. Ruined careers resulted.
Junta	In November of 1948, a Military Junta seized power in Venezuela. A clampdown of political freedom resulted. On 2 Dec. 1952 Colonel Marcos Perez Jimenez took control of government. The junta continued to exist but he essentially thrust it aside as far a governing the country. He was a cruel, ruthless tyrant, but he had some redeeming qualities. He was overthrown in January of 1958 and took up residence near Miami, Florida. He was there for many years but finally, under pressure form the now democratic

	Venezuelan Government, was repatriated to Venezuela where his liberties were greatly diminished.
Kick	Gas or high pressure oil trying to blow out of a well while drilling.
LAV	Lineas Aereas de Venezuela. An Airline.
Light plant	Diesel-electric generator for lights, cooking etc.
Liqui-Liqui	Venezuelan formal attire equivalent to a tuxedo.
Lowboy	A truck trailer with a low bed to accommodate a tall load.
LNG	Liquid Natural Gas. In this story it refers to propane, butane and pentane.
Maiquetia	International Airport for Caracas, Venezuela, then and now.
Mann Act	U.S. federal law making it a crime to transport a woman across a state line for immoral (prostitution) purposes.
Master Valve	Main shut-off on a completed oil well, usually a part of the tubing head. Also applies to a pipeline.
Matica de Cafè	Venezuelan slang. Also Matica Cafe. The end, often bitter. Death.
Mopery on the high seas	Staring at a nude woman on the deck of a battleship.
Mud Hog	High pressure oil field pump.
Mustard Cluster	Compares with Oak Leaf Cluster except it is derogatory and informal. Awarded for bombing churches, beer joints, brothels or forgetting to put the wheels down before landing.

Nipple up.	To complete operations after a casing job or a tubing job or to complete the well.
Oil leg test	When a gas cap is suspected, a well located relatively lower on structure expected to intersect the oil zone.
Oater	Western movie. Sage brush saga. Horse opera.
Oil Gravity	A measurement of the quality of crude oil expressed in API degrees. Twenty degree crude is for road tar or bunkers. Forty degree crude is gasoline grade.
Pay zone	Where one expects to find oil.
Poontang	Exotic sex.
PDQ buck slip	Pretty Damn Quick note attached to a memo or letter. Nowadays ASAP. In France, tout de suite. In Venezuela, *Ensiguida*.
Podner	Cowboyspeak for Partner.
Pup Joint	A short length of drill pipe used to pick up tools.
QRC	Quick Ram Change blowout preventer designed so that ram changes can be made in minutes. Cameron Trademark.
Rumdum	Loss of the ability to concentrate one's mind because of lack of sleep or stress. American oil field slang.
Salvoconducto	A safe conduct pass in Venezuela during troubled times. Frequently not honored.
Sandy	Poker slang. A bluff. From 'sandbag'.
Seguridad Nacional	A euphemism for a secret police force operated by the dictator, Colonel Marcos Perez Jimenez. Their job was to keep the

country calm and peaceful. They made short work of agitators etc. From 1953 until January 1958, this organization was dreaded by the average Venezuelan. The secret police were among the first organizations disbanded by the new government.

Setting pipe	Running a string of casing.
Short Arm Inspection	U.S. Army slang. An inspection of an enlisted man's penis to determine if it is dripping from gonorrhea.
Shot point	A numbered point in a line of seismic holes where dynamite is exploded to obtain a reflection from the underground strata. Reference point for exploratory drilling.
Sit a well	Geologist attending a well to inspect cuttings coming up in the mud, looking for oil.
SOCAL	Acronym for The Standard Oil Company of California. NYSE symbol was then SD
Southern Ferry Route	Winter ferry route through South America during World War II
Spud. Spud in.	To commence drilling of an oil well or a well looking for oil.
The Smoke	London. Where else?
Standing short.	Poker slang. At a disadvantage, like holding a four-flush against a full house. By extension, not having everything you need.
Stilson Wrench	Trademark for a pipe wrench

Strat Trap test	A stratigraphic trap is an accumulation of oil caused by a fault as opposed to a structural trap. Strat traps in those days, were difficult to detect with seismic surveys.
Toolpusher	Top dog on a drilling rig. In charge of operations. Term has different meanings in various oil fields of the world. A drilling foreman. A Company man. Nowadays called 'Drilling Supervisor'.
Torqued up	Angry, upset and worried, all at the same time. Derived from stuck drill pipe, which will not turn in the hole, a serious problem. A person who is 'torqued up' is to be avoided while he or she is in that condition.
Trip. Round trip.	Pulling out or running in a string of drill pipe or tubing.
Twist off	A break in the drill string. while drilling ahead. By extension, when a person makes a bad mistake.
Very Pistol	Flare gun. First used extensively in World War I and II. Nowadays used to ignite gas at the end of a flare line on a testing oil well.
Waist gun	A machine-gun in the waist of a bomber, particularly a B-17 or a B-24.
Water leg	Water underlying the oil zone. If one drills into it, it will be detected on the electric log and pipe will be set above it.
Wampas Baby	A title bestowed annually on selected Hollywood starlets by the Western

Association of Motion Picture Advertisers during the years 1922-1934. Included were: Mary Astor, Joan Crawford, Fay Wray, Loretta Young, Ginger Rogers. Many others.

Water Drive An oil field in which underlying water rises as oil is produced, thus improving recovery. As opposed to gas drive.